OF EMBERS & IVY

To those who saw the potential in me when I couldn't see it myself, thank you for encouraging me to keep going.

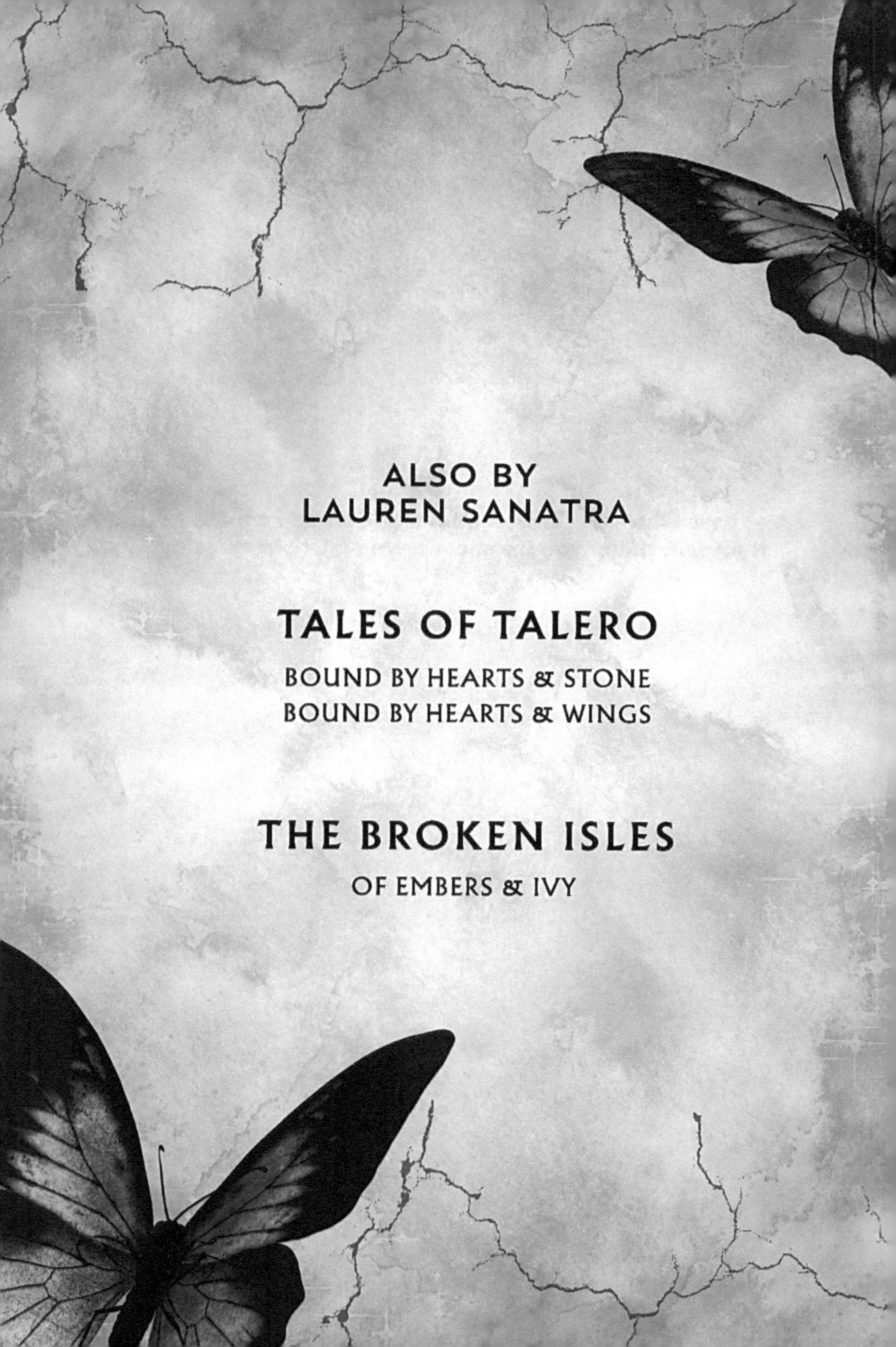

THE BROKEN ISLES

OF EMBERS & IVY

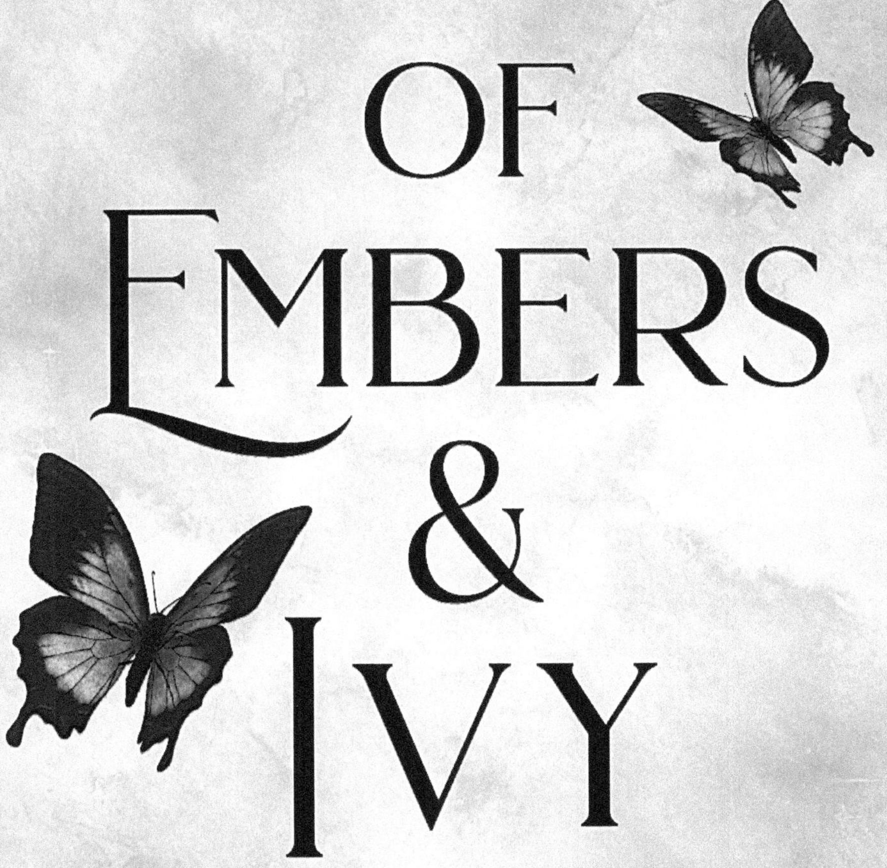

LAUREN SANATRA

MIRAVALLE BOOKS

TEXAS

Of Embers & Ivy
The Broken Isles, #1

Miravalle Books published books may be purchased in bulk discounted quantities for promotional, educational, and/or business use. Please contact your local bookseller or visit our website to learn more and/or to inquire about placing a bulk order.

Miravalle Books ™ is a trademark of Miravalle Books LLC, a Texas based Limited Liability Company

Library of Congress Cataloging-in-Publication Date

Names: Sanatra, Lauren, author.
Title: Of Embers & Ivy / Lauren Sanatra
Description: First Edition | Texas; Edinburg: Miravalle Books, 2025
Identifiers: Library of Congress Control Number: 2025945256
ISBN-13: 979-8-9926549-9-8 (Paperback) | ISBN-13: 979-8-9926549-2-9 (eBook)
LC Record available at: https://lccn.loc.gov/2025945256

Cover Design by Xielle Covers

Miravalle Books
PO BOX 731
Edinburg, TX 78540

Printed in the United States of America

10 9 8 7 6 5 4 3 2 1

OF EMBERS & IVY

1

"King Caraway and Prince Hawthorne are coming!"

Mirra's voice cut through my chambers like a bell, sharp and shrill enough to startle the dead. Her words trembled with excitement—or was it fear?—that clung to every word.

I rubbed the crust from my eyes and struggled to sit up, the warmth of my comforter clinging to me as if reluctant to let go. "What do you mean?" My voice cracked as I spoke, rough from sleep. Slowly, my vision focused on Mirra's pale face, her hand trembling as she gripped a scroll.

"They've accepted the invitation," she said, moving to perch on the edge of my bed. "The Royal family of the Ivy Isle will be coming here for your brother's coronation."

I froze, a cold knot forming in my chest. King Caraway. Prince Hawthorne. The Ivy Isle. They were coming here. To the Ember Isle. It didn't make sense. No rulers from the neighboring Isles ever left their lands. Why would they now?

I inhaled sharply, trying to steady my racing thoughts. "Are you sure?" I asked, my voice still strained with disbelief. "Did they say why?"

Mirra shook her head, her dark curls swaying with the movement. She handed me the scroll, and I took it from her, my fingers brushing the cold wax seal before I unrolled it. In the center, in bold, sweeping letters, the message was clear: *We would be honored to attend.*

I blinked at the words, trying to make sense of them. King Caraway's signature followed: *King Caraway of the Ivy Isle.* The "we" was obvious, his son, Prince Hawthorne, was included, but that was it. No other explanation, no further details.

I flipped the scroll over, hoping for something more. But the back was blank.

It was customary to send invitations to the royal families of each Isle for important events, weddings, funerals, or the birth of a new royal. We'd recently received one ourselves for the upcoming birth of the new princess from the Isle of Mist, but those invitations were always met with silence. They were more of a formality than anything else.

I had never met any fae from the other Isles, but I had always been curious. I wondered if the fae from the Isle of Mist truly had gills, as the stories claimed, or if those from the Isle of Gust possessed the delicate wings I had seen in the illustrations from my mother's bedtime tales. There was even speculation that the fae from the Ivy Isle had small thorns that punctured through their flesh like spikes. I had once believed they might be just that, stories, but now, with the Ivy Isle about to step foot on Ember Isle…

I squeezed the scroll in my hand, the parchment creasing under my fingers, as I rummaged through my closet for a robe. "Have my mother and father seen this yet?" I asked, shaking the scroll slightly toward Mirra.

"Yes, both King Keegan and Queen Alynta were present when it arrived," she replied, her voice soft as she helped tie the sash of my robe.

I could only imagine what my parents thought when they read the message. They must have been as stunned as I was. The presence of royalty, anyone from another Isle wasn't something we ever anticipated, let alone prepared for.

"Princess Eliane," Mirra whispered, as though the very mention of King Caraway's name had already brought him to our doorstep. "This complicates things."

"I know," I whispered back.

I rushed down the hall of the palace, my robe billowing behind me, Mirra close on my heels. My footsteps rang out sharply against the stone walls, quickening as I pressed forward. The flames of the ever-burning torches mounted along the corridor seemed to flicker and sway with my hurried pace, casting long shadows that seemed to stretch in warning. Mirra was still close behind me as I turned to approach the wall at the end of the hall, one that, to anyone else, would appear to be just a normal structure. I paused for a moment, letting my thoughts settle, then pressed on the stone wall where I knew one of the secret passages would open. It gave way easily, just as it always had. Mirra followed instinctively, as we'd done this countless times before.

Once through the passageway, I slipped quietly into the hallway leading to the throne room. I eased the door open and saw that a small crowd had already gathered, their low murmurs filling the space. It seemed I wasn't the only one troubled by the news of our future guests.

My mother and father sat upon their thrones, regal yet tense. My mother's dark copper hair was tightly pulled back and secured under her massive ruby crown, the sharp angles of her face set in a mask of concentration. Beside her, my father's auburn hair fell free, a contrast to her prim appearance, though his bronzed crown was more modest than her own. Both of them were as youthful as their age allowed, their beauty still evident, yet now, their hardened expressions made that beauty seem almost distant, obscured by the weight of the moment. The air between them crackled with something I couldn't name, but I felt it in my bones, a tension I wasn't used to sensing so clearly, despite my shortcomings as a fae.

My eyes scanned the room, landing on two familiar figures, Branton and Adan, my parents' most trusted guards. The father and son duo had always been steadfast, pillars of loyalty. But today, they looked out of sorts. Branton, with his dark hair streaked with grey, embodied the years he had lived. The furrow of his brow and the distinguished lines beginning to form along his face were no doubt earned through long years of service to the Crown, but there was no denying he had aged like a fine wine. Even now, he was a handsome male, his features sharp and regal in their own right. But today, something was different as I studied him, his face tighter than usual.

Standing beside him, his son Adan looked equally disturbed. Adan, younger and still in the prime of his youth, resembled his father so closely that if I squinted, I could almost see Branton as he once was, vigorous and unburdened. Adan, with his mesmerizing hazel eyes set against the bronze canvas of his smooth face, he was the kind of male who turned heads without effort. Striking, really, he could have posed for any of the great artists of the Ember Isle, become the muse of sculptors with chiseled features that seemed almost too perfect to be real. I was sure no one would complain if statues of Adan adorned the kingdom. I certainly wouldn't. But that wasn't his path.

Branton had served as captain of the royal guard since my father's coronation, just as his father had before him. Adan would take up that mantle once my brother became king. But right now, both of them looked as if the weight of the world had fallen squarely upon their shoulders.

"Eliane." My mother's voice was soft, her face peeking over Branton's shoulder, her eyes narrowing in that way I knew meant something serious was unfolding.

"Is it true? They're really coming to Hayden's coronation?"

"It's true," she answered, her voice calm, but there was a crack in it, a false sense of control. "We don't know why, after all these years, but they will be here in two days, arriving just a day before the coronation."

"Double the guards near the docks and around the palace too," my father stated. "We should also station a few more outside of our quarters as well as Prince Hayden's. For all we know, this could be a silent invasion."

I watched as a silent nod passed between Branton and my father, as if Branton were ready to summon our entire army.

"But, Keegan, the rules..." my mother began, her voice trying to steady him.

"I understand the rules, Alynta," my father replied, the frustration clear in his tone. "It's just a precaution."

We all knew the consequences of breaking the ultimate laws, the same ones carved into the petrified wood that hung above the king and queen's seats in the throne room, a constant reminder of Theodon's wrath should we ever disobey. Only two rules were etched into that ancient wood. The first, and most important, declared that no Isle could wage war on another unless there was just cause, a reason pure and unselfish enough that even Theodon himself would give his blessing. But reasons like that were rare. So rare, in fact, they hadn't been seen once in our history since the Isles split. So, surely, they wouldn't come here with intentions of attacking. Would they?

My mother stood from her throne and walked toward me, her steps measured but heavy. "You know what this means, don't you, Eliane?"

I did.

I was the Ember Isle's secret. My existence was a carefully guarded truth, known only to my family, our closest guards, and the servants who had no choice but to keep quiet. I was the secret twin. The powerless princess. The one born with so little magic that it couldn't even be called true power. The weakness that could bring the entire kingdom to its knees if the wrong people ever found out.

Being born a twin and surviving the first moments of life was unheard of. No child had ever shared a womb with a sibling and lived, at least, not since the original rulers of the Isles, The Original Four. The first High Elemental Fae, born of the union between Theodon, the Divine Creator, and his human consort, Vesta, our Divine Mother of Ainoah, before the Isles split and each kingdom forged its own destiny.

The Ember, our royal elemental gift, was the most powerful magic on the Isle, passed down through the bloodline since King Sulien's reign. But there was only one. Only enough for one child to carry the Ember. And it had chosen Hayden. Not me.

No one expected me to survive. My body, with barely a trace of magic, was not meant to live. Hayden had taken most of the Ember's power, leaving only a fragment behind for me. Just enough to keep me alive, but not enough to make me whole, It hadn't affected Hayden's power, not in the way it should have, but I carried enough of the royal shimmer from my Pyronia bloodline to look the part of a High Elemental Fae.

But I wasn't. I had no true magic.

I could heal small wounds, but it took days, sometimes weeks, not moments. Not like Hayden or any of the true fae, whose gifts weren't as dull or nonexistent as mine. Once, as a child, I had tried to fly with Hayden and Adan, hoping to emulate the fae of the Isle of Gust. We'd climbed to a cliff above the hot springs in Atsila and jumped. Only I didn't fly. I fell. I hit so many rocks on the way down, breaking my leg and tearing open deep gashes across my body.

Had it been Hayden, he would have healed in minutes. Adan, being a lesser fae, would have taken a day at most. But me? I had been forced to rely on my parents' magic. Without it, I would have spent weeks healing, if not months. My body wasn't strong enough to heal itself. That was my reality.

I wasn't even a lesser fae. I was less than that.

"Eliane?" My mother's voice snapped, cutting through the quiet.

"Yes, yes, I understand." I replied dryly, rolling my eyes as I spoke. I did understand. With royals from another Isle coming, I'd have to blend in as I always did when strangers arrived, Sending me away was always the easiest choice. But not this time. Not when this event was so important to Hayden—and to me.

"Keegan," my mother began, her voice steady and calm. "It's her brother's coronation. Surely, we can have her play part of the staff for the duration of their stay. Eliane knows those roles and how to behave."

It was true. I'd spent years acting as the extra hired help for large events. I never let anyone get particularly close to me, just moved about as the jack-of-all-trades—the person to call when a pair of extra hands were needed—and then I'd disappear. With an event this size, no one would question my presence. In fact, I was sure they'd all be thankful for the extra assistance.

"Alynta, it's too risky."

"Father, you know I will be discreet. In all these years, I've never been caught..."

"That could have been pure luck, or the fact that our guests weren't royals. No, this time my word is final," my father declared.

"Dear, how many times have you yourself scanned the crowd and been unable to find your own daughter hidden among the faces? Your own flesh and blood? Surely, if you couldn't spot her or put two and two together about who she really is..."

"If they look closely enough, they'll see her eyes. The golden shimmer is faint, almost imperceptible to those who don't know what to look for at first glance or to those who don't linger long enough. The Ironwood's, however, see that gleam in their own reflections every day. If you put yourself in a situation where they can study you for too long, if they get close enough, they might notice. It's too big a risk."

"*If* they get close enough, tell me, do you really think the Ivy King or the prince would spare a moment for a lesser fae? Do you honestly believe they'd even notice them, let alone speak to them?" my mother scoffed.

"Alynta..."

"This is the king's first visit to the Ember Isle," she pressed on, "do you really think he'll waste his time chatting with the staff? Would you, if the roles were reversed?"

My father's nostrils flared as he muttered under his breath, his jaw tightening slightly, clearly impatient with the conversation.

I knew my father wasn't cruel or dismissive toward those who worked within the palace walls. He treated them with kindness, always. But she wasn't wrong. If he were visiting another Isle as a guest of royalty, his attention would likely be fixed on matters of politics, strategy, and the land, not on the ones who merely served it.

"You know I can do this," I begged, hoping he would see reason. "I will play whatever role you'd like. Shall I be the handmaid again? Or perhaps a stable hand? A royal archer, maybe?" As much as I hated pretending to be someone else, it was still better than being locked away—or worse, sent to the safe house beyond the oasis outside Atsila.

"A female royal archer?" my father scoffed. "No, that will not do. Or even a stable hand, for that matter," he muttered, rubbing his chin as if the idea itself were foreign to him. "Especially not with the Ivy King around."

I rolled my eyes at his words. Little did he know, I had embraced all those male-dominated roles before—with Hayden's help. But I supposed now wasn't the best time to bring that up, especially since it seemed he was actually entertaining the idea, instead of dismissing me outright. Deep down, I knew he had to understand that I needed to stay.

"I think a kitchen maid would be best," my mother suggested, her voice softening as she placed a hand on my shoulder, a silent gesture of reassurance.

"Fine," my father relented. "But she must stay in the back at all times when they arrive."

"She will," my mother added with a small smile. "Besides, I know how much you love cooking, Eli."

She wasn't wrong. I had secretly hoped she'd let me be the archer, but a kitchen maid would work. Playing different roles over the years had become second nature to me, but cooking was something I genuinely enjoyed. Baking and preparing meals didn't require magic, only skill, something I could excel at without feeling inadequate. It was a task that let me lose myself, focus, and feel a rare sense of peace.

"So," my father began, running a hand through his long auburn hair, "here's the plan. When King Caraway and Prince Hawthorne arrive, you'll be on kitchen duty. We'll move some of your things to the kitchen staff's sleeping quarters."

"Would you like an extra guard stationed near that part of the castle for the Princess's protection?" Branton asked.

"I'll be fine." I had been protected my whole life; I wasn't afraid of a simple visit.

But Adan cut me off, his gaze meeting mine with a quiet intensity. "I can do it." His voice was firm, but there was an underlying softness, a promise beneath the words. "If I'm to be worthy of my role at Captain of the Guard to Prince Hayden, let me start by protecting his sister, the Princess.

His sister? The Princess?

Adan had known my name since we were children. Hell, we'd seen each other naked while skinny dipping in the pools of Solana Oasis when we were kids. Sure, Hayden was always with us, but there were those rare moments when it was just me and Adan. Times when he wasn't the son of the Captain of the Guard, and I wasn't merely the secret princess. Just moments where we could laugh and be ourselves, his smile offering me more warmth than even the blazing sun. We'd play in the sands, and he was always the one to help me up after we made Sand Fae outside the palace, using our arms and legs to shape what we imagined the fae from Gust might look like. He always lifted me up, his arms strong even then, making sure my creation was perfect without leaving any hand or footprints behind. It was annoying how now he treated me more like I was just another part of his job, and not his friend. I suppose everyone was taking this arrival very seriously.

"That would be fine, I suppose." I shrugged, trying to keep the bitterness out of my voice.

"Then it's settled," my father said, his voice echoing in the grand throne room. He rose from his throne with a sweep of his cloak, his words final, like a hammer striking the anvil. "Mirra, if you could begin moving some of Princess Eliane's belongings to the kitchen quarters, that would be much appreciated."

"Yes, Your Majesty," Mirra replied quickly, curtsying before hurrying out of the room, her footsteps fading into the distance.

"Shall I inform Prince Hayden?" Adan asked, already making his way toward the door with quick, purposeful strides.

I frowned. Where was Hayden? It had been a quiet realization, but it finally hit me: he wasn't here. All the important people in the palace seemed to have gathered, but my brother was absent. Did he already know about our unexpected visitors? Was he already preparing for their arrival, or perhaps for the coronation's royal hunt? Maybe getting fitted for a new, grand outfit? The palace was always alive with preparations, but this moment felt hollow without him.

Before I could think more on it, Adan had reached the door, a subtle urgency in his movements.

"I'll go with you," I said, stepping forward before I could second-guess myself.

"No." Adan's response was sharp enough to stop me in my tracks. "I mean, I can manage on my own."

Something was definitely off. Adan's strange tone only intensified my suspicion, as if he were purposely concealing something. Were those two involved in something I wasn't allowed to be a part of? A secret, maybe? The more I thought about it, the more my curiosity grew.

"I may be playing the role of kitchen maid in two days," I started, forcing a level of calm assertiveness into my voice, even though the tension was bubbling beneath my skin. I leaned in, lowering my voice to a whisper, "but I'm still the princess. And I will not take commands from you."

For a split second, Adan was silent. He was taken aback, I could tell. His brow furrowed in surprise, his eyes narrowing slightly as he processed my words. That brief flash of uncertainty was enough to make me feel a surge of power.

I was the princess, after all. And no matter what role I played, no matter how many kitchen maids I became or how many times they shut me out, I was still a Pyronia at my core.

Adan seemed to swallow whatever thoughts were swirling in his head. "Fine," he muttered. "But don't blame me for what you see."

What would I see? Hayden hungover and naked in his bed, surrounded by a puddle of his own vomit? That would hardly be a new sight for me. I had the unfortunate luck to walk in on him in that state more times than I care to remember. Maybe this time I would walk in on him with a female's legs wrapped around his head. What had I overheard some guards saying? Feasting on a maiden? I shook my head, trying to banish the thought. I could only hope he was still in his room because he was diligently practicing his coronation speech, however, something told me it was most likely one of the more scandalous scenarios I had been trying not to imagine.

Adan and I scurried down the hall toward my brother's chambers, and the closer we got to Hayden's room, the more a troubled look settled on Adan's face. It wasn't just in his furrowed brow; it was in the way he seemed to avoid eye contact with me, either out of embarrassment for what I might see or shame over the state his best friend could be in.

Growing up, Adan and Hayden were inseparable. The dynamic duo, always in some sort of mischief. Then there was me, Eli, not quite part of the duo, though I'd always tried. I'd done my best to join in on their antics, whether it was sneaking out at dawn to hunt unchaperoned with bows too large for our small hands or pulling pranks on the servants and guards. Pranks that always seemed to get me into trouble. Well, at least, I was the one who took the fall. I always volunteered to take the blame; to fess up and claim I was the mastermind behind it all. Sometimes, I truly was. From then on, if Hayden or Adan stepped out of line, whether I was there or not, the blame somehow found its way to me. I became the easy excuse, the one who was "acting out" because of my situation. At first, I didn't care. It felt like a small price to pay to protect them. But soon, my parents became stricter with me. They couldn't have me causing a scene or embarrassing the future king. I think Hayden and Adan knew what I was doing, and I think they even appreciated it. But appreciation doesn't take the punishment away. It was still me who faced the consequences.

I knew, deep down, that Hayden loved me and that our twin bond would always remain, but I also knew the real reason he and Adan put up with me for so long, partly because I would throw myself on a blade for them. I always sacrificed myself, and I could only hope they didn't keep me around out of pity. But as we grew older, and as my mother liked to say, as my "embers flamed," things began to shift. We started to drift apart. The isolation I had once only felt in fleeting moments began to settle in, familiar and suffocating within the palace walls.

Being a twin, Hayden and I shared a closeness that was natural, a bond forged since birth. But with Adan, it was different. With him, I became someone else. Someone who made him uneasy. Someone who couldn't even meet my gaze unless he was in his official role, guarding the Royal Family. I hated it.

While I wasn't the brightest or most beautiful flame on the Isle, I wasn't entirely unfortunate either. I knew enough to recognize that my body was pleasing to the male eye, and sometimes, even to the female one. My features were pleasant, or so I had been told. My copper curls framed my heart-shaped face, and my amber eyes, dotted with small flecks of gold, were often remarked upon. Though my eyes weren't as striking as my brother's or my parents', the amber with gold flecks was the signature trait of those born of the royal line.

Luckily, the gold in my eyes was faint enough that it wouldn't immediately give me away. It would take someone a long time to notice, which wasn't something I ever worried about. Few ever got close to me, especially in the many roles I played, or were attentive enough to catch the subtle trace of royalty hidden in the amber.

They were nothing like Hayden's eyes. His were nearly entirely golden.

But the one thing I couldn't escape were the freckles that dotted my face, small constellations of brown specks that seemed to mock my existence. My skin, too fair for someone born on the Ember Isle, stood in stark contrast to the sun-kissed, bronzed complexions of most of our people. The desert sand that surrounded us did little to warm my skin; instead, it seemed to emphasize my lighter complexion.

It was a constant reminder of my difference, of who I was and who I had to pretend to be. Not like Adan, who walked with such confidence, completely sure of himself and his future role. He never had to pretend to be anyone but himself.

As we made our way down the hall to Hayden's door, I could already hear sounds of pleasure echoing off the stone walls. It didn't take long to guess what was happening on the other side of the door. Even with the thickness of the closed door, it did not do much to drown out the moans of a female's voice. Wait maybe two? And was that a male I heard grunt? Maybe Adan was right, maybe I didn't want to know what was occupying my brother at the moment. Too late now.

Adan ran a hand through his dark hair, "I told you," He said, a smirk starting to form along his lips.

"Just knock on the door please and let's get this over with," I demanded, my face turning hot.

He slammed his fist along the large metal door, "Hay, its Adan, open up!"

"Ah fuck off Adan, can't you see, or rather hear that I am busy!" My brother's voice called through ragged breaths, another moan slipping out. "Unless you want to join us?"

Gross. While I didn't want to let my mind run wild with thoughts of Adan and my brother tangled in the sheets, I couldn't deny that I had, once or twice, fantasized what it would be like between Adan and me. I often wondered what his muscular physique looked like now that we were no longer children. I wondered how his muscles would feel under my fingers, the heat of his skin against mine as he peeled off his shirt, then his pants. I imagined that chiseled body pressed against me, every curve and plane molding to mine. I thought about where his warm, calloused hands might roam, tracing me down my body and perhaps even lower, and the sound of a moan escaping his lips, my name caught in it.

Having spent many nights alone, I had explored my own body, trying different things to find what brought me release. However, I knew that experiencing it with a partner would be vastly different. The thought of someone else's hands touching me, guiding me through new sensations, and helping me find release was tantalizing. But for now, those thoughts remained a fantasy, and I was getting ahead of myself. Before diving into anything too complex, I figured I should start with something simpler like kissing. I'd been kissed before, but it was always just quick pecks with no real emotion behind them, nothing like the passionate kisses I'd read about. The kind that sparks a fire inside and makes everything feel right. But I didn't think I could ever have that... or could I?

Another loud thud from the other side of Hayden's door snapped me out of my thoughts, reminding me why we were here. I slammed my fist as hard as I could, careful not to hurt my hand.

"Hayden!" I shouted. "Put your cock away, put on some clothes and come out, it's important!"

"Eli?" Hayden squeaked with nervousness in his voice followed by a hard thud that echoed through the hall. "Adan, why is my sister here?"

Adan put his lips to the door, "I tried to warn her, but she insisted," he replied, giving me a stink eye, "but truly Hay, it is important."

"Alright," Hayden answered back after a moment, sounding a bit disappointed.

I listened, hearing frantic movement on the other side of the door. Hayden had clearly been caught off guard, and I could almost picture him scrambling to cover himself and hide any evidence of his activities in the room. But it was too late—I was already all too aware.

After a few minutes and the sounds of buckles and shoes fastening, a parade of fae waltzed out of Hayden's room. There was a portly female about my age I had recognized as a librarian from the city, another female, clearly much older with her more wrinkled skin, though with the way the fae aged, it was hard to tell if her age was as it seemed, then lastly a handsome young fae male who appeared to still be tucking his unmentionables into his trousers. I recognized him from the stables, his long blonde hair fastened back with a gold lace. *Was he here for the fae girls, or my brother? Both?* This was not the time to ponder all of this.

Holding the door open, Hayden invited us into his room, fastening a robe around himself. The smell of sweat and cinnamon filled the air, making my stomach a bit queasy. I glanced around Hayden's large room. It was more extravagant than my own. His large canopy bed sat at the far end on the room, crimson silk sheets and a completely disheveled comforter, hanging halfway off the bed. Looking closely I could see dark stains of liquid splattered across the red. I felt bile begin to climb up my throat before taking a breath and swallowing it back down.

"Have a seat," Hayden said, motioning to the two large chairs placed around a small marble table. "Drinks?"

Adan and I exchanged a glance, shaking our heads as we denied both offers. From the liquid stains on the velvet cushions, it was evident that Hayden's activities did not stay confined to the bed.

"So, what was so urgent that I had to leave my guests so unsatisfied?"

I sucked in a sharp breath, gathering the courage to speak. "The Ivy Isle is coming to the coronation. They accepted the invitation." I blurted, finally releasing the breath I had been holding since the moment I'd learned the news.

Hayden froze. His face twisted in confusion, pinched, as if he didn't understand what I was saying. I supposed I had probably looked just as bewildered when I'd first heard it. His expression softened after a moment, and then, was that a smile? No, it wasn't a smile. It was something worse. A laugh.

A light chuckle escaped his lips, and he leaned back in his chair. "Okay, come on now. You're fucking with me, right?"

"No, Hay," Adan replied, his voice turning hard as stone, devoid of any humor. "King Caraway and Prince Hawthorne are already on their way. They'll be here in two days."

The laughs died on Hayden's lips, his face shifting from disbelief to a quiet stillness. He stared at us for a long moment, as if weighing the reality of it all. "Mother and father..." he trailed off, the question hanging in the air as he poured himself a drink from the small bar set up in the corner of the room.

I watched him take a long swig of amber liquid, then refill his glass without a second thought.

Hearing it out loud again only made me tense. I glanced down at the bar cart, thinking maybe I should have taken that drink after all. This time, I didn't wait for an invitation. I poured myself one too, though not as much as Hayden. He always drank more than he should. I wasn't much of a drinker, especially not anything stronger than a glass of wine with dinner, but this... this was different. The tension, the pressure of what we were facing, deserved something stronger.

I tossed back the drink, the burn in my throat a welcome distraction from the gnawing unease that had settled in my stomach.

"Do they already know?"

"Yeah," I answered, my voice a little hoarse and my throat on fire as I set down the now scrunched up scroll I didn't realize I was still holding. "They know."

Adan joined us by the bar but didn't pour himself a drink. Can't drink on duty, I suppose. His face turned even more serious than it had been in the throne room. I could see the hard lines etched into his face as he clenched his jaw.

"Do you think they're coming under the guise of an attack?" Adan asked, his face still hard as he read over the words on the scroll. "Or maybe trying to get information about the Isle or our armies?"

"I don't know," Hayden replied. "It doesn't make sense to come now, after all these years, unless…"

Hayden's head sharply turned toward me. I knew what he was thinking. Maybe they know about me. Maybe someone had found out about my existence and told them about my lack of powers.

One of the most important rules across all the Isles of Ainoah was that we were forbidden from going to war with one another. It was the first rule of the treaty that formed when Ainoah split into four independent Isles, each aligned with one of the four elements bestowed upon us by the Original Four. The first and only quadruplets that survived a birth, each inheriting an element, the original keepers of the Ember, the Seed, the Gale, and the Dewdrop. This division caused the fae, with their distinct elemental gifts, to naturally settle in the Isles that matched their powers when the split happened so long ago. Though each isle had its differences, they were equal in power and strength. If war were to break out, everyone would lose as chaos descended. It would bring nothing but death and suffering, especially to the innocent lesser fae, those who had been gifted only a small trace of magic all those years ago, and who would inevitably be caught in the crossfire. But if the Ivy King knew our secret, would he attempt to wage war regardless?

Our Isle had been weakening for centuries, gradually shrinking every year as a sort of sickness spread through the land and even the water around us. I assumed this was happening to other Isles too, as we are all connected by the sea. But maybe the other Isles weren't affected at all? Perhaps our very existence was accelerating the process, and maybe it was only the Ember Isle that was truly depleting. If the Ivy King somehow realized we were weaker, would that give him an opening to attack?

If the other Isles knew about Hayden and me being twins, they might see it as a vulnerability. They could assume that Hayden didn't possess the full power of the Ember, or that he would never reach his full strength, not while I survived, with even the faintest shimmer in my blood. Not while there was a small, yet absurd, chance that I carried even the tiniest fragment of that Ember within me. Which, maybe I did? We weren't sure how, or if, it affected Hayden's powers, and hopefully, King Caraway remained unaware of that as well.

"It's a possibility," Adan replied, finishing Hayden's thought. "Princess Eliane has already been advised on her role to play while the Ivy Isle's royal family and guards are on our land."

I grabbed my robe and curtsied towards Hayden, and said sarcastically, "I get to be a kitchen maid."

Hayden's body tensed as he tightened his grip on his now empty drink causing small cracks to line the glass, "What? Why aren't they sending you to the safe house?"

I reached out, guiding my brother's hand down to the table to release the glass before he completely shattered it. "I am not missing your coronation. Mother knew that despite Fathers disagreements," I started, my voice measured and calm as Hayden finally let go of the glass, his knuckles white. "We shared a womb twenty years ago and you have been my best friend and the most important person in my life ever since. I would never miss one of the most important events of your life." Not to mention I truly hated the safe house.

"If they try anything…"

"They won't!" I cut him off quickly, "I've played these parts before, I will be fine. There is still a chance they genuinely know nothing about me, about us. Plus you know the rules, I doubt the Ivy King would be foolish enough to try and harm a fae from another Isle."

Along with the "no wars" rule in the treaty, there was another very important rule carved into the petrified wood in the throne room. A life for a life. If a fae were to harm or even kill another fae from a neighboring Isle, the punishment was equal to the crime. Kill a cook from the Ember Isle? Then we get to kill one of their cooks. So if they hurt Hayden in any way, we got to do the same to their prince and so on. It was a rule that was hardly enforced due to the distance each Isle kept. Either way, I was glad Theodon and Vesta wrote it into existence amongst the Original Four.

"Hayden, as your soon to be Captain of the Guard and your friend, I promise," Adan continued as he placed a balled-up fist across his chest and over his heart, "I promise, no harm will come to her, I will protect her with my life."

It was very sweet, although I knew he was protecting me for Hayden's sake more than my own.

After a few more drinks between Hayden and I, Adan just silently observing, we finally began hashing out the plan. A few of my belongings had already been moved to the kitchen quarters, and I would follow shortly after. There were some staff who already knew about my secret, those who understood the game we'd been playing for years. But for those who didn't know me, or didn't know who I truly was, they would just think I was a new servant, an extra pair of hands for the coronation. I'd help prepare the meals and serve the guests.

A frown tugged at my lips, disappointment prickling under my skin. I would never get to wear the gown I'd had specifically made for the event, the ruby-red dress with actual shimmering rubies sewn into the bodice, each one catching the light like tiny flames. For once, I could've been the Ember Princess. Just for one night.

But I supposed the kitchen maid garb would do. It wasn't the same, but it would have to be enough.

We turned to leave Hayden's room, only to stop just before the door as he called after us. "I want to charge up your pendant before they arrive," he said, his tone serious.

"Hay, I'll be fine," I replied. I wasn't in the mood for another one of his protective gestures.

"Please, Eli," he said, the urgency creeping into his voice. "It'll give me peace of mind, knowing you'll have some sort of protection."

I hated when he asked for this. I hated needing him to drain a piece of himself for my sake. But, as much as I hated it, I knew it was necessary. That pendant had gotten me out of trouble more times than I could count.

It was no ordinary trinket. The firestone opal embedded in it was unique, crafted with my family's blood, shaped into a swirling design, the copper twisting around it like a flame. The opal shimmered with an ethereal glow, as though it contained a fragment of the Ember itself. Hayden, being the keeper of the Ember, could charge the stone with a portion of his power that I could channel as my own. It wasn't much, just some fire magic I could use for a short amount of time before the pendant was drained. But the cost to Hayden was steep. Even giving that small amount of energy left him weakened. I saw it in his face every time, how pale his skin would grow, how tightly he would clench his jaw as if the act physically pained him. But I understood why he did it.

Throughout the Isles each fae was gifted with a small trace of magic, magic that was to be respected and not abused. The royal lines of each Isle, the direct descendants of the Original Four and Theodon himself, were the most powerful and able to manipulate the element we were born bound to. Most of the lesser fae who received only a fraction of the elemental powers from the Original Four could only harness small traces of their elemental magic. But even then, it was only to be used in times of need in order to honor their gift. I wasn't sure if Hayden sharing his magic with me was frowned upon by Theodon himself, or if the act was seen as him being noble. Either way I hated that I needed his assistance in such matters.

"Fine," I sighed, begrudgingly conceding. "Follow me to my room and charge it, but please, don't give too much of yourself to

it. Can't have our future king be weaker than his powerless twin."
I teased.

"Plenty of me to go around, don't you worry," he said with a half-smile, though it didn't quite reach his eyes.

I bit back a sigh as he stepped aside, letting us pass through the door. It was time to put the plan in motion.

Over the next two days, the entire castle buzzed with frantic energy as preparations for the coronation and the arrival of the Ivy Isle guests began in earnest. But honestly, I wasn't sure which event had the staff more stressed, the coronation itself, or the arrival of our powerful neighbors. The tension in the air was almost suffocating.

Hayden was preoccupied with his princely duties, the ones that fell squarely on his shoulders as the future king. Among them was the Royal Hunt, a centuries-old tradition that required him to provide every single dish for the grand feast. Every potato needed to be dug up by him. Every piece of fruit, plucked from the trees by his hand. Every bird, rabbit, and small game had to be hunted and killed by no one but Hayden himself during the week leading up to his coronation. And, of course, there was the desert stag, the great and mighty beast that would be the centerpiece of the banquet, roasted and served for the royal table. It was always saved for last, ensuring it was fresh, tender, and perfect for the feast.

I begged Hayden to let me join him on the hunt. I had always loved the thrill of it, tracking through the scorching dunes, the stillness of the desert broken only by the rush of wind and the hunt itself. But tradition was clear: only the firstborn could participate in the hunt, and according to the royal documents, I wasn't the first born.

Never mind the fact that Hayden and I were twins and that I had arrived first, by mere minutes, but it was his name that would be crowned, not mine. His future that was destined to shine, not mine. A technicality that I often wondered would upset Theodon or not.

As for the hunt itself, finding a large enough desert stag this season was going to be difficult. The Isle had been shrinking for years. The land's natural resources were growing scarce, the great desert that stretched for miles becoming emptier with every passing year. Fewer animals roamed its depths. Even the mighty desert stag, a creature once abundant across our rugged, sun-scorched lands, was becoming a rare sight. It was a bitter reminder of the shrinking power of our kingdom, and I could see the frustration mounting in Hayden's eyes as he prepared for the hunt.

But more than that, the dwindling resources were a reminder of why my identity had to remain hidden for as long as possible. It was no secret that our isle was fading but if people knew about me, it wouldn't take long for our people's silly superstitions to focus that blame solely on the royal family. I could already hear the rumors that would swirl, the whispers in the hallways of the castle, in the taverns, and on the wind. Our people, believing my existence was the cause of the weakening magic. A stain on the bloodline. They would claim that Hayden couldn't possibly inherit the full strength of the Ember while I was alive. The slightest flicker of power within me, mere sparks compared to his fiery brilliance. It would be enough to create doubts in the minds of the people. While I knew our people adored Hayden, their loyalty could shift quickly if they felt betrayed. They could demand an alternative heir, or worse, call for both Hayden and I to be executed if they saw us as a threat to the strength of the Isle. This would ensure the Ember naturally absorbed back into my father, giving the Isle another chance at an heir who would leave no room for doubt about whether or not they held the Ember's full power. Even with that assurance, we could never predict what would come next, but one thing remained certain: chaos would only spring from the truth.

I had to live with this secret. And so did Hayden. It was just part of the gig, a burden neither of us had chosen, but one we were forced to carry.

The morning before the coronation, they arrived. King Caraway Ironwood and his retinue had, to my surprise, actually followed through and shown up as two ships showed up at our docks. The palace buzzed with activity as news of their arrival spread like wildfire. Hayden and my parents made their way to the docks to greet them, accompanied by an entourage of guards, servants, and, if the rumors were to be believed, at least a few females from the Black Cinder, the Ember Isle's pleasure hall. Clearly, the Ironwood's were being treated with the utmost care and respect. They were rolling out the royal carpet in every sense of the phrase.

And where was I during this monumental event? Deep within the heart of the palace, surrounded by the clatter of pots and the warm scents of roasting meats and rising dough. I had been tasked with preparing the tea and cakes, which, truth be told, wasn't all that dreadful. I had always loved cooking and baking. It was an art, a craft that demanded precision and patience, and one I was particularly good at. Yet, despite the comfort of the familiar, I couldn't shake the sense of longing. It wasn't just the cakes that were sweet, it was the idea of being part of something historic. A meeting between two of the great houses of Ainoah, the Ironwoods and the Pyronias. I could never have imagined that in a million years they would sit down for an intimate tea in our very own palace. The thought of such an event, rich with political significance, made my heart ache. I wanted to be part of it, to witness it, to somehow be included.

But instead, I was confined to the kitchens, my role as a mere servant more apparent than ever. I tried not to dwell on it as I continued frosting the cakes, smoothing the rich, velvety buttercream with the precise movements of my spatula.

"How are those cakes coming along?" A voice crackled from behind me, deep and surly.

Kalynda.

"I'm just finishing the frosting on the last few!" I called back over my shoulder, keeping my focus on the task at hand, my lips curling in a small, tight smile as I did.

Of all the staff in the kitchens this morning, Kalynda was the only one who knew who I truly was. The only one who knew my secret. She had worked in the palace longer than anyone could remember. She was ancient, and yet, somehow, still thrived in the bustling kitchen, always on the move, always at ease with whatever task she was given.

Kalynda had started in the palace years ago in her youth as a stable-hand. From there, she worked as a handmaid and later trained to become one of the palace's healers. She was a jack of all trades and, by all accounts, a master of every one of them. As she liked to put it, "Life's too short to only be the master of one skill. Might as well learn them all."

She wasn't kidding. Despite her silver hair and the fine web of wrinkles etched into her face, Kalynda had the vitality of someone much younger. I'd heard rumors, most of them whispered by the older staff, that she had lived for centuries, and while fae age slowly after the age of twenty, there was something about Kalynda that made me think she was older than any of us could guess. It was in her confidence and the way she carried herself. Always so sure about everything. She'd probably been alive when the Isles first split. Could she have known Theodon and Vesta, or the Original Rulers of Ainoah? If she had, she wasn't about to share any of those stories. She never did. And I wouldn't dare ask. Kalynda's age was a mystery wrapped in an enigma, and it was best left that way.

"Not long now," she muttered, peering over my shoulder, her sharp eyes scanning the cakes I was decorating with practiced precision. Her tone softened, as it always did when she gave me advice. "Make sure the cakes have just the right balance of sweetness. A touch of spice, a whisper of warmth, nothing too overpowering. Just like the tea. It's all about the balance."

I nodded, grateful for her steadying presence. Kalynda always knew exactly what to say, even if she didn't say much at all. She had a way of teaching that didn't feel like teaching, she simply made you see things differently.

It was hard not to wonder, though, what she thought of my current situation. Did she pity me? Did she think I deserved to be more than this? To have a place beside my brother, to be seen for who I truly was? Or did she, like everyone else, see me only as the secret twin, the powerless princess who wasn't supposed to be seen at all?

"They're here!" One of the young kitchen maids, Adena, squealed with excitement, her voice a high-pitched trill that sent the air around us buzzing. She nearly dropped her tea tray in her haste, only managing to catch it at the last moment. "Can I be the one to serve them? Oh please, Kalynda," she begged.

Kalynda, who was no stranger to this sort of behavior, raised a brow and answered dryly, "Yes, Adena, as long as you stop using those lashes on me like I'm a young Fae male you're trying to seduce." She handed Adena another tray, her tone not shifting an inch. "And take Tana with you. I don't trust you won't spill tea all over their royal laps."

Adena and Tana exchanged knowing glances, giggling as they fluffed their hair in the reflection of the kitchen's brass pots. They weren't subtle about it, both of them pinching each other's cheeks to create a rosy glow, before bending slightly forward to adjust the bodices of their uniforms. They had done this before. I could see it in their synchronized movements, deliberate, practiced, a little too eager. I wondered if they even knew what Prince Hawthorne looked like. Did they? They probably hadn't even bothered to ask, too caught up in their imaginations and fantasies about the Ivy Isle prince. As for me, I knew it didn't matter. I wasn't going to be part of that world today. I wasn't even allowed in the same room. I would be stuck back here, hidden in the kitchens for the whole event. It was for the best, I told myself.

The luncheon began shortly after, with Adena and Tana shuffling back and forth between the kitchen and the royal dining area, their cheeks flushed, their gazes glimmering with more than just anticipation. Each time they came back, they were touching themselves up, smoothing their skirts, fixing their hair and giggling to each other like schoolgirls. I couldn't help but roll my eyes as I refilled their trays with fresh courses. They were acting like love-struck fools, and the worst part was, they didn't even realize how transparent they were.

"He winked at me!" Tana screeched, her voice piercing the air like the clang of metal on stone. "Prince Hawthorne actually winked at me!" Her eyes were wide with excitement, and she practically bounced on her heels.

Adena's voice cut in, slightly more composed but no less enthusiastic. "Well, he told me my complexion would look most beauteous in his forests, away from all this desert sand."

I bit back a sarcastic comment. Typical. They had clearly fallen for the first string of sweet, meaningless words the prince had thrown their way.

I leaned in slightly, voice dripping with fake sweetness as I refilled their teacups. "Let me guess. He promised to take you away to his kingdom on the Ivy Isle?" I couldn't help the edge of mockery in my tone, even if they couldn't hear it.

"Well, not in so many words," Adena said, a little breathless as she met my gaze. "But he definitely seemed to enjoy our company," she added, her voice lowering into something flirtatious and self-assured.

"Maybe he'll invite us to his bedchamber tonight?" Tana chimed in, her voice just as breathy and light, as if she already imagined herself in the prince's arms. The way they spoke was almost unbearable. It was quite annoying in fact; just how silly they were acting around our guests. Guests that we shouldn't want here to begin with.

Idiots, I thought to myself.

I could already picture it. Prince Hawthorne would likely invite them to his chambers, charm them with a few more words, and have his fun. Afterward, he would move on, seeking new prey for the next day. If what these two were saying was true, it was clear the prince had no long-term intentions. The prince was a rogue, through and through. He wasn't looking for anything serious, nothing meaningful just something quick and easy. And these females? They were easy prey.

"Well," I said, handing them the now full tray with a smile that didn't reach my eyes, "I hope you three have fun tonight." The words slipped out almost without thinking, too sugary to be genuine, too bitter to be polite.

The two girls beamed at me, their giggles echoing as they bounced out of the kitchen, no doubt already planning how they would dazzle the prince. Kalynda had been right, of course. If they weren't careful, they'd spill the entire tray of tea into the royal guest's lap. But that seemed like a minor concern compared to what was coming next.

As the kitchen door swung closed behind them, I couldn't help but feel a little sorry for them. They were about to be played, and not in the way they imagined.

I found myself drifting, my focus slipping as I absently scrubbed at a pile of dirty dishes. The clink of porcelain against the sink echoed in the otherwise quiet kitchen, and for a moment, I felt as though I were a ghost, moving through the motions without truly being present. Was it jealousy? I wasn't sure. Maybe. Maybe I envied the attention Adena and Tana were getting, even if it was based on nothing more than their pretty faces and a few flattering words from a prince.

Even if those compliments were empty, just part of his act, it still stung. A part of me longed to be the one receiving those looks, to feel the flutter of someone's gaze landing on me with that same hunger. Maybe it was a naive desire, but who didn't want to be swept off their feet? Even for a moment.

Then again, wasn't that exactly what I was doing, too? Playing a part? The innocent, wide-eyed fae, yearning for something more? Something real? The thought made me laugh bitterly to myself.

That would never be me. Not while I was stuck in the shadows of my own life, hiding who I truly was. Not with the double life I led, always veiled in secrecy. The only male I knew who truly understood the weight of it was Adan. And, as much as I cared for him, I was certain he only saw me as his little sister. He couldn't possibly think of me in any other way.

Still, it didn't stop me from imagining, just for a moment, what it might be like to be like Adena and Tana, to be the doe-eyed romantic, the one who could play the part of the girl eager for love. Maybe I could pretend. At least for today. For this event. A fleeting chance to feel something other than the weight of my own secret.

"Wake up, girl!" Kalynda's voice snapped me out of my reverie, the sharp tone making me realize what had happened. My gaze dropped, and there, resting in shards across the stone floor, was a broken teacup. The faintest echo of it still lingered in the air.

"I'm sorry, I was just thinking," I muttered, not realizing until now how lost I had become in my own thoughts. "I didn't mean to—"

Kalynda didn't look upset, though. Instead, her eyes softened as she knelt to pick up the broken pieces. "It's alright, Eli. I've seen you do worse, honestly."

She was right. I wasn't exactly known for my grace. But Kalynda, ever the steady presence, wasn't one to chastise. She simply gave me a look before standing up and turning towards me. "It was those two girls, wasn't it?" she asked, her voice gentler now, though still carrying that familiar edge of insight.

I froze for a moment, before my reflexes kicked in. "I don't know what you mean," I replied quickly, pretending to focus on the dishes again. But I could feel the lie curling in my chest, the unease rising in my throat.

Kalynda wasn't fooled. "Eli," she said softly, "I've known you your whole life, do you honestly think I can't tell when you're lying?"

"I just…" I trailed off, unsure how to finish the thought.

Kalynda didn't let me linger on it for too long. She reached out, gently guiding me away from the sink and toward one of the small, worn chairs arranged around the kitchen table. "Sit," she ordered. Her tone softened, and I realized it wasn't scolding.

"You want to be there, don't you?" she asked quietly, her eyes locking with mine like she could see right through me. "You want those experiences; you want to be included. You're not wrong to feel that way, Eli." Her hands rested on my shoulders, grounding me. "You were dealt a bad hand, but it won't always be like this. You won't be this shadow that your parents created forever."

I couldn't speak at first. Her words lingered in my mind, too much for me to process all at once. It was true, wasn't it? The way I had always been pushed aside, hidden away. Forced into the shadows while others got to live their lives, their desires, their dreams.

I wanted to protest, to argue that my life wasn't all bad, but deep down I knew she was right. Kalynda always had a way of getting to the heart of things.

"You'll see," Kalynda continued, her tone softening further. "Once your brother takes the throne, things will change. All the pressure will fall on him. He'll marry, and that Ember will pass to his firstborn. No one will be questioning the royal lineage then."

Her words hit me like a jolt of cold water. It was true. Once Hayden was crowned and secured a new heir, I would no longer be a threat. I wouldn't be the ghost of Ember Isle, the supposed flaw in the royal bloodline.

I swallowed the knot in my throat. A weight I didn't realize I had been carrying was suddenly lifted, just a little bit.

I reached out without thinking and pulled Kalynda into a long, tight hug, my arms wrapping around her like a lifeline. "Thank you," I whispered. "I think I needed to hear that."

Kalynda chuckled, a warm, sound that made my chest tighten with gratitude. "You're most welcome, Eli. Now," She pulled away from the hug, her expression lightening, "finish those dishes, huh?"

I groaned, rolling my eyes. "Kalynda—"

"You may be the princess," she said, wagging a finger at me with a sly smile, "but in this kitchen, I am the queen. Now get to it."

I couldn't help but laugh as I returned to the sink. No matter how many royal duties and expectations weighed on my shoulders, Kalynda would always keep me grounded, and for that, I was grateful.

A few hours later, the dining hall finally cleared out. Though I never set foot inside, the sounds that drifted through the kitchen were oddly peaceful. There was no shouting, no glasses shattering or hasty arguments. No drunken brawls or angry words exchanged. From what I could tell, the meal had passed without incident. All the glassware had been carefully returned, each cup and plate in perfect condition. Was this a new era for Ember Isle? Perhaps the other Isles would hear about this and finally see that we could all coexist, even if we had spent centuries living separately.

I wondered if the Ivy Isle's visit might mark the beginning of something bigger, something that could bridge the divide between our Isles. After all, were we really that different? Sure, we all had our little quirks, our physical traits that separated us, but at the end of the day, we were all fae. All tied to Theodon and Vesta. Maybe this was the first step toward the unity we all so desperately needed.

With those hopeful thoughts swirling in my head, I finished the dishes in near silence. Tana and Adena had long since been distracted by their fluttering excitement over the prince's attention. I couldn't blame them, though. If I were in their shoes,

I'd probably be just as giddy, despite knowing full well that it was all part of the prince's game. A trick to lure somebody into his bed for the evening.

"The dishes are all done," Adena said with an air of lightness in her voice. She glanced over at Kalynda, a hopeful look in her eyes. "May we be dismissed?"

Kalynda, as always, was thorough in her inspection. She squinted at each plate and cup with the practiced gaze of someone who had spent years in the service of royalty. After a long pause, she gave her verdict. "Looks good enough. You may go."

Adena and Tana exchanged a quick, satisfied glance before they disappeared, their voices trailing behind them as they giggled excitedly. Snippets of their conversation echoed through the hall behind the closing doors, something about a plan involving Prince Hawthorne's chamber and a staged "accident," they were certain would give them the perfect excuse to slip into his room.

I rolled my eyes. Didn't they realize there was no need for their schemes? I had never known a male to turn down a willing, young female, especially not ones as inviting as Tana and Adena. The two of them had the kind of bodies that turned heads. Slim, yet perfectly curved in all the right places, with skin the color of rich honey and long, lustrous ebony hair that framed their faces like something out of a fairy tale.

I suppose it wasn't hard to see why the prince had been drawn to them. If their beauty standards on the Ivy Isle were anything like ours, I had no doubt that the prince would find them more than desirable.

The sound of their giggling faded as they made their way up the hall. My attention snapped back to the kitchen, where Kalynda's voice broke through my thoughts.

"I believe our guests have retired to their rooms for the day," she said, her eyes narrowing with something akin to concern. "You should be safe to move about the castle now, as long as you keep up the kitchen maid ruse."

"Great," I replied with a sharp edge of sarcasm in my tone as I rolled my eyes. "I think I'll make myself a plate of those leftover cakes and head to my room for the rest of the day."

Kalynda gave me a confused look, her gray eyes softening with something close to pity. She didn't speak, but simply nodded before turning to leave, the sound of her footsteps echoing as she departed. She knew me too well. She knew how much I hated hiding; how much I hated being shut away in my room like some delicate treasure.

As a child, that had been the solution my parents had settled on, either take me to the safe house or keep me locked up in my room, far away from any potential danger or scandal. And for years, that was what I'd done. I had spent so many nights pacing those four walls, staring at the same old pictures, the same old furniture, the same old memories. The longer I was trapped in that room, the more I felt like I was suffocating. But I hated the safe house even more. At least in the palace I had corridors I could sneak around in. I had my loved ones just a room or a floor away. But at the safe house, I was miles away from everything and everyone I loved. It wasn't that I didn't understand why they did it, it was for my protection, after all, but it never made it easier.

It was only when Hayden had pitched the idea that I could "blend in" with the staff during these important events that things had started to change. It took a lot of convincing, but eventually, my parents agreed. They had seen how much I hated the solitude, how my room had become a place of unease. If it weren't for Hayden and Adan sneaking me out to their rooms on occasion, or even setting up small slumber parties on my own to make it feel less suffocating, I doubt my room would be as bearable as it was.

Still, I was never good at sitting still, not when there was so much life happening just beyond my reach. Becoming part of the staff during these events had given me a chance to exist, to be a part of things without having to be the princess everyone tiptoed around. It also made me realize just how much effort had gone into making my family and the higher fae more comfortable, things that often went unnoticed. Though the servants were lesser fae in terms of power, they were far from lacking in other qualities. They each had strengths that I came to respect and learn from. From the archers, I honed my precision and strategy; from the cooks, I discovered creativity and adaptability; from the stable hands, I gained resilience and the power of hard work; and from the maids, I learned patience and the importance of small details. These lessons shaped me, teaching me to value what others might overlook.

As I got to know them over the years, I found that, in addition to all of these skills, they were incredibly welcoming, even when I was simply playing the part of an extra pair of hands to help. I would never think less of them, especially not after witnessing their hard work first-hand. It served as a reminder that you should never judge a book by its cover.

I took a deep breath, pulling myself from my thoughts as I grabbed a tray and filled it with the leftover cakes, their sweet scent teasing me as I prepared to take my little escape. For the moment, I was content with pretending to be someone else. I could pretend to be a simple kitchen maid, just another face in the crowd that no one would look twice at.

As I prepared to make my way out of the kitchen, I couldn't help but wonder what the next few days would bring. Would it all go smoothly, or would the tension between the Isles come to a head? Only time would tell, but one thing was certain: this coronation was going to be a turning point. One way or another, something was going to change.

I looked down at my tray of treats, each one making my mouth water. I scooped a bit of frosting off the top of one of the cupcakes with my finger and happily sucked it clean. I was never one to brag, but damn, I'd really outdone myself this time. I hoped our guests agreed. My plate now overflowing with cakes, scones, and fruit, a little tower of sweetness ready to carry me off to my room.

But just as I was about to make my escape, a voice called out from behind me, making me jump and causing my carefully balanced tower of treats to slip from my grasp and topple straight to the floor. Pastries and shattered glass scattered everywhere, a beautiful disaster.

"Ah! I'm so sorry," the voice apologized, sounding genuinely concerned.

"I-it's alright," I stammered, my voice shaking as I turned to assess the damage. "I just wasn't expecting anyone else back here."

"Here, let me help," the stranger said, appearing beside me in an instant, kneeling to gather the broken pieces of plate.

I glanced up at him. The kitchen lighting was dim, but he didn't look familiar. Although, given the polished green and black leathers he was wearing with a hint of silver intertwined into the fabric, it was clear he was one of the royal guards escorting the king and prince from the Ivy Isle. His coal-black hair was combed back with meticulous care, and there was a commanding presence about him, though his eyes were soft and warm. A royal guard, for sure. Maybe even a captain? Branton and Adan both had the same clean and composed look. Looking professional was their job, a direct reflection of the families they served. It was probably the same expectations for the guards on the Ivy Isle.

"It's not fine," the stranger said, a hint of amusement in his voice as he carefully picked up a broken piece of plate. "If I hadn't startled you, you'd still have a full plate of those delicious cakes."

Did he just call my cakes delicious? I felt a small smile tug at my lips from his confession. Wait, had the guards been allowed to sample some of the desserts during the lunch? Maybe he had been testing them for poison. Even with the "life for a life" rule, you couldn't be too careful, especially not with royals.

"I was actually down here to see if there were any leftovers I could... borrow," he said with a grin, picking up a cupcake now covered in dust and debris. "But I guess what was left of them is now scattered on the floor."

"You would be correct," I answered, sighing as I reached for the glass shards, trying to salvage something from the wreckage.

"Careful," he warned, reaching for my hand before I could touch the broken glass. "Wouldn't want you to cut yourself."

I hesitated for a moment, watching his large, calloused hand hover near mine. Of course I'd be careful. If I bled now, it would ruin everything. Depending on how good his vision was in the low light of the kitchens, the shimmer of my blood would give me away in an instant. And this stranger from the Ivy Isle? Who knew what he'd do with that information. Probably run straight to the king and prince and alert them, causing a whole chain of events we weren't prepared for. My heart fluttered nervously.

"Why?" I asked, trying to keep my voice light as I pulled my hand away from his grasp, "Does blood make you squeamish?"

"No," he replied, his teasing tone matching mine as he carefully set the remaining desserts on the counter. "I just wouldn't want to see anything pierce and stain that silky flesh of yours."

Silky flesh? Was this just how males from the Ivy Isle spoke? Maybe they were all charming rogues. I took a bit of him in, searching to see if the stories were true, but I could see no thorns in sight. Just smooth patches of skin peeking out below his uniform. For a moment I forgot I was supposed to be offended by his words, not enamored with his skin.

"Excuse me?" I asked as a sudden heat spread across my cheeks, my face surely turning a deep shade of pink.

"You heard me," he said with a cheeky grin, placing the fallen desserts on the counter. "I didn't see you at the luncheon today. Why were they hiding you back here?"

The very word *hide* felt like a cold splash of water in my face. Was he onto me? Was he starting to piece it together? I quickly shook the thought away; there's no way they could've figured it out. I was being irrational, jumping to conclusions. But why did he have to say *hide*? Why that word, of all things?

After a deep breath, I forced myself to calm down, I couldn't afford to forget the role I was playing. "I wasn't hiding," I replied, my voice steady despite the lump forming in my throat. "I was working."

"So were the others," he continued, a playful lilt in his voice as he leaned in slightly, "but they made at least one appearance in the dining room. Some curious and desperate to get a glimpse of the Ivy King and *prince*."

"Well, someone had to stay behind to make sure lunch was coming along perfectly." I said quickly, the lie slipping out easier than I'd expected. I turned away from him, hoping to hide the sudden flush of warmth spreading across my face.

"So," he continued, shifting closer to me, "what were you working so hard on back here instead of, you know, throwing yourself at the prince like the others?" He slid closer to my side, leaning in as though curious to see what I'd say next.

"These," I answered flatly, picking up one of the fallen cupcakes and examining it for any signs of imperfection other than the coat of dust and grime now on it. "I made these, along with everything else served at the tea luncheon."

There was a long pause, and for a moment, I thought he might speak, but instead he just stared at me with an intrigued expression.

"You made all of these?"

"Yes, and that's why I was busy back here, no time for pleasantries." I forced a smile, trying to mask the hurt that I didn't even realize had slipped into my voice.

"Not even for your guests?"

"No," I murmured, not lifting my gaze from the mess. The sting of being excluded from everything was more painful than I'd realized. "It's not a kitchen maid's job to greet our guests, royal or not. My place is here."

"Well, if it's not too forward of me to say," he whispered, his voice suddenly lower as his hand gently cupped my face to turn my head towards his, "I would like to express my gratitude for the spread. Everything was delectable. The best desserts I have ever had the pleasure of tasting."

His words made my chest feel lighter, though the fluttering in my stomach made me uncomfortable. It was a simple compliment, but somehow, it felt like more, like he was seeing me for something other than my role here.

"Thank you," I said softly, my eyes still focused on the countertop. I let my cheek rest gently into his palm, feeling the heat of his skin radiate through my own. For just a moment, I closed my eyes, letting the warmth of his touch lull my racing thoughts into silence. It was a feeling I hadn't allowed myself to enjoy in so long, and I almost didn't want to pull away from it.

"You're welcome," he murmured, his thumb tracing the curve of my cheek before pulling away. I blinked, and then he held his thumb up, showing me it was now coated with frosting.

"Oh no," I said, blinking in embarrassment. How long had I looked like this?

"Well, it looks like there's still some left after all," he said, smiling down at me, and slowly, deliberately, he brought his thumb to his lips.

"Delicious," he moaned as he slowly sucked the frosting from his thumb. "I think your skin may have made it sweeter."

My breath hitched in my throat, my body flushing hot with an unfamiliar sensation. He was absolutely doing this on purpose. And though I tried to remind myself that I shouldn't be affected by him, I was. I could feel my pulse quicken, and I was almost certain he noticed. His teasing was playful, but there was something underneath it, something that made my chest tighten with a mix of anticipation and nervousness.

But no matter how hard my body betrayed me; I wasn't going to fall for it. I wouldn't.

"Would you like a taste?" he purred as he slid his thumb over my bottom lip.

How did we get here? I steadied my breathing. I thought I would pull away but my body had other plans and instead I leaned into his touch. The soft pad of his thumb exploring my lips, my eyes began to close, enjoying the soft back and forth of his gentle touch. I started to open my mouth to let him in and really taste him, but then I shook my head to snap myself out of it and my body finally obeyed as I took a step back.

"I'm sorry, I did not mean to make you feel uncomfortable."

"It's alright," I quickly squeaked, my eyes finally meeting his gaze.

The air between us was charged, taut with something I couldn't quite name. As his gaze locked onto mine, a strange, unsettling sensation ran down my spine. Those eyes... those eyes were like nothing I had ever seen before. Not just green, but a green that seemed to shimmer, no, shift, as though the light itself were playing tricks on me. And then there was silver. It wasn't just a hint, not just a fleeting glimmer. Those silver flecks were deep, swirling within the emerald, as if they were liquid and flickering like stars.

My heart skipped a beat. How had I not noticed it before?

The longer I stared, the more I felt the heat of his gaze seeping into me, crawling beneath my skin. Was it the green that held the power? Or was it the silver, like tiny lightning strikes scattered through the storm of his irises? I blinked rapidly, trying to clear the haze from my vision, but it only made everything worse. His eyes pulled me in further, spinning, blending, until I could no longer tell if they were green with a touch of silver or silver with a touch of green.

I swallowed hard, the air suddenly thick, pressing against my chest. There was only one explanation for eyes like those. The rare, otherworldly eyes of—

No, no, no. Please don't let it be true.

His next words hit me like a shockwave. "Are you alright? You look like you've seen a spirit."

My blood ran cold. My knees wobbled. The world around me seemed to go still. I took a shaky step back, instinctively retreating. But I was trapped. I was backed against the cold stone wall of the kitchen, unable to move.

"W-who?" My voice cracked, a thin thread of panic cutting through my throat. My pulse hammered in my ears. "Who are you?"

He smiled. But it wasn't a friendly smile. It was something knowing, something dangerous.

"I think you've just figured it out."

My heart stuttered in my chest. *Oh no.* My mind raced, scrambling for some explanation, some way to make sense of what was happening. I wanted to run, to scream, to break free. But his presence was overwhelming, suffocating. He was too close now. Too close for comfort, too close for my own sanity.

I didn't want to believe it. I couldn't believe it. But the longer I stared into his eyes, the more impossible it became to deny. Those eyes. They weren't just unusual. As the sickening realization continued to crawl up my spine.

I quickly tore my gaze away, heart in my throat, and jerked my hand to my chest, fumbling to tuck the fire opal pendant deeper into my dress. *Please don't see it. Please don't know.*

But it wasn't just the pendant. It was my eyes, the golden flecks in the amber hardly evident, but a fellow royal would surely know. If he looked too deeply, if he knew what he was seeing, then my secret would be laid bare. Everything I had fought to keep hidden, my family's lies, the bloodline I tried to ignore, would come crashing down. I could only hope the dim light hid the faint traces of gold in my eyes, silently praying to Theodon that he didn't spot them at first glance.

His hands pressed against the wall, caging me in even more tightly. He was inches from me now, his breath hot on my skin, his presence suffocating.

"Why didn't you say something sooner?" I asked as he reached out, his fingers grazing the delicate line of my jaw. I shivered, both from his touch and the dangerous knowing in his voice. I struggled to keep control of my breathing.

"I thought you already knew who I was," a sly smile curled on his lips. "But now that you do, am I making you nervous?"

His eyes never left mine, reminding me I needed to look away, to hide my eyes. And as I stood there, heart hammering in my chest, I realized just how precariously balanced this moment was. One wrong move, one misstep, and he would know everything.

"No," I quickly replied, "but what do you want from me?" As a prince, he was probably used to women throwing themselves at him, giving him whatever he wanted, unless this was about something else entirely. Unless he already suspected my identity and was going to confront me.

His thumb brushed gently over my bottom lip, and my breath hitched. The proximity was unbearable, and yet I couldn't pull away.

I glanced up for just a second and watched as a slow, teasing smile spread across his face while he stepped even closer, his body practically pressed against mine now. His scent was like pine, fresh and intoxicating as it filled the air around me, I found myself weakening under the heat of his gaze, under the pressure of his proximity. "Well, when you didn't respond like the others, I wanted to have a little fun."

I felt the ground beneath me tilt as the world swayed dangerously out of balance. No, this wasn't happening.

"Please," I whispered, struggling to regain control of my voice. "I—I have to bow. I—"

But before I could finish the sentence, his hand moved to tuck a stray copper curl behind my ear, his fingers lingering a little too long on the soft skin of my neck. I felt my breath catch in my throat, my pulse quickening, as his touch sent a shiver down my spine.

"Why?" His voice was low, almost predatory. "I am not your prince."

I felt a flush rise to my cheeks at his words; at the way his gaze burned into me. The heat was unbearable. "You are still a prince, and I need to follow the protocol."

"Why?" he repeated, his lips so close to my ear that I could feel the warmth of his breath brushing against my skin. His words were like a soft caress, each one making my pulse race. "Why the formalities, when you're already so... close?"

My heart was pounding so loudly I could barely hear myself think under the pulse in my ears. I can't let him get too close. I can't let him see.

"I... I can make some treats for you, if you'd like," I said, the words tumbling out before I even realized it just trying to stray away from the situation I was currently in. "I can have them sent to your room."

His gaze darkened, his lips curling into a slow, wicked grin. "Only if it's no trouble."

The back of his hand brushed so gently down the side of my ribcage, following the curve of my body. The touch was almost languid, dragging as if he had all the time in the world, and with each agonizing second, I felt my resolve cracking. His knuckles brushed against my skin with maddening slowness, making every inch of my body come alive in a way I had never known.

Heat pooled in my stomach, swirling with something darker, something that scared me more than any danger I had ever faced.

I pushed him back suddenly, forcing myself to regain control, though it felt like every fiber of my being screamed to pull him closer. I took a shaky breath, my voice trembling as I exhaled the words I knew I had to say. "Alright. An hour. I'll have them ready."

Prince Hawthorne stepped back, eyeing me up and down with a gaze that was nothing short of predatory. His lips curved into a smirk, his teeth grazing his lower lip in that way that made my stomach twist.

"Looking forward to something sweet," he said, winking as he turned and exited the kitchen, leaving me alone with the dense cloud of everything I had just discovered.

I was shaking, the adrenaline still coursing through my veins. By the grace of Theodon.

This wasn't just some male from the Ivy Isle; this was the prince from a bloodline I was never supposed to cross paths with. And now, I didn't know how to get away without him unraveling everything.

I couldn't bring myself to deliver the sweets to Prince Hawthorne's chambers, despite the strange pull I still felt toward him. That look in his eyes, like a predator watching his prey. I was no fool to think I could go near him again without losing whatever tenuous grip I had on my own composure. The feeling of his skin on mine, his gentle touch. *No.* I couldn't think of that right now. I had already gotten too close today, and I didn't want to risk it again, not with everything hanging in the balance.

So instead, I sent Tana. She practically squealed when I asked her to take the cakes to the prince, and I'm fairly sure we lost a glass flute or two in the process. I couldn't help but feel a brief flare of jealousy flicker inside of me, even though I knew it was ridiculous. Tana had the freedom to live unapologetically, without the burden of responsibilities pressing down on her. She was free to explore males without fear. She didn't have to worry about the consequences of crossing paths with someone like him. But I did, and the thought of seeing him again stirred up feelings I couldn't quite control.

I had to focus on the bigger picture: tonight's feast. The last grand celebration of my parents' reign before they passed the mantle over to Hayden. Then, tomorrow, the day that should have been one of the happiest of my life, the coronation. I could handle that. Once the Ironwood royals left, I could slip back into the shadows, let the court return to its usual rhythm, and pretend none of this had ever happened.

Kalynda, as always, was overseeing the final preparations for the feast. The kitchen was alive with activity, the air thick with the scent of roasted meats, spiced breads, and simmering stews. Tana, of course, was nowhere to be found, and I had a good guess as to where she had disappeared off to. I didn't dare let my mind linger there. I had more important matters to focus on.

I stirred the pot of desert rabbit stew, trying to steady my thoughts. Hayden had returned earlier that day from another successful hunt. The wild game was impressive: birds, rabbits, even a few baskets of fish from the Solana Oasis. Hayden had truly outdone himself. The Ember Isle was mostly desert, with the few oasis spots scattered like precious jewels in the midst of barren sand, and the water had always been a source of pride. But even that was beginning to dwindle, just like everything else. The oasis that Hayden had traveled to, that had taken him the better part of the day, was one of the few places where fish still thrived. It seemed like an impossible task, and yet, there he was, with baskets full of fish and stories of how he'd braved the farthest edge of the desert for them.

Tomorrow, he would have to venture even farther to hunt the desert stag for the coronation feast, an even more difficult trek. But for today, at least, he had proven his worth.

I wiped the sweat from my brow, my apron sticking slightly to my skin as the heat from the stove intensified. "Alright," I breathed, feeling the exhaustion seep through my bones. "That should be everything."

Kalynda, ever the perfectionist, took a ladle and dipped it into the stew, inspecting it as if she were trying to analyze every flavor.

She slurped a spoonful with satisfaction, and for a moment, I held my breath, awaiting her verdict.

"Well?" I asked eagerly, my heart in my throat. Kalynda had been on the Ember Isle far longer than anyone I knew, and her approval meant the world to me. If anyone could tell if something was truly good, it was her.

"Delectable!" she exclaimed with a broad smile, licking the remnants from her lips. "You outdid yourself on this one. The seasoning is perfect, the meat tender, and the broth." She made a noise of contentment that made me proud. "You've learned well, child."

My chest swelled with pride. "Thank you, Kalynda," I said, offering a small bow as a jest, though my heart felt lighter. "If you don't mind, I think I want to see Hayden before the feast and then retire for the evening."

"If you don't mind?" Kalynda snorted in amusement. "Who am I to deny such a request to the Princess?"

I smiled at her and began to remove my apron, the fabric heavy from the long hours in the kitchen. "I thought you were the queen of the kitchen?"

"Oh, I am," she replied, stepping closer and surprising me with a sudden, tight embrace. "But I will always know who you truly are," she whispered, her arms enveloping me in a warmth that was far more tender than I was prepared for.

I froze for a second, surprised by the affection. Kalynda and I had shared only a handful of hugs over the years, mostly at times of loss or celebration. Her embrace was a rare thing, especially in front of others. But this felt different. Almost protective.

"I'm fine, really," I reassured her as I pulled back slightly, giving her a small, hesitant smile.

Kalynda studied me for a long moment, her weathered eyes locking onto mine as if she could see straight through the walls I'd so carefully built around myself. For the first time, I felt like I really saw her, not just the lines that time had drawn across her face, but the quiet strength beneath them. Her eyes, though dulled by age, still held a warmth that caught me off guard, like embers glowing low in a dying fire. Strands of silver framed her face, slipping free from the braid that hung over one shoulder, as a quiet sigh escaped her and an unspoken sadness seemed to settle across her features.

It was as though she were on the verge of saying something. I watched her mouth part, her lips trembling as though the words were caught between them, only for her to close it tightly, shaking her head slowly in a subtle, almost imperceptible movement. "It should have been you," she whispered, her words so soft I almost didn't catch them.

I blinked, unsure if I had heard her correctly. "What?"

She gave a nervous laugh, shaking her head as if to dismiss it. "Oh, just an old fae rambling," she said with forced cheer, breaking our embrace and taking a step back. "Go see your brother, and try not to sulk all night. You deserve some peace this evening."

I stood still for a moment, her words hanging in the air. *It should have been you.* I couldn't fathom what she meant. I had little magic, no ability to rule in the way my family could. I could barely look after myself, let alone an entire kingdom.

But Kalynda didn't wait for me to speak again. She simply gave me a smile before turning away to check in on the other kitchen maids, leaving me alone for a moment with the confusing turmoil of her words.

I took a deep breath, trying to shake off the heaviness that lingered in my chest. Not tonight. I had a feast to prepare for. And a brother to find.

I began to gather the few items I brought with me to the kitchen when all of the side chatter that had become white noise to my ears suddenly went silent. I turned around to see everyone in the kitchen bent at the waist in a bow. Scanning the area, I saw them, Queen Alynta and King Keegan, my parents. With them were Branton and Adan.

I felt a light backhanded slap hit my ribs. "What?" I hissed at Kalynda, who was also in a bow. "Oh, right," I mumbled and began to lower myself into a dramatic bow. In this role, I wasn't their daughter the princess. Just a mere kitchen maid.

"You may rise," my mother said in a melodious tone.

Instantly, everyone stood a little straighter, waiting for the signal to return to their work in the kitchen. My mother made a small, elegant gesture with her hand, and the others immediately resumed their duties. But then, with a deliberate motion, she crooked her fingers at me, a silent command for me to come closer.

There had to be a good reason why my parents were here. I hoped things with the Ironwoods were still peaceful, but the look on my parents' stoic faces gave no hint. Maybe Prince Hawthorne was on to me and had seen right through my kitchen maid ruse. Did he share what he discovered with his father and, in turn, with my parents? My heart began to race.

"You, girl, Eli, is it?" my mother asked, playing the part of a stranger.

"Yes, Your Majesty."

"Come this way, we need to speak with you."

I nodded and followed my parents along with Branton and Adan out of the kitchen and into the servant's passageways. To most, these halls were a maze, but not for me. With how often I had to use them to sneak around while playing a part, I could navigate them blindfolded. The hall darkened as Branton closed the passage door with only a few torches on the wall bringing in a bit of light. Branton stood guard with his son, both with concerned expressions plastered on their faces as they guarded the door.

This must be serious. I took a large gulp and spoke. "What's wrong? Is it Hayden?"

"No," my father spoke in a quiet voice while he glanced down the hall to ensure we were alone. "It's about you. Why didn't you tell us you ran into the Ivy Prince?" His eyes now filled with anger. Or was it worry?

Shit. How did they know? "I didn't realize it was him at first, and it was only for a few moments—"

"He saw you!" My mother scolded, her sharp voice echoing through the hall. "How could you let this happen? Don't you understand how dangerous this could be?"

"It wasn't on purpose!" I began to shout, my father holding his hand out to shush me. Keeping my composure, I took a deep breath and continued, "It was an accident. He was in the kitchen looking for sweets. I told him they were all gone and that I would send more up to his chambers. That's it!"

"Then why is he specifically requesting you?" My father grunted, raising his eyebrows as he awaited an answer.

Requesting me for what? Oh no. Did he really think I was some common whore he could order up to his room just like room service? That he could just bed me, no questions asked? He truly was a rogue.

"How do you know he was requesting me?" I asked, hoping they were wrong and perhaps it was Adena or Tana he was looking for.

"He asked for the company of the maiden he met in the kitchen with the wild, flame-like hair, face covered with beautiful soot. Sound familiar?" My father tapped a foot on the stone floor, awaiting my response.

Adena certainly didn't look like that, nor did Tana. But soot-covered face? Was he referring to my freckles? I couldn't tell if it was a compliment, though he did say "beautiful."

"Did he see your eyes?" My father demanded.

I replayed the events in my mind and shook my head. He couldn't have seen them, not with the dim lighting in the kitchen and the brief moments our eyes met. The flecks of gold in my eyes were so much lighter than Hayden's, barely noticeable unless someone was truly searching for them. He couldn't have seen enough to suspect anything, not after all my efforts to keep my gaze locked to the floor.

I held my hand to my chest, panic rising. "No, I barely looked at him, I swear!" That was the truth. This wasn't my fault.

"Well," my mother began, "even if his only intention was to bed you, it's still too risky. He wasn't supposed to see you let alone know you even existed. It's safer to have you leave."

"Leave!" I exclaimed, my voice growing louder again.

"Adan will escort you to our safe house outside the capital."

The words landed like a punch to the gut as a wave of panic surged through me. I looked desperately at my parents, searching their faces for any hint they might change their minds. For any sign that this wasn't real and they didn't mean it. But their expressions were blank, as if their minds had already been made up.

"When?" I asked, feeling tears pool in the corner of my eyes.

I shot a glance toward Adan as my stomach twisted inside. I hated that house, and Adan knew it. I watched as his brows furrowed, his eyes momentarily filled with a sad gaze before his composure turned stoic once again. So many times in my younger years, I was sent there feeling nothing but loneliness. Adan had heard my cries to Hayden each time I returned. It wasn't just the house, but how it made me feel. Like I didn't matter, like I was unwanted. Just thinking about it sent a wave of anxiety through my body.

"Tonight," my mother answered, her tone leaving no room for argument. She knew I despised it there, yet she was still sending me. "I am so sorry, love, but it's for the best. You will have Adan there, and you will be safe."

"No, please," I begged as another stray tear rolled down my cheek and dripped onto the stone floor. "I will be fine. My pendant is fully charged. It will keep me safe. I'll even stay in my room. I won't come out, I promise. Just please don't send me away."

My mind whirled with the memories of that place. The place that felt more like a prison than a home.

There were no personal touches or comforts, just an empty fortress for me to hide in. An unsettling quiet always hung in the air, nothing like the energy I felt here, even when confined to my room, and nothing like the joyous sounds of laughter and music promised by the coronation underway. I needed to be here. Even though I could no longer attend the coronation as a guest, I needed to be near Hayden on one of the most important days of his life. Maybe it was a twin thing, or simply a sibling thing, but I didn't want to leave. I couldn't leave. I would be content just to hear the party from my room if that was all I could get. I just couldn't be sent away again.

This was such an overreaction on my parents' part. I could stay away from the Ivy Prince, blend back into the shadows like I was supposed to. I had to change their minds. "Please don't cast me off," I pleaded, my trembling voice under control now. My glossy eyes looked toward Adan, hoping he would chime in and say something, do something.

"Eliane, you know that's not the intent," my father started, his voice soft but still stern. "We just want to protect you. It's only for a few days. Once the Ironwoods leave, we'll have Adan escort you back immediately."

"Adan," I softly spoke as I approached him and his father, still guarding the door. "You know you want to be here for Hayden just as much as I do, please don't take me there."

Adan stared at me for a long while. I could see the wheels turning in his head. I knew he didn't want to leave either. Hayden was his best friend after all. He needed to be here. I needed to be here.

After a long pause, Adan cleared his throat and finally spoke.

"Your Majesties, if I may interject, I think it would be safer for the Ember Princess to remain here."

"Son," Branton grumbled.

"If we were to leave tonight, this close to the coronation, it could be dangerous." Adan finished as he took a step toward my parents.

"Explain?" My mother said with a scowl, arms crossed at his disagreement.

"Well, until the Ironwoods leave with the entirety of their party, we really don't know who could be out and about. There is still a decent number of Ivy Guards at the docks guarding the ships. For all we know, King Caraway could have stragglers exploring the

Isle ever since they arrived. If we were to be followed, it could compromise our largest source of protection. The house is there to protect your Majesties as well and it serves as the royal family's last line of defense if needed."

He was actually on my side. Though I was sure it was for Hayden's benefit rather than my own. The way my parents' faces twisted made me feel like they weren't buying into his excuse, but after a long silence, my mother finally spoke, "And you will stay in your room, you promise?"

I nodded quickly, before they could reconsider. I had never felt so relieved to promise to stay locked in my room.

"Adan, you will stand guard at her door until the Ironwoods are off the Isle," my father commanded.

I saw a flicker of sadness cross Adan's face at my father's orders before he quickly masked it, returning to his stoic demeanor. "No," I quickly let out. "Let him enjoy the party. He's going to be Hayden's Captain of the Guard. He should be there for the crowning, it would look odd if he was not there for the ceremony." I said in one breath. "Send a different guard." I could see a little bit of relief sweep over Adan's face with my suggestion.

"Fine," my father huffed. "Branton, please find Tyson and inform him of his new assignment. And Adan, please escort the Ember Princess to her bedchamber and wait for Tyson to arrive and dismiss you." Both Branton and Adan nodded to these requests.

Branton and my parents disappeared back into the kitchens, leaving Adan and me alone in the passageway.

"Thank you," I whispered, giving Adan a light embrace while I buried my head in his chest. Another wave of tears began to flow freely.

For a moment, Adan just held me like that. It felt safe and warm; his arms wrapped around my back and his chin resting lightly on the top of my head. His smooth, warm breaths caused a loose strand of my hair to blow with each exhale. I knew he was just as thankful to stay as I was.

Finally pulling away Adan spoke, "Now," he started while his hands drifted down to my shoulders, holding me in place, "you have to promise me you will stay put."

"Yes," I agreed, "after I see Hayden."

"No," Adan quickly barked, "I was instructed to take you straight to your room, no pit stops," he finished and grabbed my hand to lead us down the passage and towards my room.

"But Adan—"

"Look Eli, I am thankful for your insistence that I be present for the coronation, believe me, but my orders were to take you straight to your chambers, and that is what I will do."

"Then send Hayden to me!" I argued and pulled my hand away from his grip. "I just want to see him before to coronation."

"I will arrange for him to visit in the morning before the Royal Hunt, alright?" Adan answered, extending his hand back out to continue guiding me down the path.

"What about tonight?"

"No, he will be too busy tonight," Adan responded with a little bit of discomfort in his voice.

I knew what that meant, Hayden was probably already deep into the whisky and deep into a female or two having a pre-party orgy. Maybe it could wait until tomorrow. My stomach churned at the idea of seeing a hoard of naked fae riding or being ridden by my brother. "Fine," I said with a huff.

Adan hurried us through the passageway, each step marked by a slight hesitation, until I finally decided to pull ahead and take the lead.

"Eli, what are you doing?" Adan scolded. "You said you would cooperate and go to your room."

"And I will, but you're going the wrong way!" I shot back. I couldn't really be angry; I knew these corridors much better than he ever would. "Let me lead the way. We'll get there much faster, I promise."

Adan was reluctant at first, a male always needing some control, but eventually, he allowed me to guide us until we reached the path to my floor. As we reached the end of the hall, Adan pushed the door open to make sure the floor leading to my room was clear. I let out a small scoff as his guard instincts kicked in, though unnecessary. No one was ever on my floor. The rooms surrounding mine were once guest rooms, but they were mostly used for storage now due to keeping my long-term presence here a secret. No one ever came to this floor except for my family or one of the few handmaidens who knew of my existence. Other than that, it was always quiet. But tonight, it would be different; I could already hear the swell of music rising from below. The party must be starting, and even though I couldn't go, I was thankful that I could hear the music and revelry down below. If I closed my eyes, I could imagine I was there.

Adan pulled me from the hall, snapping me back to reality and towards my door. "Let's make this quick before somebody sees you," Adan whispered as he placed a gentle hand on my back and guided me towards my room.

I fell into step and marched through the doorway, all the while Adan's hand never left the small of my back, his warmth burning through my clothing and onto my flesh. "You know, you can come in until Tyson gets here," I said coyly, not quite wanting to be alone yet.

Adan's bronzed face turned completely red, "It would not be proper," he sharply replied with a small crack in his voice.

He was always obsessing over protocol, worrying about every little detail to make sure everything was proper. There was something so striking about him—handsome in a way that could make anyone pause—but he often seemed like a wet blanket, so stiff and reserved. I couldn't decide whether it was his seriousness about his position that drew me in as we got older, or if it was that same seriousness that made me want to pull my hair out in frustration. Maybe it was both. I knew deep down I shouldn't feel the pull at all, but I couldn't help it.

Still, I invited him in. I knew he would never agree to what I was suggesting. After all, to him, I was basically his sister—someone to protect, someone to keep at arm's length. But still, there was a strange comfort in knowing how predictable he was, even if it frustrated me to no end. Perhaps that was the allure all along. He was familiar and safe.

Perhaps I was still worked up from my encounter with the prince or the fact that he may have been attracted to me, at least enough to want to bed me rather than Adena or Tana. Or maybe the prince was hoping for all three of us. Our bodies all becoming intertwined with one another unable to see where one ends and another began. Our breaths coming and going in shallow pants while we all found our release together as one. I could feel my flesh turning hot as the pictures of my imagination came to the forefront of my mind. Was it actually like that? I didn't have much experience to go off of so maybe my imagination was nowhere near what really took place in the bedroom. Perhaps I was completely wrong and misinterpreted the stories I had heard by passing guards. Either way, I could feel my complexion reddening at the thought of it all. Maybe being locked in my room was what was best for me tonight.

"Eli," Adan said softly before closing my door, bringing me back to the present.

I had been thinking of Hawthorne, but in that moment, I forgot about the male standing before me. "Yes, Adan?" I asked, my voice slipping into a more sultry tone, wondering, hoping that maybe this would be the moment he'd say something. He had helped me after all.

"Thank you for sticking up for me. It is important that I be there for Hayden, not only because it would look odd if the king-to-be did not have his appointed Captain of the Guard at his side, but because, truly," Adan closed his eyes as if working on a confession, "he means just as much to me as he does to you. Future king or not, I will always be there for him."

I felt my face drop as I took in his words. I wasn't sure if it was from the disappointment of realizing he wasn't here to confess some secret love for me, or the cold reminder that I would miss

Hayden's big day. I knew it was important for Adan to be there, since this was almost as much a coronation for him as it was for Hayden. He would rise in the ranks of the Ember Guard, and both of them had a big night ahead of them. But what about me?

"I truly am sorry you cannot be there," Adan finished with true sadness displayed across his handsome face. "I promise, I will bring Hayden to you tomorrow morning."

"Thank you," I breathed out as Adan shut the door, sealing me inside.

I laid back on my bed, eyes closed, listening to the music from the party drift down the hall, filling the silence in my room. The distant laughter and buzz of voices sounded so far away. Once again, I had been locked away. But this had been my choice, hadn't it? I had said I preferred this over the safe house and I truly did, but then why did I feel so angry? I had gotten my way, yet I couldn't stop the mixture of fury and sadness bubbling inside me. My eyes scanned the room, back and forth across those same four walls I had known all too well. I took a deep breath, trying to dismiss my feelings, but then Hawthorne's face flashed across my mind again. This was his fault. After so many years of silence between our Isles, of course, this had been the event the Ironwoods chose to accept the invitation for. If they hadn't come, I could have worn my dress and blended in with the crowd, no one the wiser. I clenched my teeth, holding onto that ire toward the Ivy King and Prince. At least anger felt better than sadness. For now anyways.

Time passed, and Tyson popped his head in long enough to inform me that Adan had been dismissed for the night. Good, I thought. I hoped he'd have a good time enough for the both of us.

Tyson's face fell for a moment as he glanced over his shoulder before revealing something in his hand. His voice dropped to a conspiratorial whisper. "Don't tell the king and queen about this," he muttered, sliding a small bottle through the crack of the open door.

I wasn't much of a drinker, but tonight, I was willing to make an exception. "I won't say a word," I replied, pressing a finger to my lips as he shot me a teasing wink.

After the door clicked shut behind him, I walked over to the sitting area, poured myself a large glass, and took a sip. This was the kind of wine you were meant to sip slowly, to savor. But tonight, I needed something stronger. I needed to feel something, to drown out the loneliness and the disappointment. I tilted the glass back, draining it faster than I was used to. The warmth of the alcohol spread through me, but it wasn't enough to quiet the buzz in my head or the persistent ache in my heart.

As time dragged on, my anxiety began to bubble up again. Maybe it was the half bottle of wine I had consumed too quickly, or the gnawing feeling in my gut that I was missing out on such an important evening. Everyone was down there, celebrating the end of my parents' reign in preparations for Hayden's big day tomorrow, and I was here, locked away in my room. Alone.

I couldn't just lie here. I had to do something, anything to get my mind off the situation. I swung my legs off the side of the bed, and my eyes landed on my closet door. Inside, my dress hung waiting; the ruby gown I had specifically ordered for tonight's ball leading to the coronation. It stared back at me like a cruel reminder of what I wasn't part of. I ran my fingers gently down the tulle of the skirt.

Memories of the day I was fitted for it flooded my mind. I had imagined wearing it, blending into the crowd of revelers, catching the eye of some handsome stranger who would ask me for a dance. We'd twirl through the ballroom together, our feet never tiring as the night unfolded into something unforgettable. I could have been anyone in that dress, anyone I wanted to be. Free from the weight of the crown and the life I was bound to.

Another flourish of music echoed from below, a waltz. The sound of it made my heart ache, but it also sparked something within me. If I couldn't dance with an eligible prince, or with anyone at all, then I would dance by myself.

I grabbed the dress from the closet and laid it out on my bed. For a moment, I just stared at it, taking in its beauty once again. The way the rubies sparkled in the firelight, the way the fabric seemed to shimmer as if it held its own heartbeat, a silk ribbon laced down the back, delicate and intricate. I wasn't someone who typically enjoyed grand attire, but this dress? This was different. It had been crafted for me, and it felt like a personal statement. The sweetheart neckline of the bodice was a little more daring than I usually wore, bold, even. But for the ball before Hayden's coronation? A night to celebrate the end of my parents' reign and the start of Hayden's? An accomplishment that wasn't mine, yet still felt like my own? I could make an exception. I could wear the gown, with its high slit that exposed more of my leg than I'd ever been comfortable with. For once, I could be the Ember Princess. Just for one night. It deserved to be worn, to be danced in. Even if I was the only one here to enjoy it.

I peeled off the simple kitchen maid garb, feeling an odd sense of relief as the rough cotton fell away. I stepped into the soft tulle of the skirt, feeling its lightness as it brushed against my legs. The fabric floated around my skin, its delicate layers light and airy. As I pulled it up, it flowed easily, almost weightless, catching the light with a soft shimmer. Just putting it on felt like the right choice, like I was finally stepping into the life I had been pretending to live all along. I would have my own celebration, even if it was here in my room, alone.

Lacing up the corset from the back proved to be trickier than I'd anticipated. Without Mirra to help, it was a losing battle. I tried pulling the strings, tugging them tight, but they never came out right. After several attempts, I gave up, leaving the back half undone. It was indecent, I knew that much, but I wasn't about to tear myself apart over perfection when no one would see me. Still, I couldn't help but think that if my mother were here, her heart would surely sink.

Finally, after the losing battle with the corset, I stood before the mirror, fully in the dress. I took in the sight of myself, every inch of fabric, every sparkling ruby and every delicate fold. Though it didn't quite hug my body the way it was supposed due to the loose laces I couldn't reach on my own, a smile tugged at my lips anyway. It felt right. It felt like who I was supposed to be.

Though I was locked away up here, I couldn't help but wonder how things were unfolding down there. I could bet Hayden was already being his charming self, cracking witty jokes, laughing with Hawthorne, or perhaps even bragging about all the females and males he'd bedded. The Ivy Prince seemed like someone Hayden could easily relate to, both rogues in their own way. Maybe my parents, though wary of the Ivy King, were actually getting along, both exploring this new friendship. I hadn't seen King Caraway yet, but if he looked anything like the prince, I was sure he was handsome and charming too. Was there a real alliance, or at least a friendship forming between our Isles? Maybe this was the beginning of peace. But did that mean the prince would be visiting more often? Would this open the door to hosting other Isle royals, forcing me to hide away indefinitely?

It was all too much to think about. I wouldn't let my mind wander to those uncertain thoughts, not when I had music and wine to drown it all out.

Taking a swig from the wine bottle, I felt the warmth spread through me, almost as if the drink were loosening my body and my thoughts. The music below continued to echo through the palace, the waltz weaving its way into my room. I closed my eyes and let the music surround me, imagining the world outside turning into a grand ballroom.

Before I knew it, my feet started moving of their own accord, a gentle sway that matched the rhythm. It was automatic, the steps ingrained from years of lessons I had never wanted but was forced to endure. I raised my arms, pretending I held a partner, and twirled around the room, feeling the dress swirl with me.

I always hated those lessons, the ones that had me trapped inside the palace while other children ran free just outside. I begged for lessons in sword play instead, but was always denied. But now, alone in my room, the dance lessons felt like an old friend. In my mind, the room dissolved. I was no longer in my dreary quarters but somewhere grand, somewhere filled with laughter and the sound of clinking glasses, where I wasn't just the girl in the corner but the one at the center of it all.

My movements grew more fluid, the dizziness creeping in. I wasn't sure if it was the wine or the spinning that made me feel this way, but I didn't mind. It was a nice feeling that blurred the edges of everything around me until nothing mattered except the music and the dance. I hummed along with the next song that echoed into my room, a small hiccup escaping my lips. The perfect cure for hiccups was always drinking water quickly, but I supposed more wine would do the trick.

I reached for the bottle again, tilting it to my lips, only to find it empty. A sudden pang of realization hit me. I drunk the entire thing. A full bottle of wine. Me. The one who could barely handle two glasses before falling asleep or getting sick. But here I was, still standing, still wanting more – though wobbling was a more accurate statement. I couldn't stop now. The party might be happening down there, but I was still here, still in my room, still dancing alone.

Hayden would have been proud of me, I thought, even if he always teased me about how weak my tolerance was. I had proven him wrong. Maybe I could keep this up long enough to forget how lonely it felt to be stuck up here, to forget that tonight wasn't the night I had imagined.

I just needed a little more wine then maybe…maybe I wouldn't feel so empty. I glanced at my reflection in the mirror to make sure I didn't look as sloppy as I felt. My face was flushed, my eyes glossy, but otherwise, I looked alright. If I was going to get more wine, I had to convince Tyson I wasn't already drunk. If he knew I'd finished an entire bottle so quickly, he would surely cut me off. I had to be sneaky. Straightening my posture, I took a deep breath and headed for the door.

"Tyson?" I knocked softly, trying to sound as normal as possible, though a small hiccup escaped my lips. "Tyson, can you hear me?"

The door cracked open just enough for his eye to peek through. "Yes, Your Highness?"

"Could you bring me another bottle of wine?" I asked, trying to sound as innocent as possible.

"You already finished the bottle I gave you?" Tyson scolded.

"No!" I protested quickly, another hiccup escaping. "I was dancing in here, and the skirt of my dress knocked the bottle over. I only got one glass before tragedy struck."

"Should I fetch someone to clean it up?"

"No, it's alright," I said smoothly, my lie slipping out effortlessly. "I took care of it. But with the party still going on, I just want to feel like I'm a part of it."

"And you think wine will help with that?" Tyson asked, sounding suspicious.

"Well, it couldn't hurt."

He grumbled. "Fine. But keep your door locked, and don't leave the room. I'll be back in just a few minutes. And remember—"

"I won't tell my parents," I interrupted, giving him a small, pleading smile.

Tyson hesitated for a moment, then shut the door. I heard his boots retreating down the hall. Good. More wine would be here soon, and I could continue my little party in peace.

I sat back down on the edge of the bed, holding my breath until the hiccups subsided. The music from below had started up again, and I swayed my head side to side, letting the rhythm fill me. My fingers absently toyed with my pendant. It was normally hidden beneath my clothing when I wore it, but with the bodice of my dress so low, it was impossible to miss.

To the untrained eye, it looked like a delicate family heirloom, but Kalynda had known exactly what it was when she gave it to me. The fire opal still hummed faintly with Hayden's power. Each time he charged it, it drained him, leaving him weak and pale for a short while. I hated seeing him like that, the brief body shakes that came with the power transfer always difficult to watch. Still, he was always willing, even happy, to do it. It brought me comfort just having it near. I ran my thumb over its smooth surface, feeling the lingering warmth of his energy, even though I hadn't yet needed to use it. Of all the gifts I'd ever received, it was my favorite.

Gift. That's right. I never gave Hayden his gift.

I froze, suddenly filled with a surge of panic. The small golden box had been sitting in my dresser drawers for days. I'd meant to give it to him tonight before his coronation tomorrow, but that was not happening now.

I looked inside and saw my gift safely nestled in its box. It was a piece of coal from the first Ember King, King Sulien. It was an artifact Kalynda helped me find. I had hoped it would bring Hayden the same good fortune it had brought to Sulien.

I couldn't believe I'd forgotten. Maybe it wasn't too late.

A wicked thought crossed my mind. Maybe I could deliver it tonight. Right now. Tyson was still out fetching my wine, and the secret passageways were my escape. In and out, unseen. I could leave the box in Hayden's room for him to find. The idea sent a thrill through me. No one knew the inner walls of the palace quite like me. I could do this, and no one would suspect a thing. I was sure of it.

I grabbed a quill, my fingers slightly unsteady, and scribbled a quick note: *To Hayden, from El.* Just so he'd know. Then, I slipped out of my room, the soft click of the door behind me nearly silent. The stone wall across from my chamber was seamless, but I knew where the hidden passageway was. Years of practice had me finding the secret stone with ease. One press, and the door creaked open. I stepped through the same passage Adan and I had traveled through earlier, listening for any sounds of movement in the hall. Nothing.

The passage was dark and cool, the air smelling faintly of old stone. My body seemed to know the way even if my mind was a little fuzzy. Two lefts, a right, down the stone steps. Just thirteen steps and I'd be there.

I pushed the door open slowly, poking my head out to check for any signs of life. Empty. Good.

I closed it behind me, the sound muffled, then started down the hall. Hayden's room was just ahead. Adan's room too, but I didn't need to go there. The hallway felt different tonight. Longer, like the walls themselves were closing in. When had those scarlet curtains been put up? I passed the first door, then the second, then on to the third. *Wait. There should only be two doors here, shouldn't there?* My breath caught, and I stopped in my tracks. This wasn't right.

Shit. I'm on the wrong floor.

Had I turned wrong? Two lefts, a right, or was it the other way around? The world felt off-balance, like the wine in my stomach was making the floor sway beneath my feet.

I cursed under my breath. I was too drunk to be sneaking around the halls at this hour. Maybe I should just wait until morning when the walls weren't vibrating in front of my eyes.

I turned and tried retracing my steps, but the passageway eluded me. I pressed against the stone wall, but the door wouldn't budge. My fingers fumbled over the smooth surface. I had come through here hadn't I? I started to frantically slam my palms into the stone, hoping for some sort of sign I hadn't imagined this, that there was indeed a passageway here.

And then I heard it. A giggle. Light and fluttery, echoing from the stairs below. My heart thudded as the sound of not one but two voices started to climb up the steps.

I froze, my breath catching. I couldn't get caught, not with my head spinning and my body wobbling on uncertain legs. I darted behind one of the scarlet curtains, the fabric cool against my arms. The hem of my dress slipped between my fingers as I tucked it under the curtain hiding myself further in the shadow. My heart pounded, loud in my ears, but I held my breath, praying that they wouldn't hear me.

The sounds of giggling voices grow louder and I was sure they must have been just across the hall from where I was hiding. I pressed my hand to my mouth, fingers tight on the golden box clutched in my other hand. I squeezed my eyes shut. *Please don't find me.*

But they didn't pass by. Instead, their giggling turned into soft, heavy breathing, followed by a males grunt. The sounds filtered through the curtains like whispers. I tried to hold my body still, but my heart thudded harder with each passing second. I listened in as a female's voice spoke up between pants.

"I want you to fuck me right here, right now," she whimpered. The female's voice was unmistakable.

Tana. I didn't need to hear any more to know who the male was.

I felt the heat rise in my chest, the strange pull of curiosity tightening my throat. I should've been mortified, horrified even, but I wasn't. I stood there, hidden, breath held, eyes wide. The rhythmic sounds of kissing, low murmurs, and soft, desperate pleas filled the space between us. I was frozen, caught between something wrong and something inexplicably intriguing.

The longer I stood there, the more I realized how completely present I was in the moment. How close I was to a scene I should have never been part of. How very far I was from where I was supposed to be, yet my feet stayed rooted, and I listened.

"So greedy," a smooth voice teased, and I heard the faint sound of a belt unbuckling.

I was right. The voice belonged to Prince Hawthorne. From the sounds of it, he wasn't wasting any time.

He was going to take Tana right here, just as she'd begged.

My pulse quickened. It felt so wrong to be listening to this. But it was clear they weren't heading into his chambers anytime soon, and I couldn't exactly step out from behind the curtain. I'd never live it down. This was torture.

The wet smacking of lips filled the hall, accompanied by the rustling of fabric. I couldn't help but imagine what was happening just on the other side of the curtain. My body warmed, a strange tightness pooling between my legs. This had to be the wine clouding my thoughts, it had to be.

"Your Highness," Tana gasped, breathless, her voice hitching as if something had shocked her. "Please."

"Please what?"

"Stop teasing me and fuck me already!" Tana demanded.

"As you wish," Prince Hawthorne murmured, his words trailing off into whispers I couldn't make out.

A small, involuntary sigh escaped me as I heard their voices become more distant. They were finally heading toward his room. I could escape this madness. Maybe I'd been wrong about Tana. Maybe she wasn't as deluded as I thought. Maybe the prince really was into her, and maybe, he'd give her the life she wanted. I couldn't help but feel a sharp twinge of jealousy. It wasn't logical, but it was there. I shook my head, trying to focus.

The door clicked shut. I hesitated, then peered with one eye out from behind the curtain, scanning the hall. I was safe, for now. No more lovers roaming the halls.

But then, something moved.

Vines, long, twisting tendrils, began to slip under the curtain. My heart skipped a beat. This had to be some trick of the light, or the wine playing cruel games with my mind. I blinked hard, trying to clear the fog from my vision, but the vines didn't disappear. Instead, they curled tighter around my ankles, squeezing.

I took a step back, my breath quickening. The vines twisted around my legs, inching higher, and my pulse raced. *No, no, no. This isn't happening.* Even in my inebriated state I knew this was real and not something my mind conjured up. My legs were locked in place, and with a sudden yank, the vines tugged me backward.

I fell, my head hit the marble floor with a sickening thud. The vines, like serpents, dragged me out from beneath the curtain, pulling me helplessly toward whatever fate awaited me.

"Hasn't anyone told you that it's impolite to spy," a voice hissed.

I watched as the vines now retreated back into their owner's palm, freeing my legs.

He looked down at me, shock was evident in his features. "You? What are you doing here?"

Prince Hawthorne. I should have known it was him. The Ivy Isle fae were blessed with the power to control and conjure plants, to shape them as they wished. Fascinating. Terrifying.

I remained sprawled on the floor, dazed. My heart was still pounding in my chest, my mind racing to catch up with the events that had just unfolded.

What was I doing here? How had I ended up in this mess, dressed like this, drunk, sneaking around in the dark? I tried to push myself up, but the dizziness from the fall kept me down. My throat tightened, and I knew I had to explain, but the words wouldn't come. I couldn't even look him in the eye.

I had to leave. I had to get out of here.

"I'm so s-sorry, Your Highness," I stammered, my voice shaking with a mix of panic and embarrassment. "I got lost on my way to my room, and—"

Before I could finish, Prince Hawthorne stepped closer, offering his hand to me. "Here, let me help you up."

He'd just dragged me across the hall, and now he wanted to help me? The absurdity of it made me want to pull away. "No thanks," I muttered, pushing myself off the marble floor. My legs were still shaky, and I stumbled, nearly losing my balance.

"Whoa," Hawthorne said, his grip tightening around my arm to steady me. "I'm sorry about that, how is your head?" he asked and his voice sounded like it was filled with genuine concern.

I quickly raised my hand to my head, hoping the skin hadn't split, leaving me to have to drunkenly explain my shimmering blood. My heart rate picked up as I lowered my hands, my eyes scanning every inch. Luckily it was dry. I was safe. "I'm sure I'll be feeling it tomorrow once I'm sober."

"How much have you had to drink?"

"Too much," I admitted bluntly.

His touch burned where his fingers wrapped around my arm. I leaned against the cold wall, grateful for the support, but I hated how vulnerable it made me feel.

"I thought you were leaving the capital tonight," he remarked casually.

That stopped me cold. My parents must've told him. They'd probably spun some lie about my departure to get him off my scent. But I hadn't counted on him remembering. I assumed he would have moved onto the next female he was trying to bed. That thought struck a nerve in my chest. I couldn't afford to let him see how much I was rattled. I had to lie.

"My plans changed," I muttered quickly, my gaze dropping to the floor. "I'll be leaving early in the morning, so I must be getting to bed." I tried to pull away from his grip, but his fingers tightened around my arm, holding me in place.

"I didn't see you at the party," he said slowly. I could feel his hand slide down the edge of my dress, grazing the fabric. "I would've remembered this dress. I would've remembered you."

The blood rushed to my face. Of course he would remember the dress. It was a far cry from my usual attire. "I... drank too much wine too fast and felt ill," I said quickly, my voice faltering just a little. "That's why I left early." It wasn't completely a lie, but it wasn't exactly the full truth either.

He didn't seem convinced. His eyes flicked to mine, narrowing slightly as if he were weighing the sincerity of my words. "What are you doing here then?" He glanced around, taking in our surroundings. "This isn't the kitchen maid quarters."

I froze. My throat went dry.

"Explain to me why a kitchen maid would have even been invited to such an event as a guest, and in an expensive dress no doubt?"

Shit. I was caught. There was no graceful way out of this. Why *would* I be there dancing amongst the guest and not tending to my kitchen duties for the evening? Panic fluttered in my chest.

The room seemed to close in around me. My vision blurred around the edges, spots of light dancing in the corners of my eyes. I had to think of something, anything, to throw him off. But my mind was spinning.

I couldn't form a lie fast enough. I could feel his gaze pressing down on me, scrutinizing me, dissecting every word, every movement. I had to say something, or this whole thing would unravel.

The prince still held me up by my arm while I tried to place my other along the wall, needing something to physically ground me. I went to press my hand along the wall but in my grasp was Hayden's gift I was still holding tightly. That was it. Hayden. This would give me an alibi.

"I was invited by Prince Hayden," I said, not technically a lie. "I got sick but I was trying to find his room to drop off this coronation gift." I finished raising the golden box towards Prince Hawthorne to inspect.

"To Hayden from El," he read. "I'm assuming you are El?"

"Yes." I replied, my eyes still refusing to meet his.

"Is that why you truly did not come when I requested you? You already have a prince in your bed?'

"No!" I shouted, appalled at the idea, "I…the Ember Prince and I are just friends."

"Well in that case my offer still stands," he said with a wink.

The audacity of this male. This devastatingly handsome male. And he knew it too, which made it worse. Maybe it was the wine loosening my tongue, but I wasn't about to let him slide.

"If I'm not mistaken, wasn't that Tana with you? And unless I'm seeing things, I'm guessing she's not exactly fully clothed in there, huh?" I asked while I gestured towards the abandoned pile of fabric down the hall.

"You can join if you'd like?" Hawthorne whispered as his body pressed against mine, his shirt already unbuttoned. "Or I can send her away if you want me all to yourself," he said softly as his lips grazed my ear.

My heart felt like it was going to beat right out of my chest. I felt that warm sensation between my legs begin again. I knew I should keep my eyes down but I needed to look at him. My eyes dragged up his body taking in every detail before settling on his face until our eyes finally met. There they were again, just as beautiful as they were before, that green with wisps of silver.

"Your Highness," I said breathlessly.

"Hawthorne," he corrected as he pushed further into me, the undeniable bulge in his trousers pressed against my stomach.

"Hawthorne," I replied, looking down again, this time out of curiosity of his exposed body rather than fear. I studied the lines of his muscled torso; impulse mixed with some liquid courage taking over as I reached my hand out the trace those lines.

"El," Hawthorne moaned under my touch. "It is El, right?"

"Yes," I replied as my hands continued to explore lower.

"What do you say to my offer?" He grabbed my wandering hand from going lower while awaiting my answer.

With my hand halting, the rest of my mind started to catch up. I needed to stop this; I needed to collect myself and get out of here.

"I'm sorry, but I can't."

"Because of Prince Hayden?" he asked with a bit of disappointment in his voice as he released my hand.

"Yes." Which was true, just not in the way he thought it was. "I need to get back to my room, early morning start tomorrow."

"Can I escort you?" he asked while he peeled himself away from my body. The heat between us still lingering as he offered his hand to me.

"No, that's alright, I'll manage," I mumbled as I felt the warm air between us drift as Hawthorne moved further away. "Besides, you don't want to leave Tana waiting."

"She would wait all night if I asked her."

She probably would. Still, I couldn't let him escort me to my room, my actual room without yet another lie and another story. "Tana is very sweet, please don't hurt her," I replied and I began to walk past the prince and down the hall.

"Wait," Hawthorne commanded as he seized my wrist with surprising strength, twirling me back toward him and causing me to stumble until I was flush against his chest. The sudden force made my breath catch in my throat, and my pulse hammered wildly beneath my skin.

I froze, panic twisting in my chest. "What are you doing?" I asked, the words coming out more frantic than I intended. My heart pounded in my ears, and I had to fight to keep my composure. *Does he know? Did he see through me?* The thought made my stomach churn and I dropped my gaze to the exposed skin of his chest. I held my breath, as if even breathing around him was dangerous. I needed to get away, but I was too distracted by the pressure of his hand against my arm and the heat radiating from his body so close to mine.

"You're undone," he said.

In a fluid motion, he turned me around as I felt him gather my untamed hair to one side of my shoulder as he went to work. I could feel his fingertips brush lightly against the exposed skin of my back as he tugged at the loose laces of my bodice. His movements were methodical, practiced, and I had no choice but to stand there as he deftly began to tighten the corset that was only half-secured, leaving me vulnerable in my half-dressed state.

"If you insist on wandering these halls without an escort, at least make it look like you belong here and not as if you were some drunken maid sneaking back to her quarters after a night of fucking" he added, his voice teasing, but the way his fingers glided over my skin sent a jolt through me. There was something calculated in his touch, almost like he knew exactly what it was doing to me. The reality of the situation hit me again like a wave. This was all wrong. But there I stood, completely unable to move.

"Trust me," he murmured, his fingers brushing a little too close to my spine, making my whole body tense under the slow pressure. "I know how drunken males think."

My mind was sluggish, struggling to grasp the full implication of his words. "How do they think?" I asked, the words falling out before I could stop them. My voice was softer, more breathless than I intended. The heat of his body pressed against mine seemed to amplify the warmth already spreading through my own skin, sending a tremor through me. Every movement, every breath of air between us felt charged.

"They think like any sober male," he explained, his voice becoming darker. "Except they lose that little voice that tells them to stop."

I swallowed hard, trying to ignore the way his hands now traced down my back, the skin of my spine tingling under his touch. My mind told me to pull away, to resist, but the heat of his breath, the heat of his skin, had me frozen in place.

Don't look at him. Don't look at him. But my body betrayed me. Slowly, my gaze drifted upward as I craned my neck back, taking in the fine tailoring of his shirt and the sharp cut of his jaw. He was so close. And those green eyes with a storm of silver, caught mine, holding me there in a trance. I couldn't look away.

"What's wrong, El?" he asked, his lips curving into a teasing smile. The softness in his voice only made my heart race faster. His fingers slowly tightened the final knot in the laces, the fabric pulling snug against my ribcage. I felt the soft pressure of his palm on my back as he finished tying the bow, and my breath hitched at the sensation.

His hands lingered there, moving just a little lower, tracing the curve of my waist. My body felt like it was burning under his touch, each caress of his hand leaving a trail of heat in its wake.

"I should be going," I forced out, barely recognizing my own voice. It was strained and breathless, and I hated the way my body responded. I needed to get away from him. Now.

But Hawthorne didn't pull back. Instead, he leaned in, his mouth brushing close to my ear. His lips barely grazed the sensitive skin, and I could feel the heat of his breath against my earlobe. "Yes, I suppose you should," he murmured, his voice husky and full of an undercurrent I couldn't quite place. Then, in one smooth motion, he turned me around, my back now to the wall as he reached for my hand and brought it to his lips, pressing a lingering kiss to the back of it.

His touch was soft, almost too soft for the storm that brewed inside me. "Goodnight, El," he said, and there was something almost intimate in the way he said my name. "Safe travels tomorrow."

I had to force myself to step away. It felt like every part of me was being pulled toward him, as if by a gravitational force. Yet, I managed to step aside, my legs giving way slightly beneath me, as though I were tumbling out of orbit.

I couldn't shake the feeling that something had shifted, that we had crossed a line. And that line was still there, lingering between us, electric.

Just before I could walk away, I stopped myself, a final bit of hesitation gripping me. "Um, Prince Hawthorne?" I asked softly, trying to make my voice sound meek, like I hadn't just nearly fallen apart in his arms. "If you could... keep this little secret, the part about me going to see Hayden, it would be much appreciated."

Hawthorne looked at me, his eyes glittering with an unreadable expression. A small, dangerous smile tugged at his lips. "I never saw you," he said smoothly, and the glint of amusement in his eyes sent a shiver down my spine.

His words hung in the air. I could feel his gaze on me as I turned away, and I couldn't help but still feel the lingering tension between us.

With that, he disappeared into his chambers, and I was left standing alone in the quiet hall, my heart still racing. I took a deep breath, trying to steady myself, but my body was still shaking, whether from the adrenaline or something else, I couldn't tell.

I pressed my hand against the cold stone wall, grounding myself. Focus. I needed to get back. Tyson was probably in full panic mode, and I could only imagine how I'd explain this mess.

With shaky hands, I located the hidden passage, thankfully, more sober now after the shock of the encounter. As I stepped inside, the air seemed cool, but the heat of what had just happened still lingered under my skin. My mind raced. I had to get back to my room, and quickly. Hayden's gift could wait until morning.

One more lie. That's all it took.

I just hope I could keep all the lies straight.

I woke to the sound of pounding, though I wasn't sure if it was coming from my head or somewhere else. My skull throbbed as if it had been struck by a hammer from last night's fall, and the faint scent of stale wine clung to the air. Oddly enough, I wasn't as hungover as I expected. Probably thanks to Tyson's long, drawn-out lecture when I finally staggered back to my room last night. He was furious, of course, but at least he hadn't alerted my parents yet. I guess he knew he would have to be the one to explain how I got past him in the first place.

His punishment had been swift and effective; he'd confiscated my second bottle of wine and made it clear that it was for my own good. Honestly, I was relieved. I didn't have the energy to drink any more, after everything that happened last night. The rest of the evening had passed in a blur when I made it back to my room. I didn't even have the strength to undress, instead I kept the gown on and crawled under the covers before I collapsed, my body weighed down by exhaustion and regret.

The smell of wine and sweat still clung to the sheets, my head was throbbing, reminding me of everything I shouldn't have done. What time was it? The heavy silence of the room made it feel like I'd been asleep for days.

Knock, knock, knock.

That wasn't in my head. Someone was actually knocking.

I jumped out of bed, feeling the disorientation of a night's worth of wine and poor decisions wash over me. The pounding in my skull worsened as I stumbled towards the door, my bare feet dragging across the floor.

"Hayden?" I called out as I flung the door open, already smiling in anticipation.

But my smile faltered when I saw the figure standing in the doorway. Adan.

"Where's Hay?" I asked, confusion and disappointment creeping into my voice. "You said you'd bring him to me this morning."

Adan stepped inside, his expression unreadable as I took a step back, trying to make room for him to enter. He was taller than me, his presence filling the space like he always did. But today, his posture was rigid, his movements tense, as if something had happened to throw him off balance.

"He's not coming," Adan said quietly. His eyes narrowed slightly as he scanned the room, and his nostrils flared as if he could smell something foul. "Were you drinking in here all night? And what the hell are you wearing?" He crossed the room in a few swift strides, his gaze moving from me to the half-dressed bed, taking in every detail of the disarray. His eyes flicked to the empty wine bottle on the side table before narrowing again, clearly appalled by the state of things.

I looked down at myself. Aside from needing to smooth out the skirt, the dress was still nice and tight around my body after Hawthorne had laced me into it. Rather tightly I might add.

"Long story," I muttered, pulling at the fabric of the dress as if that would somehow make me feel less exposed. "Did Hayden already start the hunt, then?" I asked, trying to change the subject and refocus. "Has he left already?" I asked again, my voice coming out sharper than I intended.

"No," Adan replied, but his tone was cryptic, like he was holding something back. He leaned in closer, his eyes scanning the room as if he expected someone else to jump out from the shadows. He lowered his voice as if we were conspiring, though I wasn't sure what about. "That's why I'm here."

I frowned, a knot of tension forming in my chest. My heart rate quickened as a sudden wave of panic washed over me. *Why are you being so secretive, Adan? What do you know?*

"Is he okay?"

What if Hawthorne saw my eyes more clearly last night? My memory was hazy at best, but I was sure I'd looked up at him for just a second longer than I should have. He had been so close, and I couldn't stop myself from staring.

Adan seemed to pick up on my anxiety. He studied me for a moment, his eyes narrowing before he let out a quiet, almost dismissive breath.

"He's fine," Adan said, though there was a tension in his voice that didn't match the calmness of his words. His gaze softened, "but I'm afraid you look like the brightest ember compared to him."

Great. Hayden had managed to get himself utterly plastered last night and probably had a wicked hangover, and on his coronation day, no less. I pressed my lips together, frustration simmering beneath my skin. I wasn't in any position to judge, not with my own head pounding like it was, but it still irritated me. Hayden could be so incredibly moronic at times. He was brilliant in so many ways, but there were days when I honestly didn't know if he was ready for the responsibility that was being thrust upon him.

I sighed, running a hand through my tangled hair. "What can I do to help?"

Adan gave me a sidelong glance, one brow raised, his eyes calculating. "Well, he's not exactly in a state where he can get himself together." He paused, then shrugged. "Can you come with me to his room and get him back on his feet?"

I blinked in surprise. "You'll take me to him?" My voice wavered at the thought of sneaking out of my room under Adan's watchful eye. My parents would never approve, but it wasn't like they could stop me now. "Are you sure?"

"Trust me, the last thing I want is to get caught sneaking you around the palace. But I've done everything I can to help him, and you know you've always been better at getting Hayden back on his feet than I ever was. Plus, you have that twin connection with him, Eli. He always listens to you. If anyone can bring him back to his usual self, it's you."

My heart gave a small, relieved flutter. Of course, I would help Hayden, especially today of all days. Plus, Adan wasn't wrong. Hayden and I shared that unspoken twin connection, that raw understanding of each other. He needed me now, and I wouldn't let him down. "Let's go," I said without a second thought.

Adan and I moved quickly through the secret passageway, the narrow stone hallways echoing faintly as we made our way to Hayden's room. My steps were quieter this time, and I could see clearly the exact route I'd taken last night, the places I'd gone wrong.

We arrived at Hayden's door, and I felt an odd mixture of dread and concern. I hesitated for a split second before gently opening it.

The moment I stepped inside, the smell hit me. It was overpowering, whisky mixed with the unmistakable scent of sex. Salt, sweat, and something sharper, something almost like bile clung to the air. I winced, my stomach twisting as I tried to ignore the nauseating scent.

I scanned the room quickly, my eyes immediately locking onto the evidence of Hayden's reckless night. There were skirts and torn bodices scattered carelessly across the floor, mixed in with discarded trousers. My brother was nothing if not an equal opportunist, and it was clear that his usual antics had carried over into the early hours of the morning.

I lifted the hem of my dress, stepping carefully over puddles of whisky and other liquids I couldn't quite identify. My nose wrinkled in disgust. I hoped to Theodon it was just curdled cream. Instinctively, I pressed my arms tight against my body, shoulders raised in a protective gesture. I wasn't taking any chances.

"Hayden," Adan called out as he approached my brother's bed. Hayden lay sprawled halfway off the mattress, his body twisted and tangled in the sheets, his face flushed with feverish sleep. "Wake up. Eli's here."

There was a muffled groan from Hayden as he slowly stirred beneath the sheets. "Eli?" he mumbled. "I don't want her to see me like this."

I stepped lightly through the mess, trying to avoid stepping on anything that might disgust me even further. "Oh, come on, Hay," I teased lightly, trying to ease the tension in the room. "I've absolutely seen you a lot worse than this." I let out a little giggle to lighten the mood. "Remember the night after the Blaze Ball when you drank so much you were vomiting all over the dance floor? At least you aren't doing that."

As if on cue, Hayden let out a strangled noise and, with a violent lurch, vomited onto the floor, right onto Adan's boots. Brown liquid splashed onto the floor with a sickening sound.

"Sorry," Hayden groaned, barely able to open his eyes, his voice muffled by the hangover.

"It's alright, Hay," Adan said, his face twisting in disgust as he took a step back, holding his nose. I couldn't help but smirk. Poor Adan was usually so composed, but even he couldn't keep his cool in the face of this disaster.

I turned away, heading over to the small bar area Hayden kept stocked with liquor, trying to get my mind off the scene unfolding in front of me and the pungent smell that lingered in the room. I poured Hayden a large glass of water, knowing it would be the only thing I could truly offer to save him from the brutal hangover he was facing. Getting a healer to make a tonic this early wouldn't give us enough time to get him on his feet, not to mention the shame I was sure Hayden would feel if anyone saw him in this state. Water was my best option right now. The water wouldn't cure it, but hopefully it would help.

I brought the glass to his bedside, my voice firm. "Drink," I commanded, holding the glass in front of him.

Hayden blinked up at me, his amber eyes were glazed over, making his golden flecks stand out even more. He closed his eyes before he weakly grabbed the glass, swallowing the water in one go. He gasped for air once it was gone, his face still pale and sweaty. "Another, please."

I poured him another glass, bringing the pitcher to the side of his bed. "After a few more, you'll be good as new," I said, trying to keep my tone upbeat. He needed to hear that, needed to believe it.

But Hayden didn't move. Instead, he collapsed back into the bed, his red curls sprawled out along his pillow as his body sank into the softness of the mattress like he couldn't hold himself up any longer.

"I can't," he muttered, a note of defeat in his voice as he closed his eyes again.

Adan shot me a look that clearly said, *do something*. His eyes flicked back to Hayden, concern still clouding his features. Hayden couldn't possibly be in any condition to carry out his task today. Not in his current state. He might not even have the strength to lift the sacred bow, and he certainly wouldn't be able to leave the palace gates unless he got his act together.

"I'll do it then," Adan said without hesitation. "I can hunt the desert stag in his place."

I looked at him, stunned. Despite Adan being a capable candidate, he had to know the consequences that could follow if anyone found out. Not to mention, he wasn't blood. "The bow won't work if you use it," I reminded him. Only Hayden could wield it. He was the one chosen to perform the Royal Hunt, the one who needed to kill the stag.

The Pyronia bow and arrow was sacred, a symbol of our bloodline's power, and for good reason. The magic embedded within the weapon was tied to our family, passed down through the generations. It could only be wielded by a direct blood relative of the Ember. It wasn't just any weapon, it was the key to a tradition that had been followed for centuries. Each new king or queen was expected to hunt the desert stag before their coronation feast. The hunt wasn't just about providing food for the people; it was about honoring Theodon and Vesta, ensuring their blessings upon the kingdom and the new ruler. The stag had to be hunted by the new ruler alone, using the sacred bow.

I wasn't too superstitious, but even I knew better than to tempt fate on a day like this. Hayden needed to complete the hunt, and it needed to be done with the Pyronia bow. If he failed, it could mean disaster for the kingdom's future, especially with the feast to follow. This was more than just a royal tradition, it was essential for the blessings to flow, for the kingdom to thrive under his reign.

Adan always ready to act before thinking when it came to my brother, was already looking for an alternative. "I'll just use my own bow," he said, voice filled with frustration. "No one has to know."

"No," I snapped back immediately. "It has to be Hayden and it has to be the Pyronia bow. You don't understand, Adan. The food needs to be blessed by Theodon and Vesta. If it's not him, if it's not his blood, they might not accept it and they might not accept him as the future king."

Adan's jaw tightened. He wasn't giving up so easily. "He'll never sober up in time," he argued. "And he's in no shape to go out into the sands like this. I don't even know if he can hold the bow, let alone use it."

He was right. Hayden's state was beyond bad, he couldn't even keep his head up, let alone wander into the desert, aiming for the elusive stag. This was a disaster. I could see my brother's anxiety, his fear of failure, hanging over him like a shadow. I knew how hard he worked to prepare for this day, and to see him unravel in front of me, his future slipping through his fingers like sand broke my heart.

"Hay," I said gently, kneeling beside his bed, putting my hand on his shoulder. His skin was cold and clammy with sweat, but I could feel the tremble of his body as he fought to rise. "This is your big day," I continued softly, trying to offer comfort where I could. "You're going to be a king. A fantastic one, I know it. You just need to take a shower, drink some water, and hunt the stag. After that, you can sleep until they announce you to the court at the feast. They'll understand. But we need you on your feet, now."

"I don't think I'm ready," Hayden mumbled, his eyes glossy, looking far younger and more vulnerable than I'd ever seen him. "Look at me," he added, voice cracking. "I'm a mess."

I could hear the pain in his voice, the crack of uncertainty in his words. My heart clenched for him, but I refused to let him wallow. Hayden wasn't a mess. He was just scared of what lay ahead, and the weight of the crown heavy on his mind.

"You just had a good time last night," I said, my voice soft and reassuring. "Maybe a little too good. But I know your heart, Hay. You love your people, our people. You're ready for this. I know you are."

I paused, trying to gauge the storm of emotions churning in his eyes. My brother was always so confident, so sure of himself, that I'd never guessed just how afraid he truly was. But as the tears welled up in his eyes, it all made sense. Hayden was terrified. And like many, he turned to the bottle when he couldn't face the truth. When he didn't feel enough.

"What if I'm no good at being king?" Hayden asked, the doubt in his voice so raw, so real, that it tore at me. Another stray tear traced down his cheek. "I'm too young, no other heir has taken the throne at my age."

I reached for him, brushing his hair back from his forehead. "You are going to be a wonderful king," I reassured him, forcing a small smile. "It's just nerves, Hay. You've got this."

Adan spoke up then, his voice earnest and steady. "Eli's right. You're just scared. It's completely natural. You just need to get through the hunt."

Hayden let out a choked sob, his face crumpling as more tears spilled down his face. "I'm letting everyone down, aren't I?"

It hurt to see him like this. I wanted so much to fix everything, to tell him that he was enough, but in that moment, all I could do was watch him suffer. The future king, so full of promise, so capable, but trapped in his own doubts. I hated seeing him like this, but I knew one thing: I couldn't let him fail today.

I glanced over towards the stone clock in the corner. It was already a bit past eight. He didn't have the luxury of time. Not anymore. Something needed to be done and fast.

I turned toward Adan, my mind racing. "I'll get the stag," I declared, my voice suddenly clear, like a light had gone on inside me. "I'll hunt it."

"What!" Adan and Hayden said in perfect unison.

"I'll do it," I repeated, more firmly this time. I was already heading toward Hayden's wardrobe. "I share your blood, Hayden," I said as I pulled out the sacred Pyronia bow and arrows, feeling the familiar hum of magic beneath my hands as I traced the delicate fletchings sticking out of the quiver, they felt soft yet powerful beneath my fingertips. The bow was wooden, yet enchanted with golden markings that made it immune to fire. Much like the arrows, the bow sent small sparks of electricity through my flesh. It was like the bow had recognized my touch, a small but noticeable vibration that traveled up my arm. I couldn't help but smile. This was the answer. "Besides, I've always been a much better shot than you," I teased.

Both of their eyes widened in shock, as if the idea had never crossed their minds. It hadn't crossed mine either until now. But as I held the bow, I could feel the connection to our bloodline, the ancestral magic that flowed through it. There was no turning back now.

"You'll do it?" Adan asked, his voice tentative, but there was a flicker of hope in his eyes. "You're really going to—?"

"Yes. I'll make sure the hunt goes as planned. No one will know the difference. I'll use the bow. It's still Pyronia blood, let's just hope Theodon can forgive this minor last-minute change."

Hayden stared at me, the disbelief slowly melting into something else. Relief, maybe? It was hard to tell, but he was starting to look less defeated. "You're going to take my place?" His voice cracked, still hoarse from the alcohol and tears.

"Yes, Hay," I nodded. "You've got enough to deal with today. Get some rest. I'll bring back the stag. You just focus on being ready for the coronation."

"El," Hayden started as his voice became serious, "You can't!"

"And why can't I?" I challenged.

"Well," Adan spoke up, "for starters you aren't even supposed to be out of your room let alone gallivanting though the sands on a hunt!"

"That's why you will need to cover for me," I said as I swung the bow over my shoulder to join the quiver of arrows, "I will use the secret passage to get out of the palace, and you just need to volunteer to keep guard at my room and no one will even know I left."

"I know Hayden won't like it, but let me just get the palace healer. Just wait until we get that handled before you make any rash decisions."

"No, it would take too long to wait for the brew to be made and we've already lost too much time. It has to be me."

"I don't think this is a good idea," Hayden groaned, a look of concern on his face.

"Then sober up and meet me out there!" I scolded him. "Adan, get the healers to start brewing a tonic now, and I'll get a head start. And Hayden, once you're on your feet, meet me out there."

I could do all the hard work and at least track the thing which would be the most time-consuming part of the hunt. Once Hay felt sober enough and met me out there, I would gladly hand the bow over to him to take the shot. As much as I wanted Hayden to feel better, I was kind of excited about this task. It was something I could contribute and only I could do. I had a role in this coronation. I would provide the meal and by the way the bow vibrated in my hand, I knew I had its blessing. Let's just hope I had Theodon's as well.

"Fine," Hayden breathed out, "but please don't let yourself be spotted and I will be out there as soon as this pounding in my head ceases."

I gave Hayden a hug, being careful not to squeeze him too tight in fear he would throw up again and I was back in the passageway armed and ready. Adan followed me through, all the while muttering his concerns for my plan. It didn't matter, I could do this, for Hayden and maybe a little for myself.

We reached the end of the passageway that led to the back of the palace grounds, which resembled a ghost town. Fortunately, it seemed that everyone was still asleep or nursing a hangover from the revelry of last night.

"Wait." Adan spat the words out as he pulled me back into the passageway. "You're going to hunt in that?" He motioned up and down at my dress, disbelief clear in his voice. "I thought you'd at least change first."

"There's no time," I said, my frustration creeping into my voice. "I'm already at least an hour behind. I need to find a horse and leave."

"What about shoes?" Adan asked, pointing to my bare feet.

I looked down and saw my bare flesh gleaming back at me, but before I could come up with a solution to my shoe predicament, Adan bent down, removed his boots, and handed them to me. They were at least two sizes too big and still had a bit of Hayden's vomit along the heels, but there was no time to go back, especially if everyone started waking up.

"Thanks," I muttered as Adan helped me lace up the boots, still warm from his skin.

"Here." Adan swiftly unbuckled his guard leathers, handing them to me. "At least throw this over it. That red dress is bound to send a flare up to anyone who's looking." He wrapped his leather coat around my shoulders.

"It's too hot," I complained, tugging at the edges of the coat.

"Well, with your fairer skin and that barely-there dress, you'll burn in the first hour of sunlight."

I hated that he was right. My skin was much lighter compared to most on the Isle. That's what happens when you're locked indoors for most of your life, away from the glorious sun. Sweating in the thick leathers would be uncomfortable, but a sunburn? That would be worse, unbearable even.

"Alright, fine," I said, annoyance still lingering in my voice. "Get Hayden on his feet, then return to my door like you've been guarding it all morning."

"Be careful, Eli." His voice softened as he gave my shoulder a light squeeze.

His tone was sincere, and it made my heart lurch unexpectedly. Part of me would always have a crush on Adan, and moments like this made me wonder if maybe he felt the same. But Adan was impossible to read. I couldn't afford to waste time on that now. There was a job to do.

I pushed the thought aside and walked across the powder-soft sand, each step sinking slightly into the ground. The path to the stables was as empty as the courtyard. Had everyone truly overindulged last night? For a second, I almost forgot that I, too, had woken up with a foggy head and a heavy body. But now, the task ahead of me cleared my mind. Or, at least, I hoped it did.

7

I hadn't had much experience with riding horses, but I knew enough to get by. Fintana, my white filly, was the one I always practiced on. She'd been a gift from Hay three years ago. He'd told me it was more of a plan than a gift, hoping that by giving me a horse, our parents would allow me out more often, perhaps for riding lessons or to explore the isle with him. His plan was clever, but it hadn't exactly gone the way he'd imagined. My parents thought having a horse that was easily identifiable as one from the Ember Palace would only rise more suspicion. Even with a horse and the riding lessons, my parents kept my riding confined to within the palace walls. This was particularly unfair to Fintana, as she had been eager to leave the grounds just as much as I was. Luckily, Hayden was able to take her out routinely so she could stretch her legs. I suppose it was fine, though. I had preferred to walk anyways, feeling the earth beneath my feet, the heat of the sand between my toes. If it weren't for the fact that I had to bring back an entire stag, I would've chosen to walk to the oasis. But we didn't have time for that. So, Fintana it was.

I saddled her up quickly, my fingers moving through the familiar motions as I adjusted the straps. Fintana shifted beneath me, her coat gleaming in the early morning light. The horse's steady rhythm and the warm morning air almost made me forget the tightness in my chest, the weight of the task ahead. But there was no time for distractions.

The Ember Isle was truly beautiful. I often wondered what fae from other Isles thought of this place. I imagined they assumed we were nothing but an island of endless sand, stretching on for miles with no end in sight. I doubted they ever imagined the hidden pockets of greenery we had. Oases dotted the landscape, with the largest just outside the capital city, the Solana Oasis. That's where I would go. The still waters, as smooth as glass, surrounded by clusters of palm trees, were sure to hold at least one stag. The Isle might be slowly fading, but for now, there was still enough game to go around.

My copper hair whipped across my face as Fintana picked up her pace, responding to the gentle pressure of my heels against her sides. I didn't want to risk anyone in the city seeing me

Once we crossed the boundary beyond the city's walls, I felt a surge of relief. We were finally out of sight. To the left, the sand stretched toward the smaller towns scattered across the Isle, to the right lay the "Forgotten Desert." A barren stretch of land so inhospitable it was almost as if it had been cursed. No water, no trees, no animals that we knew of. Just sand, harsh and endless. It was a place reserved for the worst criminals, those cast out to die, left to face the relentless emptiness.

The desert had no means of survival and no one ever came back from it. No one was sure how it had become so infertile, though many had tried to revive it over the years. But nothing would grow. Water evaporated too quickly, and the sand was coarse and grainy, nothing like the soft, golden grains of the rest of the island. It was just as unpleasant as its purpose.

I'd read in our history books that the Forgotten Desert hadn't always been that way. Once, it was as thriving as any other part of the Isle. But over time, the land slowly withered, like an infection spreading through the earth. Each year, it crept farther. My parents had been meticulous about marking its borders, tracking its spread. It was so slow and subtle that sometimes I wondered when it had first started, when the change had really become noticeable. Maybe it was the same kind of slow fade that was happening across the Isle. I wondered if the other Isles were experiencing a similar effect on portions of their lands.

But no one, not even us, would ever admit to the fading. To do so would show weakness, and we couldn't afford that. The other Isles thought of us as powerful, our land as fertile as our people. If they knew we were fading, they'd see an opportunity to strike, to conquer.

I didn't go left, and I certainly didn't go right. Instead, I went straight, the path leading to the oasis. Beyond that lay smaller towns, patches of fresh water, and enough greenery to keep the island's heart beating. That's where our family's vacation home was. In truth, it was a safe house, my safe house. The bitterness I felt for the place made it hard to see its beauty, but I had little choice. Fortunately, I wouldn't need to venture that far. If my hunch was right, a desert stag should be waiting in the first oasis.

Fintana trotted steadily, her hooves making soft prints in the sand until we finally reached the edge of the greenery. I tied her to a sturdy tree near the entrance, taking care to secure her reins. From here, I would go on foot. I couldn't risk the filly making too much noise among the trees. Stealth was essential if I was going to locate the stag. I would find it, shoot it, and haul it back. That was the plan.

I patted Fintana gently on her side, the soft pressure of my hand grounding me before I reached for my bow and quiver. The bow settled comfortably against my back, its weight a reassuring presence as I turned toward the dense cluster of palm trees towering over me. I hesitated, then instinctively raised my hand to my chest. My fingers brushed over the cool surface of the fire opal hanging just above my breast. Still there. The stone pulsed faintly, warm against my skin, a quiet promise of protection. I let out a sigh, my shoulders loosening. As long as the opal held its charge, I'd be safe, no matter what dangers lurked in the wild.

The Isle wasn't lacking in creatures. Most of them could be found across the world. But here, the magic in the air had twisted some into monstrous forms. The Loa was one of the worst, a beast whose origin was unclear but likely tied to ancient feline bloodlines. I had never seen one before in person, but I had seen plenty of illustrations in books and heard enough stories. It was a massive, spotted cat that could breathe fire. To most fae on Ember Isle, it might not seem like much of a threat, but to me, with my lack of magic, it could be deadly if it overwhelmed me. Its claws and teeth were dagger-like, sharp enough to slice through flesh and muscle, and even fae healing abilities may not heal someone in time before they began to bleed out or succumb to infection.

I remember one day, when I was standing in as an arrow bearer for the archers, overhearing a story that made my blood run cold. One of the new archers in training had ventured too far into the oasis and was attacked by a Loa. Loas were rare, and sightings had been unheard of for years. But that day, one decided to take a fae's life.

He was a lesser fae, still holding onto some magic, but even that wasn't enough to save him. The Loa struck swiftly, its claws raking through the air, tearing through the fae's defenses as if they were paper. The story was detailed, too detailed, and I could almost hear the fae's desperate cries as the creature's massive jaws closed around him, his blood staining the sand.

That incident led to a strict rule: no archer or hunter in training was allowed to enter the oasis without a veteran fae. The thought of it all made my stomach churn. If he hadn't survived, lesser fae or not, there was no way I would have. Luckily, I had my opal. It was my lifeline, fueled with Hay's magic, and should shield me long enough to escape if I ever encountered a Loa.

I strung the bow, the taut string biting into my fingers as I crouched low, scanning the sand for any sign of movement.

Though I could handle a bow, I wasn't a skilled tracker, not like Hayden. I cursed under my breath, eyes sweeping over the ground. The prints were faint, barely discernible. But then I spotted them, small, delicate hoof-prints in the sand. Too small for the stag I was hoping for. A fawn, maybe. The sight of them stirred a flicker of hope in my chest. Life, however fragile, still moved here. A subtle reassurance that the Isle wasn't as barren as it sometimes felt.

I moved deeper beneath the shelter of the palms, sand kicking up around my boots as I made my way toward the water. Hayden had always told me that water was a good place to find game. Animals needed to drink, after all. It seemed like a safe bet.

I'd been searching for what felt like hours, though I'd long lost track of time in the silence. No rustling, no chirps, no calls. The air hung heavy, thick with heat and the quiet. I tugged at the collar of Adan's coat he leant me. The leather stuck uncomfortably to my skin, and beads of sweat formed at my brow. I sighed and pulled the coat off, draping it over a nearby rock, the light breeze bringing me instant relief as the air brushed over the sweat that had gathered on my back.

Now that my skin was exposed, I needed to be cautious about long exposure to the sun. While my skin held a light tan, it was nothing compared to the rest of the fae on the Isle. I would surely burn before my skin had any time to absorb any real color. The shade of the palms would have to do for now, though the sun was relentless, still high and burning in the sky. Sometimes the sun and I would fight, but I truly did love it. The sun gave us life, gave us beautiful painted skies at each sunrise and sunset as it produced some of my favorite colors. I could stare at it all day if I knew I wouldn't go blind.

Continuing, I scanned the horizon again, my eyes flicking from the trees to the water's edge, listening for any hint of movement.

Then, it came.

Crunch, crunch, crunch.

The sound wasn't like the subtle scuffle of a small animal, it was too deliberate, too fast. My heart skipped. It was too big to be a mere creature. A person? Or something worse? My fingers trembled as they instinctively wrapped around the fire opal at my chest, its heat burning through my skin, vibrating with raw, untamed power. My pulse hammered in my throat, each beat syncing with the chaotic rush of Hayden's energy flooding into my palm. Another piercing sound echoed through the oasis, sending a cold spike of panic shooting through me, making my heart race even faster. Maybe it was the relentless hangover, or the suffocating heat pressing down on me, but my thoughts spiraled uncontrollably, sinking deeper into the darkest corners of my mind. My survival instincts surged to life, and I allowed the borrowed magic to flood my senses, desperate for anything to keep me safe and grounded.

In the span of a heartbeat, I reacted. A rush of flame erupted from my fingertips, streaking through the air like a living thing as I aimed toward the source of the sound. The fire flared up, twisting into a towering pillar of bright orange, flooding the shadowed trees with a sudden, intense glow.

The moment the fire shot from me, instant regret hit. I hadn't even considered who or what might be behind me. What if it was Hayden, trailing behind me to catch up? The flame would sting at worst. But what if it wasn't? What if it was a Loa, or something even worse... someone from the Ivy Isle, who would surely find my presence here with the Pyronia bow nothing short of suspicious? My breath caught in my throat. Better to be safe than sorry.

I stood frozen, the heat of the flames still curling in the air, my chest tight, waiting for whatever, or whoever, was out there to reveal itself.

"Hello?" I called out, just in case it was another fae. "Hay, is that you?"

The silence lingered, dense and unnerving. I reached for my pendant once more, my fingers brushing against the smooth stone as I conjured a ball of fire in my palm. The warmth spread up my arm, tingling with the promise of destruction if necessary. "If you value your life, you will come out this instant!" I shouted, my voice sharp, aimed at the now blackened and charred foliage ahead.

I kept my focus on the flame, my fingers clenched around it, ready to throw it at whatever dared to reveal itself. The faint sound of something moving reached my ears, metal clanging, barely perceptible through the still air. The creature was approaching, cautious and deliberate, stepping through the trees with a kind of measured precision. Not a creature, I realized, but definitely another fae.

"Please don't hurl that at me," a deep, husky voice called out from the shadows, its owner unmistakably male.

"Who are you, and why are you out here?" I asked, my grip tightening around the fireball.

The stranger stepped into view, his eyes scanning me with an intensity that made me feel strangely vulnerable. He was tall, his dark clothes frayed and worn as if he had been traveling for a long time. There was a wildness to his appearance that suggested he didn't belong here—at least not in the same way I didn't. His eyes flicked to the fire in my hand, then back to me, and I saw the faintest glimmer of something in them, curiosity, maybe, or amusement.

"I didn't mean to scare you," he said, his voice calm, almost too calm for someone who'd just been threatened with flame. He raised his hands slowly in a gesture of surrender, as though trying to ease the tension in the air. "I'm just passing through."

I wasn't sure where this male had come from, but his pale skin, made me suspicious. He couldn't be from the Ember, not with that complexion, and definitely not with those clothes. Although his attire was a bit ragged, it looked like it was made of thicker material. No one on Ember would ever wear something so impractical, not with our blazing heat. As I scanned his clothes again, I still couldn't place where they might be from, making me wonder why he was even out here to begin with.

"You don't look like you're from here," I said bluntly, still keeping my flame at the ready.

The stranger took a cautious step forward, and the light reflected off the silver strands of his messy, unkempt hair. Despite his apparent dishevelment, there was a certain elegance to his features, sharp cheekbones, a strong jawline, and eyes that seemed to burn with an intensity I couldn't quite place. He looked young, no older than me, though his silver hair had the faintest patches of black giving him a salt-and-pepper look. But with the fae aging process, it would be hard to tell is exact age.

"That's because I'm not from here," he said as he took another cautious step closer. His hands remained raised, fingers slightly curled, as if ready to defend himself if needed.

"Where are you from?" I asked, my voice steady but guarded. I could feel the energy of the fireball in my palm starting to wane. Every second it drained the pendant's power, and if things escalated, I might need that energy to protect myself.

The stranger sighed deeply, lowering his hands slightly but not fully. "Look, I'm not going to hurt you. I'm just trying to pass through and disappear. You'll never see me again."

"You still haven't answered my question."

He let out a long, almost defeated breath, his gaze shifting briefly to the ground before meeting mine again. "I'm originally from the Isle of Gust," he said slowly, as though choosing his words carefully. "But I was taken prisoner by a ship from the Ivy Isle. They brought me here against my will."

I frowned, trying to piece it together. His story didn't add up. fae from the Isle of Gust were mountain dwellers, secretive and isolated, hardly ever leaving their cliffs and caves. They were a reclusive people, proud, self-sufficient, and known to avoid interactions with outsiders.

"Where are your wings then?" I had heard the Gust fae possessed wings of sorts, but this male clearly had none.

"Not all fae from Gust have wings, mostly just those closest to the royal bloodline or High Fae, but sometimes other fae are blessed with them as well, though it is rare." The stranger explained to me as if I were a child. "Trust me, if I had wings, I never would have been caught by the Ivy ship."

King Caraway's fleet must have caught him as he sailed for our Isle. Still, things did not add up. Not much was known about the mountain fae from Gust, as they pretty much kept to themselves, living in isolation in the rocks of the Isle. The only thing I could recall was the story of their missing princess I read from a few scrolls and texts in the palace library. It was said that Queen Camira and her wife Queen Zariyah's first daughter Princess Auretta, the holder of the Gale, much like our Ember, disappeared many years ago before I was born. They were never sure if she ran away of her own accord or was captured, but fifteen years ago they were sure of one thing. Princess Auretta was dead.

With the Gale absorbing back into the wind before returning to the last holder of the gift, this gave the Queens an opportunity to have another heir to pass on the Gale to, the young Prince Eurus. While it was uncommon for a royal fae to perish before passing on their power, there was a provision set in place by Theodon himself to ensure the gift would be passed on. If Hayden were to die before passing on the Ember, it would automatically be absorbed back into the flame and back into the last holder of the Ember, my father. That would give him an opportunity to try and pass it on again to ensure our line was continued. The Isle of Gust Queens were the first in many years to have to conceive again just to secure their line.

They never discovered what truly happened to the princess, but with the life for a life law, no one would dare kill a princess from another Isle without damning their own. Her fate would remain a mystery. Much like the reason this male was out on the open water before being captured. What crimes had he committed to end up imprisoned and dragged along with them? Another mystery.

"What were your crimes?" I asked boldly, my voice steady despite the gnawing unease in my chest. I had to know, especially with him so close. What if it was something like murder? Or worse, rape. I was alone out here, with little hope that Hayden would show up in time to save me if things went wrong. But I couldn't let that show. He was still a stranger.

"Thievery," he answered plainly, closing the space between us without hesitation.

I hadn't even realized how close he had gotten. Now, with him mere paces away, I could see the scar that ran across the corner of his silvery-grey eye, slicing through the bridge of his nose and across his cheek. His gaze, though intense, was striking. His eyes were sharp with the cool gray that it seemed to glow in the fading light, with a sliver of green on the inside of his iris, just around the pupil. The imperfections and uniqueness only added to the allure of his face, an undeniably handsome face that clearly held a story.

"Th-thievery?" I stammered, instinctively taking a step back. I wasn't sure why I felt so flustered. Was it the sudden proximity? Or the fact that this was the second beautiful stranger I had encountered in two days, both of whom left my heart racing and my legs feeling weak. Maybe it was just the isolation catching up with me, the years of being cooped up, seeing no one my age except Adan and Hay. But still, I couldn't shake the feeling that something was off.

"Yes," he confirmed, his voice low and steady. "Not the horrendous crimes you're probably imagining," he added, casually tucking a stray silver lock of hair behind his ear. "I told you, I mean you no harm. If you'll put that fireball away, I'll be out of your way."

"What did you steal?" I asked, still skeptical, but curiosity getting the better of me.

"Fish," he replied quickly, crossing his arms with a slight smirk that tugged at the corner of his mouth.

"From the Ivy King's ship?" I asked, incredulity creeping into my voice. Why would anyone risk stealing from a royal ship?

"As I said, yes," he said with a shrug, his smile widening. "Now, may I pass?"

"Why?" I asked, genuinely curious. "Why would you steal from a king?"

The stranger let out a small, exasperated sigh, though there was a glint of amusement in his eyes. "Look, I don't know if you're just bored or starved for attention, but I've got somewhere I need to be before King Caraway's guards realize I've slipped through their fingers."

"I'm not asking for a story," I said, trying to keep the annoyance out of my voice. "Just answer me, and I'll let you pass."

He seemed to consider it for a moment before muttering, "Fine." He shifted his weight slightly, clearly preparing to give an explanation. "I was out with a small crew, looking for food. Our Isle's resources are dwindling, and things are getting desperate. We weren't having any luck, and that's when we saw the ship. We didn't know it was royal, hell, we didn't even care. We boarded it out of desperation, and my crew, well, they didn't make it. The Ivy King threw them overboard to the sea's mercy and I was taken prisoner for questioning."

His voice faltered just slightly at the mention of his crew, and I noticed the distant, haunted look in his eyes. It wasn't a facade. He'd lost people, people he cared about. I could hear the weight of his words and see the tension in his posture. This wasn't just a story; it was the reality of his survival.

"I've been stuck on their docked ship for the last two days. This morning, I managed to knock out a few guards and make a run for it." He paused for a moment, glancing away. "Now I'm just trying to get as far as possible before they come after me."

So, it wasn't just my island suffering. His was, too. The famine, the dwindling resources, it wasn't just affecting us. So, what did that mean for the other two Isles? Were they struggling for resources as well? It couldn't be a coincidence that two of the four Isles were depleting. I'd need to tell my parents, tell Hayden. This was a bigger problem than just my own Isle.

I felt a pang of sympathy for the stranger. I extinguished the fireball in my hand, the embers flickering out until only faint sparks lingered on my fingertips. Then, with a reluctant step to the side, I mumbled, "You may pass, then."

"Well, little fire girl," he said with a light chuckle, "that was exhausting."

"Don't call me that!" I retorted, irritation bubbling to the surface.

His grin widened, unbothered by my frustration. "How about Sparks, then? Yeah, I'm going to call you Sparks, unless you'd like to share your actual name?" His tone had that teasing lilt again, and despite myself, I felt my cheeks flush.

"I thought you were leaving?" I shot back, trying to mask the betrayal of my emotions. "Didn't you say you had to get as far away as possible?"

"I do," he replied with a mischievous gleam in his eyes. "But now it's my turn to ask *you* some questions."

"Me?" I asked, trying to sound innocent, but already bracing for whatever he'd say next. After all, I had no reason to be out here alone either, and I was starting to wonder if he'd realized that too.

"Yes," he answered smoothly, his eyes glinting with amusement. "What is a girl in a ball gown doing all the way out here alone, and armed with a bow and arrow, no less?"

"I'm not alone" I snapped, suddenly defensive.

"With the Ember Prince, then?" he asked as he began to circle me slowly, studying me like a hawk.

I could easily feed into his assumptions. If I told him I was with Hayden, he'd likely back off, not wanting to risk the wrath of another royal. "Yes," I lied, my voice sounding more confident than I felt. "How did you know?" I tried to sound casual, but the question caught me off guard. Had he seen Hayden? Maybe Hay was on his way now.

The stranger shrugged, unfazed. "I overheard the guards talking about a royal hunt this morning. They mentioned it was something the Ember Prince had to do alone, prove his worth, provide for the Isle. But here you are, and where's the prince? "

Shit. How was I going to explain this? He might be a passing stranger, but in the short time I'd known him, it was clear he had a knack for conversation. There was no way he could know the bow I held was bound by the Pyronia bloodline just by looking at it. But if he told anyone he found me out here, a female dressed more for a ball than a hunt, holding a bow and tracking a stag, what would people say? I needed a story, and I needed one fast.

"I'm just holding this," I said, gesturing to the bow with a sharp flick of my wrist. "The prince is out tracking."

"Why you, though?" The stranger leaned against a palm tree, folding his arms as his eyes studied me with that unnerving intensity. "You don't exactly look like one of his guards."

A lie formed in my head, a disgusting one, but the best I could come up with. "He wants to bed me," I said, trying to sound nonchalant, though I felt the bile rising in my throat.

His lips curled into a sly smile. "Well, considering you're still in last night's gown, and with hair that can only be described as 'sex hair,' I'd say the prince already had his fun with you last night."

That made my stomach churn, but more than that, it made me self-conscious. My hair must've looked like a tangled mess, and suddenly I felt the intensity of his gaze, as if it could see right through me. But I pushed the discomfort aside. I had to stick to the lie. "No. I got sick last night. Nothing happened," I groaned, injecting just enough truth to make it believable. "But I promised Hay—Prince Hayden—that if he brought me on the hunt, I'd let him do whatever he wanted with me after the kill. However and wherever he likes." I pressed a hand to my stomach as nausea twisted inside me, both from the disgusting lie I had just told and the lingering effects of last night's drink.

The stranger pushed off the tree and took a slow step toward me, that smug grin still in place. "Can't say I blame him," he purred, his eyes flashing with some unreadable thought. "I'd probably let you tag along anywhere if you made me that deal. I bet you taste delicious."

His words sent a strange flutter through me, like butterflies in my stomach. But it only made the nausea worse. I quickly turned away, pressing a hand to my mouth, willing myself not to vomit. *Not here, not now.* I didn't want to embarrass myself in front of him. Why was he still hanging around?

"Hey, you okay?" His voice softened, and suddenly, I felt his hand on my shoulder, gentle yet steady. "I was just joking. Didn't mean to offend you."

"I'm fine," I muttered, pulling away from his touch. My stomach churned again, and I forced myself to stay composed. "Do you have any water?"

"I've got something better." He grinned and reached for a flask hanging from his belt. "If it's a nasty hangover you're dealing with, try this." He held the flask out to me.

I eyed the flask warily. "What's in it?" He was still a stranger, and I didn't like the idea of taking anything from him without knowing what it was.

"It's not poison," he chuckled, "though, I suppose that's up for debate. It's just some gin with a hint of peppermint I stole from King Caraway's ship. Take a swig, it'll clear your senses and ease your stomach."

I'd heard of that old saying, "the hair of the dog." It had worked for Hayden before, and honestly, I was desperate. Anything to stop the nausea that was threatening to overwhelm me. I accepted the flask almost too quickly now.

"Cheers," I muttered, already regretting it, but too far gone to back out now. I took a long swig, feeling the burn of the alcohol crawl down my throat.

"Cheers," he replied, lifting a smaller flask to his lips, the grin never leaving his face. The flask was so small, it looked like it only had a sip or two in it.

I swallowed the gin and immediately regretted it. My stomach lurched, and I dropped to my knees, trying to fight off the urge to vomit. My hand flew to my mouth, and I kept my face turned down, praying I could keep it down. I wasn't a fan of gin, but I didn't have much choice.

"Not a gin girl, huh?"

"Not exactly," I croaked, taking a deep breath to steady myself. The gin seemed to settle in my stomach, the nausea slowly beginning to subside.

"Feeling better at least?" He asked, his tone shifting to something a bit softer as he placed his smaller flask back on his belt.

I handed his flask back, still shaky, but the worst of the nausea was passing. "Yes," I answered truthfully, removing my hand from my mouth. "The nausea's subsiding. Thank you."

He offered me his hand, and after a brief moment of hesitation, I took it. I wasn't sure I trusted him entirely, but I had already accepted a drink from him, so I supposed there was no harm in letting him help me up.

"You're welcome."

I let go of his hand, feeling a little awkward as I began smoothing out the ruffles of my dress, trying to focus on anything but the odd tension in the air.

I glanced at the flask he'd replaced on his belt. "What was in yours?" I asked, nodding toward the small silver flask still hanging there.

He ran a finger over the design of the flask with a smirk. "Mine? Oh, now that *was* poison," he said lightly, as though it were nothing. "You wouldn't have liked it."

"You're probably right," I said with a nervous laugh, unable to hide the slight tremble in my voice. I wasn't sure if I should be relieved or concerned.

The silence stretched on between us, thick and palpable. The mountain fae were masters of seclusion, just like me, but they liked it. This male, however, had left his Isle. He said it was for resources, but maybe there was more to it—maybe he was trying to escape the isolation he'd lived with. Perhaps he was running from loneliness or looking for a reason to experience something beyond the solitude that clung to him.

I could feel his gaze, but I wasn't afraid to meet it. There was something oddly comforting in staring into the eyes of this stranger, a sense of calm I hadn't expected.

I doubted he'd been close enough to any royal fae to understand what the gold flecks in one's eyes meant. And with mine being so minimal in my amber eyes, I doubt he'd notice. Besides, with the sun shining, it would be easy to blame any gold on its streaking rays.

As I studied his face, I noticed something more than the cocky, smooth confidence he projected. There was sadness there, buried under the sharp lines of his jaw and the glimmer of mischief in his eyes. It was the kind of sadness I knew well. I saw it every day when I looked in the mirror. A sadness that only those who had known isolation could recognize, the quiet grief carried in the smallest of gestures.

"My name's Reed," he said, breaking the silence that had stretched a beat too long.

I blinked, momentarily caught off guard. "What?" I asked, dragging my eyes away from his face, suddenly self-conscious of how long I had been studying him.

"Reed," he repeated. "That's my name."

I raised an eyebrow, still confused. "Why are you telling me?"

He shrugged with a grin, a devil-may-care look in his eyes. "Well, you'll probably never see me again. And when you tell the Ember Prince about meeting the devastatingly handsome stranger who nearly got incinerated, I don't want to be known as that *random escaped prisoner.*"

A small laugh escaped me, despite the strange tension that crackled in the air. "What makes you think I'll even tell him about this?" I teased, taking a small step forward, closing the gap between us. Theodon, what was wrong with me? It had to be the gin. That's the only explanation.

Reed's grin widened. "Do you love him?" he asked, his voice lowering as he took a step forward too, mirroring my movement, matching the closeness with a slow, deliberate pace.

My breath caught in my throat, and I instinctively found myself holding his gaze. "Yes," I answered, the word slipping from my lips without hesitation. It was true, in a sense. I loved Hayden, but not the way Reed probably thought. The way I had made it seem. But that didn't matter now.

"Then you'll tell him."

"What if I don't want to," I replied, my voice becoming breathy, "what if I just want this moment to be ours, a secret I could hold onto?" What the hell was I saying? Did a bit of gin really make me that forward? That brave?

Reed took another step towards me closing the last bit of space between us. "And what exactly would we do in this moment that you would want to keep secret from the prince?"

"I don't know," was all I was able to get out. I knew what I wanted, what I wanted to say, what I wanted to do, but I couldn't bring myself to speak it. Maybe it was best if I just acted on it.

"Maybe I can give you a few suggestions?" Reed whispered.

I stood so close to Reed now that the heat from his skin radiated against mine. My pulse quickened, if I stood on my toes, our noses would brush, maybe even our lips. His gaze was fixed on my mouth; his eyes darkened with a mix of something I couldn't quite place. My heart pounded so loudly, I was sure he could hear it. But I didn't care. I was too lost in the moment, in the closeness, in the feeling that had risen between us, that magnetism I couldn't explain.

This was the second time in just a short while I found myself standing so close to a male, and yet there was no fear this time. Not from him. He didn't know my secrets, nor did I think he was particularly interested in them. And I didn't mind that. We were both strangers, bound by nothing except this fleeting moment. The same moment that would slip through my fingers as soon as he left. The same moment I could surrender to, just for now. He would be gone soon, a memory, and I'd never see him again. No awkward run-ins. No risk of anyone finding out.

His eyes finally left my lips and slowly made their way back up to my eyes. There was a search in his gaze, something that made me feel exposed, but not in the way I was used to. This wasn't the usual unease. This felt like understanding. His stare moved side to side, as if looking for something. I didn't look away, not like I usually would. I wanted him to see me. In this moment, I didn't care who I was. I wanted to be someone who could be kissed by a handsome stranger, someone who could let go of everything else, if only for a heartbeat.

I placed my hands on his arms, feeling the hard muscle beneath the fabric. He was solid like marble, like something unmovable. I nudged him closer, the tension between us thickening, needing to break. And then his hands were on my waist, pulling me toward him, and I knew we were both on the same page. Or so I thought.

But then, just as the space between us seemed to disappear, Reed slowly pulled back. His hands left my waist, his expression shifting to something more concerned, more serious.

"Are you alright?" he asked, his voice full of concern.

I blinked, the moment suddenly shattered, and I stumbled to find my words. "Yes?" I said, though it came out more like an uncertain statement. "Why?"

Reed's eyes scanned me with a sharpness I hadn't noticed before. "You're trembling," he said, his voice softer now, almost as if he were seeing me for the first time. "And considering we're in the middle of a desert, I don't think it's because you're cold."

It was only then that I became aware of the trembling in my hands, the nervous quiver that had spread through my body. I wasn't scared, not really. Nervous, yes. Nervous about the unknown, about the potential of this moment. If things had gone the way I hoped, this would've been my first real kiss, the kind sparked by lust and longing, a moment of release. I was ready for that. Ready to feel something. To feel him. But my body betrayed me. I had wanted to be confident, but instead I felt raw, exposed and inexperienced.

"Have you done this before?" Reed's voice broke through the fog of my thoughts, and I could hear the sincerity in his tone. He wasn't mocking me.

My heart skipped a beat, and I answered too quickly, trying to cover the uncertainty I felt. "Of course I have!" My voice was too sharp, too defensive. "And I've done a lot more with plenty of other males." The lies flowed out easily, a quick fix to cover up the cracks. "Remember, I'm the prince's plaything," I added with a forced casualness. "I have him wrapped around my finger."

The words sounded hollow, even to me. But I had to keep going. I had to sell this lie.

Reed chuckled, but there was something in his eyes that made me wish I had kept quiet. "Oh, I remember," he said, as he took a small step back, causing the heat between us evaporate like water on hot sand. "Perhaps that's why we should stop now. I would hate for the Ember Prince's wrath to pour down on me."

A strange mix of disappointment and relief surged through me. I had ruined this. Ruined everything with my nervousness, my lies and my own self-doubt. It was better this way, I knew it was. But I couldn't stop the sting that came with it. I wanted him. I wanted anyone, really, to make me feel something, anything but this suffocating loneliness. First with Adan, then Prince Hawthorne, and now this stranger. But I couldn't beg him for a kiss. I couldn't make myself that pathetic…could I?

I stood up straighter, forcing a coldness into my voice, though the words tasted bitter as they left my mouth. "You're right. Prince Hayden would probably incinerate you if he found out you were kissing what was his."

The words felt wrong, too possessive, too cruel, but I couldn't back down. I couldn't let him think this was his decision. I had to make him believe it was me who was pulling away, not him.

"I think it's best you be on your way," I continued, trying to sound confident. "Prince Hayden should be back from tracking the stag soon, and he most likely would turn you over to King Caraway's guards if he finds you here."

Reed paused, his eyes studying me for a beat before he nodded. "You're probably right, Sparks," he said, the nickname rolling off his tongue like a soft caress. He reached for my left hand, lifting it to his lips and pressing a gentle kiss to the back of it. His lips were warm and soft, but it didn't last long enough to make me forget the ache building in my chest. "Good luck on the hunt."

And with that, he pulled away, walking back toward the thicket of trees. I stood frozen for a moment, my heart thudding in my chest, my mind trying to catch up with the fleeting moment. His kiss lingered on my skin, but I couldn't focus on that now. I had to find the stag.

"Reed," I called out before he could vanish completely. He turned his head back, his gaze locking with mine.

"If you find yourself heading back to Atsila," I warned, "avoid the Forgotten Desert. The signs on the decaying palm trees just beyond the marker are there for a reason. No one who enters ever comes back."

He raised an eyebrow, a half-smile on his lips. "Noted. Thank you." With a small nod, he disappeared into the trees, his form swallowed by the shadows.

I let out a long breath I didn't realize I'd been holding as I watched him leave. The whole encounter felt surreal, like something out of a dream I would wake from at any moment. But the lingering warmth on the back of my hand, the way my pulse still raced, reminded me that this was real. Reed was real.

I shook my head, attempting to rid myself of thoughts of the male. I was here for a reason. I had a task to complete. The stag was out there somewhere, and I didn't have time to dwell on the ache in my chest or the emptiness left behind by Reed's departure. I could feel the time slipping away. I had to focus.

Another hour passed. No stag. No Hayden. The oasis stretched out before me like a labyrinth of water and trees, and my feet felt heavy as I walked deeper into it.

I retraced my steps, following the footprints in the sand, back to the place where Reed and I had crossed paths. I stopped for a moment, shaking my head as memories of him flooded back. He had been a distraction, a welcome one at that, but a distraction all the same. The memory of his smile, the warmth of his hands on my waist, made me want to forget what I was here for.

No, I had a job to do. I had to find the stag. I couldn't afford to fail again.

I pushed the thoughts of Reed out of my head as I moved toward the entrance of the oasis since going deeper in wasn't getting me anywhere and I was in no shape to get lost out here all day. I was failing at this task and I let everyone down. But mostly, I let Hayden down.

I dragged my feet back toward the entrance, defeat heavy on my shoulders as the heat of the sun left me feeling tired and exhausted. I failed. I had one chance to do something, and I couldn't do it.

It felt like the morning had been a complete waste. I had already almost given our secret away by letting Hawthorne get so close, not once but twice. Maybe I was truly useless, never meant to contribute to this Isle, let alone help Hayden. If he was deemed unworthy because of me, I wasn't sure I could live with myself. He was going to make a great king, of that I was sure, and this was my chance to help him get there, yet I had still screwed it up. My self-doubt lingered, growing stronger with every defeated step that crunched under my boots in the sand. Maybe I should have just left, listened to my father, and disappeared like I always did, the only thing I had ever been useful for.

A rustling sound broke my thoughts. A crunch, like something shifting in the sand in the distance. My breath caught. Was it a Loa? I wouldn't stand a chance if it was. I froze, heart pounding, hoping it was just the wind, a trick of the desert air or perhaps another handsome stranger. Slowly, I turned my head.

And then, there it was. The desert stag.

A wave of relief flooded through me, drowning out the tension I was holding. The stag stood tall in the distance, a magnificent silhouette under a cover of shadows. Its massive antlers branched wide and high, far grander than any ordinary stag I had ever seen, each point catching the faint light like gilded ivory. Its powerful, sleek body moved with a grace that seemed almost unreal, muscles rippling beneath its glossy coat. I had found it. This was it. The moment I had been waiting for.

I took a steadying breath, pulling an arrow from my quiver. My hand felt steady now, more certain than it had all morning. It was further than I was used to, but I was a great shot. I could do this. I could bring the stag down quickly, without pain, without hesitation. I loaded the arrow, drew it back, and aimed carefully.

Release.

The arrow sliced through the air with a hum, hitting its mark with a clean, sharp sound. The stag crumpled to the ground with a graceful, almost reluctant fall.

A wave of triumph swept through me. I had done it. I had actually done it.

Tears stung the corners of my eyes. I had accomplished something. I could feel the weight lifting off my chest, the anxiety melting away. Hayden would be proud. I smiled, still breathless with excitement, as I slung my bow over my shoulder and made my way toward the stag. My heart raced.

But as I got closer, my smile faded. My stomach twisted in disbelief.

It wasn't a stag at all.

It was a fae.

My stomach dropped.

No. No, no, no.

Please don't let this be happening.

I stood frozen, too afraid to move, my body slowly unraveling as I finally willed my feet forward and walked closer to the unmoving body. I was sure. I was sure it had been a stag. My heart hammered against my chest as I approached the figure on the blood-soaked sand.

Please don't be Hayden. Please don't be Reed. Please don't be anyone I know.

But as I got close enough to make out small features, my worst fear was confirmed. It wasn't a stag, and it certainly wasn't a stranger. It was Prince Hawthorne.

I choked on my breath, a strangled sob escaping my throat. The crimson blood, shimmering silver against the desert sun, puddled around him, staining the sand a deep shimmering red. My knees gave out, and I collapsed into the sand not able to move myself any closer. Shock took over and I was too horrified to even scream.

Tears flooded my eyes, blurring everything around me. How had this happened? Why? What was he even doing here? He wasn't supposed to be here. He couldn't be here.

I couldn't breathe. I couldn't think. I couldn't move. My hands trembled uncontrollably as panic seized me, suffocating me from the inside.

"I'm sorry," I gasped, barely able to form the words between ragged breaths. "I'm sorry. I'm sorry." The words kept repeating, but they did nothing to soothe the horror gnawing at my soul. *He's dead. He's dead because of me. Because of my mistake.*

More of the shimmering blood pooled beneath him as it dripped down the sides of his torso. I felt bile rise in my throat as the weight of what I had done crushed me. I was going to be sick.

Suddenly, I couldn't keep it in anymore. I retched, the bitter taste of gin and peppermint still lingering in the back of my throat. What had I done? Was the gin to blame? Had it clouded my judgment and made me see things that weren't real? I hadn't felt drunk, hadn't felt dizzy, but with the heat exhaustion coupled with the alcohol I couldn't be sure.

"El?"

A familiar voice pierced through my haze. Hayden.

I looked up and saw him. Though still a bit disheveled, his hair out of place in certain spots, he looked every bit the king he was soon to be. Meanwhile, I sat in the sand, a flushed, tear-streaked mess, guilt consuming me faster than I could process.

I scrambled to sit up, still shaking uncontrollably. "Hayden," I whimpered, my voice cracking. "I killed him."

Hayden was beside me in an instant, wrapping his arms around me with comforting strength. He pressed me against him, murmuring soothing words into my hair as I cried uncontrollably into his shoulder.

"Was it self-defense?" he asked, his voice soft but tinged with something darker underneath. "Did he try to hurt you? Did he try to take advantage of you?"

"No," I gasped between breaths, unable to even think straight. "It was an accident."

Hayden pulled back, his hand trembling slightly as he wiped my tears away. His eyes widened, disbelief flashing across his face as he looked down at me. Then his gaze shifted to the stag, no, the fae, lying on the ground. His jaw tightened, unable to fully comprehend the sight before him. "El... that's not just any fae," he breathed, his voice barely steady. "That's Prince Hawthorne."

"It was an accident," I said again through sobs.

Hayden loosened his grip on me as he sniffed the air. "Have you been drinking, Eli?" he asked, his tone hardening slightly.

I nodded weakly, barely able to speak. "It was just a sip of gin from a male I met earlier—"

"A stranger?" Hayden's voice rose, a thread of anger lacing his words. "What the fuck were you thinking, Eli?"

I watched as his body began to tremble, his ragged breaths matching my own. His fists clenched at his sides, and his jaw tightened as fury and fear warred across his features. He was furious with me, sure, but I could also see the terror in his eyes, terror at what this meant for him, for me. His gaze darted frantically between us, and I knew I had to explain. I hadn't done this out of carelessness. I would never have intentionally killed someone, let alone the prince.

"I didn't feel drunk," I tried to explain, though I knew it was no excuse. "But maybe there was something in it. Maybe it was laced with something... something that made me hallucinate. I saw the stag, I swear I did. I wouldn't have released the arrow if I knew it was Hawthorne. I wouldn't have hurt him."

"How would you have known it was him?"

I hadn't told him about my encounter with the Ivy Prince. I suppose I just assumed Adan or our parents would have mentioned it, especially after I had been missing all of last night, locked away in my room and completely avoiding the kitchens.

I hesitated, searching for the right words. "We spoke briefly," I began, but as the words left my mouth, I saw Hayden's expression change.

Hayden's eyes narrowed. "You've met the Ivy Prince?" His tone grew more suspicious.

I hesitated. Should I tell him everything? That would open a whole new world of complications. Instead, I nodded slowly, barely able to make eye contact. "Yes."

Hayden stood, his eyes still filled with fear. "Stay here," he ordered. "I'm going to check to see if he's really dead. If you missed his heart, he could be healing as we speak."

I wanted to believe Hayden's words, wanted to cling to the fragile hope that maybe I'd missed the heart and that somehow Prince Hawthorne was still alive. But the way he lay there, motionless and unmoving, I knew deep down that it was too late.

I squeezed my eyes shut, praying to Theodon for a miracle. A blow to the heart would kill a fae instantly, but still, I held on to a sliver of hope. I opened my eyes slowly, the tremble in my hands betraying the panic rising inside me. All I saw was Hayden, walking back toward me, his head lowered, shaking.

"Well?" I asked, my voice barely more than a whisper as I wiped the tears from my cheeks.

"He's dead," Hayden said bluntly, and another wave of grief hit me, crashing over everything else.

Anxiety clamped down on my chest. The thought repeated over and over, like a mantra and I knew I wouldn't be able to live with myself after this. I couldn't breathe. I couldn't think. But then, the realization slammed into me with a sickening clarity.

The law. A life for a life. I had killed a prince. And as the law demanded, King Caraway would ask for an equal life in return. They would take Hayden. A prince for a prince.

"Hayden," I forced myself to stand, my legs weak and unsteady. "Hayden, the law—"

"I know," he replied, his voice soft and shaky, his normally strong jawline tense with fear.

"But you didn't do this. I did." My voice faltered as the words felt like they were suffocating me.

"Eli," Hayden's hands gripped my shoulders. "I need you to listen to me. You need to get back to the palace. Go to your room and lock yourself in. Now."

"But, Hay—"

"You were never supposed to be here. It was me. It was my arrow that struck the prince. You were never here. Understand?"

"No!" The word escaped my lips in a sharp, desperate snap as I realized what he was trying to do. "You will not take the fall for me. I'm a princess. They'll take me as payment for this. The law says they can take me as the equal life!"

"I can't let you do that, El." His voice was strained. "This is my fault. If I hadn't been hungover, if I'd just said no, you would never have had to cover for me. I should have stopped you. I should have—" His voice cracked, but he pushed on, fighting for control. "This is my fault, and I will pay the price."

I looked at my brother, his face empty of all but resolve. He was holding it together, but I knew the truth. He understood the gravity of what we were facing. King Caraway would demand blood. The law was unyielding. A life for a life.

"The kingdom needs you, Hay," I said quietly, forcing the words out through the lump in my throat. "It needs you to survive this. It has to be me."

Concern, deep and unsettling, etched itself across Hayden's face. He knew I was right. No matter what he wanted, he couldn't protect me from this. Not now. Before I could say another word, Hayden grabbed the bow from the ground and strapped the quiver to his back. He had made up his mind.

"Go. Now," he urged, as he began to move toward the prince's body.

I backed away slowly, so many thoughts and emotions swirling in my head, until one thought clung to me: I would go. But I had a plan, and I knew what I needed to do.

My head was spinning with a mix of disbelief and horror as I made my way back to where I had tied up Fintana. I had killed someone. I had taken a life. And Hayden would pay the price for it. This felt like a nightmare I couldn't wake up from, no matter how many times I tried. No matter how many times I pinched myself or shook my head, the reality stayed the same. I was still here, racing toward the palace grounds on Fintana, my heart thumping, my tears drying faster than they could fall. I had to get there quickly. I needed to reach Adan before the news of the prince's death spread, before Hayden could do something reckless in an attempt to protect me.

I was the one who needed to pay the price. Whatever punishment King Caraway demanded, I would accept it. I deserved it. I was a murderer.

We finally approached the palace, but there was no time to return Fintana to the stables. Fortunately, it seemed some of the staff had already risen, and I quickly passed her off to a stable hand before making a frantic dash through the hidden passageway, racing up to my floor. The adrenaline coursing through me kept my legs moving faster than I thought possible, carrying me through the winding corridors and back to my room.

I didn't stop to check if the coast was clear as I stepped into the hall leading to my floor. I didn't have time to be cautious.

"Adan!" I screamed, my voice raw and frantic.

"E-Eli?" His eyes widened in shock as soon as he saw me. He stumbled back, startled by my sudden appearance, then quickly crossed the hall toward me, his eyes scanning my face, looking for answers. "What happened? Are you okay?"

"No!" I shouted, unable to keep my voice down. "It's my fault! I did it, not Hayden!" The words spilled out in a frenzied rush.

Adan's arms wrapped around me, pulling me into a tight embrace, trying to steady my shaking body. "Slow down, Eli," he said softly, his voice laced with concern. "Breathe. What happened?"

"I killed him!" I repeated over and over, the heaviness of my own confession crashing down on me with each syllable. "Please, Adan, help him! Help Hayden!"

"Hayden?" Adan's voice was filled with panic. He pulled back from me, his hands tightening on my shoulders, fear flashing in his eyes before he promptly released me and sprang into action. "Is he all right?"

I realized how those words must've sounded to him. I could see the panic starting to settle in his gaze as he was thinking the worst. I had to explain, and quickly, before he completely spiraled into panic too.

"I killed Prince Hawthorne," I said, the words tumbling out of me without a second thought.

"What?" Adan barked, grabbing my arm and guiding me toward my room. Once we were securely behind closed doors, Adan's attention went back to me.

I hadn't even realized how openly I had spoken the truth, but thank Theodon for Adan's quick thinking. The floor was usually empty, but I couldn't risk a passing maid overhearing me. Not today. I was a mess. My mind was unraveling, and I needed to pull myself together.

Adan slammed the door shut behind us and locked it, then turned to face me, his expression a mix of disbelief and concern.

"What do you mean, you killed the Prince?"

"It was an accident," I said quickly, struggling to regain some control over my racing thoughts. "I thought it was a stag. I mean, it was a stag, but it wasn't." I began pacing, trying to keep my mind focused. "When I got closer, it was Prince Hawthorne. He didn't move, he…" My voice faltered as I realized I couldn't finish the sentence. My chest tightened, and my breath grew shallow as I felt the walls close in. I needed to calm myself before I lost control.

Adan's grip was firm as he grabbed my arms, steadying me. "It was an accident."

"But I still did it!" I sobbed, the reality finally hitting me. "I still killed him."

Adan's expression softened with understanding. "I know you, Eli," he said softly, "you'd never hurt someone on purpose. You don't have a malicious bone in your body. It was an accident."

I knew I wasn't malicious, but that didn't change what had happened. That didn't change the price Hayden would pay. I needed to fix this. "We need to help Hayden!"

"Hay…" Adan stopped mid-sentence as we both heard a loud cannon fire in the distance.

We rushed to the window, my heart sank as I saw a group of Ivy Guards marching toward the desert, heading for the oasis. They knew. Of course, they knew. King Caraway had probably felt the pulse of power, of the Seed return to him as soon as the prince's life force left his body.

They would find Hayden near Prince Hawthorne's lifeless form and demand the payment of an equal life.

"Adan, listen to me," I said, my voice shaking. "Hayden is out there, and he's going to take the blame for me. We can't let him do that.

"A life for a life," Adan murmured, and I was certain he understood what it meant. His face was pale with dread. "They're going to kill him."

I grabbed Adan by the shoulders, forcing him to look me in the eyes. "Unless we can stop it."

"How?" Adan's voice broke, a tear slipping down his cheek.

"We trade me in his place," I said, the words coming out in a rush. "That's where I need your help."

I quickly explained my plan, and after much debate about me taking Hayden's place, Adan finally agreed. He knew the kingdom needed Hayden, more than they would ever need me. He was the future of the Isle, and I was just a powerless nobody. If my plan worked, King Caraway and the entire Ember Isle would know who I really was and what I was, or rather, what I wasn't.

The palace was buzzing with urgency after the sudden departure of the Ivy Guards. Even from my empty floor, I could hear the stampede of guards rushing up and down the corridors above and below. They were no doubt making their way to the throne room to assess what was happening, why King Caraway had ordered such a drastic move into the desert. I knew my parents well, if they hadn't already planned their own counterattack, they would be on the verge of it, thinking we were under siege. They had no idea how justified this attack was. Because of me.

"We have to tell my parents what's going on before they launch their own attack and we end up in more life debt," I said, my voice strained with urgency. I turned and ran toward the hall. "You know what to say to King Caraway, right?" I asked, looking over my shoulder to make sure Adan was still on board with the plan.

"Yes," he answered, his voice shaky but resolute. "Now we need to hurry."

We didn't bother with the secret passages this time. After everything that had happened, after everything that was about to happen, it wouldn't matter who knew I existed or not. We were about to open the floodgates to the darkest secrets my parents had kept hidden, and the truth was going to hit everyone hard. I couldn't imagine the shock it would bring to those inside the palace, but the people of Ember Isle? Our neighboring Isles? The whole world would soon know who I was. And when this was over, I would be dead. I would die to repay the life debt I owed.

I couldn't think about that now. If I let myself give into my panic, I'd chicken out. I'd hide, as I always did, and condemn Hayden to a fate he didn't deserve. No. I couldn't let that happen. I needed to see this plan through, no matter the cost.

Adan and I continued to race down the corridors, my pulse pounding in my ears. The entire palace turned into chaos. Guards were flooding to the throne room, some gathering to protect my parents, others to find shelter, unsure of what was really happening. I wanted so badly to assure them that the Ivy Guards weren't here to harm them, that they were just fulfilling their duty to avenge their fallen prince. But there was no time to explain. And even if I did try, who would believe me? Most of the people here didn't even know who I was. The ones who did would only recognize me as a palace servant, someone with no voice or power to speak for herself.

Adan pulled me along, faster than I could manage on my own, until we reached the throne room doors. There, a guard I didn't recognize blocked our way.

"The room is full," he said, eyeing me warily. "Adan, you may pass, but the girl will have to take shelter in her own quarters."

"Let her pass!" A voice boomed from the crowd. My mother.

The guard immediately stepped aside at his Queen's command, and Adan and I rushed through the throngs of people, moving toward the platform where my parents stood. At the top, my mother, father, and Adan's father, Branton, were surrounded by guards. The room was packed to the brim, the heat of so many bodies pressing together making the air feel thick and suffocating. The atmosphere was filled with panic, guards with weapons drawn, others holding torches and flames ready to fight if the need arose.

"Eliane," my mother's voice rang out softly, and I felt a brief wave of relief when I heard it. "They have my permission to pass," she said, looking to the guards surrounding her. "Step aside."

The guards parted at her order, and Adan and I moved forward, heading straight for my parents.

Instinctually, I ran into my mother's arms, pulling her into a tight embrace, then moved to my father. I held them both tightly, knowing very well this was the last time I would ever get to feel their warmth, to breathe in the comforting trace of my father's natural musk or the sweet scent of freshly bloomed desert flowers that always lingered around my mother. I glanced over at Adan and Branton. Instead of a hug, the father and son duo merely tilted their heads toward one another in silent acknowledgment. It was such a stoic gesture, no words, no comfort. I realized then where Adan got it from.

After what felt like an eternity, I finally managed to break away from their embrace. "We need to talk, now" I commanded in a harsh whisper, my voice trembling.

"What's going on?" My father asked, his brow furrowed as he pulled Adan and me closer, his tone full of concern. "Do you know why the Ivy is attacking?"

"They aren't attacking us," I quickly spat out, clutching my pendant for comfort, my fingers fluttering against the cool stone.

"We saw them heading into the desert in packs, straight toward where Prince Hayden was hunting," Branton replied, his voice tight with anger. "What other reason would they be doing that if not to harm him or use him in some plot to seize the lands? I knew letting them come here was a bad idea."

"We already sent a troop to hopefully retrieve your brother before the Ivy Guards get to him," my mother added, her lips trembling as she spoke. "The last thing we need is for them to use Hayden against the kingdom."

They truly believed we were under attack. From the moment King Caraway had accepted the invitation to the palace, they had suspected this was all a trap, a way to take over our Isle. But they were wrong. They weren't the villains here; we were. I was. King Caraway had every right to call in the life debt. It didn't matter that they were guests in our home; we had wronged them. I had wronged them, and they deserved their justice.

"Prince Hawthorne is dead," I blurted out before I could stop myself. The words felt like knives in my throat.

My parents went silent, their faces going pale. Adan gave me a reassuring nod, urging me to continue. I took a steadying breath. "I killed him, but it was an accident. And now King Caraway is calling in the debt. He needs an equal life to pay for the loss of his son."

"Hayden's life," my mother whispered so softly that I wasn't even sure the words had left her lips. "What happened?"

I explained the events of the morning: the hungover hunt, my taking Hayden's place, and my eventual accidental killing of the prince. I expected to feel numb by now knowing I had to live with my actions. But it was all still so raw. I felt the lump in my throat rise again, and before I could stop myself, I began to sob. I needed to pull myself together, though. We were running out of time.

"It's not an attack," I said. "It's an arrest. They went out there to retrieve Hayden."

"But why would they assume Hayden did it?" my mother asked, her face still frozen in shock, trying to process the reality of what was happening.

"It wouldn't matter," Adan interjected, his voice heavy with the same despair that I felt. "Regardless of who killed Prince Hawthorne, the debt would always fall on Prince Hayden. They knew he would be out there doing the royal hunt."

The life-for-a-life debt was always strange that way, no one ever seemed to care who the true criminal was. All that mattered was an equal life to replace the one lost. In my twenty years, I'd never seen the debt truly paid, largely because we had no significant interactions with fae from other Isles. But I had heard rumors of accidents or missteps. No matter the circumstances, the debt always needed to be paid in fear of Theodon's wrath coming down on the guilty party's Isle. Perhaps our Isle would deplete faster? Or Theodon would take the Ember away from our Isle, leaving us powerless and vulnerable. Killing a prince had to equate for a much bigger punishment if not rectified.

My parents' faces twisted in horror, both looking as though they were watching their world crumble around them. I could see it in their eyes, the understanding that, no matter what, the price would be paid. They would lose a child tonight, but it wouldn't be the one they expected.

"I'm going to take his place," I said quickly, my voice unwavering.

"Eliane," my father started, his expression softening as he reached for my hand, his voice gentle but filled with concern. "You can't."

"And why can't I?" I challenged, my heart hammering in my chest. "The life debt says it must be repaid with a life of greater or equal value. I am the Ember Princess. That makes me of equal value."

"Love," my father hummed. "King Caraway will never agree to that. He will demand our heir in place of his own." I watched as his lip quivered before they became tight with anger again. "We will have no choice but to approve his request and let the Ivy King take Hayden to die on his lands, just as his son died on ours. There is no other way."

"But there is," Adan spoke up, his voice steady despite the desperation in his eyes.

"Son?" Branton scolded, though Adan ignored him.

"Princess Eliane has an idea, one I think will work. Let me be the speaker on your behalf when King Caraway comes to claim his debt. I know what to say." Adan's voice was filled with conviction, and I could feel my hope stirring as he spoke.

"So, I am to lose a child regardless?" my mother said with a shaky voice, reaching up to stroke my hair as tears pooled in her eyes.

I hated seeing her cry, but there was no other way. "Yes. But I did this. I caused this, and I'm ready to pay the price."

"What do we need to do?" My father's voice was firm now, a sense of urgency filling it. I knew he loved me, but I also knew that if it came down to it, they would always choose Hayden, heir to the throne, their legacy. And I would too. I would always choose him.

"First," I began, my voice steadying, "You need to have everyone leave and return to their homes or quarters. We can't appear as though we're about to start a war. You need to ensure that everyone stays calm and that no one does anything rash."

"Branton," my father commanded, "see to it that everyone calmly returns to their respective areas and inform the troops they are not to harm any Ivy Guards when they make their return."

"Yes, Your Majesty," Branton bowed and immediately set off to carry out the task.

"Now," I breathed, my plan starting to feel like it might actually work, "get Kalynda. We're going to need her."

It took some time before Branton and the guards were able to calm the chaos amongst the crowd, but eventually, things began to settle. The tension in the air was still lingering, but the frantic energy had dissipated somewhat. My parents still had a larger than usual entourage of Ember Guards within the throne room, just in case things went awry. As for the majority of the palace workers and servants, only a select few remained mixed in with those who knew my true identity. They would be necessary witnesses if my plan went south, while the others were in for a rather large surprise.

Looking around the room, there were only a few I recognized by name. I caught sight of some fae from the stables I'd worked with in the past and a couple of handmaids, including my own, Mirra. There were also a few from the kitchen staff who were aware of my secret. Among the unfamiliar faces, I noticed a couple of too-forward males, who I'd crossed paths with while on hunting duty.

It wasn't unusual for me to take on the role of a hunter but it was the role I stepped into the least. Some of the males didn't like it. Perhaps it was because I was female, or maybe because I was 'new' to the palace and they assumed I didn't deserve the position, or worse, that I had "slept my way" into it. I shut them up the first day I managed to shoot a rabbit clean through its head, right between its beady eyes. That silenced their taunts about my skills, but not their crude advances or lewd comments. I was sure that once they learned the truth about who I really was, they would replay every past conversation in their minds, probably preparing for the worst of my parents' wrath. Good, let them squirm.

As I looked around the room again, most faces were somber, heavy with the knowledge that today they would lose their heir and they were powerless to stop it. But there were two faces in particular that stood out, both marked by the echo of soft sobs. Adena and Tana. The beautiful girls seemed to have an endless stream of tears running down their flawless cheeks. I was sure their sorrow wasn't just for the loss of Prince Hawthorne, but for the future that had just been taken from them. When I looked at them again, Tana was practically falling apart in Adena's arms. Maybe it was because, between the two of them, she was the one who had been intimate with him, already developing feelings for someone she couldn't have then and certainly couldn't now. She was the one who had actually spent the night in the prince's bed, though I wouldn't put it past him if Adena had joined them later. Any hopes of becoming the Ivy Prince's consort and leaving the Isle were now gone. Perhaps they had truly loved him in the brief time they'd known him, but I had a feeling it was more about their own futures than their affection for him.

I stood on the platform beside Adan and Kalynda. My mother and father sat upon their thrones, regal as ever, their postures poised and their heads held high. They may have been facing a monumental loss, but they would not show weakness. They were not above the law, but neither were they cowards, and they knew how to stand firm under the demands of duty and expectation.

Branton stood between the two thrones, his hand resting on the hilt of his sword, ready to defend them if needed, but also prepared to stop them if they tried to prevent King Caraway from claiming Hayden or I. Preventing it would start a war, and we couldn't afford that. Not with so many innocent lives at stake.

The room grew eerily silent as the sound of heavy footsteps echoed through the halls. The Ivy Guards were drawing closer, their boots thundering on the marble floor as they neared. The tension thickened, a knot in my stomach tightening. Everyone froze, awaiting their arrival. In the silence, my mind conjured images I desperately hoped were false. Images of them dragging Hayden in, bloodied and bruised. Of his lifeless body slung over a guard's shoulder, limp and cold.

But no, they wouldn't do that. King Caraway would not be that rash. The law required him to execute the equal life on his own Isle, as his son had been killed on ours. Even in his grief and rage, he would understand that. As a king, he knew better than to bend the law in the heat of the moment, especially if it meant risking Theodon's wrath and punishment. Yet still, I couldn't help but fear that in his grief, he might do something reckless, something unforgivable.

The doors to the throne room flew open with a sudden crash, and there they were, the Ivy Guards, tall and imposing in their dark armor and leathers, marching in with grim determination.

The Ivy Guards filed into the throne room, forming a direct line toward my parents. The last to enter was King Caraway, flanked by a guard dragging Hayden by the chains of an iron collar. The sight of his bruised body sent ripples of cries and gasps throughout the room. They stopped just before the platform where my parents sat, and where I stood, frozen in place. My eyes locked onto Hayden, searching for signs of injury. Luckily, there was no blood spilling from his wounds, a sight that could ruin our plans right now if the Ivy King saw the shimmer. His left eye was swollen and a few developing bruises were painted on his normally tanned skin, which seemed to grow paler and paler under the influence of the collar around his neck. The iron collar he now wore made it impossible for the bruises to heal. Iron had that effect on us, it drained our power, rendering us weak, powerless. A feeling that was all too familiar to me, but so new to Hayden.

"Your Majesties," King Caraway hissed through clenched teeth. "Your son owes me his life." On cue, the guard yanked roughly on the chain, pulling Hayden to his knees. "He owes the Ivy Isle his life for the death of my only heir, my son, taken from my people. Taken from me!"

This was the first time I laid eyes on the Ivy King. He was tall, clad in regal green leathers, with a silver leafed crown resting atop his head. He was the spitting image of his son. His face handsome, chiseled, but weathered by time, bore a strong resemblance to Prince Hawthorne's, down to the sharp jawline and the emerald eyes flecked with silver. The only difference was the small beard of stubble on his chin and the silver strands threaded through his black hair. In that moment, he could have been Hawthorne's elder twin.

I stared back into his eyes, expecting to see the anguish that would bring on another wave of my tears. But there was nothing. Only hatred. The raw, fiery kind that threatened to consume everything in its path. Somehow, that was worse.

"We understand," my father began, his voice calm, measured. "But—"

"No!" King Caraway interrupted, his voice a thunderclap of fury. "You know the rules. As his family, no matter your status, you are not allowed to bargain for his life." His hands balled into fists so tight, his knuckles turned white. "Who have you selected to speak on your behalf to sort out the punishment, to settle the official record?"

"I will," Adan's voice was cool, detached. He played his part flawlessly. "I was meant to be the Captain of the Guard for Prince Hayden's reign. I am neutral, and I will uphold tradition and policy, including the life-for-a-life debt."

"Then you understand," Caraway's voice dripped with scorn, "that I am within my rights to take the Ember Prince back to the Ivy Isle and execute him on our soil to repay the debt."

"Yes," Adan replied, unfazed. "But as the mediator, I must hear your exact demands, in front of the court, in front of my King and Queen." He shot me a glance, his gaze steady, before taking a deep breath. This was the moment. The critical moment. "For all to witness, King Caraway, are you demanding the blood of the Pyronia's firstborn in place of your own?"

I glanced at Hayden, who visibly stiffened as Adan's words registered.

"Adan, no!" Hayden shouted, struggling against his chains, but the guard yanked the collar, pulling him back down to the ground.

"Hush!" Caraway snarled, silencing him with a sharp command. "There is no saving you from this fate."

"King Caraway," Adan's voice cut through the tension like a blade. "Is that the price for the debt? The Pyronia's firstborn in blood for the loss of yours? We need to hear you agree to the terms, since we have already acknowledged our obligation to the Ivy crown."

"Yes!" Caraway shouted, his fury reaching a boiling point.

I stepped forward, every muscle in my body rigid with resolve.

"King Caraway," I said, my voice steady, "As you commanded, the price will be paid. But now, you must release Prince Hayden from his iron collar."

Caraway's face twisted in confusion, his guards equally perplexed. "And why would I do that?" he snapped.

"Because," I took a deep breath, swallowing the lump in my throat, "he is not the firstborn." I stood as tall as I could, forcing my wobbling legs to remain steady. "I am."

The room erupted in a cacophony of disbelief. There were murmurs, gasps, and even a few mocking laughs. The noise swirled around me, until it was almost deafening.

Hayden's voice rang out, desperate and panicked. "She's lying! Don't listen to her!"

Caraway turned to my parents, his fury growing. "Explain yourselves!" he demanded. "Do you really think your lies could save your son? What kind of fool do you take me for?"

I remained still, my gaze unwavering. I would not falter. I would not show weakness. "Everything I've said is true," I said firmly, refusing to let fear or doubt seep into my voice.

"I was not talking to you, you imposter bitch!" Caraway spat, his eyes blazing.

My father stepped forward, his voice calm and authoritative. "She is our firstborn. We have not deceived you, King Caraway. We've simply kept her existence a secret, known only to a select few."

Kalynda, who had remained silent until now, spoke up. "I can vouch for her," she said, her tone resolute. "I was the one who helped bring her into this world. As the royal doula, I have delivered many members of the Pyronia line, including King Keegan himself, among many others. Eliane is, in fact, the firstborn of the Pyronia bloodline. I swear this to you or may Theodon smite me right here and now."

The crowd was in an uproar now, murmurs of disbelief rippling through the room. Even some of our own people seemed unwilling to believe it.

"Proof," Caraway demanded, his arms crossed in disdain. "I require proof that she is of royal blood and is in fact the first born."

We had prepared for this. I knew King Caraway would not take our word alone. Kalynda pulled a knife from her belt and raised it high, the blade gleaming in the sunlight. "I can show you. Eliane, come here, my dear."

I stepped forward, my heart pounding in my chest. I held out my hand, bracing for the sharp sting. Kalynda slid the blade slowly across my palm, the pain immediate as the blood began to drip down my arm. The room fell into stunned silence. The gold in my blood shimmered under the cascading rays of sunlight that filled the throne room, catching the eyes of every onlooker. This was it, the proof that could not be denied.

I watched as Caraway pushed through the crowd, eager to get a closer look. But the unmistakable shimmer of my blood had to be proof enough.

"How do I know this isn't some sort of trick?" The Ivy King demanded, his fist clenched. He took a step closer to inspect the blood. "Let me see that knife!"

He lunged toward Kalynda and me, but a guard quickly intervened, blocking his path.

Kalynda wiped the blade clean with her apron, her voice steady as she added, "If this is not enough, just look into her eyes. They are flecked with gold, a gift from the Ember and the Pyronia blood line."

"But the prince's eyes are also flecked with gold," the Ivy King argued.

"They are," Kalynda agreed. "The result of a simple blood spell, like those used many years ago to create decoys that protected the royal families before the treaty."

As a king, he should have known that such things happened all the time. It wasn't common for it to occur between family members; the strategy was typically used with body doubles meant to protect the royal family, especially the keeper of the Ember—just like I was sure his family had done to protect the Seed in darker times before the treaty. It was the perfect way to safeguard the royal family, particularly the heir. Since the treaty, that kind of magic had no longer been necessary, and decoys were no longer a requirement. Still, the magic existed and could be used, nonetheless. We could only hope he believed us.

It felt like a plausible enough explanation for why Hayden, though second-born, was acting as the prince, with magical influence easily accounting for his eyes. But if the king demanded to see his blood, there was no amount of magic that could hide the truth. Blood magic couldn't change or disguise blood. I had to hope that what he saw in me would be enough to convince him

A stunned silence filled the room as the truth settled over the crowd. I was who I said I was, the hidden princess of the Pyronia line. The tension in the room thickened as I took a deep breath, preparing for the final step of my plan. Hayden, kneeling before us all, looked sick. His face was pale, and his eyes held a mix of guilt and helplessness. He knew without a doubt that it would be me who paid the price, not him. I could feel his pain, the desperate need to protect me, but this was something I had to do. I had no choice.

I took a step closer, presenting my still-bleeding palm, hoping this closer look would serve as the final, undeniable proof. A chill spread through me as Caraway's dark glare pierced me while he inspected my blood, barely inches from his eyes. His eyes darted away before flicking to Hayden as he stepped back, putting distance between his hard gaze and my dripping blood. His body relaxed for a moment, and once he seemed satisfied, I balled my fist to staunch the bleeding, hiding the fact that the cut was far from healed.

"So," I began, forcing my voice to stay steady, "please release my little brother from that iron collar and take me instead."

King Caraway stood motionless, his gaze fixed on me as a thousand thoughts seemed to race across his mind. I could tell he was still unsure, still trying to make sense of the situation. If my blood, my eyes, and Kalynda's testimony weren't enough to convince him, I had one last trick up my sleeve. I could still summon Hayden's power from the pendant around my neck. A last spectacle, a final demonstration of my royal strength.

Before I could make my move, Caraway spoke again, his voice low, almost calculating. "Why? Why hide her? Why was she a secret rather than the rightful heir?"

It was a question we had anticipated, one we had prepared an answer for. Adan and I were able to craft an excuse for this very question. Hopefully, it would be enough.

"We wanted a boy," my father began, "Eliane was our firstborn, and she was the one to inherit the Ember, but much like the Ivy Isle, we feel a male is better suited for the throne. It has been quite a few centuries since the Ember picked a female ruler, so the birth of Princess Eliane came as an unexpected shock to both my wife and I. We love her with all that we are, but we were simply unprepared for a female to possess the Ember."

The lie stung, because deep down I knew there was some truth to that statement. Still, it was necessary. The truth was too dangerous, too complicated to reveal.

"My *daughter* was born first. But the Ember Queen and I worked to have a male heir as soon as she was able. We kept Eliane's existence a secret, hoping that we would carry on the line once our son was born. This is why we hid her from the world."

King Caraway's expression darkened, but his interest seemed piqued. He stepped forward, a sharp glint in his eye. "And what of the Ember, and your line's future?"

My mother spoke then, her voice as steady as my father's. "We agreed that, when the time came, Princess Eliane would bear an heir and pass them off as Hayden's child. This is not the first time the Pyronia line has done such a thing, to ensure that a male would always hold power. As I'm sure the Ironwoods can attest to their own history of maintaining a male heir on the throne to further your legacy."

I knew the words were true, at least in part. There had never been a female heir to the Ember or Ivy. But hearing it spoken aloud, hearing it laid bare for all to hear, sent a chill through me. Was this what my family had done? Was there some truth to this story and perhaps that was why I denied the role of the heir?

But there was no time for second-guessing. Not now. The Ivy King still wasn't convinced.

Caraway's eyes narrowed. "Well," he started again, his voice soft and dangerous, "If she is the true holder of the Ember, why fight so hard for her to take the place of this one?" He gestured roughly toward Hayden, yanking his head up with a violent jerk, forcing my brother to meet his gaze.

My father's voice remained calm, though a quiet anguish underlay his words. "We understand the law, Caraway and we would not risk Theodon's wrath by not giving you our first born to pay the debt," he said softly. "We love our daughter, but truthfully, she never wanted to rule. That's why she let Prince Hayden take her place and agreed to the ruse all these years. But we always knew she would be the spare. A powerful fae, should anything happen to Hayden, or if our Isle was ever under attack. She was our secret weapon."

King Caraway's face twisted in disbelief. "Prove it," he demanded, stepping forward. "Let's see those *powerful skills*."

I'd known he would demand a demonstration, and I'd prepared for it. The opal pendant around my neck still held a spark of Hayden's power, and it was just enough to put on the show of a lifetime. I glanced at Adan for support, and he gave me a single nod, his face impassive.

I turned to Hayden next. His head shook violently, his iron collar clinking against the chains with each movement. He pleaded with his eyes, but I couldn't let fear sway me now. I had to do this. For him. For the kingdom.

"Stand back," I commanded and the crowd parted, creating a wide gap between me and the rest of the room.

I discreetly reached for the pendant nestled between my breasts. My fingers brushed the cool surface of the opal, and I closed my eyes, drawing every last ounce of power from the stone. I focused on the fire that ran through my veins, the heat that swirled inside me, and I let it loose.

A wave of fire erupted from my hands, sweeping over the crowd. It danced and flickered, a violent, burning wave that crashed together with a deafening roar. The flames soared upward, licking the ceiling and consuming the marble walls in a fiery embrace. The temperature in the room skyrocketed, and I could feel the heat pressing against my skin as the flames circled above us, wild and uncontrollable.

I willed the flames to grow, to swirl in a chaotic crescendo. The air grew thick with the scent of smoke, and the Ivy Guards shrank back, moving closer to the center of the room to avoid getting too close to the walls. The heat was unbearable, and I could hear the faint hiss of steam rising from the marble as it absorbed the flames.

I held the flames in place, hovering just above everyone's heads, watching as the crowd stared, wide-eyed, at the spectacle I created. I could feel my strength waning, but I couldn't stop now. I had to make them believe.

King Caraway stood frozen, his expression unreadable, but I could see the spark of confusion in his eyes. The fire danced in the shadows, casting long flickers of light on his face. For the first time since I had revealed myself, I felt as though he was beginning to understand.

I harnessed the flames for as long as I could, every ounce of strength poured into the fire that had once felt like an extension of myself.

But eventually, the flames flickered and died, their warmth slipping from my grasp. Hayden's power, which had fueled my magic, drained from the pendant and left my body hollow, empty. A shell of who I was moments before.

The weakness washed over me, but I couldn't let anyone see it. I couldn't let the king know that my magic was borrowed, that it had drained me completely. I had to stand tall, no matter how faint my strength felt.

I took a deep breath, steadying myself, and forced my spine to straighten. "Proof enough?" I spat out, the words sharp, though my head still swirled with dizziness.

"Yes." King Caraway replied, his voice laced with astonishment. But then his gaze sharpened, and he leaned forward, a question forming on his lips. "But I have one question, why let her surrender so easily?"

"If she dies," my father said, his voice cold, calculated, and empty of any real feeling, "the Ember will reabsorb into the flame and return to me. This gives my wife and I another chance to try for a male heir who will hold the Ember. In the meantime, we will stay on the throne until our future son comes of age."

"And Hayden's coronation?" Caraway probed.

"Cancelled," my father said bitterly, "for obvious reasons now. We cannot have a future king until the Ember is secured into another heir."

The words hung in the air, and King Caraway gave a low grunt, almost sounding like a laugh.

"Well, then, I suppose I may not kill her right away. Perhaps I could have other uses for her," he mused, his lips curling into a vicious smile as his gaze raked over me.

I stiffened, cold dread crawling up my spine.

The plan had never been for me to become the Ivy King's prisoner or his slave and definitely not his whore. I was meant to be brought to Ivy Isle and my blood was to be spilled to appease Theodon. But now, standing before this male, I realized how easily those plans could shift. This wasn't part of the deal. I could accept death, but not the degradation he threatened.

I could feel my chest tighten as shallow breaths rattled in and out. I had to stay in control. I couldn't show weakness.

"King Caraway," my father said, his voice low but laced with restrained fury, "we understand that you are grieving the loss of your son, and that the debt must be paid. Eliane will pay it with her life, by the sentence you yourself declared. She has already agreed to this punishment." His voice rose as he continued. "But do not ever fucking imply that you plan to violate my daughter again!"

His words rang out, loud and clear, echoing through the room, but King Caraway remained unmoved. The bastard actually laughed, short and mocking. It was obvious that he was enjoying the rise he'd gotten out of my father. I could only hope his cruel words were nothing more than a twisted game.

"Oh, calm down, Keegan," Caraway sneered. "I wouldn't dare touch the female you were so ashamed of that you felt the need to hide her away."

"Please," Hayden pleaded, his voice raw with desperation, "just take me. Kill me. Leave her out of this."

"It's too late, Prince Hayden," Adan's voice cracked with emotion. "The debt has already been agreed upon, so please, King Caraway, take that iron collar off my prince. He is no longer your prisoner."

"Adan!" my brother shouted, but I could see the storm of emotion brewing in his eyes. He was furious, desperate, but trying to stay in control.

"And here I thought the king was the emotional one," he taunted, his words dripping with mockery. "You two lovers are agonizing to watch."

"Shut up!" Adan roared, stepping forward, his fists clenched in fury.

Caraway only sneered in response. "You only prove my point," he spat, his gaze narrowing.

His son had just died, and yet here he was, standing unfeeling and amused, making crude comments as though this were all some twisted game to him. He was an absolute bastard.

"Guards," Caraway barked, his voice cutting through the tension, "release the Ember Prince from his collar and bring me the girl." He turned his eyes toward me, and that wicked smile of his returned.

The guards stepped forward, pulling Hayden from knees as the collar was removed. His powers slowly began to resurface, the familiar energy of him returning in slow waves. Hopefully the king did not see how quickly he was recovering or he may suspect that Hayden did indeed possess the Ember.

Though he was healing quickly, he was still not at full strength. Watching him like this, so weak, so vulnerable was like a knife to my heart. I didn't want to watch him suffer, but I knew that once this day was over, Hayden would be whole again, and this nightmare would eventually be over for him. For me, however, it was only beginning.

I walked forward, meeting the guards halfway. I wouldn't give them the satisfaction of dragging me. I would go willingly, even if the thought of what lay ahead nearly made me sick.

The cold iron of the collar closed around my neck, the metal biting into my skin. I couldn't help but shudder at the sensation. My untamed curls bringing me slight relief as strands were caught under the collar. For a moment, it felt like the very air had been sucked from my lungs. The iron would irritate me, yes, but unlike more powerful fae, it didn't burn me the way it had with Hayden. The effects of it were only uncomfortable for now, but over time the long exposure would start to burn my skin. For now I let out a small hiss, playing up the pain, giving the illusion that it hurt more than it did.

I cast a quick glance at my brother as the guards tugged at my chain, causing me to stumble to the floor. Hayden moved in an instant, rushing to pull me back up.

"Don't try anything, Prince," one of the guards barked, his grip tight on the chain.

"Let me say goodbye to my sister!" Hayden snapped, his voice shaking with a fury I knew all too well. "At least let me do that!"

The guard hesitated, glancing at King Caraway for permission. Caraway gave a curt nod. I couldn't waste time saying goodbye to everyone, but I couldn't leave without saying goodbye to Hayden. He was my twin, my other half, and the thought of parting from him like this left a bitter ache in my chest. He would carry on. He would lead. He had a future, one that I wouldn't be a part of.

Hayden pulled me into his arms, holding me tight, careful to avoid the collar that now wrapped around my neck. His embrace was strong, his heartbeat frantic against my cheek. He whispered, his voice so soft that I almost couldn't hear it. "Eli, listen to me. Stay alive as long as you can. He may want to interrogate you about our kingdom, our armies —"

"But, Hay," I whispered back, choking on the fear that threatened to break me. "I don't know if I can —"

"Lie," he interrupted, his tone urgent, "make yourself valuable until the next full moon. Give him a reason to keep you alive. I will come for you."

I nodded, not trusting myself to speak. His words hung between us like a thread, fragile but strong. The next full moon was almost a month from now. Could I survive that long? I had no choice but to lie, to feed Caraway whatever fake information I could about army strategies I didn't know, about secrets I didn't possess. Or maybe I could even use my body, play his game to stay alive. It sickened me to think it, but if it would buy me time, I'd do whatever I had to.

Hayden would come for me.

Wait, no. That can't be the solution. I needed to repay the debt. If I escaped, Caraway would likely demand Hayden's life again, and this would all be for nothing. I had to snap myself out of the fantasy that this could end any other way than with my blood being spilled. I had already accepted this fate. Hayden needed to accept it too.

"No, Hay," I loosened our embrace. "There's no saving me. I have to pay this price."

"Eli," Hayden growled through clenched teeth, his grip tightening, "I am not going to let you die, and by Theodon, I swear, I will kill you myself if you give up." His eyes, glazed with emotion, locked onto mine. "I will come for you. We'll figure this out, together."

Hayden looked like he was going to be sick. I didn't want my last memory of Hayden to be of us arguing. I nodded, my throat tight, unable to say more. I loved him, and I knew he meant well, but I couldn't let him play the hero when he might not even survive the attempt. This was his last hope, and I couldn't take that from him.

"Okay," I whispered, barely a sound.

Caraway snapped his fingers sharply, commanding. "Take her to the ships and lock her in the cell. I want to leave this cursed Isle." His guards stirred, and once again I was jerked forward, nearly losing my balance in the process.

"Wait!" My mother's voice rang out, raw with pain. "Don't we get to say goodbye?"

King Caraway slowly turned around, his face cold. "Did I get to say goodbye to my child?" The room fell into an oppressive silence. "That's what I thought." With that, he turned to leave, his guards trailing behind him as we were herded out the door.

I glanced back, my gaze locking on Hayden's tear-stricken face. His eyes were wide, brimming with unspoken emotions. I held his stare as we marched forward, each step pulling me further and further away from him. Before we were completely out of the room, I saw Hayden's lips move. He mouthed a single, desperate phrase: Full moon.

I would always root for my brother, no matter what he set his mind to. But this was one task I had hoped he would fail at.

11

I was forced to march behind the guard's horse, trudging across the palace grounds and then through the unforgiving desert sands. My legs ached, but I had no choice but to keep up the pace, my pride too stubborn to let myself be dragged. The long hem of my dress, still clinging to me from the night before, didn't help matters. With each step, the fabric caught on the rough ground, tearing and ripping beneath the constant friction of sand and my stride. The dress, once symbolizing my hope for change, now felt like a cruel reminder of how much had already been lost. I had told myself it would change things when I wore it, and I wasn't wrong.

Passing through so many places heavy with memories only made my chest tighten further. Places I would never see again, moments I would never get to create, and recollections that stung all the more as we passed the oasis where it had all begun, the guilt burrowing deeper and deeper within me.

We finally reached the outskirts of the Isle, where the docks awaited. One ship had already set sail ahead with its cargo, the body of Prince Hawthorn. The other ship remaining was a large, imposing vessel, black as midnight with emerald sails that shimmered in the light. As we drew closer, I couldn't help but notice how massive it seemed, its hull towering over us.

The guard who had held the chain of my collar in the throne room once again gripped it tightly as he dismounted his horse. "This way, Princess," he said mockingly, reveling in the control that came with his new role as my warden.

He was a large male with dark brown hair, not quite black like the Ivy King's, but close enough to give him an almost sinister appearance. His eyes were dark and empty, as if the world had stripped him of any softness, leaving only the hardness of his role in the king's guard. There was no kindness in them, no empathy. Though he grinned at me throughout the journey, his smile was anything but sweet. It was feral, predatory. I did not trust this fae male one bit.

"Orrin," King Caraway called sharply toward the guard holding my leash. "Take her below and lock her up. I want to get home as soon as possible."

"Yes, Your Majesty," Orrin replied, his voice cold, followed by a rough yank on the chain that made my collar dig into my skin.

Orrin. Now I had a name to pair with the brute.

He shoved me roughly along the bridge leading to the ship. Once aboard, I clutched the railing and took a long, lingering look at the shore, the place I had once called home. A final glance. I knew I would never see it again. No more soft sand between my toes, no more warm, clear waters to soak in. No more mother, no more father. No more Hayden. The thought left a bitter taste in my mouth.

The deck creaked beneath my feet, slick with sea spray. Sailors moved with practiced precision, hauling ropes and adjusting sails, their shouts cutting through the wind. Ivy Guards patrolled, armor clinking, their eyes filled with anger and judgment whenever they glanced my way, though I knew it was well deserved as their watchful eyes pressed in on me, a reminder that I was no longer in the safety of the Isle I knew.

The swaying motion of the ship made my stomach lurch, and I gripped the railing tighter as the deck tilted beneath each wave. Everything familiar had shrunk into a panorama of memory, framed by the endless blue of the ocean.

A sharp tug at my collar snapped me back to reality. Orrin was pulling me away from the railing and below deck, no doubt toward the prison cells.

It was dark and musty down there, the air filled with the stench of rancid seawater and moldy wood. I pinched my nose in an attempt to hold back the nausea rising in my throat. The smell was unbearable. I could barely breathe, but I had to endure it. This would only take a few days, I told myself. I could hold my nose for that long, right?

We paused at the cell, and before locking me inside, the words "I'm sorry" replayed over and over in my mind until, I suppose, I let them slip from my mouth, since Orrin's voice cut through my thoughts.

"It's your brother who should be sorry," Orrin hissed. "He should be the one in here, but I have to say, I'm not exactly hating the view in this switch, at least not until the debt has been paid." He sneered, and my blood turned cold. "It was rather brave of you to demand to take your brother's place, a quality I quite admire." His lips curled into a wicked smile.

"There's nothing to admire," I said through clenched teeth, "not when I was the one who shot—" I stopped myself, realizing it might already be too late.

"What was that?"

"Nothing," I said, clamping my mouth shut. I wasn't sure if the truth even mattered at this point, but I didn't want to experience the king's wrath if he knew it was truly me who killed his son.

"You know, we saw someone riding off very fast from the oasis earlier, someone matching your description," he said, smiling like he knew. If he knew, who knew what he would do with that information? Maybe if I just apologized, he would see my sincerity, that it was truly an accident and that I was prepared to pay.

"It was an accident," I said, the truth bubbling out quicker than I could stop it.

"So it was you?" Orrin questioned. "Is that why you took your brother's place?" He paused, then asked, "What else are you hiding?"

"Nothing," I quietly replied, determined not to reveal any more secrets, but the truth gnawed at me. I wondered just what exactly Orrin would do with that information. "Are you going to tell your king?"

Orrin's wicked grin returned as he said, "This can be our little secret, Princess. But what will you give me in exchange for my silence?" he reached out and ran his rough fingers along my lips.

I gasped and recoiled, my shoulder slamming into the metal bars. Orrin stalked closer, his hand dropping to trace the bodice covering my breast. I was paralyzed by fear, not only from the contact, but because I knew I couldn't fight him off, especially not with the collar's chain still in his grasp.

"King Caraway may actually keep you alive out of spite," Orrin growled. "You're going to want someone on your side, Princess." He squeezed my breast hard, causing me to gasp in pain, then slid his hand lower, lifting my skirt. "I can make things more comfortable if you cooperate."

I had to stop this, preserve my dignity and virginity. I deserved death, but not this. Summoning my courage, I struck out my knee making contact with his most sensitive area. Orrin collapsed with a grunt, pulling me down with him. As he struggled to his feet, his face red with pain, he shouted, "You little bitch!" And yanked the chain, nearly snapping my neck.

Towering over me, Orrin's hand flew back and landed on my cheek with such force that I tasted blood and my ears rang. He threw me into the cell, muttering, "After what King Caraway has in store for you, you'll beg me to fuck you in exchange for comforts. You'll need me to survive, and I won't be gentle about it."

I closed my eyes tightly, wishing this were all just a nightmare. But when I opened them, all I saw was the cold, unforgiving cell. Orrin was already ascending the steps. "Sleep tight, Princess," he called, closing the door behind him.

I was alone in the dark, and I wasn't sure whether I should be thankful for it or terrified beyond measure. Being alone with my thoughts was never a good thing. This was my fault. Everything that would likely happen to me, and to my body, was my fault. I killed Hawthorne. I was a bad person, and no matter how much I told myself I didn't deserve this, a part of me knew I truly did. I had stolen an entire family's future, an entire kingdom's future, because I made a mistake. A mistake that could have been avoided if I hadn't been so eager to play the hero, insisting I take up the hunt. I wanted so badly to prove my worth, and look where it had gotten me. I was an idiot for taking a drink from a stranger, no matter what it was. My poor judgment had landed me here, even if what Reed had given me was only gin.

Reed. Oh no, I wondered if this was the very same cell he had sat in. The cell where he'd likely felt the guilt settle in, knowing he was responsible for his crew's deaths. *No.* Not him. Caraway. Caraway was the one who killed Reed's crew when all they were doing was trying to feed their families. Wherever Reed had ended up, I hoped it was far from Caraway's reach.

I needed to sleep. It was the only way to silence my mind and drift away from these guilt-ridden thoughts. I lay on the cold, damp floor, wrapping my arms around myself for warmth, occasionally wiping at my still-bleeding lip. There was no bed in this cell, not that I would deserve one anyway. I took deep breaths, trying to quiet my mind. Behind closed, watery eyelids, I could still see the shimmering blood pooling on the desert sand. The arrow lodged in the prince's chest, standing upright like a cruel reminder. My mind fled to the memory of his fingers gently wiping frosting from my cheek, to his tender touch as he laced up my dress. The dress

I was still wearing, heavy with bad memories. I just needed to shut everything out, focus on my breathing, and let the world fall away. My tear-soaked eyes grew heavy, and finally, there was release as I slipped into the darkness of sleep.

When my eyes began to lift, I was disoriented for a moment, unsure of where I was. The sharp, musty smell of mold filled my nostrils, instantly grounding me in the reality of my surroundings. I was still on the ship. How long had I been asleep? How much longer until we reached the Ivy Isle?

Slowly, I propped myself up, my body still weak and sore from being dragged behind the horse that morning, or was it yesterday? The lack of any natural light in the cell made it impossible to tell. My eyes strained toward a small flickering glow as my vision began to clear. At last, my gaze fixed on the only source of light, a single torch propped against the wall. That's when my blood froze. There, just outside my cell, stood a dark, looming figure. Orrin.

"Finally awake, are we?" he muttered as I watched him tuck something into his trousers.

Oh no, was he watching me sleep? Was he touching himself while I laid here unconscious? What if I hadn't woken up? I felt bile begin to climb up my throat as I tried to shake the thought.

"Looks like that pretty little mouth of yours is going to bruise," he said with a grin.

I raised my hand to my swollen lip. Just a gentle touch, but the instant pain shot through my face, I couldn't suppress the flinch. I couldn't let him see it, though. I cleared my throat, trying to sound steady. "How long have we been at sea?" My voice was hoarse, barely a whisper.

"It's only been a day," Orrin said, crouching down to meet my gaze, his eyes gleaming with a twisted amusement. "We still have at least a few more, weather permitting. And then," he smiled viciously, his teeth sharp in the dim light, "and then, Princess, it will be time to pay."

I said nothing. I wouldn't give him the satisfaction of hearing my fear. It was clear from his smirk that it was exactly what he wanted. So I nodded, pretending indifference, and crawled into the shadows of the back of the cell, as far away from him as I could get.

"You know," he called, his voice dripping with malice, "my offer still stands." He moved closer to the bars, leaning in as if we were sharing some secret. "You're going to want at least one friend on the Isle."

I didn't respond. He didn't need to hear my thoughts on his idea of friendship. I would rather endure every torture he could imagine than give him what he wanted. His silence while I slept told me that he'd probably been given orders by Caraway to keep his hands off me for now, orders he would probably need my consent to override. Consent he would never get.

"You'll reconsider," he said, straightening. "Trust me, Princess. Hell, you'll be begging for my help once we arrive. You'll see."

With that, he turned and climbed back up the stairs to the deck, his heavy boots echoing on the wooden planks. Despite having slept for what must have been at least eight hours, I still felt like I hadn't slept at all. Sleep was the only thing that offered me a brief reprieve from the pain, the guilt, and the fear that haunted me. Just a blank canvas where I could hide from it all. That's what I craved now. So, I curled up on the cold floor again, using my arm as a makeshift pillow. I closed my eyes, hoping to escape into nothingness once more.

"Princess, wake up! They have arrived!" A voice, sharp and shrill, pierced the fog of my sleep.

My eyes fluttered open, and for a moment, I didn't know where I was. The familiar feel of satin sheets wrapped around me, the warm glow of sunlight filtering through my curtains. It felt like home. I sat up, a wave of relief crashing over me. Marble walls streaked with gold and copper. My room. My closet. My bed.

I was home.

"Come on, it's time to meet them. They're waiting in the throne room!" The voice shrieked again.

I looked up. It was Mirra. She was here. It was all just a bad dream. I wasn't in that dark, cold cell. I wasn't on a ship headed toward the Ivy Isle.

"Meet who?" I yawned, still groggy from sleep.

"Prince Hawthorne and King Caraway," Mirra replied, her eyes wide with excitement. "They're asking to meet you specifically."

Meet me? "What are you talking about? They don't even know I exist."

Mirra paused, giving me a curious look as she began to pull the covers off me, the satin slipping against my skin. "You're the princess and heir to the Ember throne, of course they know who you are."

This had to be a dream. I was the powerless princess, not the heir. This couldn't be real. But if in this dream I was allowed to be seen, then maybe it meant things were on a different path. Hayden was safe, I was safe, and Hawthorne was alive.

"Okay," I said, standing up and grabbing a robe to cover myself, "Let's go meet them."

"Is Hayden already there?" I asked, my mind still hazy as I pulled the robe tight.

"Who?" Mirra asked, furrowing her brow as she helped me tie the robe around my waist.

"Prince Hayden," I chuckled softly, "My brother."

"Oh," she said slowly, her eyes flicking away from mine, "You mean your twin? The one you killed?"

The words hit like a punch to the gut. "What?" I gasped. "I didn't kill him. I killed Hawthorne." The words came out bluntly, almost too harsh to bear.

I blinked.

Suddenly, I was no longer in my bedroom. Instead, I was back in the oasis. The sun beating down on the desert sand, and before me lay Hawthorne's lifeless body, blood pooling around him in a horrific stain. But this time, I wasn't standing far away. I was hovering above him, so close that I could feel the heat of his blood on my skin.

"You killed me, El," Hayden's voice whispered into my ear, forcing me to turn. His face was twisted in rage, his eyes black with fury. "You just couldn't stay hidden, could you?" His voice dripped with venom, each word cutting deep. "Is this how you would get rid of me?"

"No," I choked out, stumbling backward. "Hay, what are you talking about? It was an accident."

"You've been jealous of me and my power since birth," he continued, his hands balled into fists. I couldn't help but notice how every muscle in his upper body tensed, his broad chest and powerful arms flexing with the kind of strength that made him look like a warrior ready to strike. "And now that you've found the perfect opportunity to get rid of me, you took it, didn't you?"

"I don't care about the crown. You know that," I spat, my body beginning to shake.

Now, I was certain this wasn't real. Hayden would never say these things to me. But why did it still hurt?

"I'm going to pay the debt, and you'll be fine," I said, my voice shaking, "Everything will be fine."

"Equal or greater life, right, El?" Hayden's voice oozed with bitterness as he moved toward Hawthorne's lifeless body. "Do you really think your life is equal or greater than his?" He wrenched the arrow from Hawthorne's chest, blood spraying and painting his skin.

Hayden stalked toward me, his grip tightening on the arrow. His knuckles turned pale as he moved closer.

"Hayden," I said, my voice steady despite the bile rising in my throat from the sight of the blood.

"After they torture you and find out how worthless you really are," Hayden yelled, "they'll come for me!"

"They won't find out. I p-promise," I stammered, backing away, though I wasn't sure if I was trying to convince him or myself.

"Shut the fuck up, Eli! You've damned me and this entire kingdom, all because you couldn't handle the shadows."

"Please, Hay, listen to me," my words caught in my throat as I held my hands up in surrender. I had never seen my brother like this, so consumed by rage, so full of hatred. I wanted to wake up. I needed to wake up.

"No!" he shouted, his face inches from mine, his breath hot against my skin. "If I'm going to die for a crime *you* committed, then it's only fair that I commit that crime," he twisted the arrow in his grip, the sound of the shaft scraping against the metal sending a shiver down my spine.

"What do you mean?" I whimpered, realizing I was trapped, sand at my back and Hayden at my front, his presence suffocating.

"If I'm to pay the price for killing a royal," he muttered, his tone cold, "then I might as well kill one." His eyes were wide, burning with that sick, twisted logic.

"Hay," my voice was barely a whisper, but before I could say another word, I felt it. I looked down, pain surging through my body, as Hayden took a step back.

There it was, an arrow in my chest. The same arrow I had used to kill Hawthorne. The pain was immediate and the agony felt all too real. Warm blood streamed down my chest, seeping into my gown. The warm, sticky liquid slid down my belly, making my heart stutter.

I could barely breathe. My lungs screamed for air, but my chest felt crushed under the intensity of the pain as I stumbled backward, leaning against the familiar trunk of a palm tree for support

I focused on anything but that. Anything but the overwhelming, crushing ache that consumed me. My vision blurred, but I stared at Hayden, his form growing taller. I thought maybe I was just losing my mind, but then I realized I was slipping. I was sliding down the palm tree behind me. Had I wanted everything Hayden had? No. I shook my head, trying to force the thought away. I didn't want the crown. I only wanted Hayden to be happy.

And once this whole thing comes to an end, hopefully he will be.

"Wakey wakey, Princess," a gruff voice muttered, pulling me roughly to my feet, dragging me out of the haze of sleep. "Time to go."

I blinked rapidly, trying to shake the darkness from my vision. My mind felt sluggish, but I could make out the shape of the male standing before me. Orrin. Of course, it was him. There was no escaping this bastard. King Caraway had clearly tasked him to be my shadow, staying close until my blood was spilled.

"Are we on the Ivy Isle?" I croaked, my voice hoarse from days without water. At least, I think it had been days. Time had lost meaning in the dank cell, and I hadn't even touched my feet to the soil of the Ivy Isle yet.

Orrin tugged the chain on my collar and yanked me out of the cell. "We're docking as we speak," he said, his grip tightening on the chain. "Hope you rested those legs of yours. You'll be walking behind the horse all the way to the castle. It won't be an easy journey."

"I can take it," I spat, the words dripping with disdain as we began climbing the stairs. I already knew where this conversation would end up, and I was sick of it. Sick of being treated like some plaything for the male who held my chains.

Orrin stopped us on the landing before he opened the cabin door, finally letting me see what time it was. As the door creaked open, the cool night air hit me, and I was grateful for the first signs of the outside world.

He wrapped the chain around his wrist, pulling me closer, reducing the space between us. "You know, if those little legs are still sore, you could ride with me," he said, his fingers brushing my cheek. "I'll even let you sit on my lap."

I recoiled sharply, a sharp whimper escaping me as the collar pressed painfully into my throat. I sucked in a breath, trying to steady myself, to fight back the pain.

"I'd rather walk than let you anywhere near me," I hissed, each word laced with fury. I'd face my punishment, but not at the cost of this male touching me.

Orrin gave the chain another vicious tug, his fingers digging into the chain of my collar, reminding me just how little control I had. "Remember who holds your leash, dog," he sneered. Another pull, and another wince of pain escaped my lips. He had the power, and I had none. "Let's get moving, and we'll see how long you last."

I turned my gaze to the sky, the stars barely peeking through the darkening night. The evening was still young, and I prayed we wouldn't be walking all night. The dense forest ahead loomed ominously. I could make out the faint outlines of crooked, curving trees through the shadows cast by the torchlight. Under different circumstances, I was sure this place would be beautiful, but right now, there was only a growing unease in my chest at the slightest hoot of an owl or chirp of a cricket. I hadn't studied much about Ivy Isle, but I knew enough to understand that, beneath its beauty, it was a land of dangerous magic and beasts that had evolved over centuries, much like the Loa. If we were attacked, I stood no chance, not with these chains, not without magic.

I could only imagine how little Caraway would care if I died out here, though he'd probably be upset he didn't get to deliver the final blow himself.

Caraway led the front of the group while Orrin kept me close, walking just a few guards behind his horse. Another line of guards on horseback brought up the rear. If we were attacked from behind, I could hope one of the Ivy Guards would slay whatever beast dared to approach me. If it attacked head-on... well, I could only pray the guards would spot it in time to protect their king. The thought offered me a shred of comfort, but it wasn't enough to ease the pain that shot through my legs with every step.

It must have been hours by now, but I had no idea how much longer we'd be traveling until we reached Ivy Castle. The king only allowed brief stops, mostly for the horses, not for the guards, and certainly not for me. The sky had darkened, the faint glow of the crescent moon and the shimmer of stars offering the only light in our way. Despite everything, I couldn't help but think about my old dreams of seeing the Ivy Isle. I'd read stories about its thick, enchanted forests, places so green and vast you could easily lose yourself in their depths. The ancient trees, their towering trunks stretching skyward, were said to protect anyone beneath them from the sun's blistering heat. A heat I rarely minded and often welcomed whenever I could.

As we moved deeper into the forest, I strained my eyes, trying to make out any shapes in the darkness. But it was impossible. The only thing I could clearly identify was the intoxicating scent of the forest, the damp earth mingled with the sharp, soothing pine. It reminded me of how Prince Hawthorne smelled. It made sense, of course. He was from this island, the scent of its trees and soil must have absorbed into his skin like a second nature.

I shook my head sharply, trying to dismiss the thought before it could take hold of me. I didn't want to think about him, not now. I couldn't let myself cry again. Not in front of them. Not in front of the king.

Caraway raised his hand sharply, signaling the guards to halt. "Water the horses quickly," he ordered. "Then we'll make the final stretch home."

We must have been near a stream or a pond, though in the dark I couldn't tell. I seized the opportunity to crouch down onto the cool, dewy grass. The soil felt like heaven beneath my bare legs, which had been exposed after the rough journey. My once floor-length dress had been torn and shredded at the hem, now hanging unevenly around my legs with one side reaching mid-calf, the other just below my knee, giving the fabric a jagged look. The branches and thorns of the forest had snagged at it along the way, but I found myself oddly grateful for the shorter length. It had made walking easier, and for the last hour, I hadn't tripped over the hem once.

"Stay here while I water the horse," Orrin commanded, guiding the animal toward what I assumed was the stream.

As if I could run. Even if there were no guards, my legs, aching, weak, and quaking, would never carry me far enough to escape. I collapsed onto my back in the cool grass, savoring the brief comfort of stillness. I stared up at the stars, wondering if this would be the last time I saw them. I'd heard stories about the constellations, how each pattern told a story, passed down through generations. The only one I remembered clearly was the tale of Theodon and his human wife, Vesta.

It was the story of how all of this began. Theodon, a God, had created all of Ainoah in his solitude, centuries before the Isles had split. For years, he shaped life from nature, watching his creations grow, evolve, and build. But as he observed them, he also saw their darker side, their hatred, their capacity for destruction. The story always spoke of Theodon's ambivalence, how he could never quite decide which trait of his creations he admired more, their love and creativity, or their hatred and ruin. Both sides of the coin were necessary, after all. One could not exist without the other.

Theodon would often shape shift to other forms to get a front row seat of his creations in action. That would have been a nifty genetic trait to have, I could imagine the endless possibilities that it would give me. Unfortunately, it was a trait that never made it to his four children. Most likely because he had multiple elements to bend and shape within himself, and once the quads were born, each element split off and was assigned to one of the Original Four. A pity.

The story spoke of a day many years ago when Theodon took on a human form, as he often did to experience the life he had created. This time, however, things were different. Witnessing how far hatred had spread, something within him snapped.

While walking the land, Theodon stumbled upon a village he had never before explored in his long years. He was always curious to discover new places, to watch as the world changed around him. It was in this village that he saw Vesta.

She was tied to a pillar in the center of the market square, surrounded by a large, jeering crowd. Her dress was torn open at the back, and a whip cracked down upon her again and again. The crowd watched, some with pity, others with amusement, as the lash struck her skin. According to the stories, Vesta's father was the one holding the whip. Over the centuries, the details of their story had become blurred, yet the core of it remained the same. Vesta's father took pleasure in abusing his only daughter, and the abuse continued until she became pregnant with his child.

The accounts diverged at this point. Some stories claimed that Vesta had deliberately caused the death of the child within her womb painting her as a villain. Others said the babe had died on its own, a miscarriage caused by the cruelty she endured. Regardless of the details, one thing was clear: Vesta's father was enraged by the pregnancy. In that time, females were seen as nothing more than property, treated with the same disregard as livestock. Males were free to do as they wished, and females had little choice but to endure.

Theodon watched from the edge of the crowd, a front-row seat to the hatred and destruction unfolding before him. A seat he usually enjoyed, but not on this day. He could see Vesta's back, bloodied and raw, with each lash. Her cries tore through the air, and soon they tore through him. He couldn't stand it anymore. This was the very kind of suffering he had created. Hatred and pain, cycles of violence that would never end.

Theodon had sworn, long ago, never to intervene in the lives of mortals, to let them chart their own course. But standing there, watching Vesta's torment, something inside him shifted. In his human form, he was subject to human emotions, and they overwhelmed him. Sympathy and compassion consumed him. He couldn't just watch anymore.

He stopped the punishment and took her from that life.

This was how their love began. This was my favorite story in the stars. The story of a creator falling in love with his creation. If that meeting had never happened, the fae would never have existed. The love between Theodon and Vesta gave birth to the first four Elemental Fae. When the Original Four were born, a strange and powerful phenomenon occurred, one that would shape the future of the fae. As the babes uttered their first cries and let out their first laughs, the energy they exuded wasn't just felt, it was absorbed. Those who were closest to the newborns, within mere miles of their presence, felt the full force of this power. The humans nearest to them absorbed the bulk of this energy, and depending on which elemental wavelength they absorbed first, that was the exact elemental power the newly made fae possessed. They became the High Fae.

But as the ripple of power spread further across the land, the strength of the gift began to wane. Those who were miles away, too far to feel the full intensity of the babes' power, absorbed only a small amount of the magic. These humans, though touched by the same gift, could not tap into the same depth of power as a High Fae. From then on, they became what we now know as Lesser Fae, still bound to the magic, with extraordinary gifts, just not as powerful.

Then there was me. Something even less, with only the faintest whisper of magic. But that didn't matter now.

A rough voice pulled me from my thoughts.

"Get up," it commanded. "Time to get going."

I didn't have the energy to respond to Orrin. Using my arms for leverage, I slowly pushed myself up from the cool grass, already mourning the loss of its gentle touch against my skin, even if it had left my flesh a little itchy. I stood still while Orrin attached the iron chains to my collar, ready to drag me along once more. Fighting would do me no good. I just wanted to get to the castle and end this nightmare.

We continued through the forest, the stars growing brighter as the evening wore on. I tried once again to take in my surroundings, as I knew they might be the last things I saw. The darkness had spread, casting a heavy blanket over the trees and obscuring the path ahead.

"Almost there," a guard muttered from horseback, his voice barely audible.

Thank Theodon. My legs were on the verge of giving out, but I could make it just a little farther. I could see the vague shape of the castle now, a silhouette against the night sky. We were close, at least thirty more minutes, and I would either be dead or thrown into a cell. Either way, the agony in my legs would finally end.

The castle came into view, clearer and more distinct as we drew nearer. In the darkness, it looked as though it was made of dark metal, its jagged edges wrapped in ivy that sprouted like veins from the soil. It had an eerie, almost sinister presence, like something straight out of a ghost story. I had always imagined the Ivy Isle to be a place brimming with greenery, life, and color, but this castle… this place looked lonely. Hollow, even, as if it hadn't been cared for in years.

We approached the front gates, and King Caraway dismounted from his horse, striding toward Orrin and me. Was this it? Was this where it all ended?

His eyes never left me as he passed Orrin, a cruel smile twisting his lips. "Welcome to the Ivy Castle, Princess," he said, his voice dripping with mockery as he stepped closer. I flinched involuntarily, the proximity of his body sending a cold shiver through me. "Before your mind starts racing," he continued, his tone dark and sinister, "I won't kill you just yet, though you deserve it, after what your brother did to my son."

A lump formed in my throat, tight and painful, but I swallowed hard to try to loosen it. "I know," was all I managed to say, my voice barely above a whisper.

Caraway took a step back, his eyes scanning me, no doubt measuring which parts of me would bear the brunt of his vengeance. He seemed to enjoy the thought of it, taking his time as though savoring the moment. I deserved it, I knew. Whatever punishment he saw fit, I would endure it.

"Orrin, take her below to the dungeon cells," King Caraway finally commanded, his voice cold and final. "I've got a few questions for our prisoner, but tonight, I need some rest."

With that, he dismissed himself, turning away without a second glance.

Orrin nodded and guided me through the castle's entrance. Inside, the contrast to my palace was stark and unsettling. The air was clouded with dust, and the cold, rough stone beneath my feet was a far cry from the smooth marble and stone floors of the Ember Palace, often streaked with lines of gold and copper embedded into the marble. This place was dark, with only a few flickering torches lining the walls of what appeared to be the main hall. In the hall, I could make out some scattered chairs and a long table near the entrance, but from the looks of it, the place hadn't been bustling with life in quite some time. Shadows stretched across the room, casting long, eerie shapes that made my skin crawl. As we moved further through the castle, I glimpsed the throne room, or what I assumed was the throne room, marked by an iron chair in the center. I tried to scan the area, wondering if, like the throne room back home, King Caraway had the laws of Ainoah posted up. But from what I could see, it was just a very bare room. I had imagined a throne room lush with greenery and vibrant with life. But instead, this place felt oppressive and abandoned, as though the life once here had been stripped away. Dark vines crept up the rough stone walls, curling like forgotten memories, and there was a sense that even nature itself had turned its back on this castle.

"This way," Orrin shouted back at me, pulling me from the dream-like fantasy of a castle I had built in my mind.

We moved through several more rooms, the cold stone underfoot echoing with every step, until we reached a long hall with a heavy metal door at the far end. I watched as Orrin wrapped his bare hand with a strip of cloth before pulling open the large door with ease. I guessed it was made of iron, designed to keep prisoners locked inside. Not that I had any escape plans. At least, none that I could or would ever carry out, despite Hayden's hopeful words.

We continued down a narrow staircase that descended deeper into the castle, the air growing colder with each step. Orrin moved behind me now, forcing me to lead the way. The darkness around us was thick, oppressive, and every step felt more dangerous than the last. The only light came from the small torch Orrin held behind me, casting shadows that seemed to move and writhe like living things. I could barely see the stairs in front of me. One wrong step and I could fall, shattering my skull on the stone. Then again, I had no doubt that if I did fall, Orrin would yank on the chain hard enough to snap my neck.

Finally, we reached the bottom, and the temperature dropped sharply as a cold draft brushed against my exposed skin. I squinted into the darkness, trying to make sense of the shapes and structures around me. All I could make out were faint outlines of four cells. Two on the left, two on the right. The space was cramped and small, and the air had a stale, damp smell that made my stomach churn. It looked like I was the only prisoner here, though I couldn't decide if that was a blessing or a curse.

It was good, in a way. Who knew what kind of crimes the other prisoners had committed to end up in such a dirty, suffocating place. But it was bad too, because I would be locked away here, alone, with only the sound of my own thoughts for company. I had no idea what the king's plans for me were, but it wouldn't be long before the loneliness set in. It was only a matter of time before I might find myself begging for death, just to escape the isolation and despair. I knew that made me weak, but in a land where I had no one, who was there to impress by pretending to be strong? My fate was already sealed, and I had nothing left but the waiting.

"In you go," Orrin commanded, pulling open the iron bars of the cell door. His bare skin was still wrapped in cloth.

He undid my chain and I stepped inside without hesitation. Honestly, I didn't have the energy to fight or argue. I was beyond that. All I wanted was to get through this, to survive long enough until I was judged by Theodon in the afterlife.

The screeching of the cell door closing echoed behind me, reverberating through the cold, damp space. I surveyed my surroundings, but in the dim light cast by Orrin's torch, all I could make out was a dusty broken cot with no blankets, covered in cobwebs, and a small bucket, presumably for relieving myself. That was it. The barest essentials.

I plopped down in the far corner of the cell, choosing the stone floor over the cot. Even if it had been clean, even if it had a blanket, I didn't deserve such comforts. The floor was my place, where I belonged. I curled in on myself, wrapping my arms around my body for warmth. I waited for Orrin to leave, so I could finally give in to the tears that had been building up inside me.

I didn't care if he saw my tears, but I couldn't bear the thought of giving him any more reason to stay. This was the one time I longed for solitude, no matter how much it hurt, just to escape his presence.

"Sleep tight, Princess," Orrin's voice echoed with amusement. He chuckled darkly before ascending the steps, taking the last bit of light with him.

As soon as I heard the heavy iron door slam shut, sealing me in complete darkness, the floodgates opened. My tears began to flow freely, and I started to rock gently, as if the motion might soothe the ache in my chest.

I killed him. It's my fault. I killed him. I'm a bad person and I deserve this. I killed him, it's my fault. I killed him. I'm a bad person and I deserve this.

The words repeated over and over in my head, a mantra of guilt. I didn't know how long I had been lying there, crying and murmuring to myself. Without any natural light to guide me, like the dimness I had on the ship, I couldn't tell if it had been minutes or hours. But by the time I noticed the cold puddle of tears beneath my cheek, my throat was raw from the constant repetition of my self-loathing.

If I focused on my guilt, it might drown out the anxiety creeping in from the suffocating darkness. Thankfully, exhaustion won.

I wasn't sure when or for how long I drifted into sleep, but it found me eventually. Thankfully, there were no nightmares. Only darkness. Silence. Numbness. I hated to admit it, but for the first time in what felt like forever, it was peaceful.

Maybe this was death? Maybe King Caraway had killed me already, and I just didn't know. Or perhaps this was the in-between, the place between life and judgment, before Theodon decided my fate. I knew I was damned. But maybe twenty years of good had outweighed this one bad. It was doubtful, but I had to hope.

A sharp pain yanked me from my slumber, searing along my wrist. My eyes snapped open, and instinctively, I pulled my hand back, cradling it against my chest. The iron bars. I must have rested my wrist against them without realizing. Iron didn't hurt me as much as it would a normal fae, but it had been there long enough to leave its mark. I couldn't see anything through the darkness, but the pain was unmistakable, hot, raw, and relentless.

I ran my fingertips gently over the sensitive spot, and a jolt of pain shot up my arm. It felt like the skin was seared, raw from contact with the metal. The pain would linger until the collar was removed. Even though my healing was slower than others, a few hours without the collar would likely ease the burn.

I pushed myself into a sitting position on the cold, hard stone beneath me, my body aching from the unforgiving surface. I still felt exhausted, but the pain radiating from my arm made it clear I had been asleep for a while with it pressed against the iron, long enough for it to burn this badly.

Wiping the dried tears and dirt from my face, my thoughts drifted back to home. I couldn't help but worry. Had I left my parents with too much trouble now that the kingdom knew our secret? Would my father truly cancel the coronation, or try to keep it hidden from the other Isles?

Maybe they would have to announce another heir, or at least pretend to, while Hayden quietly took the throne. Would the people still accept him as their king, or had my taking his place already made him appear weak?

Or perhaps it made him seem strong, even ruthless, for letting me take the fall for the good of the kingdom. If his coronation still went forward, I wondered if, when they inevitably cleared out my room, Hayden would find the gift I had never gotten the chance to give him. The one meant to bring luck and good fortune to his reign. A gift that now felt like nothing more than a cruel joke, because if it truly carried luck, it had failed me.

A chill swept through me at the thought of what awaited my home—my family. I rubbed my arms, trying to coax warmth into my skin, but the burn along my wrist flared with every movement, a constant reminder of my captivity.

The iron door above the steps creaked open, letting in a sliver of light. My heart began to race, knowing that this was it. The time had come. I looked down at my dress in the faint light to make sure I was still covered. I didn't want Orrin getting any ideas, no quick looks, no lewd touches before they executed me. From what I could see, my chest was still covered, the laces of my gown tightly fastened in the back still. My skirt, now torn and ragged, left my legs exposed from the knee down, but the rest of me was mostly intact.

Orrin's heavy footsteps echoed off the stone walls, growing louder as he descended the stairs. "Sleep well, Princess?" he mocked, fumbling with a ring of keys. "Seems the iron bars found you," he chuckled, his hand moving to his wrist, as if pleased with the irony of it all.

I stayed silent, refusing to engage with him. He took too much pleasure in my pain, and I refused to give him the satisfaction of a response. In my mind, he had become less fae and more monster. I couldn't help but wonder if this cruelty was reserved just for me because of the circumstances, or if this was his usual behavior with every female he encountered. He wasn't much to look at, and with a personality like his, it wasn't surprising he felt the need to prey on innocent females. Even fae from places like the Black Cinder would probably shun him, if they had any sense at all.

"Nothing to say?" Orrin sneered, letting out a low laugh. "I'm sure that'll change once the king's done with you."

With a jangle of keys, he unlocked the cell door and stepped inside, chain in hand, ready to fasten it to my collar.

So here it was, time for the interrogation. For once, I was thankful I didn't know anything about my parents' war strategies or the intel on our armies. Though the Isles had never waged war, thanks to the strict law prohibiting it, every Isle had prepared for the possibility. Now that my secret was out, who knew what King Caraway might have planned? And the fact that he had bought into our lies about Hayden not actually possessing the Ember, it was a relief in some ways, but it was a dangerous gamble. If word spread to the other Isles, it could be an open invitation for them to invade. I feared the chaos and bloodshed that would follow, a war that could have been avoided, but I had no control over that now.

The chain connected to my collar with a sharp click, and Orrin let his cloth-covered fingers linger on my neck. He traced the quick beat of my pulse with disturbing calm, and I instinctively pulled away, earning a low, mocking laugh from him. He tugged me forward, my feet stumbling as he dragged me toward the stairs.

My body ached with every step, the exhaustion from the journey and the unyielding stone beneath me taking its toll. We reached the top of the stairs, and Orrin pulled me through the hall. My heart sank when I saw the door at the far end of the hallway. I hadn't noticed it before, but now it felt like an omen. The dark wood of the door seemed to whisper of pain, of suffering that awaited beyond it. Something about this floor, the deafening silence, the heavy air, told me everything I needed to know.

Orrin opened the door and shoved me into the room. The cold, damp air hit me immediately, and the gloom was suffocating. My eyes scanned the space, landing on chains and other grim devices bolted to the walls, hanging from the ceiling like some twisted, macabre display. In the center of the room stood a wooden chair, its arms and legs fitted with shackles, designed to restrain a fae. My stomach lurched. This was the place, I realized. The place where they would break me, where they would force me to answer whatever questions the king had.

And there, standing next to the chair, was King Caraway. His expression was unreadable, his face stripped of all emotion. A stone wall, just like his kingdom.

"Have a seat, Princess," he said, his voice cold, devoid of any warmth or hint of mercy.

I didn't fight it. There was no point. I slowly sank into the chair, my body heavy with exhaustion and fear. Once I was seated, Orrin wasted no time, securing my ankles and wrists to the cold metal with cruel efficiency. Luckily the chains were long enough that I could still move my limbs freely enough. When he grabbed my burned wrist, pain shot through me like a bolt of lightning. I bit my lip, trying not to flinch, but I was sure the pain showed in my eyes. Thankfully, the cuffs were not made of iron. I felt no burn as they fastened around my limbs, but the rawness of my wrist left me trembling.

"Remove her collar," Caraway commanded, his attention shifting to a small table next to him.

Orrin retrieved a ring of keys from his belt, the soft jingle of metal filling the room. He fumbled through the keys, finally stopping when he found the right one. There was a quiet click, and with a sharp twist, the collar fell away from my neck. Almost immediately, I felt a faint lightness in my head and a slow, steady return of energy to my body.

But when I ran my fingers over my neck, I couldn't tell how red or irritated the skin was from days of wearing the collar. I had expected the pain to be sharper, but strangely, the area didn't burn as badly as my wrist. I didn't have the strength to contemplate why, and I certainly hoped Caraway wouldn't think to investigate further.

"Why remove it?" I asked, my voice hoarse. The night had been long, my mind lost in repetitive guilt, and my throat ached from the silent sobs that had wracked my body.

Caraway didn't look at me as he answered. "Because you're not stupid enough to do something foolish."

I glanced at the table, and my stomach twisted into knots. There were several sharp objects laid out, each more sinister than the last. Most of the weapons were unfamiliar to me, but one thing was unmistakable: a gleaming silver dagger, its blade reflecting the flickering firelight. And next to it, an odd object, a rough stone, roughly the size of a large grape. What was that for? Maybe to bludgeon me to death slowly, I thought. But I didn't really want to know what any of these implements were designed for. I would behave.

King Caraway picked up the dagger, his fingers caressing the hilt, which was encrusted with small diamonds and a large emerald at the center. The blade reflected in the low light, silver as moonlight. My pulse quickened as he approached, his eyes never leaving mine.

"What are you doing?" I demanded, panic rising in my chest. I had expected torture eventually, but not yet, he hadn't even asked me any questions.

"Just a simple blood test," he answered, his voice smooth and cold.

Before I could react, he pressed the edge of the blade to the palm of my hand. I sucked in a breath, but the pain was nothing compared to what I'd endured before. He dragged the blade across my skin, opening a shallow cut, and crimson pooled at the surface.

Caraway dipped his finger into the wound, collecting my blood, and raised it to the light. A small smile crept across his face as he examined it. "Needed to make sure your blood still shimmered after all you've been through. Can't have you too weak."

I looked down at my palm, watching as the blood dripped, mixed with tiny flecks of gold. My shimmer. It was weaker than Hayden's, always had been, but it was still there. It was enough to satisfy the king. I clenched my fist around the wound, trying to hide how slowly it was healing. I couldn't let him see that.

He wiped his finger clean on a piece of cloth, the smile never leaving his face. "Still strong enough for now."

A quiet silence settled between us, and I took in a shaky breath, focusing on controlling my emotions. It was easy to forget for a moment that I was trapped, restrained, and helpless, as long as I focused on the pulse in my hand, the thudding of my heart.

Caraway broke the silence, turning to Orrin. "You may leave us. I'll call for you when it's time to collect her."

Orrin hesitated, glancing back at me. "She doesn't have a collar on," he said, concern lacing his voice. "Is that wise?"

Caraway's eyes flicked to me, then back to Orrin. I knew his decision had nothing to do with me, not really. It was about control, about ensuring that even without the collar, I would feel the pull of his power. His gaze turned calculating. "No. I don't think this one will act up. Especially if it means putting her brother in danger."

My body tensed, muscles tightening at the mention of Hayden. My thoughts spiraled. The debt. I had to make sure it still stood. I couldn't—I wouldn't—let him find a loophole. If I kept the ruse up, if I lied well enough, maybe I could buy Hayden more time. Once I was dead, the debt would be settled, and my brother would be safe.

"I will cooperate," I said, my voice rasping. I knew it wasn't convincing, but it was all I could manage in that moment.

Caraway's smile widened, as if pleased by my resignation, which only caused my fear to spike.

"Orrin," Caraway started, "Please leave me and the Ember Princess to 'discuss' a few things." He said with a smile that was anything but sweet.

"Of course," Orrin nodded, slipping out of the room. The door shut with a soft click, leaving me unsure whether the creeping feeling was more panic or relief now that it was just me and the Ivy King.

After dismissing Orrin from the room, he reached down and pulled a lever beneath the chair. Suddenly, the chair tilted backward, its upright position morphing into a horizontal plank. The shackles on my arms and legs pulled taut, tightening painfully around my limbs, sending fresh waves of discomfort through my body.

My heart began to race again as I realized that the position I was in was meant for something more than a simple interrogation. I closed my eyes, focusing on my breathing, trying to calm the rising tide of panic in my chest. I remembered the comment Caraway made in the throne room about using me in other ways, and I had hoped—prayed—that he had more honor than that. But even if he tried to violate me, I knew I couldn't fight back. Not without putting Hayden in even greater danger. Not without condemning him to suffer torture, or worse.

"Don't worry," Caraway's voice was soft, almost too calm, "while you seem lovely, I don't plan on touching you in that way."

I opened my eyes and looked at him, confused. He was mixing something together on the table, his movements deliberate.

"But," he added, his eyes glinting with something darker, "if you wish for a quick fuck before you die, I can oblige."

"No thank you," I muttered, my voice barely a whisper. I forced my gaze forward, focusing on the wall ahead of me, anything to avoid looking at him. At least he said he wouldn't force himself on me and I only hoped that rule extended to his guards as well.

Caraway made a dismissive sound. "Suit yourself. Never heard any complaints."

I felt his presence hover above me. The air seemed to thicken as his fingers brushed aside the pendant at my throat, revealing the exposed skin of my chest. A chill ran through me as he began to spread the paste along my skin. The smell was earthy and strong, almost nauseating. I couldn't tell what it was, but I knew I didn't want it on me. It wasn't painful yet, but the way he moved with such practiced precision made me feel like it was the calm before a storm.

"What is that?" I asked, trying to lift my head to get a better look at the brownish paste.

"It's a mixture of plants from each Isle, blended with water and dirt, all natural elements," Caraway answered, not meeting my gaze as he continued his even spreading of the paste. "A recipe passed down for generations."

"Why are you putting it on me?" I asked, my voice tight with anxiety, fully expecting the pain to follow any moment.

"Do you know the story of the first Elemental Fae?" Caraway asked, his tone shifting to something colder, more detached. His eyes remained on me, though, calculating.

"Yes," I answered, dread coiling in my gut as I realized where he was headed.

"They were born as quadruplets, four children who should've perished in the womb or shortly after birth, but they survived. And each was given a different magic, the very essence of the four elements." Caraway continued, almost as if lost in the history. "Maren, the first Queen of the Isle of Mist, Blaer who harnessed the power of wind and air, ruling over the Isle of Gust. Sulien, your first ruler, King of the Ember Isle, and then there was my ancestor, King Sylvan, ruler of the Ivy Isle."

His words struck me like a slap, my heart stuttering in my chest. *He knew. He knew.* And he was about to expose everything, wasn't he? The mention of Sulien's name was a bitter reminder of the twisted fate I shared with Hayden, and the secret we had kept from the rest of the world. The truth about our blood.

"So?" I managed, my voice hoarse, barely able to keep the panic in check.

Caraway's eyes locked onto mine, intense and calculating. "Each child was given a gift at birth. They each harnessed an element that would spread to the humans when they cried or laughed in those first few days of existence, their power was transferred to the humans through those first sounds." He continued spreading the paste over me, his words becoming more like an incantation, a ritual.

I knew the story. It was how the fae came to be, how the first human generations were forever bound to the four elements. The humans of the Ember Isle had received the gift of fire from King Sulien when he was just a baby, as had my ancestors. Caraway's people had received their gifts from his ancestor, King Sylvan, and so on, across the generations.

"I'm sure you know the story of Theodon, the creator, falling in love with a human."

"Yes," I answered, my heart beginning to hammer in my chest.

Caraway finished with the paste and leaned back, wiping his hands on a cloth with the casual air of someone who had completed a necessary chore. "We just need to wait for it to dry, so it can begin to pull." His voice was chillingly calm, as if this was all part of some ritual he had performed a thousand times before.

Pull? What was it going to pull? The blood from my chest? Would the magic in this paste be strong enough to rip my soul from my body? My mind raced with terrifying possibilities. Whatever this was, it couldn't be good. But still, there was no pain. Not yet, at least.

A few minutes passed, each second crawling by as I waited for the inevitable. Still, nothing.

Caraway's gaze dropped to the paste on my skin, and he spoke with a quiet urgency, "Can you feel it yet?"

I shook my head, but his expression darkened with visible disappointment. "We can wait a bit longer then."

He clenched his fists, and began pacing in the dim light, clearly growing frustrated. I could feel the tension in the room thicken as his movements became sharper, more agitated. If this thing wasn't working, whatever it was, what would he do next? The thought made me shiver.

Desperately trying to keep his focus away from whatever he was planning, I asked, "Why were you asking me about Theodon and Vesta? Is there more to their story than what is in the ancient texts?"

A smile curled at the corners of Caraway's lips, and his eyes darkened with something I couldn't place. "The text is correct, as far as we know," he said, and I saw the smile grow even wider as his gaze flickered toward a small rock on the table. He lifted it in his hand, holding it up to the light. The stone shimmered faintly in the dim glow, like something ancient and powerful. I could see some sort of symbols etched into the small stone, but it was so tiny that I couldn't make out what they were.

I swallowed hard, my throat dry. What was he planning to do with that rock? My mind raced with grim possibilities, though the idea of him using it to beat me didn't seem likely due to its size.

"What's with the rock?" I asked, my voice barely above a whisper, though I wished I could be louder, stronger.

"It's the key to everything," he replied, his voice suddenly soft, almost reverent. His eyes glowed with an unsettling light. "I'm guessing you remember the part of Theodon and Vesta's story where he proposed to her, after they fell in love?"

I nodded. Their story had always been one of legend, a tale passed down through the generations. A romance that had captured the hearts of fae and humans alike. How Theodon—a God—saved Vesta from the wrath of her cruel father. How, in his pure joy and love for her, he lost control of his power, causing the stars themselves to dance in the sky. One fell, hurtling toward the earth, and landed between the two lovers.

Vesta had confessed that every night, she wished upon that star, asking for a better life, for love and happiness, for escape from the pain her father had caused her. The star became a symbol of their love. Theodon had taken pieces of it, fragments of the celestial rock, and crafted her wedding ring. That ring would serve as a reminder of how much they loved each other and of how Vesta had overcome the darkness of her past to become the most powerful woman in history. A mere human. The mother of life as we knew it.

It was a beautiful, tragic tale. And in many ways, I felt connected to it. Like Vesta, I had been powerless. But also, like her, I had the potential to change my stars. The idea of it, the hope in that story, had always given me a spark of strength.

But now, as Caraway's voice lowered, I could feel the echo of his words suffocating the air between us.

"I had always wondered," he continued, his tone edged with a dark kind of pleasure, "if that star that fell from the sky is still here. Still alive in some way. After all, it was the physical manifestation of Theodon's joy. The symbol of their bond, of their power." He paused, watching me with a glint in his eye. "Do you know what that star truly is, Princess?"

I swallowed again, trying to keep my expression neutral. What did he mean? Was he suggesting that star still existed?

"Vesta changed her stars," Caraway said softly, almost to himself. "She became more than human. She gained immortality once she became pregnant, but she was still Vesta. The human girl who wished for something better."

I tried to keep my emotions neutral at the mention of her humanity. It was a connection I felt deeply between us, and I couldn't let any of my emotions reveal how much I admired the human woman who didn't let her shortcomings define her or her true power. I had always admired Vesta's strength, her ability to transcend the human limitations placed upon her. She was powerless yet powerful, something I longed to be.

Caraway looked down at the small rock in his hand again, his smile widening, but now it was darker, knowing. "It's funny, isn't it? How all stories lead to the same place. It's a matter of power. Who holds it. Who wields it."

I stared at the rock in Caraway's hand, still gleaming in the dim light. It appeared utterly plain, just a tiny, inconsequential fragment. *Could it really be?* I swallowed, a sick feeling pooling in my stomach. "Is that the star?" I asked, my voice barely above a whisper. "The one Theodon gave to Vesta?"

Caraway's laugh was dark and low, almost condescending. "It's not the ring he gave her, obviously," he said, his eyes narrowing as he tightened his grip on the rock until his knuckles whitened. "But yes, this is a fragment of the very star that fell from the heavens, the same one he used to craft her wedding ring." He glanced down at it with an almost reverent expression, his fingers curling around it possessively. "The star that changed everything."

He leaned over me then, the rock still clutched in his hand, hovering just above me before he finally placed it on my chest. His voice lowered, almost a hiss. "Anything yet?" His breath was hot against my skin as his eyes flickered to mine, waiting for a response.

I could only shake my head, my pulse quickening in fear. "It just feels cold."

"Perhaps you aren't meant to feel anything, then." Caraway's expression soured, a frown creasing his brow. He muttered to himself, frustration creeping into his voice.

I couldn't hold back the question any longer. "What does this stuff have to do with the star, and where did you even get it?"

"Vesta was wearing a piece of the star when she conceived," he began, his eyes never leaving the rock. "It's believed that because of the star's natural powers, its connection to the heavens, that when Vesta wore the ring, it caused her to become pregnant with four powerful children." He paused, the words hanging in the air like smoke. "The power of the star mixed with Theodon's essence, dividing the elements into each child, making them vessels for each of the four powers. Wind. Water. Earth. Fire."

I blinked, trying to process the implications of his words. The first Elemental Fae. The ones who shaped the Isles, who held dominion over the elements, each of them carrying a part of the star's power. But now, a fragment of that star was on me. And in the pit of my stomach, I realized what Caraway was getting at.

The horror of it struck me like a blow to the chest. Caraway was hoping to repeat whatever had happened with Vesta. But with me.

I swallowed hard, panic rising in my throat. "Please don't. Not like this." My voice cracked, and before I could stop myself, I whispered, "I still have my maiden-head." The words felt like a betrayal as they left my lips, a desperate plea. But the tears began to flow anyway, the reality of the situation hitting me all at once. He planned to impregnate me while I had the star fragment on my body. Use me as a vessel to create something new, something powerful.

Caraway's eyes darkened with a flash of amusement, and he wiped a single tear from my cheek with his thumb. "I already told you, my dear. I have no plans of touching you." His voice was silk, but there was a venomous edge to it.

I tried to control my breathing, to steady myself against the terror that was bubbling up from within. But the words, the implications of what was happening, were too much. If he wasn't trying to duplicate what Vesta had done with the star when she conceived, then what did he plan to do with me?

There was a moment of tense silence as I composed myself, sucking back the tears away as best I could. Caraway stared at the rock on my chest, his brow furrowing in concentration.

"What's supposed to be happening, then?" I asked, trying to keep my voice steady despite the tremor in my limbs.

Caraway's jaw clenched, and for a brief moment, I saw a flicker of uncertainty pass across his face, an emotion I hadn't expected from him. "This is my first time trying this," he admitted, his voice almost betraying a hint of frustration. "Do you truly feel nothing?"

I barely managed a whisper, "No."

Without another word, Caraway grabbed the rock from my chest, his grip tightening so harshly that the rock seemed to crack under the pressure. His face flushed with anger, and I knew that whatever he had been trying to achieve hadn't worked.

"Orrin!" Caraway yelled out the door.

Orrin's heavy footsteps echoed from the hallway as he quickly appeared in the doorway, his expression a mix of concern and obedience. "Yes, sire?"

Caraway snapped his fingers impatiently. "Take her back. Leave the collar off. She needs to heal, and she won't try anything foolish." He turned to me, his gaze cold and menacing. "Will you?"

"No," I quickly responded, though my voice wavered. The fear in my chest hadn't abated, not even a little. The questions swirled in my mind. Why let me heal? What was his game here? But I was too terrified to ask. Too terrified to even breathe too loudly. I had no idea what he wanted, but I knew that whatever it was, it wasn't good.

The Ivy King stormed out of the room, leaving me alone once again with Orrin. The way his dark eyes lingered on me, I could already tell what he was thinking. "Don't fucking touch me," I growled.

Orrin loomed over me, his hand sliding slowly down my arm, sending a shiver through my spine. "You're in no position to order me around, Princess."

I spat back, "No, but your king ordered you to take me back to my cell."

Orrin let out a low, mocking laugh as his fingers tapped against the metal cuffs around my wrists. He reached into his pocket and pulled out a key, unlocking each cuff with practiced ease. "Try any of that fire magic on me, and I'm sure the king will have no problem with how I decide to punish you."

I said nothing. He was right, and I knew better than to defy him. I had no magic to use anyway, but they didn't need to know that. I had to keep up the illusion of compliance.

We moved down the hall, Orrin keeping pace behind me. I was relieved that the collar and chain were gone, though the bars of my cell still loomed ahead, cold and unyielding. At least my neck was free now-small victories mattered in a place like this.

Orrin opened the cell door and before he could bark any orders at me, I stepped through, immediately curling up in my corner on the floor. I turned my back on him and began scraping off the now-hardened paste from my chest. I still didn't know what it was or what the king had intended with it, but it was clear this had a long-term purpose and I didn't trust it.

Orrin's voice cut through the silence. "What's wrong with the cot?" he prodded as he locked the door behind him. "Not good enough for you, Princess?"

"I'm on the floor where I belong," I muttered, hoping he would just leave so I didn't have to endure his mockery.

"Considering you killed my prince, yeah, you're exactly where you belong." His voice was flat, brimming with hate. "I'll be back to fetch you tomorrow. Sleep tight."

I didn't respond. Orrin knew it was me who had killed his prince, not Hayden, though he hadn't shared that with the king yet, thank the stars. If he had, I had no doubt the king's twisted experiments with that paste would have been much worse. He claimed it was made from plants native to each Isle. Did that mean the Ivy King had already set foot on them all, with Ember as his final destination? Or had he simply sent others in his place? Whatever the case, I still didn't know what the paste was actually supposed to do. I couldn't help but wonder what would have happened if Hayden had been the one shackled to that chair instead of me.

Whatever his plan was, I knew it had something to do with the Ember he thought still burned within me. I wondered if he was truly trying to use me, believing I possessed it, keeping me alive long enough to ensure my parents never regained access to the Ember, giving him an opening for a war and leaving our Isle weak and vulnerable. So what was with the paste and the star fragment then?

The king had promised to try again. This time, I'd have to lie about the paste. He was uncertain about what was supposed to happen, which meant I could say whatever I wanted about its effects. Maybe if I made him believe his experiment was working, I could learn more about what he was really after. For now, though, all I could do was wait for him to decide when I was healed enough to endure his next round of tests.

I had to rest and let the faint magic still lingering in my veins work its slow healing. A good night's sleep would help, or at least that's what I told myself as I closed my eyes and let the dark of the cell swallow me whole.

14

I awoke with a faint sense of renewal, my body feeling less like a cage of aches and more like something that might be whole again. The collar was gone, and for the first time in what felt like ages, I had slept through the night without nightmares gnawing at my mind. No iron bands biting into my skin, no cold walls pressing in on me. A torch burned dimly on the wall, its soft orange glow flickering against the stone, casting long shadows that stretched like quiet fingers across the room. The warmth from the flame was a small comfort, restoring me in ways I didn't even realize I needed.

I glanced down at my palm the king had slashed the day before. The red streak still marked my skin, a jagged line of raw flesh that had scabbed over but not fully healed. If I were Hayden, or any other fae, really, it would be smooth by now. Hopefully Caraway wouldn't notice the lingering scab during his next little experiment.

With a groan, I rolled over, avoiding the cold spot on the floor where my back had been pressed for most of the night. The remnants of a meal sat near the door: a tin plate and cup, both scratched from use. It must have been Orrin who had left them. I hadn't even heard him come in, though I had been in a deep enough sleep to lose track of time. The idea that he might've been here, watching, made my stomach churn. I couldn't help but shudder, imagining what else he might've done while I was unconscious. I forced the thought from my mind, focusing instead on the food.

Not wanting to rise just yet, I dragged myself to the plate, my arms weak and sluggish. The bread was dry, its surface hardened, and the meat, if it could even be called that, was stiff and leathery. I sniffed the cup. Water, thankfully. Though I doubted its cleanliness, I could hardly afford to be picky. My body craved hydration, thirst a constant, relentless thing.

I tore at the bread with my teeth, breaking it into smaller chunks so I wouldn't choke on the dryness. Each bite scraped across my throat, rough and unsatisfying, but it was food. The meat was no better, tough and stringy, but I managed to tear off small pieces, swallowing each down as if it were the last thing I'd ever eat. I washed it all down with the water, its coolness a blessed relief. It was filthy, I was sure, but it tasted like the sweetest thing I'd ever had, sliding down my throat like heaven, soothing the rawness in my chest.

When the plate was empty, I was still hungry – starved, in fact – but I wasn't foolish enough to believe the king had fed me out of kindness. No, he needed me strong for whatever twisted plan he had for me and that damn rock. The thought of the stone made my stomach tighten, a knot of dread twisting into my gut. Whatever his endgame was, I knew I was a piece in it, nothing more.

I stretched out again on the cold floor, staring up at the flickering torch. The light danced like a weak flame of hope, fragile and desperate. I missed the sun. The heat of home. My body ached for it, longed for it, but here, in this darkness, I could only watch the faint, wavering flame and remember what warmth felt like.

The hunger gnawed at me again, not just for food, but for escape. For release. My thoughts spiraled into darker places, and for a moment, I wished for my own end. I thought of how simple it would be, how sweet it would be to just disappear. To move on, to wherever Theodon thought my soul deserved to go. I pulled myself back from the edge of those thoughts, forcing myself to breathe.

The king had every right to make me suffer. I had taken his son. Caraway was justified in every way, even if he didn't know the truth. I had murdered Hawthorne, taken away the child he loved so deeply, and now I was paying the price. The guilt sat heavy on my chest, but I knew it was nothing compared to the pain the Ivy King must have felt. I was the monster in this story, not him.

I tried to focus, to steady my breath, as my gaze remained fixed on the flickering flame. I didn't hear the door open at first, not until it creaked on its rusty hinges, a soft groan that cut through the silence like a threat. The sound of footsteps followed, heavy and deliberate. I knew who it was.

Orrin's voice broke the quiet, mockingly bright. "Feel refreshed?" His keys rattled as he fumbled with them, and I didn't answer. What was the point?

I stayed silent, refusing to give Orrin the satisfaction of a response. Whatever it was the king wanted from me, I'd comply, but I didn't have to entertain this bastard.

"Silent treatment again?" Orrin's voice oozed mockery as he grabbed my arm, his grip tight and unyielding as he tugged me toward the door. Before we ascended the steps, he leaned in, his breath rank with the sour sting of tobacco and stale whiskey. "I'll have you screaming once the king's through with you," he whispered, his words slithering over my ear like venom. He took a long, unnecessary sniff of my hair, and I recoiled inside, feeling the skin on my neck prickle with disgust.

I kept my face impassive, refusing to let him see the effect his words had on me. I focused on the cold stone underfoot as I started to climb the stairs. His gaze on my exposed back made me feel raw, as though my skin had been peeled open for him to gawk at. The red dress clung to my form, barely offering any coverage to my backside and legs. I really needed to get out of this thing.

At the top of the stairs, Orrin stepped in front of me, yanking my arm again and dragging me toward the room I'd been in yesterday. Caraway was already there, standing by the wooden chair, his posture stiff with impatience. His face was a mask, but I could see the lines of frustration, the edges of something darker beneath the surface.

"Welcome back, Princess," he said, the words carrying none of the warmth of a greeting. "Have a seat."

I followed the order without a word, lowering myself into the chair. It creaked under my weight, and as I sat, I felt the cool metal of the cuffs being fastened around my wrists. This time, they weren't as tight, a subtle change that hinted at the king's desire to keep me comfortable. I felt the strain of his expectations pressing against me, but I wasn't fooled. My body still ached, muscles and bones screaming in protest at every movement. I wasn't healed, not by a long shot. But I couldn't let them know that. I had to appear whole, at least for now.

Caraway pulled a lever beneath the chair, and it snapped flat like a board, my back pressed rigid against the hard wood. "Palm," he commanded, his voice cold and businesslike, as he picked up the same dagger from before, the blade gleaming under the dim light.

I hesitated for a fraction of a second before deliberately moving my left palm across to the far side, making sure to draw attention to it. The chains rattled as I shifted, and I felt his gaze sharpen as he watched my every move. The other hand still carried the scab, the telltale mark of my previous injury, and I couldn't afford for him to see it.

With a subtle shake of my hand, I presented the left, and Caraway leaned forward without hesitation, as he slashed my palm. I winced at the sting, feeling the warmth of my blood well up against my skin. It coated my hand in a slow trickle, the familiar gold shimmer dripping to the floor in small, rhythmic drops.

"Good," Caraway muttered, his voice betraying no hint of emotion. He didn't linger over the injury, but his eyes didn't leave my palm as he observed the blood. It wasn't the kind of satisfaction that came from watching someone in pain, it was the cold, clinical observation of someone waiting for something to happen.

Caraway waved his hand dismissively, sending Orrin out of the room with a few muttered words. And then, it was just the two of us again. The silence between us stretched, as Caraway moved to prepare the paste once more. He worked with methodical precision, stirring the mixture in the bowl, his eyes fixed on the task with an almost obsessive intensity.

"Feeling rejuvenated?" he asked, his voice still absent of warmth, his focus entirely on the paste.

"Good as new," I shot back, sarcasm dripping from the words as I squeezed my left palm tightly, trying to stanch the bleeding before he noticed it was still seeping when it should have already begun healing.

I watched as the king set the bowl of paste down, the thick substance still clinging to the sides in irregular clumps. He reached into another bowl on the small table beside him, and I felt a jolt of panic when I noticed the steam rising from it, curling in soft, haunting tendrils. The water in that bowl was scalding hot.

He must have known that such heat wouldn't harm an Ember fae, but for me, it would be agony. The initial pain would be unbearable, a searing burn that would flare through my skin before the smallest sparks of power in my veins could fight it off. By then, the damage would be done. Was this some kind of test? A cruel experiment to see just how much power I had left? I could already feel my pulse quickening, the blood pounding in my ears.

As the king reached for the bowl, I couldn't help myself. "What's that for?" I asked, my voice shaky despite my efforts to keep it steady.

He smiled, a tight, calculating thing that didn't reach his eyes and dipped the cloth into the steaming water. My breath caught. I braced for the worst, but all he pulled from the bowl was a cloth, the fabric heavy and dripping with the hot liquid. I exhaled in relief, barely able to suppress a shudder of dread.

"You still have dried paste clinging to your skin from yesterday," Caraway explained calmly, his voice soft, but with an underlying edge. "For this to work, I need to clean the area."

I relaxed just a fraction, as he gently began to wipe the remnants of the dried paste from my chest. The cloth was still hot but not unbearable as it clung to the material. I winced as it brushed against my skin. I'm sure the king saw my discomfort and assumed it was from his physical contact; the unwanted touch I had made abundantly clear I didn't want.

Once the king seemed satisfied with his cleanup, he moved aside my pendant with careful hands, his fingers brushing the delicate chain before he began to apply the paste to my chest in slow, deliberate motions. Each new dollop of the substance sent a sharp, earthy scent into the air, the smell so strong it stung my nostrils, nearly choking me. I resisted the urge to cough. The king didn't seem to notice my discomfort, but I knew it was far more than just a simple substance. I could sense that the paste had some kind of purpose, something tied to me, to my power, though I still couldn't fathom how all of this connected to the first Elemental Fae or Theodon.

He finished with the paste and took a step back to inspect his work, his expression unreadable. Then, without looking at me, he asked, "Feel anything yet?" There was a note of hope in his voice, though it was carefully controlled, as if he were trying to keep his emotions in check.

I had to lie. I couldn't afford to show weakness, not now. Not when I still didn't understand what was truly going on. "A little," I groaned, keeping my voice steady. "It's like a warm, tingling feeling near my heart."

I made sure to meet his gaze as I spoke, hoping that my answer would be the one he wanted to hear. The smile that spread across his face told me I'd said the right thing, though I knew it wasn't true. There was nothing warm or tingly about the cold knot of dread twisting in my stomach.

"What is this all for?" I asked, pushing a little further, testing the waters. I needed to know more. The more I knew, the better I could prepare.

"For the good of Ainoah," Caraway replied, his voice as cold as ever, but now carrying a trace of something, an almost reverent note that made the words feel hollow. He placed the rock carefully on my chest, as if the very act of laying it on me was a sacred ritual. "To bring us all back together, united as one."

His words struck a familiar chord, and I felt a bitter laugh curl in my throat. "Yeah, that's what everyone says. You think you're the first ruler to try such a thing?"

"Of course not. But they lacked the knowledge I possess, knowledge that could unite us all. Perhaps your brother murdering my son was the turning point in everything. There must be some silver lining to this tragedy. Everything happens for a reason, and by Theodon, I believe you are the answer."

"Is that why you haven't killed me yet?" I asked, trying to piece things together. "You think I'm part of some divine plan?"

I needed to understand at what point he would abandon this foolish notion and let me pay my debt. I didn't even want to think about how Theodon was punishing my Isle for my survival. Unless there was a loophole, since it seemed the Ivy King *wanted* me alive, for now at least. I needed more information about what the hell was really going on.

"I suppose we shall see," he answered, his voice almost filled with awe.

"And does that rock also have something to do with it?"

"We're about to find out."

Given that I felt nothing at all, it was hard to take him seriously. Whatever he was attempting clearly wasn't working, but I couldn't let him see that.

For the good of Ainoah. I had heard that line before, in every speech, every peace treaty, every leader's proclamation. It was the same old rhetoric: the promise of unity, of peace, of bringing all the kingdoms together under one banner. But history told a different story. Treaties were written, signed with pomp and circumstance, but the small print was always a trap. Whoever held the pen always wrote the terms in their favor. No one trusted each other, and the rule of no war between the Isles was a fragile law, barely holding together the fabric of a world constantly on the verge of conflict.

I couldn't help but think of Vesta, who had been so heartbroken over her children's war that she had divided Ainoah into four Isles. It was meant to stop the fighting, to bring peace to the world by separating the elements, by giving each child their own corner to rule. The plan had worked for a while. But the truth of it was, the Elemental Fae had always dreamed of bringing the world back together, of uniting the Isles under one rule. But whenever they tried, it led only to death and destruction. Each not wanting to give up their own rule and power.

Caraway, for all his noble talk, was just another in a long line of rulers who believed that unity could be achieved by force. And somehow, I was right in the middle of it all, still unaware how I fit into this plan.

I wondered if Caraway had any idea of how much chaos he was inviting. The thought of bringing the Isles together again, of wiping away centuries of division, seemed as dangerous as it was naive. Maybe he thought he could pull it off, but something told me that no matter how much he believed in the purity of his goal, he relished the idea of control, of power over the four corners of Ainoah.

I watched him, trying to read the king's mind, but his face remained an inscrutable mask. Whatever his plans were with the paste, the rock, and me, it was clear that he thought this was the key to achieving his vision of unity.

I realized Caraway had been staring at me, his eyes shifting from my face to the rock on my chest, back and forth. I was just lying there, lost in thought. I'd forgotten I was supposed to be reacting to the paste and the star. I quickly began to writhe as though pain were shooting through my body, exaggerating my breathing by quickening my breaths.

"Can you feel it?" Caraway's face lit up as he watched me. "Is it working?"

"I don't know," I whimpered. "It feels hot... like I can't breathe." I took a sharp, shallow breath to keep up with the story. I really hoped this was what was supposed to happen, because truthfully, I felt nothing.

Minutes dragged by as I continued my ruse. I squeezed my eyes shut as if I were in unimaginable pain. Each time I opened them slightly, I saw the smile on the king's face. Whatever was supposed to happen, it was meant to be painful. I let my body twist and turn under the shackles. When I thought I'd been at it long enough, I let out a final breath and let my whole body go still. I just hoped whatever was supposed to happen at the end of this experiment wasn't my death, because that was one thing I couldn't fake.

He snatched the star fragment off my chest and held it up to the light. I wasn't sure what he was looking for, but from the aggravated grunts I heard while he inspected the stone near the torch, it was clear he wasn't pleased.

"What happened?" I asked weakly, still committed to the bit. "I don't feel so well."

Caraway slammed the stone in his hand back onto the table, replacing it with a dagger, and stormed toward me. "What did you do?" he shouted, his green eyes full of fury. "Tell me!" He pressed the blade to my throat. This was it. It was finally happening.

I wasn't sure what to do, so I stuck with my lie. "I didn't do anything," I replied, my voice genuinely shaky. "What was supposed to happen?"

"What did you feel?" he demanded, the dagger digging into my flesh so hard I feared he'd draw blood.

"It was warm, almost suffocating," I lied. "Maybe I just haven't healed enough?"

"Bullshit!" Caraway spat, his face twisted with rage. "If you and your family tried to pull one over on me—"

"No," I quickly replied, "I am the powerful one. I am the true heir and I hold the Ember. I tried not to sound too desperate, but I had to convince him I was the right sibling before he found some loophole and went back for Hay.

Caraway yanked a lever, and instantly the board I was shackled to shifted back into a chair. The sudden motion sent a jolt of pain through my body where the shackles dug into my skin.

"Show me," Caraway commanded, undoing the cuff on my right wrist. "Show me your power."

"W-what?" I stammered. I had nothing left. He was going to find out, and I couldn't act my way out of this.

"I want to see your fire magic. Now! Show me now or I will kill you slowly!"

I rotated my wrist, hoping for a miracle. "Um, I think I'm drained from the star—"

"NOW!" he bellowed, so loud I was sure the whole castle could hear him.

I'd screwed everything up. Now, not only would he probably kill me anyway, but he'd also demand Hayden's life once he found out we'd tricked him. He would know that, even though I was technically the firstborn, things on Ember Isle had shifted, blessing the second born instead. If he believed we had deceived him, he might try to start a war, especially if he didn't feel his son's death was truly justified under the law.

I raised my palm and focused harder than I ever had before. I knew the magic I had left was minuscule, but I hoped Theodon could help me in this moment—even if I was a murderer.

Heat started to form in my palm, and I cracked an eye open to see a fireball taking shape. It was smaller and weaker than my usual flames, but it was slowly growing. I could feel the ball vibrate in sync with my pendant. This was Hayden's magic, but how? I thought I had drained it all during the demonstration.

I thought back to that day as the flame grew in my palm, and it hit me. The hug. Hayden had held me so tightly in the throne room, giving him the perfect chance to charge my opal. No wonder he had looked so weak afterward. It had been quick, so I was sure this magic would be short-lived, so I had to once again play pretend.

"Back up!" I yelled. Caraway obeyed, and I hurled the fireball from my hand, sending it flying to scorch the stone wall.

I stared at the now charred and blackened wall, my heart heavy with the hope that it was enough to sustain my charade. My gaze flicked toward Caraway, who cowered in the corner. His expression shifted from fear to a cold, burning rage.

"It must be the star that's the problem then," he muttered under his breath, his voice tinged with disbelief. He flipped the small table in a fit of frustration, sending the bowl of paste and a rock crashing to the stone floor. "Orrin!" he screamed, and within moments, the guard stalked back into the room.

"Sire?"

"Retrieve her collar and lock her back in the cell," Caraway commanded, his voice sharp. "And when you're finished, have my horse saddled and ready for departure."

"Will I be accompanying you?" Orrin asked, a hint of uncertainty in his voice.

"No. You'll stay and guard her. It's either a problem with the star or it's her. Either way, I'm going to get to the bottom of this."

Nothing made sense anymore, but one thing was certain: it wasn't the star. It was me. I still wasn't sure what the star was supposed to do or how it would bring unity across the Isles. But Caraway was convinced that the star fragment and I were crucial to his plan, one that I hoped didn't end with me somehow giving birth to four babes. I couldn't help but wonder if things would have been different if Hayden were in this chair instead of me, especially since he was male. Perhaps trying to replicate what Vesta had achieved wasn't the end goal after all, but then why use the star? And why wasn't it working? The star certainly looked ancient, with symbols carved into it, still too small to decipher without a closer look. I was sure it had some sort of magical properties, and it seemed that Caraway believed the same. But now that it wasn't working to achieve whatever his desired objective was, I wasn't sure what he would do next.

Orrin roughly placed the collar back around my neck, and this time, it burned more fiercely than before. Not enough to really hurt me, but enough to make my skin crawl with discomfort, especially with the thought that I'd be wearing it for who knew how long. The power of the pendant must have dulled the pain but now it was drained and empty.

Once again, I was dragged from the room. The dried paste on my chest made each movement feel tight and itchy. We descended the steps back to the dungeon prison cells, and Orrin shoved me inside.

"Is the Ivy King leaving?" I asked, trying to confirm whether I'd have a few days of peace before he tried this twisted experiment again.

"That's none of your business," Orrin grumbled as he locked the door behind me.

I knew he had to be aware that I was in the room when the king ordered his horse, but I tried to pry for any other scraps of information. No luck. He wasn't about to budge.

"Why doesn't he just kill me and be done with it?"

"The Ivy King has a plan. And for whatever reason, you're a key player." He moved toward the torch, extinguishing its light before grabbing another from the wall.

I wondered just how much the guard actually knew about the king's *plans*. Was he simply a well-trained dog following orders, or did he know something more.

"So, you don't know his plan?" I teased, but he didn't respond.

Orrin remained silent as he climbed the steps, slamming the door behind him, taking the last flicker of light with him. Once again, I was plunged into darkness, left alone with my thoughts. It would have been useless to beg him for the small comfort of a nightlight, but part of me still wished I'd tried. I hated the eerie quiet that settled around me.

Caraway was scheming, and I had a sinking feeling it wasn't anything good. I was still alive, for reasons unknown, and that, too, felt like a curse. I curled into my usual spot in the corner, wiping away what little paste I could with my mostly healed hand, keeping the other one carefully tucked away to avoid infection. With the collar back in place, healing was out of the question. No wound, no matter how small, would ever heal in time as long as it was on.

I tried to process the events that had just unfolded, attempting to piece everything together. The star fragment definitely had something to do with it all, but it hadn't worked. I knew I had very little magic in my veins, but I did have a small trace. Shouldn't I have felt something? Anything? It seemed like I was supposed to, but all I felt was the crusted paste and the cold texture of the star. Unless he was wrong. Perhaps it wasn't a star fragment after all? Maybe it was just a regular rock that the king had somehow convinced himself was the sacred artifact, driven by his lust for power or his so-called noble mission to unite us all. If he tried whatever he was attempting again and it failed, suspicion might rise. He might return to the Ember Isle demanding answers. Was that where he was headed now? Was he sailing back to my home? Everything felt so confusing when it was supposed to be simple. I was supposed to die, and that was it. Yet here I was, caught in what seemed like some bigger scheme.

I closed my eyes, forcing myself to remember why all of this was happening. I didn't want to sink into sorrow, so instead, I clung to guilt. The guilt of my actions, the choices I had made that brought me to this hellish place, the pain I deserved. It was easier to hold on to guilt than to let despair flood in. So, I held on tight to the bitterness, letting it numb me. I let my mind go blank, as the darkness closed in around me.

15

The heavy sound of boots echoed down the stone steps, making my eyes flutter open. Shadows from Orrin's torch danced along the wall I stared at, stretching and shrinking as the flame swayed. The footsteps were accompanied by the jarring rattle of chains swinging and clinking with each step. Had the Ivy King already returned? How long had I been asleep this time?

I huddled in the corner, pressing myself closer to the wall, trying to make myself smaller, my back cold against the damp stone. My body had grown used to the relentless heat back on Ember, where even the harsh desert sun offered some solace. In this dark, damp cell, though, no light reached me. The air was cooler and my teeth chattered. Whether it was the cold or the fear that tightened around me like a vice, I couldn't tell. Neither offered comfort. All I could do was hold me knees to my chest and cling to the meager warmth I could summon.

The familiar jingle of keys broke the silence, followed by two voices, but it wasn't my cell the keys were unlocking. Instead, I heard the door to the cell next to mine screech open, and Orrin's grunt echoed through the air. "Get in there, you fucking thief!"

A loud thud resonated as someone was thrown into the neighboring cage. I remained perfectly still, unsure of who my new neighbor was.

"Fuck you!" the male voice spat out.

"King Caraway will deal with you when he returns," Orrin laughed as I heard the distinct click of the lock sliding into place, followed by a loud crash of metal striking the bars of my own cell. I flinched involuntarily, and I was certain Orrin had seen it. "Don't you forget, Princess," he added with a mocking edge, "you've also got a date with the king when he returns."

Orrin stalked back up the steps, and once again, the light from the room was swallowed by the shadows of darkness. I had a new cellmate, and I wasn't sure whether that made me feel relieved to no longer be alone, or even more terrified. I heard Orrin call him a thief, so hopefully, the male in the cell next to mine wasn't too dangerous. I had never been more thankful for the iron bars that separated us. I remained quiet, hoping he would follow suit.

"Princess?" the male voice called out, his tone curious, followed by the shuffle of footsteps as he moved closer to the bars that connected our cells.

At least I was positioned in the corner farthest from him. I was in no mood to talk, but I wasn't in the mood to pretend to be asleep, either. "Leave me alone," I croaked, my throat dry again, the burning sensation from the collar still biting into my skin.

"Why are you in the corner on the floor?" he asked. He must have seen me when Orrin had brought him in.

"This is where I deserve to be," I said flatly, hoping he would take the hint and just stop talking.

"I heard about you, you know, on the ship." His voice had an edge of curiosity, and I tensed. I didn't remember seeing another prisoner on the ship with me. "You're that princess the Ember King and Queen kept hidden, huh?"

"I guess word gets around."

"So, why'd they keep you hidden? Are you deformed or something?" He continued to prod, his words blunt and unkind.

"Or something," I muttered. It seemed he wasn't going to shut up anytime soon, so I decided to ask a few questions of my own. "I don't remember seeing another prisoner on the ship."

"I was on the other one," he replied nonchalantly. "The one they sent ahead with the Ivy Prince's body. Compliments from your brother, or so I've heard." His tone was oddly casual, as if discussing a dead body were no more significant than talking about the weather. "Which makes me wonder, why are you here rotting away in this cell, and not him?"

His words struck a nerve. I had to force my emotions down, reminding myself to keep up the lie that had been carefully crafted, even with a fellow prisoner. Even if I wanted to tell him the truth, I couldn't risk it. He might have loose lips, or worse, he could be a spy. If he was questioned or tortured, he might reveal what he knew, whether or not it was valuable.

"The Ivy King demanded the life of the firstborn, and, well, that was me."

"Sounds like your brother got away with murder, leaving you to pay the price." He snorted a laugh, as if he found the entire situation amusing. "Some noble prince he is."

Anger surged in my veins, boiling beneath the surface. I pushed myself up from the floor, my shaky wrists wavering as they bore my weight. "Hayden would have taken my place if he could," I hissed, the rage in my chest bubbling over, "but the Ivy King demanded me, so I had no choice. And even if I did, I would still choose me over Hayden!"

"Alright, alright, calm down. He just seems to have everyone wrapped around his finger, especially females."

The audacity of this asshole to speak so casually about Hayden. He had no idea what he was talking about, nor did he have any right to judge him. Who was this prisoner, anyway? When had he even met my brother? I let his words settle in. He'd mentioned being on the other ship that had arrived ahead of mine. That meant he had been on Ember Isle when Hayden was arrested. He couldn't be from my kingdom, Caraway wouldn't be so reckless as to take an Ember fae prisoner without a trial. But if he wasn't from my kingdom, then who exactly was he?

My mind drifted back to that day in the oasis. I remembered meeting a male thief, someone taken prisoner by the Ivy King.

"They caught you?" I blurted out before I could stop myself.

"Clearly," he replied flatly, "hence my current 'home address.'"

I took a deep breath, praying I was wrong. The fae I'd met hadn't been a criminal, he'd been trying to feed his people back home. I needed to be certain.

"Reed?" I whispered.

There was a long pause, the silence pressing heavily between us before he finally answered, "Do I know you?"

That was all the confirmation I needed. The voice, the words, it was him. I couldn't see his face, but the voice was unmistakable. I couldn't believe I hadn't recognized it sooner. My thoughts rushed back to our conversation, to that almost-kiss, the gin…

Fury ignited once again, hot and sharp in my chest. "What was in that flask?" I demanded, recalling the sickness it caused me, how it had clouded my judgment, causing me to make that fatal mistake and take Hawthorne's life.

The silence stretched out once more, heavy with realization. I could almost hear him piecing it together, just as I had. "Sparks?" he asked hesitantly, his voice now laced with recognition.

I never gave him my name, but that's what he had called me. "What the hell are you doing here?" he asked, his voice strained with urgency and concern.

I remembered telling him that I was out there with Hayden because I was trying to sleep with him, and now that Reed knew the truth, that I was actually his sister, he was probably assuming the worst. I braced myself for whatever twisted thoughts he might entertain, but I needed to set the record straight. "I lied to you that day," I began, cutting off the path my words could take before his mind went to some sick place. "I wasn't out there to sleep with the

Ember Prince. I was, helping my brother, now answer my question," I pressed, my voice rough from the burning collar, "what the hell did I drink?"

"It was just gin, I swear," he responded, the sincerity in his voice unmistakable. "Sorry, I'm just... I'm so confused. I thought you were a—" He stopped himself mid-sentence, like he'd realized the direction he was heading.

"What?" I started, and, despite my discomfort, crawled closer to where our cells met, my fingers brushing against the cold iron bars causing a brief sting. "One of his whores? Is that what you were going to say?"

"No!" he spat out quickly. "I just... I thought maybe you were a servant or something."

"Why would you think that?"

"I thought you were some desperate female who was below the prince's station, hence why I thought you were following him around like a lost puppy. Like you were just trying to rise in society."

I couldn't fault him for thinking that. Just a few days ago, I had been pretending to be a kitchen maid, blending into the shadows, unnoticed and unimportant. He hadn't seen the truth, the royal fae hiding behind the veil of a commoner. He had met me armed in a ball gown, standing in the desert, and yet he still assumed I was just a servant. I had been playing that part for so long I had become the lie.

"That was just the role I was cast in," I said quietly, the words settling over me like a cloak. "To protect the Ember." There was more truth in that statement than he knew.

"So, Sparks," Reed's voice was laced with disbelief, "it's true? You're the actual royal fae who carries the Ember?" He paused, clearly still struggling to process it all. "Why would you give yourself up so easily, then?"

I could hear the skepticism in his voice, the disbelief. I understood why, after all, it didn't make sense. The lie was far safer.

"I was protecting my younger brother," I said, my voice steady, though the words felt like a knife in my chest. Hayden wasn't just my younger brother, he was only three minutes younger than me, but the truth of that would only complicate things. There was no point in telling Reed we were twins. No point in letting anyone know that we had shared a womb. Better to let everyone think we were simply siblings.

"A mistake was made," I continued, the words heavy on my tongue. "And I couldn't let him pay the price." I paused, my breath catching in my throat. "Plus, as I said before, it was me the Ivy King demanded. A first born for a first born. So here I am."

The last sentence came out quieter than I intended, and my voice cracked as I focused on the word mistake. I had made a mistake. Saying it out loud again only brought the raw emotions to the surface, and I struggled to keep my composure. It had never been easy to admit the gravity of my decisions. But there I was, trapped by my own choices.

I lingered by the bars that connected our cells, feeling Reed's presence still there in the darkness. I could feel the heat of Reed's body through the bars and his breath, a warm mint-scented cloud that washed over my skin. There was something about his presence that made the cold seem less biting. Maybe it was the loneliness, or the memory of how we almost kissed before, but in this moment, I was kind of glad he was my cellmate. Selfish, perhaps, but I wasn't sure I could bear being alone in this place again.

"I'm sorry," he said, his voice soft but sincere. "I'm so fucking sorry this is happening to you," he murmured, as I felt the warmth of his hand brush against my face. I flinched instinctively, pulling away from his touch. I wasn't the victim here. I didn't deserve comfort.

The sudden jerk of my neck made the iron collar dig deeper into my skin, and I hissed at the sharp pain that followed.

"I'm sorry, did I hurt you? My calloused hands can be a bit rough."

"No, just this stupid collar," I replied quickly, hoping that would be enough to explain why I pulled away.

There was a rustling sound from his side of the cell, followed by the soft tear of fabric. "Here," he said. "Feel for my hand and take the cloth."

"Why?" I asked, even as I obeyed, reaching out into the darkness. My fingers brushed against the cool material, unsure of what he intended.

"Wrap it around your neck, under the collar," he instructed. "That's what I did on the ship. It won't take all the pain away, and your magic will still be dormant, but it'll protect your skin against additional pain."

I carefully followed his directions, feeling the fabric between my fingertips as I wrapped it under the collar. He was right, the cloth helped. The bite of the iron lessened and the pain dulled just enough for me to breathe easier. "Thank you," I said, my voice softer than before. I was still guarded, but his presence, his willingness to help, felt like the first kindness I had received in too long.

"So, how did they catch you?" I asked, my curiosity slipping through the cracks of my defenses.

"When the Ivy Guards went to round up your brother, they found me too," he said, irritation lacing his words.

"I'm sorry," I whispered, guilt tightening around my chest. If it weren't for me, if it weren't for what I had done, he would still be free.

"It's not your fault, Sparks," Reed reassured me, his voice warmer now. "Besides, once they realized I'd escaped, they'd have been looking for me anyway."

"So where have you been the last few days?" I asked, confused. "Is there another dungeon or prison area in this castle?"

"I've been on house duty," Reed replied, the frustration clear in his voice. "Basically, I've been working as a servant by day then locked up in a cell upstairs at night. The cells above aren't as desolate as these ones though. But with the king leaving for a few days, I guess they want me in a more secure cage, while I wait to face trial."

It sounded like the same system my kingdom had. If a fae committed a crime, they couldn't be punished until the king or queen decided their fate. Reed would be stuck here until the king returned to make his judgment.

"I have stable duty in the morning, though," Reed added, and the fleeting hope I had of spending more time with him fizzled out. I was happy he'd get to be outside, in the sun, but the thought of being alone again, after just getting a taste of companionship, made my stomach tighten.

"Oh," I managed to say, the disappointment creeping into my voice despite my best efforts to hide it. I crawled back to my corner, the warmth of his presence already feeling like it was slipping away.

"Maybe I can see if they'll put you to work somewhere too?" Reed's voice carried over to me, filled with a hope I couldn't bring myself to feel.

"I appreciate that," I started, doing my best to keep the sadness from coloring my words, "but I doubt they'll let me. Especially with Orrin around."

Orrin would never allow it; I was sure of that. Not unless I did some "favors" for him, and as much as I missed the sun, I could never bring myself to debase myself like that. Although, part of me wondered just how long I could hold out before I broke. It was a terrifying thought, knowing that I could easily give in to the pressure, but I didn't want Reed to know what kind of bargain Orrin had already struck with me in exchange for a little comfort. It was all too much to bear right now, and I needed to push it to the back of my mind.

"Yeah, he's definitely a dick, huh?" Reed's voice cut through the tension, light with a chuckle.

"Yeah," I muttered, my voice barely above a whisper. I didn't want him to ask anything else about me, not when I feared I might slip up and reveal more than I intended. As much as I enjoyed the company and conversation, I was still so drained, my body aching in ways I couldn't explain. "Reed?"

"Yeah?" His voice softened, as though sensing my fatigue.

"I know it's selfish, but I'm glad I'm not alone," I confessed, the words slipping out before I could stop them. The silence that followed felt heavy, and I prayed he didn't take it the wrong way.

"Me too," he said quietly, and there was a warmth in his voice that soothed me.

"I know we can't see each other in this darkness, but if you could see me, I'm sure I'd look awful right now," I continued, the burden of my circumstances crashing back down. I hadn't seen my reflection in days, but I could feel the grime on my skin, the dried blood and dirt caked into my dress. The smell was unbearable, and I knew I must look like a mess. "I need to sleep."

"Doubt you could ever look awful," Reed replied with a gentle laugh, "but yeah, if you need to sleep, I won't disturb you, Sparks."

The nickname he had given me made something warm flicker in my chest. "Eliane," I whispered, realizing I had never told him my real name. "But you can call me Eli."

"I think I prefer Sparks," he said with a chuckle, "but Eli suits you too. Goodnight, Eli."

I curled into myself as best as I could, trying to conserve warmth. The comfort of having someone nearby, even though it was only through bars and shadows, sent a small wave of heat coursing through my veins. Maybe it was because I wasn't alone anymore, or maybe it was Reed's presence that made it feel safer. Either way, in this hellish place, I felt a little less exposed, a little more protected.

I closed my eyes, and for the first time in days, sleep came easier.

My eyes fluttered open, and I was outside. The sun beat down on my face with its overwhelming warmth, and for a moment, I let myself get lost in the ecstasy of the light. I was free.

I shot up, hands pushing against the ground, only to realize it wasn't the soft grass of the Ivy Isle's forest beneath me, it was sand. Powder-soft sand. I was home. I couldn't make sense of it, but somehow, I was back.

I glanced down at myself. The red dress was still intact. It was clean, not torn, and not stained with blood or dirt. There were no signs of my recent struggles. I was whole again. I looked around in disbelief. The oasis stretched out before me, still the same, still the place where I had once met Reed, still brimming with memories that felt more dreamlike than real.

My head spun, and the nagging doubt crept in. This had to be a dream, or was everything that came after some kind of illusion? I must've passed out here, somewhere between the heat, the hangover, and the exhaustion that weighed my limbs.

"Eli," a familiar voice rang out. "I found you!"

I whipped around, my heart leaping. It was Hayden.

Without thinking, I bolted toward him, throwing myself into his arms. "Hay!" I whimpered, almost desperate for the comfort of his presence. "You're here!"

Hayden chuckled lightly, peeling me off of him with a grin. "I told you I just needed some time to sober up." He glanced around, and then his eyes sharpened, his tone shifting. "So, any sign of the stag?"

I studied him, his smile radiating against his sun-kissed skin, glowing with warmth as if the very ray had settled there. His curly, copper locks were wild and disheveled, just like always, an untamed mess that he never seemed to care about. His amber eyes, flecked with gold, sparkled with life, shining with an energy that seemed to defy the exhaustion I knew he'd felt just hours before. Despite being hungover and bedridden earlier, the strength in his posture and the solid, defined muscles of his body told a different story. He looked every bit the Ember Prince he was, standing tall, poised, and ready to claim the crown with undeniable confidence. In that moment, he was here, I was here, and I knew I was truly home.

This was real. Everything, every horrible thing, was just a bad dream. I almost wanted to laugh at how easily my mind had conjured it all up. I quickly handed Hayden the bow and quiver of arrows, trying to push the fear of what might happen out of my mind. I didn't want to be near the weapon anymore, not after everything it had led to.

That's when it hit me. If none of that nightmare had been real... then Prince Hawthorne was still alive. Reed hadn't been caught, and everything I feared, everything I had imagined, might not have happened at all. The thoughts swirled in my head, and all I could think of now was getting out of this desert and locking myself in my room, away from all of it.

"Well?" Hayden's voice pulled me out of my spiraling thoughts. "Did you see it?"

"No," I answered, rubbing my temples as the headache from my hangover or maybe just the confusion, settled in. "No, I haven't seen it. Have you seen Prince Hawthorne?"

Hayden shrugged, nonchalant. "Yeah, he was at the palace before I left. I think he had a good time last night." He winked at me, but his expression shifted, concern creeping into his voice. "Why, did he see you? Does he suspect something?"

"No," I answered too quickly, hoping my voice didn't betray me. "I just wanted to make sure he wasn't around here, so I could slip back inside without notice." It wasn't a complete lie. His answer confirmed what I had hoped, Hawthorne was safe, and so was I.

"Well, if what the kitchen maids were talking about is true, I'm sure he's exhausted." Hayden threw me another wink, and I rolled my eyes at him in response.

"Well, I'm going to head back. Fintana is probably ready to get back to the stables," I said, a bit more serious now. "Good luck, Hay."

I started to turn away, but Hayden called out after me, his voice carrying a note of urgency. "Eli," he said, digging into his boot. "Here, take this."

I looked at him, puzzled, but reached out as he handed me a small dagger. The blade was embedded with rubies, its deep red glow almost hypnotic in the sunlight. My fingers closed around it instinctively.

"What's this for?" I asked, though the answer was probably obvious.

Hayden gave me a half smile, a mix of affection and something else. "For protection. In case you need it. You never know what might be out here."

"I have magic," I explained, my gaze fixed on the dagger gleaming in the sun. "My pendant is still charged up." The last thing I needed was another weapon in my hand right now.

"Please, just take it," Hayden insisted. "There could be Loas out here, and you know fire magic won't kill them."

He was right. Loas. I had forgotten about them. The predators of this land, their shadowy spotted forms hiding in the trees, their hunger relentless. I could feel my heart race as the reality of the situation set in. It wasn't a long walk back to Fintana, but if I was truly being given another chance at life, I couldn't waste it by being stupid.

"Fine," I muttered, reluctantly taking the dagger from his hand. It felt cold and unfamiliar in my grip, the weight of it awkward in my fingers. There was nowhere to hide it in my dress, so I let it hang loosely by my side, ready in case I crossed paths with a Loa. "Now, go get that stag," I added, my voice strained with both gratitude and unease.

Hayden flashed me a grin and nodded before disappearing between two palm trees, his form swallowed by the shadows of the oasis.

I followed the path back to where I left Fintana and my head was still whirling. I prayed to Theodon all the time as a child, mostly for silly things like, wishing my parents would get warts for grounding me, or wishing Hayden's hair would fall out when Adan said his was prettier than mine. Just things that Theodon would never have time to answer. There was always the added prayers of wishing it was me who had the Ember and not Hay, but as we got older and I could see how big Hayden's heart was and how much he loved this kingdom, I knew Theodon chose right.

Though Hayden often found himself in scandalous situations, his heart was always in the right place. From a young age, he seemed to have devoured every textbook on history, law, and diplomacy. How he retained all that knowledge after what must have been countless nights spent drinking whiskey, I'll never understand, but he did. He had his share of fun, but he always put our people first.

Hayden would often visit the more impoverished areas of the land, which, honestly, were few and far between. He did not make these appearances for the sake of image; he genuinely cared. He listened to the concerns of the people, acting as a sort of ambassador for my parents, and made sure results followed.

Though he was probably the youngest fae to ever be thrust into a kingly role, he always knew it was coming sooner rather than later, as my parents had been preparing him from an early age. He handled it all with grace and understanding.

It wasn't until this morning when he let his guard down that I ever saw doubt flood through him, but he pulled himself together and he showed up. He was here and he would find that stag and I was blessed with a redo.

As I neared the edge of the oasis, my heart stopped. Fintana's loud whinny echoed through the air, sharp and frantic. Instinct kicked in, and I sprinted toward the sound, adrenaline surging in my veins. I didn't know what I would find, but I knew I had to get to her.

When I reached the clearing, I was met with silence. Fintana stood there, still tied to the tree, but there was no sign of the danger. My chest tightened. Had I just been imagining things? Was it me who had spooked her?

I approached cautiously, still holding the dagger in my hand. "It's just me, girl," I muttered, my voice barely above a whisper as I closed the distance. Fintana seemed fine, her coat gleaming in the sunlight. It was probably nothing, just the lingering fear from everything that had happened. Or hadn't happened. I still couldn't make sense of it.

"Let's go home," I said, giving her a soft pat on the side. I moved to untie her, the knot coming loose quickly under my shaking fingers. As soon as she was free, I heard it.

A deep growl rumbled from the heart of the oasis, vibrating the very air around me. My blood turned to ice. It was too late. I was already too exposed.

"Fin," I whispered urgently, my voice trembling, "we need to go."

I scrambled to saddle her, but my shaking fingers fumbled the reins. The dagger slipped from my hand and fell to the ground.

"Shit!" I cursed under my breath, bending down to retrieve it. But before I could even straighten up, a searing pain shot through my ankle.

The world tilted as I was yanked backward, a powerful force dragging me through the sand. My scream cut through the air as I looked down, horrified to see sharp teeth clamped around my ankle. The creature was strong, its head thrashing from side to side as it pulled me toward the dark heart of the oasis. Its sleek body moved with the fluid grace of a feline, muscles coiled and rippling beneath shadow-dark fur that shimmered faintly in the sun. Its eyes glowed like twin embers, feral and wholly predatory, but as I searched for markings to identify it as a Loa, there were none. Maybe it was not a Loa at all. Maybe it was something else, something newly evolved from the Ember Isle. My skin scraped and tore as the beast's grip tightened like a vice, dragging me mercilessly through the burning sand.

"Run, Fin!" I screamed, my voice raw with panic, watching as my beloved horse bolted into the distance.

The pain was blinding. I felt as though my very flesh was being ripped from my bones. My heart pounded as the beast continued to drag me, its growls deafening in my ears.

"Hayden!" I screamed, my voice hoarse. "Hayden, help me!"

But I knew it was useless. He was deep within the oasis by now. I had no idea if he could hear me, or if he was even safe. I could only hope that, somehow, he would make it out of this alive.

The dragging finally stopped, and I knew I had to act fast. I reached for my neck, but my pendant was gone. It must have fallen off during the struggle, somewhere in the sand. Not that it would have helped me much if it was a Loa.

I gripped the dagger in my left hand, the coolness of the hilt grounding me in the moment. I hadn't even realized I was still holding it. I tightened my grip, my knuckles turning white, the skin stretched tight over my bones. I held on like it was the only thing keeping me tethered to this world.

Then the pressure shifted. The creature's teeth wrenched free from my flesh with a searing sting, tearing a line of fire across my skin. My body jolted as the dragging ceased, sand grinding against my skin until everything went still.

Flipping onto my back, I glanced down at my legs. The sight made my stomach churn. My flesh was torn open, gold and red blood soaking into the sand beneath me. My face stung, raw from the sand scraping against it as the creature dragged me. I couldn't hold back the scream that tore from my throat. Pain radiated from every part of me. It felt as though my whole body was screaming in agony, a wave of suffering so intense it consumed me.

I couldn't breathe. I was losing blood fast, my chest constricting as each breath became harder to take. My body was shutting down and my vision was beginning to swim. I couldn't focus.

I looked around, frantic, but it was nowhere in sight. I had to get out of here, had to keep moving.

I tried to push myself up, but my legs wouldn't respond. They were shredded. The flesh was torn all the way to the bone. A weak whimper slipped from my throat as the tears flowed freely, blurring my vision.

"I don't want to die like this. Not now." I cried out, my voice cracking with desperation.

I wanted to fight, but in that moment, I was utterly defeated. My legs were useless, completely non-functional, and there was no way I'd heal them in time. My only hope was that Hayden would find me before the creature did, or before I bled out here, alone in the sand. Even if he arrived in time, it would take so much of his strength to heal the damage done to me that it could drain him dry. Then we'd both be weak and vulnerable; sitting ducks out here in the open.

I flipped onto my stomach and began to crawl. It was all I could do at this point. I didn't know why the creature had left me alive instead of finishing me off, but I wasn't going to waste the second chance I had been given. I still had fight in me, even if it felt like it was slowly slipping away. I couldn't afford to give up, not when survival was still a possibility.

The dagger was clenched tightly in my hand, the hilt pressing into my palm as if it could somehow hold me together. I was ready for when the creature returned, but I needed to steady my breath first. Panic threatened to overtake me, but I fought it back, forcing my lungs to expand slowly.

My arms moved, dragging the weight of my broken body forward. Every muscle screamed in protest, and my jaw was clenched so tightly I thought my teeth might crack from the pressure. Pain shot through me with each movement, the sharp sting in my legs threatening to overwhelm everything. My tears blurred my vision, and every sense felt muffled, as though I was underwater, struggling to make sense of the world around me.

The soft humming melody filled the air again. I shifted my eyes around but saw nothing. Was this death, coming to claim me? I searched, trying to find that silver hair and those eyes that matched mine, but all I saw was sand. Whether by claw or by song, death stalked me all the same, and I would not be fooled by the comfort in her voice.

I had to get out of here.

I could feel my blood pooling beneath me, seeping into the sand where the creature had dragged me. As unsettling as it was, it meant I was heading in the right direction. The trail of blood was my map now. The thought of that sent a wave of nausea rising in my throat, and acidic bile began to burn at the back of my mouth. I choked it back, pushing forward despite the weakness, and the raw fear gnawing at my insides.

In a quick moment, the humming stopped and was replaced by a rustling sound. It was soft but fast, and it was coming up behind me.

My heart stopped. The creature was coming back.

I froze, knowing there was no running, no escape. The only way out was to fight.

I felt a rush of air, a gust of wind stirring around me, and I knew the creature was about to pounce. Despite the overwhelming pain, adrenaline surged through me, sharpening my senses. I twisted quickly, every muscle protesting, and brought the dagger up, aiming it blindly, desperately, into the space around me. I squeezed my eyes shut and drove the blade into whatever I could.

The feeling of the blade slipping into flesh was sickeningly smooth. There was a brief, sharp spray of blood that hit my face, and I wiped at it frantically, my breath coming in ragged gasps.

When my eyes cleared, I looked up, expecting to see the beast, but instead I was met with a sight that made my stomach drop. It wasn't the creature I had stabbed.

It was Prince Hawthorne, his eyes wide in shock. The dagger I had meant to plunge into the creature's throat was now buried deep in his flesh.

"No!" I whimpered, my voice breaking as I looked into his eyes, green with silver, once so full of strength, now filled with a raw, unspoken terror. He stumbled backward, hitting the ground with a sickening thud. The dagger was still buried deep in his throat, and blood poured from the wound, spreading like a dark silver stain on the sand beneath him.

"No, no, no, no!" I repeated over and over, my heart pounding in my chest. My body was trembling. "Hold on! Please, just hold on. I'm going to help!"

I forced my shaking arms to move, pushing myself closer to him, each inch more agonizing than the last. What was he doing here? Where was the Loa? My thoughts were a jumble, but there was no time to question it. I couldn't think.

His breath was ragged, and the air was filled with wet gurgling sounds as he choked on his own blood. The horror of it twisted my insides. I had to get that dagger out.

I reached him, my fingers trembling as they touched his skin, slick with blood. His face was pale, his lips barely moving as he tried to speak. But the words never came, just more blood, spilling out with every desperate breath.

"I'm going to pull it out, okay?" My voice was barely a whisper. He didn't respond, but his eyes flickered to mine. His eyelids fluttered shut as he braced himself. "On the count of three." His eyes met mine for a brief moment, and then he nodded weakly before shutting his eyes again.

"One… two… three."

With all the strength I could muster, I wrenched the dagger free. Blood surged from the wound in hot, thick spurts, coating my hands and splashing across the sand. I pressed my palms to his throat, feeling the warm blood seep between my fingers, but no matter how hard I pushed, the bleeding wouldn't stop.

I could feel my own blood slipping away from my wounds, my vision dimming at the edges. I was fading, too. But I couldn't let him die. I couldn't.

Maybe this was why Theodon had given me this second chance, not to save myself, but to save him. To save Hawthorne. It felt like a cruel joke, like some twisted punishment, but if this was the price, then I would pay it.

No matter what I tried, the bleeding wouldn't stop. His blood kept spilling through my fingers, and no matter how hard I pressed, it wasn't enough.

"Please," I begged, my voice breaking as the tears flowed freely down my cheeks. "Heal yourself," I cried, frantic now. "You can't die. You can't, not now."

His eyes fluttered open one last time, locking with mine, his eyes full of pain as he croaked out, "heal me please."

Tears once again rolled down my face, and I could feel the strength draining from my weary body. The pressure from the brace around the wound in his throat grew weaker, slipping looser and limp in my trembling hands. He couldn't heal himself, and his desperate gaze fixed on me.

"I can't," I sobbed, my voice cracking under the strain of it all. "I don't have any magic, so please, keep trying."

He responded with a slow, dull shake of his head. I knew it then, deep in my bones. I was losing him, and there was nothing I could do to stop it.

"I'm sorry," I whispered brokenly, my voice wavering with grief, before my sorrow turned into a guttural scream of anguish. I felt his body go still beneath my blood-soaked hands, and he was gone.

I stared down at his lifeless face, my vision clouded with tears, and all I could do was repeat over and over, "I'm sorry, I'm sorry..." until my own strength started to slip away. My breath became shallow and ragged. I could feel life draining from me, too. I was going to die here. I had failed Hawthorne, and now Hayden— Hayden would die too without me to offer myself in his place. No. This couldn't be happening.

"Sparks?" I heard a voice in the distance, full of concern. "Sparks, are you okay?"

Reed. It was Reed. I didn't know how he was here, but his voice cut through the haze of despair like a lifeline.

"Help," I whimpered, choking on a sob. "Please."

"Sparks, you need to wake up," his voice was insistent, yet gentle. "It's just a bad dream. You need to wake up."

A dream? My mind was too tangled to make sense of anything anymore.

"Eli!" Reed shouted, urgency seeping into his voice. "Please, wake up! You're scaring me!"

I jerked awake, gasping for air as it rushed into my lungs. I squeezed my eyes shut, but when I opened them again, darkness surrounded me. I was back. I was back in the cell, and all my senses came rushing back as though they'd never left. It hadn't been real. It was a nightmare, a cruel trick of my mind. But even though I was awake, the nightmare was far from over.

"Sparks?" his voice called again, more fragile this time. "Please, answer me. Are you okay?" The fear in his voice only heightened my own panic, and my breath quickened.

My lungs felt like they were being crushed as I struggled to drag air into my body. "I c-can't breathe," I stammered, my words barely escaping as the pressure in my chest increased. The bodice of my dress felt impossibly tight, as if it were squeezing the life out of me. I frantically reached behind me, desperate to loosen the laces, but my fingers were shaking too violently to find any purchase. It was still tied as tightly as the night Hawthorne had laced me up in the hallway. The thought of his face, the memory of that night, only made the panic worse.

"I can't untie it," I cried, my heart hammering painfully against my ribcage.

"Untie what?"

"My dress," I wheezed, struggling for each breath. "The bodice... I need to untie the laces. It's crushing me."

"It sounds like you're having a panic attack," Reed said, his voice steady despite the situation. "You need to focus on your breathing. Slow, deep breaths. In through your nose, out through your mouth."

I tried to follow his instructions, my breaths shaky and uneven but I couldn't focus. All I could think about was getting out of this damned dress. My hands were still shaking as I reached for the lacing again, but it felt like the harder I tried, the tighter it became. The mere thought of being trapped in this corset-like prison only added to the crushing feeling in my chest.

"Breathe with me, okay?" Reed's voice was softer now, full of concern.

"No!" I shouted with a gasp. "I need it off, I need it off, I need it off!" I said repeatedly each time growing louder and louder, my fingers still fumbling helplessly at the laces.

"Come to the bars that connect our cells, I can help you with it."

I didn't hesitate. I crawled toward his voice, my hands outstretched in the pitch-black darkness. I flinched when I felt a hand touch mine.

"Reed?" I shrieked, my voice trembling as my hand reached out hoping to make contact.

"I got you," Reed said as his hand wrapped around mine. "Now, turn around carefully. Don't let your skin touch the iron bars and remember to focus on your breathing."

I nodded, my mind too frantic to respond. But his calm voice helped anchor me as I turned toward the bars, the crushing weight on my chest still there, but now, at least, I wasn't alone.

I scooted back as far as I could, my heart pounding in my chest, until I felt Reed's hand gently press against my back, signaling that I should stop before I collided with the cold iron bars. "The lace starts at the top of the dress." I frantically let out.

"Got it," he said, his voice steady as he moved to work on the knots. I focused on controlling my breathing, trying to steady myself in the overwhelming darkness. "Whoever tied you in this thing really didn't want you to get out of it, huh?" Reed said with a light laugh, his attempt to lighten the mood barely breaking through my tension.

"Hurry," I gasped, my voice barely more than a whisper, but desperate.

"Top lace is almost done," Reed murmured, his fingers nimble against the fabric. "I'll work my way down to loosen the rest."

But it wasn't fast enough.

"Just rip it if you have to," I commanded, my voice sharp with urgency. I didn't care that I had nothing else to wear. I just needed to be free of the remnants of that day, to feel the tight grip of the past loosen.

"Almost got it."

"Reed, please!" I hissed, my panic growing with every passing second. I was sure he sensed it, because the next sound I heard was fabric tearing apart.

I inhaled deeply, my lungs gasping for air like I had been underwater for hours. Now only hanging by the front stitching, the bodice slumped forward, loose around my chest. I yanked it down further, desperate to free myself from its suffocating grip, wanting to erase every trace of its confinement from my body and my thoughts.

"Let's try those breathing exercises again, alright?" Reed said gently. "It'll help with your heart rate. In through your nose for a five count, and out for a ten count."

I followed his instructions, breathing along with him as he set the rhythm. Gradually, I began to feel my heart rate steady, my breath coming easier.

"Feeling better?"

"Yes, thank you," I whispered, pulling the bodice from my body completely, the top of me now exposed. My arm shot across my chest instinctively, desperate to cover myself.

"Can you see anything in this dark?" I asked, suddenly self-conscious and aware of my vulnerability, wondering if fae from Gust had better night vision than those of Ember.

"No, not a thing," Reed answered firmly, his voice reassuring. He understood my hesitation, and for once, I was grateful to be cloaked in darkness. I didn't know what would happen if Orrin came down here and found me like this, but I didn't want to think about that now.

"Here," Reed said softly, and I heard the sound of fabric brushing against skin. "take my shirt so you can cover yourself."

"What about you?" I hesitated, still feeling exposed, as I reached out and took the shirt from his outstretched hand.

"Well," he chuckled lightly, "I think I'll be safe from any ogling by the male guards at the sight of my bare chest."

His attempt to lighten the mood worked, just a little. A small smile tugged at my lips, and for a moment, I wasn't so consumed by the pressure of everything. Reed's sense of humor was the only thing that could keep me grounded in this darkness.

A small laugh escaped my lips as I pulled the shirt over my head. The scent of mint filled my nose, its fresh, cool aroma providing me with a small sense of comfort. I practically felt like I was swimming in it, but regardless, I kept my red dress on beneath it, despite the bodice now being tattered and torn. At least the skirt was still fine, covering enough of my lower body to maintain some semblance of modesty.

"Thank you," I murmured, the words barely escaping my lips.

A long silence stretched between us as I mentally sorted through what to say next. I wasn't sure how much I had mumbled in my sleep, nor could I tell how much Reed had actually heard during my nightmare. I didn't know how to explain it. How could I tell him why my nightmare was what it was? Taking a life was something that had broken me, and even in sleep, I couldn't escape it.

"I'm sorry," I began, as I cleared my throat. "For waking you, and then yelling at you when you were just trying to help."

"Eli? Are you okay?"

"It was just a bad dream."

"Sparks, that was more than just a bad dream."

His words sent a cold shiver down my spine, and I realized that he must have heard everything.

"What I heard from you... that wasn't just a nightmare. You were screaming, saying 'no' over and over again. Was someone hurting you?" His voice was filled with worry, and I could feel his concern even through the darkness.

Yes, torn apart by a creature, but that wasn't what hurt the most. I couldn't tell him the truth. I couldn't say that I had killed the prince, that the guilt had been eating me alive ever since.

It haunted me even in my sleep, even in my dreams. Hawthorne wasn't Reed's prince. In fact, considering he had been imprisoned by Hawthorne's father, I doubted Reed even cared about the prince's death. But still, I needed to keep quiet. Reed could still be a spy. Even if he wasn't, I couldn't tell him about what I had done. For all I knew, Caraway could torture him for any information about me. He did see me in that oasis with the bow, a place I wasn't supposed to be, and revealing that might slowly shatter the lie I had built. Once that truth came out, what other truths might I accidentally expose? Truths that, for all I knew, Reed could use against me. There were too many "what ifs".

"I don't want to talk about it," I replied, my voice quieter now, hoping he would respect my boundaries.

"It's okay," Reed continued, his tone softening. "If you ever want to talk about it, I have nowhere else to be." I could almost hear the small, reassuring smile in his voice, as if he were trying to make light of our situation, of our shared captivity. "Do you think you can sleep?"

"No," I replied honestly. I was terrified. Terrified that if I closed my eyes, I would slip into another nightmare, or worse, into some alternate reality where nothing felt real. For all I knew, I could be in another reality right now, and Reed might not even be here. The thought made my stomach twist. Drifting off alone was the last thing I wanted.

"I have an idea, if you're willing to try."

I nodded, forgetting he couldn't see me in the dark, but the gesture felt right anyway. "Okay," I said. I had nothing left to lose at this point.

"When I was younger, I had my fair share of nightmares," Reed began, his voice lowering to something more personal. "I didn't have anyone to hold me or comfort me, but I had Buttons."

"Buttons? Like buttons on a shirt?"

"No, Buttons was my teddy bear," Reed said with a small chuckle, and I could almost picture the faint smile on his lips. "I wasn't very creative with names as a child, but I held onto him tightly after every bad dream. He was my anchor, the one thing I could trust to remind me what was real and what wasn't."

"Are you telling me you have Buttons in that cell with you?"

"No," Reed laughed, "I'm afraid I haven't seen Buttons in years. But I figured you could use me as your anchor."

"How?"

"Here," Reed said gently, and I felt the warmth of his hand brush lightly against my arm as he reached out toward me. "You can hold onto my hand throughout the night. Let it be your reminder of what's real and what's not."

I hesitated before reaching out. I still didn't really know who this male was. What if he was here to harm me, extract information I didn't even know I had? Was I just a pawn in someone else's game? Would he use me as leverage for his own freedom, now that he knew I was important to the Ivy King?

Then I reminded myself of the simple truth. We were both locked in cells. He had no way to reach me, no weapon in hand, and even if he did, I could always retreat to the far corner of my cell.

Still, even if there was no malicious intent, he was still a stranger. The thought of holding someone's hand throughout the night felt strangely intimate, maybe too intimate, given my experience, or lack thereof. But the idea of an anchor made sense. I thought back to the many sleepless nights I'd experienced growing up. The only ones that had been bearable were the nights when Hayden would sneak into my room, or I to his. His closeness, his warmth, helped calm me and chased the bad dreams away. Maybe Reed could do the same, simply by me holding his hand. This didn't have to be weird or intimate. It could just be an act of kindness.

I let the idea turn over in my mind, considering it from every angle, before finally answering, "Yes, I think I would like that." His fingers were still lightly resting on my arm, and I slowly slid my arm away until my hand found his.

"You're so warm," I said, my voice barely above a whisper.

"And for someone from the Ember Isle, your skin is as cold as ice," he replied with a light chuckle, and I felt his fingers interlace with mine, squeezing warmth into my hand. "Do you want to grab your blanket from the cot?"

"I don't have one," I breathed out, my chest tight with both the lingering panic and his soothing touch. "Lucky me was just given a dirty broken cot."

"A cot that, if I recall, you said you didn't deserve?" he pressed gently, his fingers still massaging small circles into the back of my hand.

"I don't," I dryly replied, a sense of self-loathing rising in me once again. "I'll be fine."

"Hold on," Reed said, his tone turning serious, and he pulled his hand away. The instant warmth left my skin, and my fingers longed to reconnect with his. "Here," he added, and I heard the rustle of fabric before he pushed a blanket through the bars. "Take my blanket."

I stared at the blanket in the darkness, momentarily stunned. "First, you give me the literal shirt off your back, and now your blanket? Why?" I asked, my suspicious thoughts swirling in my mind yet again.

"You're a good person, Sparks," Reed replied softly, reaching for my hand once again, his fingers finding mine in the darkness. "You're here paying your brother's debt for a life he took. If I had a sister in your position, I would hope someone would show her kindness as well."

There it was again, the guilt of someone seeing me as the victim. I wasn't the victim. I was the monster. And while I probably deserved each and every nightmare that was coming my way, in that moment, I needed to be selfish. I wanted to be selfish. I wanted, at least for a few hours, to escape my reality, to escape this hell. If this kind stranger was offering me a solution for that, I had to take it.

"Thank you, Reed," I murmured, my voice heavy with sleep as I laid down, careful not to disturb our connection. I kept my fingers entwined with his, both of us making sure to avoid the iron bars separating our cells. I could smell his mint-scented breath, warm and soft, drifting toward my face. If there had been light in the room, I was sure we would have been lined up perfectly, eye to eye. He would probably see the blush staining my cheeks, growing deeper with each lazy stroke of his fingers as they continued their soothing circles across my skin.

"I'll be right here all night," Reed assured me, his voice a quiet comfort in the darkness.

"Thank you," I whispered again, my eyes already fluttering closed.

"Goodnight, Sparks."

"Goodnight, Reed."

17

A hint of light slowly flooded my vision as my sleepy eyes began to crack open. I was still in the same spot on the floor, my hand outstretched through the bars, but it was empty. Reed was gone.

I propped myself up on one elbow, my body stiff from the cold, and glanced down at my clothing, inspecting it as if searching for proof that last night had really happened. I let the blanket that had been draped over my shoulders fall, exposing a dirty shirt that must have once been white, though it was nearly impossible to tell now. The fabric was stained, and near the bottom, there were tears where Reed had ripped strips to help me wrap beneath the iron collar.

All the evidence was there. Reed had been here. He had comforted me. He had been real. But now, he was gone.

I turned my gaze across to his cell. I could actually see now, there was light in the room, soft but steady. Whipping my head toward the front of my cell, I spotted one solitary torch lit, casting just enough glow to illuminate my surroundings. Next to my torn bodice, I found a plate of food and a cup of water. The sight of it made my skin crawl. The thought of Orrin delivering it while I slept was unsettling. Had he seen Reed and me, our hands clasped through the bars? Maybe that was why Reed was gone. Maybe seeing me take comfort in someone else, especially someone who wasn't him, had made him jealous, or angry.

Or maybe just the idea of me having any kind of connection with another person was unacceptable. After all, I was supposed to be suffering for my crime.

My thoughts drifted to worries that maybe my assumptions were true. Reed said he was assigned some servant tasks the day before the king left, something about being on stable duty today, so maybe that's where he was now? It would make sense. He was probably doing some kind of chores upstairs, and would return when he was done, I tried to reassure myself, but the gnawing discomfort wouldn't ease.

I reached for the cup and took a swig of the liquid. The water was stale, but it was welcomed nonetheless, the coolness soothing my dry throat. My eyes fell on the food. A piece of bread, the edges of which were already starting to darken with mold, and a slab of cold meat that was mostly fat. No doubt, whatever I was given had been the leftovers from whatever meal they had dined on the night before.

As the day went on, my thoughts became more unsettled. I could sleep all day and hope it would numb me, but there was always the chance of a nightmare. And without Reed here to tether me, I wasn't sure I could get through it. So instead, I decided to stay active, doing laps around my cell. It was a small space, but it helped quiet my mind.

The sound of a door opening abruptly halted my mindless pacing. My skin prickled in anticipation. Was it Orrin escorting Reed back to his cell, or was it just Orrin coming to pester me some more? In case it was the latter, I grabbed the blanket and sank into the furthest corner of my cell. I wrapped it around myself, trying to make myself as small as possible, though I knew it wouldn't do much good. Orrin knew I was here, and with the king gone, who knew what he might do.

I listened intently, straining to hear if there were two sets of footsteps descending the stairs or just one. But I couldn't make it out over the rapid beat of my own heart hammering in my ears. The jingling of keys grew louder, and I realized the final step had been reached. I craned my neck forward, my pulse quickening, hoping to see who was about to round the corner.

When I saw it was Reed with Orrin trailing behind him, my blood seemed to warm.

"In you go," Orrin said in a tone that was surprisingly pleasant, a tone I had never heard directed at me. "I'll be back to collect you tomorrow." He finished speaking and locked Reed's cell with a metallic clang.

I remained huddled in my corner, hoping Orrin would just leave. To my surprise, he did. No comments, no taunting, just a sly look, and then he was gone. He didn't even take the torch with him. I had thought it was left lit by accident, but Orrin didn't seem to care as he exited. Maybe the king had ordered him to keep me "comfortable" while he figured out whatever it was he was doing with that star fragment. The idea seemed far-fetched, but I couldn't think of another explanation.

"Sparks?" Reed's voice echoed from the other side of the bars, pulling me back to the present. "You okay?"

"Yeah, why?" I responded, trying to sound normal.

"Because you look like a scared little bird huddled in the corner," he said, his voice lacking humor.

I didn't want to tell him how much Orrin frightened me, so I decided to give him a half-truth. "Well, I am in a prison cell with a death sentence," I said, moving closer to the bars connecting our cells. "Every time someone comes down here, it could be to march me to my execution." I tried to force a smile, but the tension in the air was thick. Especially now that I could finally see Reed in the flesh again, his rugged handsomeness as striking as it had been in the oasis.

"Well," Reed huffed, moving closer to the bars on his side, "lucky for you, the king's still gone, and probably will be for a few days, so you should be safe for now."

I studied Reed's face as he spoke. Despite the scar running across it, from one side to the other, it was still handsome. But there was something else in his expression: lingering sadness, maybe even guilt. His eyes looked as though they were hiding some unspoken pain, a hardship he'd been carrying. I recalled his story about how he ended up in the Ivy King's clutches. He was supposed to return with food for his people, and he had failed.

Looking at him now, I decided not to bring it up. I wouldn't comment on it, not wanting to make things worse for him. Instead, I quickly shifted the conversation. "So, what did they have you do today?" I asked, genuinely interested.

"Stable duty," he said dryly, "shoveling shit all day."

"At least you got to be outside for a bit?" I offered softly, trying to help him focus on the bright side.

"Trust me, I would've rather been here, talking to you, than knee-deep in manure."

I felt my cheeks turn warm at his response. He enjoyed my company? Or maybe he was just so lonely that even I would do. I quickly looked down, hoping the dim light would hide my pink cheeks. I cleared my throat and took a deep breath. Surprisingly, Reed didn't smell, at least not of anything foul. Just the familiar scent of mint he usually carried.

"Are you sure you were around livestock all day?"

"No, I was lounging around the castle," he said sarcastically. "Why?"

"You don't smell," I said, sniffing the air again. My nose was practically trained to detect manure after years of playing the role of a stable hand back home. I could smell it from a mile away, but there was nothing. Reed's clothing was fresh and clean, without a trace of the earthy, pungent odor that usually clung to me for days if I didn't wash right away.

"I was able to bathe before returning," he replied, "Well, 'bathed' is a bit of a stretch, it was more like being hosed down. Can't have me dragging manure through the castle, I suppose."

The mere idea of a bath sounded so tantalizing. Hell, even being hosed down to wash away the filth that coated my skin felt like a dream. "I would kill for a bath," I mumbled absentmindedly under my breath.

"Well, maybe they could give you a chore or something so you can get hosed down like the rest of us. Though I doubt a proper princess such as you would appreciate showering in such a way," Reed teased.

Any kind of shower would feel like heaven right about now, but the thought of having Orrin or any of the Ivy Guard for that matter hose me down made me feel uneasy. I couldn't give Orrin even the slightest invitation to my body. I quickly shook those thoughts away, not wanting Reed to sense my discomfort or ruin the playful energy in the air.

I plastered on a smile and said, "I'm in no position to be picky," adding what I hoped was a convincing giggle that seemed to work as Reed joined me.

Our laughter slowly faded, but our gazes stayed locked on each other. I watched as the sadness from earlier crept back into his face. I had to distract him, keep the mood light. "So, were you mostly outside all day?" I asked, my voice soft.

Reed nodded. "Under the hot sun the whole day."

"Can you tell me about it?" .

"The shoveling shit part?" he let out another laugh.

"No," I also giggled hoping his smile wouldn't fade so quickly, "the sun, tell me about the sun and the sky." Perhaps it was just an Ember fae thing, but I missed the warmth of the sun. I missed the colors that painted the sky at sunset, the pinks and purples that would bleed across the horizon.

Reed hesitated for a moment before responding. "I heard from the guards about you being locked up and hidden back on Ember, is that why your skin is lighter compared to others on your Isle?"

Why had this conversation turned back to me "Partially," I began, trying to recall the story we'd come up with. This part of my life was true, or at least mostly true, just exaggerated in motive. "I was hidden away from my kingdom because I didn't want the throne."

"So, you were punished for not wanting to rule?" Reed asked. "Or was it because the Ember King and Queen preferred a male heir on the throne?"

"No," I replied quickly, feeling a small sting in my chest at his words. If things had been different, and I had been the one to inherit the Ember, I was sure my parents would have been as proud of me as they were of Hayden. Wouldn't they? Ruling was never something I considered, but was that because I knew I wasn't going to be the heir, or because it was simply rare for a female to rule over Ember at all? The thought lingered in my mind more often than I liked. "It was for my brother's safety and to ensure he was accepted as the true heir and keeper of the Ember."

"So no one knew about your existence? How did that work?" Pity laced his tone, and it made my stomach twist uneasily.

"A few did," I said, my voice dropping low as I thought of those closest to me. "I mainly just stayed out of the way."

"But if you were their daughter, you were still the Ember Princess. Why go through all that trouble to hide you?" he pressed. "If you and your brother were close enough in age, why not just present you as a second-born, or adopted?"

The questions hit like a storm, and I realized I didn't have answers. I couldn't tell him the truth about me having no magic and that was the reason I was hidden. But maybe there *was* another way to go about it? It's not like anyone would demand to see my magic, as we used it sparingly and not to make a spectacle of ourselves. My mind scrambled for a response, but all I could do was replay that day in the throne room. What had I said back then? Had anyone asked this? There was no perfect answer, only the cold truth that I wasn't ready to speak. I swallowed hard and knew I had only one way out. I had to commit to the lie. "Because," I said, louder than I meant, my voice shuddering, "because you were right."

Reed stared at me, confusion clouding his face. I could feel my lips tremble as I fought to keep my emotions in check. "What was I right about?" he asked softly, his voice full of concern.

"They didn't want me," I said, my gaze dropping to the floor, afraid to let him see the hurt in my eyes. "You were right. They wanted a male. So, I was locked away and kept a secret." I knew this was still part of the story we had crafted, but the more I said it out loud, the more my mind started to believe that maybe the story we had made up was closer to the truth than I wanted to admit.

How did everything shift so quickly? I had been trying to comfort him, distract him from his pain, but now it was my sadness that filled the room. The words stung, and I knew they weren't entirely true. My parents loved me. They had to have. But Reed was right, too. Why hadn't they just claimed me as adopted? Or said I had been born later? That way, they could have hidden me for a year at most and kept up the lie. As an adopted child, no one would demand that I prove my worth and power because I wouldn't be from their bloodline. It would have been an easy excuse to just pass off small tricks here and there with my pendant. They had options and didn't take them. But now, everything felt too late to change. I never hated my life, regardless of the unhappiness my circumstances brought, but the different choices that could have been made have slipped away, and nothing could reverse the past.

"Those bastards," Reed growled.

"It's fine," I whispered, my eyes still fixed on the floor.

"Look at me Eli."

Slowly, I lifted my head up to meet his gaze. I fought to hold back my tears, but I could feel the wetness in my eyes, reflecting everything I felt inside. When our gazes finally locked, I saw a new kind of sadness in his face, not for himself, but for me.

"It's not fine, you sacrificed yourself so they could keep a male heir on the throne. You're paying the price for what your brother did. Even now, your parents are still on his side."

The words hit too close to home. I couldn't tell him that it was my idea, my choice, to create the lie that I was the true holder of the Ember. I was the one who agreed to the deception. I was the one who sacrificed my own future for my brother's safety. Yet, somehow, his words still felt like a wound that wouldn't heal. They echoed in my mind, digging deep, making me wonder if I could have had a different life. A life where none of this pain had to exist.

A single tear slipped from my eye, and I knew I had failed in my attempt to comfort him.

"Hey," Reed's voice was gentle, breaking the silence. He reached his hand out to catch the tear that had fallen down my cheek. His touch was warm and soft, the kind of comfort I hadn't felt in so long. "The sun was beautiful today."

I choked back a sob, nodding to hold myself together. "Yeah." I could barely speak, still fighting the emotions that threatened to overflow.

"Yeah," he continued, his voice soothing, almost wistful. "It was warm today. But when I went out to watch the sunset, it was magical."

"Can you describe it for me?" The question slipped from my lips before I could stop myself. My body moved almost instinctively, and my hand reached out between the bars, seeking his.

Reed's hand found mine without hesitation, and he gripped it gently. His eyes never left my face, and I could feel his sincerity in the way he spoke next. "The sky was cloudier than it's been the past few days. But as the day went on, the sun started to peek through." He paused for a moment, his voice becoming dreamy. "It was perfect."

"Not too hot?" I asked softly, closing my eyes as I tried to picture it. I could see the faint light of the swaying torch through my closed eyelids, which only fueled my imagination, all the while feeling the heat of Reed's hand in mine, his touch grounding me.

"No," he replied, a small sound of contentment escaping his lips. "Just perfect. And by the time the sun started to set, the clouds kind of spread out, soft and light, like feathers. Still connected, but scattered enough to let the light shine through."

"What color was painted behind them?" I hummed, lost in the imagery, a smile tugging at the corners of my lips.

"Mostly pink," he whispered, his thumb rubbing gently along the back of my hand, the tender gesture making my heart flutter. "But with the yellow and orange of the sun, it turned into this rose gold, like it was glowing."

"That sounds beautiful," I said quietly, my voice soft with longing. I had seen countless sunsets in my life, but the ones that turned the sky into pinks and golds, those were always my favorite.

I opened my eyes, and there, on Reed's face, was a small grin, mirroring my own. The sadness that had lingered in his features had softened, replaced by something else, something like hope, or at least a fleeting happiness. For a moment, I forgot everything else.

"Thank you," I said softly, giving his hand a light squeeze, appreciating the comfort his words had given me.

"You're welcome," Reed replied, his voice quieter now. But then, without warning, he pulled his hand away, and I immediately felt the loss. The warmth, the connection, it was gone, and I couldn't help but miss it. He cleared his throat, as if shaking off some of the vulnerability. "So, what did you get up to today?"

"Oh, you know," I said, trying to keep the mood light despite the awkwardness in the air after Reed's retreat. "Slept in all day, had some room service delivered to my chamber, just princess things."

"Sounds like the life." His voice carried a hint of envy, but I could hear the exhaustion beneath it.

"Yeah," I replied, my voice falling flat despite my effort to stay upbeat, "it is."

We both began picking at the food that had been delivered earlier. It was always some combination of bread and meats, though the quality and freshness were always questionable. Reed's plate looked fresher than mine, and without hesitation, he kindly swapped my meal for his. Biting into the soft bread, as opposed to my stale piece, was like heaven. Reed was definitely favored by someone in this place, of that, there was no question. But then again, Reed didn't have blood on his hands the way I did. Still, I was grateful for his generosity, and I couldn't help but glance up every now and then, wondering if regret would flicker across his face when he realized just how disgusting my plate of food was. But he said nothing, and for that, I was grateful.

Reed continued telling me about his day, and honestly, it didn't sound too bad. Physically exhausting, sure, as he let out a yawn here and there, but nothing terrible. "I'm surprised they haven't had you breaking your back up there yet, to be honest."

"Orrin would never let me, not without making me pay a price."

I regretted saying it as soon as the words left my mouth. I hoped Reed wouldn't press, but I could see his expression shift.

"Does he hurt you?" Reed asked, his voice turning serious. My blood ran cold at the question.

I had just opened that door, hadn't I? I didn't want to get into it, not with Reed. Orrin had hurt me, and I had the bruises to prove it, though most of them had healed by now, or at least faded enough that I didn't feel their sting anymore. Still, I didn't need to burden Reed with that. He had enough on his plate. He didn't need to hear about my suffering. Besides, I wasn't the victim here. I had brought this upon myself. I was the villain, I reminded myself, and whatever pain I endured was nothing compared to what I deserved.

"Sparks?" Reed's voice broke through my thoughts.

I took a deep breath, steadying myself. "He hasn't been kind," I admitted. "But I'm a prisoner on death row, so I can't exactly expect kindness." I forced a small, tight smile, trying to keep the conversation light, even though I could feel the shadow of my words. "I was surprised he even left a torch down here so we wouldn't have to be in the dark."

Reed scoffed. "Probably just got tired of having to bring one down each time," he muttered. "I doubt there were any kind or noble motives behind it."

"Yeah, well," I shrugged, "I'm thankful for it. I'll sleep better." I tried to shift the conversation, but it wasn't easy.

There was a pause before Reed asked, his voice quieter now, "Does that happen a lot? The night terrors?"

I froze for a moment. The idea of explaining my nightmares, of explaining why they haunted me so consistently, made my chest tighten. I hadn't told Reed about the deeper reasons for my terror, not because I didn't trust him, which I guess I still didn't fully, but because some things were too difficult to share. He hadn't given me any reason not to trust him, but there was still so much I hadn't revealed. So much I couldn't.

I decided to tread carefully, giving him just enough to satisfy his curiosity without opening myself up too much. "Just recently," I said, my voice quiet, careful. "Ever since I was taken," I hesitated, catching myself. "I mean... ever since I left my home. To pay my life debt."

Reed didn't say anything for a long time, and I could feel his gaze on me, searching, but I couldn't bring myself to look him in the eye.

Finally, he broke the silence, his voice soft. "I'm sorry, Sparks. I can't imagine..."

I nodded, quickly changing the subject before I could let myself slip into the darkness of the memories that still haunted me. "It's okay. Really." I cleared my throat and shifted, trying to keep my tone light. "I'm just glad we're not in complete darkness down here."

Reed didn't respond right away, but the silence between us was no longer as heavy. At least for the moment.

Reed seemed content with my answer and didn't push the subject further. "I get them too sometimes," he said, his voice laced with empathy. "That's how I knew keeping yourself grounded would help. Physical contact is usually the best way to keep the night terrors at bay."

I nodded slowly, unsure how to respond to that. "What are yours about?"

Reed let out a small laugh, a teasing edge in his voice. "I'll tell you mine if you tell me yours," he winked. "Well?"

I sighed, reluctant to delve into it. "Let's just agree that nightmares are horrible, and I'm glad there's a method that works to ease them."

"That's fair," Reed yawned, clearly growing tired. He moved back into his cell and plopped down onto his cot, which looked far more comfortable than mine. At least he had a mattress. The cloud of dust that followed his movement made me want to laugh and gag at the same time.

"Let's make a deal," he said, his voice muffled by his position on the cot. "If I get a night terror, I get to wake you up so you can tether me to reality. And vice versa. Deal?"

"Deal," I agreed, a small smile tugging at my lips as I began moving toward my corner. I made a nest on the floor with the blanket Reed had given me the night before. It was surprisingly thick and large enough to cover the entire area where I intended to sleep, with plenty of extra material for me to wrap myself up in. It was far more comfortable than anything I had expected to be placed down here, though I couldn't help but feel a bit of resentment at how much Reed had been favored. Better food, an actual cot, a mattress, and now this blanket, while I was left with barely anything. He was charming, I'd give him that, but who exactly was he making friends with up there? I knew it wasn't Orrin. Maybe he was using that charm of his to flirt his way into better accommodations. He was rather handsome, after all. Or maybe he had to do something more degrading and unspeakable, using his body in exchange for better treatment... I shook my head, not wanting to think about it any longer.

I wasn't tired yet, though Reed clearly was. He had worked all day, and sleep seemed to pull at him, but I couldn't shake the feeling of anxious restlessness in my chest. I would have traded his exhaustion for my anxiety any day if it meant I could just be outside. He needed his rest, though, and I didn't want to take that away from him. But I also wanted him to know how much I appreciated his company.

"Reed?" I said, my voice quiet in the stillness.

"Hmm?" he murmured, clearly half asleep.

"I know it's selfish of me to feel this way, but I'm glad they put you down here. I'm glad I'm not alone."

There was a long pause before he answered, and I feared I'd said the wrong thing, that he might be angry or uncomfortable with my admission. But then I heard his voice. "Me too, Sparks. Me too."

We weren't alone, we were in this hell together, even if it was temporary. I knew that in the morning, I'd wake up alone again, and Reed would go off to whatever work he had. But at least I knew he'd return. I could hold onto that.

For now, though, I needed to get through the night.

I stared through the bars, my eyes catching the two torches now lit on the stone wall across from my cell casting more light into the room. Last night had been a bit easier. I had only one small, panic-filled dream, though I couldn't remember the details. All I knew was that it was bad enough to wake me in a cold sweat, my heart racing. Reed had already been awake by then, and as usual, he'd offered me his hand through the bars. His touch had comforted me enough to fall back asleep, and for the rest of the night, the nightmares didn't return.

By the time I woke up again, Reed was gone. He must have been taken from his cell while I slept. Once again, I was alone down here. Another plate of food was waiting for me, but it looked even worse than yesterdays. I glanced over at Reed's cell, and my eyes caught sight of his plate, pushed up against the bars that connected our cells. It wasn't a lot, but the food looked so much better than mine.

I wasn't sure if he had meant to leave it there for me or if it had just ended up that way, but seeing as mine was practically inedible,

I decided to help myself to his meal. I figured if I was wrong, I could apologize later. After all, Reed had been kind to me, offering comfort without asking for anything in return, I doubt he would be to upset about it.

As I ate, my thoughts drifted to home. I missed it, missed my room, the quiet of the palace, even the bustling halls. I missed the familiar faces. But more than anything, I missed the certainty of being there. Here, in this prison, everything felt strange, disorienting. Time felt impossible to track now. I had no idea how many days had passed since I left home, six? Maybe seven? I should have kept track, marked the walls. But it didn't matter much. The days had melted together, just like everything else.

I wondered about Hayden. He had said he would arrive by the next full moon. I still wasn't sure how much time had passed, but I couldn't help hoping he had given up on his rescue mission. He wouldn't make it here, and I knew my days were numbered. Even if he did, I couldn't go with him. I wouldn't. I couldn't put him in danger, not when it meant risking Theodon's wrath. It was hard to imagine, but I had accepted my fate.

Yet, there was still a part of me that hoped if Hayden ever found a way here, he could take Reed with him. Reed didn't belong in this place. All he had done was steal a few fish, and yet they had him imprisoned next to me, a murderer. Though, I suppose the Caraway didn't know that. Still, Reed's crime and mine didn't even compare, yet here we both were, stuck in these cages.

Reed deserved to be free. He had a family, or someone he was trying to care for. Perhaps Hayden could take him back to the Ember Isle and give him a fresh start if he'd prefer. Our Isle was sick, too, but if Hayden took him, I knew he'd ensure Reed and anyone he was looking after would be cared for. If there was anyone left, that is. I knew Hayden would welcome them on my behalf. My room was empty now, hell, the whole floor was. Reed could stay there if he wanted; I'd see to it.

If he wanted a job, maybe he could even train to become an Ember Guard. He would look incredible in the red, gold, and black leathers, a sword at his side, fierce and proud. His unique eyes, those striking colors, would make him stand out. The thought made me smile despite everything. He deserved more than this prison, more than the life he had been handed.

The next few days passed in a quiet, monotonous rhythm. Reed was always gone by the time I woke up, leaving me to eat my breakfast alone in the silence of my cell. But he never failed to leave his plate of food, fresh and untouched, at the edge of the bars that separated our cells. He never explicitly said it was for me, but he never stopped me from taking it either. I'd eat, my mind wandering as I counted the bars that lined the walls of my cell, then moved on to the bars that separated me from Reed. Back home at least I had books and projects to occupy my time, but here there was nothing except the bars.

My mind drifted back to when I would try to catch the invisible breeze. I'd watch the firelight in my room, counting how many times a silent gust would blow by, causing the flame to dance and sputter. I'd count the seconds until the next sputter, like measuring invisible breaths in the air. I focused on the torch on the wall, my gaze fixed on the flame. One, two, three, eleven, twenty-one... *sputter.* One, two, twenty-five, forty-six... *sputter.* The air down here was definitely inconsistent, yet this game held my attention, offering a simple distraction to pass the time.

Though I did not like being alone, this was preferable to the Orrin's presence. Every time I heard a noise from above, my heart would stop, expecting it to be Orrin coming down to harass me again. But his visits grew less frequent, his presence becoming a rare thing as the days passed. I suppose he figured I wasn't much of a threat, and that I wasn't going to try anything reckless like escaping.

The days blurred into one another, turning into nights. I could only mark the passage of time by the sound of Reed being escorted back to his cell, tired from the day's work. We would share a simple dinner, and he'd tell me about his day, always eager to describe the sunsets he saw. I started to notice the barriers between us slowly lower, inch by inch, as we found comfort in one another's company. Our conversations turned to stories of home, each of us trying to one-up the other, debating which place was more beautiful.

His stories of the Isle of Gust, with its towering snow-capped mountains, had me doubting the beauty of the Ember Isle. The way he described the peaks, how they seemed to rise like the very bones of the earth left me with a sense of awe. The snow, he said, was soft like powder, and the air there had a crisp, clean bite to it. The image of those frozen heights lingered in my mind, and I couldn't help but think that, in that moment, Reed had won the contest of beauty. I gave him that one.

"I've never seen snow," I admitted quietly, almost as if the thought itself embarrassed me.

"Well, maybe you just need to be a bit more well-traveled like me," Reed teased.

"Once you hit the Isle of Mist, you can cross world traveling off your bucket list," I said with a small giggle."

"This is true, though I hope if I ever visit there, it's under better circumstances." He laughed. "But I will say, maybe I'm biased, but no sand or dirt could ever compare to a blanket of fresh snow. You'll have to see it in person sometime."

"What's it like?" I asked, intrigued.

"It's like the sand on your home, but softer, and, colder, of course." He laughed softly.

"I hope you get to see it again someday," I said, my words coming out softer than I intended, hoping they didn't sound too heavy.

"If we both survive this," Reed said, his tone suddenly serious, "I'll take you there."

"Promise?" I asked, holding out a pinky, a playful challenge in my voice.

"I promise."

He linked his pinky with mine, sealing the deal. I knew, deep down, that it would never happen. But for a moment, it was enough to believe in something, even if it was just a distant fantasy. It was a small flicker of hope in the otherwise dark and endless days. I held onto that warmth as sleep claimed me, unaware of what awaited when I woke.

I opened my eyes in a rush, my heart racing in my chest. For a moment, I was disoriented, tangled in the nightmare that had taken hold of me. The muffled sounds of pain and quiet pleas reached my ears. At first, I thought it was part of the nightmare, a lingering echo of my own fears. But then I realized—this wasn't my nightmare; I hadn't had one. I had slept through the night, yet the small, muffled screams were still there.

"Please…stop, don't take them... don't cut them..."

Reed. My heart stopped, and panic surged through me. This time, he was the one suffering. I listened as his voice trembled with fear, trapped in his own nightmare. I hadn't believed him when he said he had nightmares too. I'd thought he was just trying to make me feel less embarrassed about my own, but there he was, in his cell, shaking with fear.

I pushed myself up, needing to get to him. If I could just wake him up, pull him from his sleep, the fear could stop. He'd been my anchor through the worst of my own dreams, always there to pull me back from the edge. We had a deal and now, it was my turn.

"Reed!" I called, my voice hoarse, barely more than a whisper in the cold, damp air of the prison.

There was no response. I strained my ears, listening to the sounds of his quiet suffering. He was shaking, his body vibrating as if caught in the grip of some unseen torment.

I moved toward the bars separating us. I could hear him muttering, his words broken and ragged. Whatever was happening in his dream, it sounded terrible, painful, even.

"Please, don't take them," he whimpered, and the sound of it sent a sharp pain through my chest. "They're all I have left of her... don't... don't take them."

"Reed, please," I whispered, desperation creeping into my voice as I reached through the bars, stretching my hand toward him. My fingers brushed against his as I reached for his hand, hoping my touch could be his tether to reality, pulling him from whatever nightmare he was trapped in. His hand was cold and clammy, slick with sweat that only a large amount of fear could muster in these cold cells.

"Reed, please wake up! It's me!" I cried out, my heart pounding as I tightened my grip on his hand.

For a moment, nothing changed. Then, with a sudden jolt, his hand squeezed mine back. But it wasn't the comforting grip I was used to. His fingers slid from my grasp with unnatural force, and a sharp pain shot up my arm as he twisted my wrist to the point of almost breaking. I gasped, my breath catching in my throat.

"Reed!" I whimpered through gritted teeth, trying to pull away. "Let go!"

His eyes snapped open, and the fog in his gaze cleared only slightly. For a moment, I saw nothing but confusion, fear, and a hollow emptiness in his eyes. The person I knew, the one who had been there for me in my nights of terror, seemed so far away.

"Sparks?" he said, his tone filled with confusion, all the while his grip on my wrist was still relentless, causing another whimper to escape my lips as I tried to pull my arm back.

"Sparks," he muttered, his voice strained, his grip loosening as he realized what he had done. "I didn't mean..."

He let go completely, and I pulled my wrist closer, the ache still pulsing through me. But I didn't care. I didn't want him to feel guilty. I was used to pain. I'd always been used to pain.

He backed away, retreating into the shadows of his cell. The distance between us seemed unbearable now, like some invisible wall had risen between us.

"I'm sorry," he whispered.

"It's okay, I was just worried," I said as I rubbed my wrist, the pain still lingering. "Please come back to the bars."

"I don't want you to see me like this," he said, his voice low.

I swallowed, trying to ignore the sting in my wrist, the way my heart twisted at the thought of him retreating further into himself. I didn't want him to hide.

"Like what?" I asked. He told me he had night terrors. He knew I would know that him waking up like this was a possibility.

"Weak," was all he said.

"It's okay to be weak, Reed," I said softly, my voice barely above a whisper. "It's okay to show vulnerability. I understand that more than most."

I was all too familiar with weakness. I understood what it meant to feel powerless and to have no control, and whatever Reed was dreaming about, it was clear someone was hurting him.

I got closer to the bars and reached my hand out. "We made a deal, remember? If you helped me through my nightmares, I'd help you through yours."

He didn't move, and my chest tightened. I couldn't stand seeing him like this, alone, hurting, and unwilling to let me help.

"It's... it's nothing," he muttered, but I could hear the cracks in his voice. "Just a dream. It doesn't matter."

"It does, Reed. Please, let me help you," I begged, my voice breaking.

He looked up at me, his eyes dull with the remnants of his dream, distant and lost. "What did you hear?"

I hesitated for a moment, unsure if I should tell him or just lie. I could just say I heard him thrashing around on the floor or heard various groans of pain. But I needed to know what was happening in there. Though he never pressed me for the details of my nightmares, and even if he did, I probably wouldn't tell him, maybe Reed would feel comfortable enough to tell me about his. I had to be honest with him.

"You were begging someone to stop," I said quietly. "You were asking them not to take… them. Who were you talking to, Reed? What were they taking?"

His face grew pale, his gaze shifting to the floor. He seemed to shrink further into himself, folding in on the pain that had haunted him for years. "We're talking about dreams now? Tell me, Sparks, do you want to go first?"

I never told him what mine were about, how every time I closed my eyes, I could see Hawthorne's dead, bloodied body with an arrow protruding from his chest, or sometimes a knife in his throat, or sometimes being stabbed in the belly by my own hands. My inner guilt and shame always played out in my nightmares. I never told him how, in my dreams, I prayed for death to take me and just get it over with, anything to ensure my home, my family, and Hayden were all safe. How I just wanted my worthless life to be over so Theodon could judge me for my actions. No, I couldn't tell him that. I didn't want him to see me as a murderer or as someone who had already given up, not when there was still a chance that Reed could get out of here.

"I suppose not," was all I could say without opening that box. Still, I wanted to comfort him. "You don't have to tell me if you don't want to, but please let me be your tether," I said, sticking my hand out further for emphasis, even though his gaze remained on the floor, still clearly trying to work through whatever had happened in his nightmare.

"Why?" he asked quietly, as I watched his head lift slightly.

"That was the deal, wasn't it? Or are you going back on it?" I let out a small laugh to ease the tension. "Guess I'll have to find my own stuffed bear to pull me back to reality when the dark dreams take over."

"No," he said as he finally looked up at me, my hand still outstretched. "I can still be your tether."

"Then let me be yours."

He didn't move any closer. Instead, his eyes went to the floor. "Was I really talking in my sleep?" he asked, his voice filled with what sounded like shame.

"Yes, and whatever was happening, it sounded painful."

"It was."

"What happened?" I asked one more time, hoping he would trust me enough to just tell me, to just open up a small amount, and realize he could confide in me. I would not judge him. I would only listen and understand and be there for him after it was all said and done.

"I'd rather not talk about it," he said, his voice quiet, eyes still locked on the cold stone floor beneath him.

I nodded slowly, respecting the boundary he'd just drawn. He didn't owe me his pain, not unless he was ready to share it. And the thought of pushing him felt wrong, like prodding at a wound still raw and bleeding.

"That's alright," I said gently. "But if you want to talk about something else... we can do that too."

"You should go back to sleep, Sparks," Reed muttered, though his voice lacked the usual sharp edge.

"I'm not tired," I replied, settling in a little closer to the bars that separated us.

Whatever he'd see in his dreams had left a shadow on his face that lingered even now. I just wanted him to know he wasn't alone. That down here, in the cold and the quiet, we still had each other.

"You know," I said, trying to lighten the mood, "since neither of us is in the mood to talk about nightmares... how about we talk about the other kind of dreams? The good ones. The strange ones. Anything to chase the shadows away."

For a while, he didn't respond. His brow furrowed, like the idea of 'good dreams' hadn't crossed his mind in a long time. But then, slowly, I saw a flicker of something in his eyes, something softer, almost amused.

"I don't know," he said eventually, his lips curving into the faintest smirk. "Can't say I remember many."

I leaned in, hopeful. "Come on. Even you must've had one decent dream. Or a strange one at least. I'm not picky."

He shrugged. "Maybe," he said, teasing now. "But I'm not sure I'd want to tell you."

From where I sat, I could see his body start to relax. The tension in his shoulders eased as he slowly leaned closer to the bars between us. His eyes softened, the sharp edge of whatever nightmare he'd had beginning to fade. Just talking seemed to be helping him let go of it, even if only a little.

"Well," I offered, "why don't I start?"

Reed gave a small nod, and I knew I was breaking through.

"Hmmm. There was one I used to have a lot. Probably a dozen times, if not more. I was getting married."

"Typical," he muttered with a dry chuckle.

"Yeah, yeah," I said, laughing softly. "Fine, it's a cliché. But it was one of my favorites."

"So?" he asked, lifting a brow. "Who was the lucky groom?"

"It was always my brother's best friend, Adan," I said, the name stirring a swirl of warmth and ache. Thoughts of home, of family, flickered through me, but I pushed them aside. This wasn't about me. I was here to comfort Reed, not spiral into my own mess of memories. "I had the biggest crush on him when I was younger."

Reed smirked, teasing again. "Was he one of those many males you claimed to have kissed and done plenty more with back in the oasis?"

I blinked, caught off guard. I'd forgotten I'd even said that, but somehow Reed remembered. I didn't want to lie, not when this was about being honest with each other. If I wanted him to open up, I had to be willing to do the same. So, I decided the truth was the best way forward.

"No," I said quietly, my eyes drifting to my boots, *his* boots. "Adan was just a crush. Someone I knew I could never have. Besides, I don't think he ever really saw me that way."

"Then he was a fool," Reed said simply, like it was the most obvious thing in the world.

I looked up and realized he had moved closer again. Our eyes met, and something fluttered in my stomach. I wasn't sure if it was his closeness or his words, but I knew one thing for certain: I was glad he was here.

"So," Reed said, his voice gentler now, "tell me more about this wedding."

I smiled faintly, letting the dream wash over me like warm sunlight. "It took place in the Ember Palace's throne room," I began, my voice soft. "The entire space was transformed with walls draped in silk, gold and ruby accents catching the light from the chandeliers above. It was like stepping into a sunrise. Even my dress was something out of a fairytale with golden thread woven through every seam and tiny ruby stones sewn into the fabric so that when I moved, it sparkled like fire. The scent of desert lilies filled the air, one of my favorite scents. They were tucked into every corner, spilling from vases, even braided into my hair."

I paused for a breath, letting the image settle between us before continuing.

"Everyone was there. The entire kingdom, and for once, I wasn't hiding. I wasn't trying to shrink myself down or disappear into the background. I was seen. Truly seen. It was my moment to shine, and I stepped into it like I belonged."

I paused, letting the memory dance in my mind.

"For once, I was stepping into the sun, the center of everything. Walking down the aisle, all eyes on me, not with judgment, but with admiration. And Adan… he always looked so handsome in black and gold. I was happy to be marrying one of my closest friends, but it was more than that. It was about being seen. Being me. Fully and without shame."

I lingered in the warmth of the dream a moment longer, until Reed's quiet voice brought me back.

"I'm sorry your parents made you feel like you had to live in the shadows. And I'm sorry that the first time you stepped into the light… it brought you here."

I shrugged, brushing away the ache threatening to rise. I didn't want to go there, not tonight.

"Alright," I said, clearing my throat and offering him a small smile. "I told you one of my favorites. Now it's your turn. What's a dream you often find yourself replaying in your mind?"

He hesitated, his gaze drifting back down to the floor. Silence stretched between us for a few heartbeats, and I could tell even the thought of sharing something good, something that might bring him peace, felt foreign to him. Like happiness wasn't something he was used to handling out loud.

Finally, he spoke.

"There's one I have," he said, his voice softer than before. "It's more of a memory than a dream. At least, I think it is. Over the years, the details have started to blur, and now I can't tell which parts are real and which are just things my mind added in, still, it's my favorite."

"I'm listening," I said gently, crossing my legs on the cold stone floor, settling in like we had all the time in the world.

He stared past me, not really seeing me anymore, as if the memory had pulled him away.

"I was really young," he began slowly, "back home on Gust. My mother and I lived in this small cabin near the upper ridges of the mountains. The air was always crisp, and the clouds would sometimes sit low enough that they'd kiss the roof. We lived quietly, tucked away from the rest of the world. Most fae from Gust prefer it that way, the solitude and the silence. But this day was different."

His expression shifted, softening with the memory. I could almost see the child version of him in his eyes.

"My mother woke me up before the sun had risen. I remember the way the cold nipped at my skin when I pulled on my boots, and how the sky was just starting to turn gray with morning. She said we were going down the mountain, and I was instantly wide-eyed. I'd never gone that far before. I was practically bouncing with excitement, just to see something new, anything beyond the snow-covered trees and stone paths I knew like the back of my hand."

He paused, a quiet laugh escaping him.

"She made it fun. We didn't take the main roads, we traveled through narrow back paths, ducking between trees, staying low, keeping to the shadows. She told me we were on a secret mission. Like spies," he said, with a faint, wistful smile. "She was dramatic about it, too, creeping around, whispering like we were being hunted. I played along, loving every second of it. But even then, I could tell it wasn't just a game. She needed us to stay hidden, and I didn't understand why."

I leaned in a little, caught up in his words. "So where was she taking you?"

"In Gust, when a fae child is born with wings, they're celebrated," Reed said, his voice distant, like he was speaking through the veil of memory. "But the real moment, the rite of passage, comes when they turn ten. That's when they take their first flight. By then, their wings are strong enough to carry them. It's more than just a family event, it's a public ceremony, a tradition. Fae from all over Gust come to watch, and even the royal family attends. They use the event to observe the children, and sometimes they'll offer positions in the Gust Guard to those who show real promise."

My eyebrows lifted in surprise. "I think I remember reading something about that in a textbook once... but I didn't realize how significant it was. I had no idea the kings and queens were involved, or that it was a sort of scouting process."

Reed gave a small nod. "A choice to join the guard is always given, never forced, but it is a huge honor to be asked. My mother kept us at a distance, but I could still see everything, every detail like it was painted in light. Fae after fae climbed to the peak, leapt off... some fell for several terrifying seconds before their wings finally caught the wind and they soared. Others didn't make it on the first try. I remember watching one fall hard as he hit the slope and had to be healed immediately. But once he was mended, he climbed again. And this time, he flew."

He paused, the memory clearly vivid in his mind. "Watching them rise into the clouds, wings stretched wide... it was the most beautiful thing I'd ever seen. It wasn't just about flight, it was about being unbound. I remember tugging on my mother's sleeve and telling her I wanted to do that someday. That I wanted to fly. To be that free."

I could hear the warmth in his voice, the wonder of a boy who'd dreamed of the sky.

"She looked at me," he said quietly, "and her face lit up. Like she saw something in me. She told me that one day, I'd be capable of amazing things. That I'd soar in my own way."

I tilted my head, curiosity tugging at me. "But... you don't have wings?"

"No," he said simply, the smile fading from his voice. "I think she meant it differently. That one day, I'd do something worth being celebrated. Something for the good of Gust." His voice trailed off, growing smaller. "How am I doing, Mother?" he said suddenly, raising his hand to gesture around at the cold stone walls of the cell. His tone was laced with sarcasm, but beneath it was pain.

My heart squeezed. I didn't want him to carry that weight alone.

"I think she would be proud of you, Reed," I said, meeting his eyes. "The reason you're here, what brought you here, was noble. That alone, I believe, is something she'd be proud of."

"I'm not always so sure," he whispered, barely loud enough for me to hear.

"Reed, look at me," I said softly. "You're going to get out of here. You're going to go home, or wherever it is you want to be. And you will make a difference in this world. In fact, you already have."

"How?"

I drew in a shaky breath, struggling to find the right words. "I... I know I don't have much longer in this world. But what I do know is that having you here, through all of it, is the only thing that's kept me going. Honestly, I'd probably still be curled up in that corner, like the first night you saw me here, if it weren't for you. So, please, just know I'm grateful you're here. And I believe, with everything in me, that one day, you'll do something extraordinary."

I extended my hand through the bars, hoping he'd take it. "And if that nightmare tries to take hold of you again," I added, my voice resolute, "it'll have to go through me first."

He didn't speak right away. His eyes stayed on the floor, tracking invisible patterns, like he was trying to absorb every word I'd just said. Then slowly, his gaze met mine.

"Okay," he said at last, and his hand found mine.

A sharp pain shot up my arm, and a faint whimper escaped my lips before I could stop it. I'd forgotten about the injury to my wrist. I tried to steady my breathing, tried not to show it, but the moment I saw the worry flash across Reed's face, I knew he'd noticed.

"Fuck," he said, as he dropped my hand. "I'm sorry... I didn't mean to hurt you when you woke me up. I... I wasn't... I didn't know where I was..."

"It's alright," I said, cutting him off. "It's fine, see?" I flexed my wrist, biting my lip from the pain to save him from any shred of guilt he might feel.

"It's been so long since those night terrors have found their way to me," he said. "I just get so lost sometimes. I would never purposely hurt you like that, Eli."

"I know." And something in me truly did know that. "Now, please come back here and gently take my hand so you can get some sleep."

After some consideration, he did as I requested, his hand becoming warmer now. The feeling offered me some relief from the tinge of pain in my wrist that was slowly disappearing.

"I didn't mean to wake you, Sparks," he said, as he let himself lie on the floor, pulling me down with him.

"It's alright. I just wanted to make sure you were okay."

"I am," he said. "I mean, I should be fine now. I hope you can get some more sleep."

"That's the thing about confinement and nothing to do all day," I joked. "You get plenty of rest."

"Yeah, I suppose so."

The room went silent, just the sound and hum of our breathing echoing off the stone walls. My eyes began to drift closed as Reed's thumb rubbed soothing circles over my wrist, and I did the same to the back of his hand, just wanting him to know I was there.

"Sparks?" Reed whispered.

"Hmmm?" I mumbled, almost half asleep.

"I truly hope that one day you can step out from the shadows and be seen," Reed said, his voice full of sincerity. "Your people don't know what they're missing, the amazing person they never got the chance to know. The brave fae who could've been the brightest ruler Ember has ever seen."

His words settled into the silence like a warm blanket, wrapping around the cold edges of doubt inside me.

"That was never my future," I murmured, my voice growing soft as sleep began to pull me under. "But... thank you for thinking it could've been."

As the evenings stretched on, Reed was able to sleep through the nights, while my own nightmares became fewer and fewer, thanks to his presence. I had to admit, there were nights when I woke up, not from a nightmare, but because I just wanted to be near him. There were a few times when I found myself reaching across the narrow gap between our cells, my hand stretching through the bars as if instinctively seeking his warmth. He never said anything, never mentioned it, but a small part of me wondered if he needed that connection, too.

It became a comforting routine, this fragile bond between us. But when I awoke in the mornings, Reed would always be gone, and I would find my hand, empty and outstretched, still resting between the cold metal of the bars.

My thoughts had been drifting to Reed all day, and they didn't stop even when I fell back asleep. I found myself lying on a soft patch of grass, gazing up through the trees that arched above me like a canopy. The sun-streaked golden beams between the branches, warming my skin and contrasting with the coolness of the grass beneath my back. I was in the forest on Ivy Isle, or at least, that's how I imagined it during the day.

As the sun began to fade, a figure hovered over me, blocking its warmth from my skin. It was Reed above me, his body pressing into mine, gently pinning me to the ground.

"Enjoying the view, Sparks?" he teased, his voice like a familiar whisper.

"I am now," I replied, my voice husky.

His hands sculpted around my face, brushing back my untamed copper hair as though he were trying to get a better look at me. The softness of his touch trailed down my throat, then continued down my ribcage. His fingertips were like whispers against my skin, sending a shiver through me that made me arch into him. It had been so long since I'd had a dream like this. Most nights, it was Adan above me, his hands on my skin, making me moan. But this? This was different. It was new. Unfamiliar. Maybe even dangerous. But I didn't care.

His eyes burned into mine, and I felt more desired than I ever had.

"I love this dress on you," Reed murmured softly, his hand sliding up the fabric of my skirt.

I let my gaze slip down to meet his. I was back in my crimson dress, but it was like new again, like the first night I wore it. I felt beautiful in this gown, and with the way his hands were gliding slowly up my bare thigh, teasingly slow, I knew he thought so too.

"Is this okay?" Reed whispered, his fingers almost reaching the delicate, sensitive part of me at my center. I nodded, no hesitation. A small smirk curled on his lips, and I felt the tension in my body shift.

His hand froze for a moment, but only to rest on my inner thigh, the other clutching a handful of fabric from my skirt. Before I could ask what was happening, his lips were on mine. The kiss was gentle at first, but I felt the pressure of his grip tighten on the skirt, while the hand on my thigh began to squeeze. Not too tight, but enough to send a clear message: he wanted both tenderness and something much more primal. I had no real sexual experience beyond a kiss, but I'd learned to satisfy myself over the years. I knew what I liked. But the thought of having someone else experiment with me sent a thrilling wave of heat through my body.

Reed's kiss turned from gentle to possessive. His tongue pushed into my mouth, invading me with a demand that mirrored the heat flooding through my veins. My hands traveled beneath his shirt, up his back, dragging my nails across his skin. He matched my rhythm, his grip tightening as his other hand slid further up my inner thigh.

"Reed," I moaned softly, the sound escaping me as his fingers found my sensitive spot. He circled it lazily, his touch sending ripples of pleasure through my body. I couldn't help but squirm beneath him, the weight of his body pushing me into the earth.

"Already so wet for me," Reed teased, his lips curving into a smirk.

My hands shot to the ground, fisting handfuls of dirt and grass beneath me. I held on as his fingers continued their maddening exploration.

He maintained a slow, steady pace, drawing small, tantalizing circles.

Occasionally, his finger would trace the outside of my core, teasing my entrance but never quite giving me what I wanted. It was like he was testing my limits, playing with my body in a way I couldn't fully control.

As I tensed, my thighs clamping together in response to the pleasure building within me, Reed removed his finger. I stiffened, the absence of contact sharp, and I couldn't stop myself from clenching.

"We can stop," Reed said softly, beginning to pull away from me.

"No," I breathed, my voice desperate as I wrapped my arms around him, pulling him back toward me. I kissed him fiercely, bruising his lips with my own. He withdrew his hand from under my skirt, and I couldn't decide whether to feel relieved or disappointed. The disappointment faded quickly when his hands found a new place over my breasts. I felt the heat of his palms through the fabric of the dress, but the pressure wasn't enough. The fabric was in the way, and I needed it gone.

I surged up, pushing myself into a sitting position. Reed leaned back, surprised by my sudden movement.

"Can you help me with the laces? I still can't reach them," I said coyly, turning my back to him.

"I'd love to."

With each pull of the ribbon, I felt my heavy breasts slowly becoming free from the fabric. My nipples hardened, anticipating the moment when Reed's hands would soon be on them.

Reeds warm breath tickled the back of my neck, sending a shiver that began at my spine and rippled down to my core as the fabric fell away.

I slowly turned to face him, feeling no shame or embarrassment in my nudity. But then my eyes went wide when I saw it wasn't Reed in front of me. "Hawthorne?" I choked out.

"El, you're undone," he said in a sly teasing voice.

I took a deep breath, trying to steady myself.

"This isn't real," I said, needing to remind myself.

"Not real?" Hawthorne questioned, his lips curling into a smirk before pressing them to mine. My breasts flattened against his chest as he held me tight. "Is this real enough for you?"

His kiss felt almost identical to Reed's, only his taste was more earthy and full of pine rather than Reeds usual mint.

Hawthorne was undeniably handsome, so maybe it didn't matter who pleasured me in this fantasy. Maybe this was just what my body needed, a release, no matter the source.

"Hawthorne," I moaned into his lips as he deepened the kiss.

"I'm glad you finally took me up on my offer," he murmured, his breath warm against my skin.

His lips trailed down to my neck, starting with soft, gentle kisses that sent shivers across my skin. My breathing quickened as his hands caressed my bare stomach, causing my body to tense under his touch.

One hand gripped my waist, while the other slid up to my exposed breast. His mouth became more insistent on my neck, his teeth grazing my skin, sending a sharp thrill through me. The sudden roughness matched the squeeze of his hand around my breast, pinching my nipple between his fingers.

"Oh Theodon," I gasped, closing my eyes and throwing my head back as pleasure coursed through me. My arms wrapped around his body, pulling him closer, needing him closer.

"Sparks," he moaned into my neck.

When I looked down, I saw shaggy salt-and-pepper hair pressed against my skin.

"Reed?" I asked, completely confused, as my mind scrambled to reconcile the shift from Hawthorne to Reed.

"Who else would it be?" he asked.

A knot tightened in my chest. The confusion swirled within me as I tried to make sense of it all. Having them both here, in my mind, Reed and Hawthorne, felt like a bad omen and I couldn't shake the feeling that this might turn into something darker. I had to wake up before that happened.

"I want to wake up," I whispered, my voice strained with unease.

"No," Reed said, his tone steady as he pressed his lips to mine once more. No not Reed, he was Hawthorne again. I was kissing Hawthorne now. My resistance faltered, and I melted into him, caught up in the intensity of the moment.

But then, the clarity hit me again. Murder. I had murdered someone, and now, that very someone was here, in my dream, offering me pleasure. I didn't deserve it. This moment, this dream, was a lie. My guilt clung to me, and I knew the pleasure I felt could never erase what I had done.

I pulled away from him, my heart heavy. I saw the sadness in his eyes, but I couldn't let this continue.

"I'm sorry," I whispered. "But we can't."

I reached for my bodice, pressing it to my chest as if that simple action could shield me from my emotions. "I need to wake up before this becomes something worse," I added, my voice trembling as I closed my eyes.

When I opened them, Hawthorne was no longer there, it was only Reed. I watched as he held out his hand, reminding me of his tether, and said, "I can protect you from it, remember?"

"You can't," I replied, shutting my eyes tight and focusing on waking my body up.

I took a deep breath as my eyes flew open, and I found myself back in my cell. I already missed the dream, but I knew it was for the best. Slowly, I let my hands travel down to my core, checking for any physical evidence of the dream. Sure enough, I was drenched and now left wanting. But I would not act on my desires, not here. I didn't deserve that release.

A hearty laugh echoed off the stone walls, and I spun around quickly. Orrin was sitting on a stool at the front of my cell, and the bulge straining against his leathers made it clear he had been watching me sleep for some time.

"You moan in your sleep, you know," he began, his voice sending shivers through my body. "Sweet dreams, I suspect?" He placed a hand over his covered erection and gave his leather pants a squeeze.

I retreated to the back of my cell, putting as much space between us as possible. His presence utterly repulsed me, filling me with unease and discomfort. I felt violated, uncertain of what he may have witnessed or overheard while I slept.

"Reed, huh?" he sneered. "Dreaming of your little cellmate? And was that Hawthorne's name I heard? Seems the innocent little flame has a dark side to her," he said, letting out a sinister laugh. "Wanting to fuck the dead Ivy Prince hmm?"

I remained silent, refusing to give this repulsive individual any further attention. I should have felt ashamed, but instead I was consumed by anger and fear. This male had terrified me from the moment we met, and with the king still absent, I feared what a desperate, defiant male might do. I would simply let him vent his taunts and jeers, hoping he would eventually lose interest and leave.

"You know," he said, continuing to grope himself through his leathers, "my offer to service you is still open, if you're interested. Just a little trade in pleasure and flesh."

"No, thank you," I replied through gritted teeth. I didn't want to engage further, but I hoped that repeating my refusal would compel him to back down.

"I can make it real good for you, Princess," he groaned, reaching to expose himself fully. "Despite my unsavory appearance, I can be quite gentle," he said, stroking himself slowly. "Or I can be rough," his hand now moving faster, "whichever you prefer."

His actions turned my stomach.

"I said no, thank you," I reiterated, drawing my knees to my chest in the hope that he would finally take the hint.

Orrin stood up, towering over me outside my cell. "I believe I only gave you two options, gentle or rough," he said. He added with a smirk, "I'll even let you call me Reed when you moan, or how about Hawthorne?"

I glared at him defiantly. "You could never make me moan like Reed or Hawthorne with a cock that small!" I hissed, my anger boiling over.

Orrin's eyes narrowed, his voice rising with fury. "What did you say?"

"Keep your disgusting little cock away from me, or I'll tell King Caraway and he can punish you as he sees fit for touching his prisoner!" I spat.

Orrin let out a dark laugh. "You think the king gives a fuck about what I do to you? Just as long as I don't kill you." He paused, then spoke again, menace dripping from every word. "So, for the last time what'll it be, gentle or rough?"

"Fuck you!"

"Rough it is then," Orrin said, unlocking my cell and throwing the door open.

I was backed into a corner, with nowhere left to go. The rage burning in his eyes, coupled with his still-erect arousal, sent waves of panic through me. In a desperate attempt to fight back, I began furiously kicking my legs towards him. When faced with the choice of fight or flight, I chose to stand my ground like the fae I was. My kicks landed a few times before he caught my ankle and yanked me closer.

"Knock it the fuck off!" he yelled as I struggled to free myself from his grasp.

"Let me go!" I screamed as Orrin pinned me to the floor, his body trapping mine.

"You're only making me want you more, Princess," he moaned. I spat in his face, continuing to fight against his grip, but it was futile.

The grim reality of the situation was setting in. He was too strong, and I had no chance of fighting him off. Tears stung my eyes as I resigned myself to the inevitable. My first time with a male would not be the sweet, passionate experience I had hoped for, but rather painful and terrifying. "Please," I whimpered, "don't do this."

"I gave you the option for it to be gentle, but then you had to open your fucking mouth," Orrin said, his legs forcing my thighs apart. "You know, I overheard your confession to the Ivy King about still being a virgin." He leaned down, sniffing my hair as he whispered in my ear, "The first time always hurts, but if you behave, maybe next time I'll actually make it nice for you. You might even find it pleasurable."

I watched as he reached towards his waistband. Seizing the moment, I scratched at his face with my free hand. Warm droplets hit my skin. I had drawn blood, and a sense of pride washed over me.

"You bitch!" Orrin recoiled, creating an opening. I snapped my knee up, connecting with his groin. He yelped and doubled over. This was my chance. I scrambled back, clearing his body, and rushed to my feet. I had no plan beyond escaping Orrin; running was far better than the alternative.

I slammed the cell door behind me and frantically searched for the keys to lock him in, but they were nowhere to be found. Precious time for my escape was slipping away. Orrin still writhed in pain, but I knew he'd recover soon. The only exit I saw was the door up the steps, leading into the castle halls. I'd rather risk getting caught by another guard than be trapped here with this rapist.

I raced up the steps, my stiff legs protesting after days of inactivity. Driven by fear and adrenaline, I pushed forward. But halfway up, something rough and leafy clamped around my ankle, yanking me back down. My face slammed into the hard stone stairs with a sickening crack, plunging me into darkness. As Orrin's vines dragged me back down, my vision slowly returned, but the rough steps tore and bloodied my face with each agonizing inch.

My broken nose pulsed with pain, blood pooling on the steps where I finally came to a stop. "Please," I weakly pleaded, but Orrin just sneered. He yanked down my underwear, exposing me to the cold air.

"You had your chance!" he hissed as I felt him pull at my hair, the chain of my pendant snapping.

Orrin pressed his body against mine, trapping my front against the stone steps. "Looks like I got myself a little gift," he laughed as my chest felt bare where my pendant once rested. "Now scream for me," he growled, as I felt his arousal slipping through my folds, searching for my entrance.

Gritting my teeth, I prepared to let out the scream he wanted, a scream I didn't want to give him. However, before he could push himself into me, before I could utter a sound, the door at the top of the steps flew open. I raised my head as much as I could, blood dripping down my chin, and saw Reed at the top being escorted by another guard.

"What the fuck?" a male voice exclaimed, though I couldn't tell if it was Reed, the new guard, or even Orrin.

"Help," I groaned weakly, my plea punctuated by the warm liquid flowing down my face. I couldn't tell if it was more blood or a flood of tears.

Suddenly, I saw the guard at the top of the steps tumble off the open side, landing with a thud on the stone floor below. A strong gust of air rushed past me, and the weight pinning me down vanished. As I started to flip my body over, I heard a voice that sounded a lot like Reed's yell, "You fucker!" followed by the unmistakable sound of knuckles hitting flesh.

"Stop! I yield!" Orrin's voice cried out.

I rapidly blinked my blurry eyes and surveyed the scene at the bottom of the steps. Reed was straddling Orrin, delivering a flurry of punches to his smug face. Vines had spread over Reed's hands, and I realized Orrin had attempted to use his elemental magic to hold him back. "Hurt her again and I'll kill you," Reed screamed, his fists relentlessly pummeling Orrin's face.

Orrin was using his vines to try and restrain him, but it didn't look like he was truly fighting back, not even trying to stop Reed's fists as they pounded into him again and again. I couldn't tell if that was a testament to Reed's strength, even with the iron collar, or if Orrin was holding back out of fear he might kill him without the king's orders.

"Reed?" I whimpered, needing confirmation this was real and not a dream.

"Eli," he replied as he whipped his head towards my direction, his voice pained as he took in my battered appearance, his gaze shifting down to my thighs where my underwear still clung after Orrin violently pulled them down, leaving me bare and painfully exposed.

Orrin lay motionless beneath Reed. Once Reed tore his eyes from me, I saw his fist clench. "You're a fucking rapist monster!" he screamed, landing one final, sickening blow. A crunch echoed off the stone walls, and Orrin's lifeless body began pooling with blood. Reed's last punch had been fatal.

I groaned, my vision blurring from either blood dripping in my eyes or a concussion starting to form. "What did you do?" I asked. If he had killed the guard, then someone from Reed's home would pay the price. Not to mention the punishment and pain the Ivy King would surely bestow upon Reed as soon as he returned. Caraway may even deem Reed's life a worthy repayment for Orrin's death, and he could be killed.

I tried to push myself up from the steps, but my body began to fold in on itself. "Whoa," Reed said, catching me before I tumbled down the stone steps. "I am so sorry, Eli," he gently whispered as he cradled me in his arms, lifting me from the floor.

My eyes scanned the room. Orrin's dead, bloodied body lay still on the ground, and the other guard, who must have been escorting Reed to his cell, was also on the ground, but his slight groans and movements indicated he was still alive. The last thing I noticed was the open door at the top of the stairs. Reed's chance to escape and avoid his inevitable punishment. I knew I would have to stay to fulfill the debt, but Reed could be free to sail away back to the Isle of Gust, away from this horror story.

"The door," I groaned, "the guards are down."

"There's more in the castle," Reed cut me off quickly, carrying me back to my cell. "We would never make it out, especially in your condition." He laid me on my makeshift bed, wiping some of the blood from my face onto his sleeve.

"Not me," I winced. "You. You can run, leave before they find out what we did."

"What *we* did?" Reed's face turned red with anger. "This isn't your fault, Eli. Don't you ever sit there and blame yourself for what that piece of shit tried to do." His expression quickly shifted from anger to anguish. "*Tried* to do," Reed said again. "I got here in time, right?"

I nodded and tightly clenched my eyes, a flare of pain overcoming my face as I realized what he was truly asking. "He wasn't able to," I paused, unsure of how to continue. "You got here in time." Reed took a deep breath, and I knew he understood.

"Not soon enough though," he muttered as he continued to wipe the blood from my skin.

"You need to leave, Reed."

"I'm not leaving you, Eli," he said, his face twisting in pain, no doubt from the sight of the gashes that now marked my face. His fingers trailed to my iron collar, and I knew he realized I couldn't heal. "Fuck!" Reed stormed out of my cell and headed back towards Orrin's body.

"What are you doing?" I asked, flipping myself around to get a better view.

"We need to get that collar off so you can heal. Orrin must have the key."

I watched Reed frantically search Orrin's body. Part of me hoped he wouldn't find it, so I could delay the inevitable of revealing my uselessness and weakness without magic. The last bit of power Hayden had charged my pendant with was gone, in fact the entire pendant was no longer hanging from my neck as I saw it clenched in Orrin's dead hand. I needed someone to heal me, someone willing to exhaust their own magic on me. *The prince slayer with a life debt.* This wasn't a wound I thought I could die from, but it would be painful to suffer through as it healed on its own, leaving permanent damage to my face.

"Fuck!" Reed yelled, kicking Orrin's corpse, signaling to me that he had been unsuccessful in finding the key.

"It's okay," I assured him, rolling onto my back as the pain in my face throbbed through my entire head. "Royal blood or not, I'm too weak anyway. I would need someone to heal me with their own magic to avoid the scarring."

"Okay, I can try," Reed breathed out, running back to my side.

"You have your collar on too, but thanks for offering," I let out a small humming breath, hoping to distract myself from the pain that seemed to be overtaking my consciousness as my eyes felt heavy.

"What the fuck happened?" A hoarse voice yelled from the entrance to my cell.

Another gust of air rushed past me, drawing my attention to the unfolding events. Reed was no longer by my side in the cell; instead, he was now grappling with the guard who had entered, his fists gripping the guard's leather uniform.

"You need to help her!" Reed commanded. He had just killed an Ivy Guard, and now it seemed he was threatening another. Did he have a death wish?

"Looks like she got what she deserved after what she did to Orrin," the guard sneered at me, shoving Reed off him.

"*I* killed Orrin!" Reed pushed the guard back.

"You what?" the guard screamed in Reed's face and then suddenly, a physical altercation broke out between the two.

Through my hazy vision, I could see the guard's vines wrapping around the two as they continued to brawl. If Reed didn't overpower this guard as well, I knew it would be the end for him. He'd be tortured or executed for trying to save me. I wished I had the ability to fight, even some small amount of power like the lesser Ember fae, so I wouldn't be so helpless. Not like that would help me now, not with this iron collar still clamped around my neck.

"Reed!" I called out weakly, trying to crawl across the floor towards the fight. I had no plan, I just needed to reach him.

I made it to the front of my cell, but it slammed shut in my face. Another guard stood there, ramming the door closed. It must have been the guard Reed pushed down the stairs.

"Eli!" A shape turned towards me at the sound of the slamming cell door, it was Reed, and he seemed to be winning the fight. But with the new guard involved, I wasn't sure how much longer he could hold out.

"What do you think you're doing?" the new guard hissed at Reed.

"You need to help her! I command it!"

I watched through the bars as the guard below Reed flipped him to the floor, pinning him down. "Oh, you command it, do you?" the guard now on top of him mocked, while the other approached.

It was two against one now. Reed killed one Ivy Guard and assaulted another. There was no way he'd escape unharmed, not with more guards patrolling the castle.

I kept watching as the guard straddled Reed, holding him down.

"Let him go!" I screamed, summoning the last of my strength to push the cell door open, praying it was just closed and not locked.

Closing my tear-filled eyes, I focused every ounce of power I had, and the door inched open, just slightly. Progress. But time was running out. They'd hurt him, or worse, kill him, and I'd be alone again.

"Enough of this," the standing guard commanded. "Get off of him, he is not yours to punish. He belongs to the Ivy King!"

No, no, no. Reed needed to escape, or at least try, no matter how many guards awaited him. Death was inevitable if he stayed.

I opened my eyes, but through the blur of tears, all I could make out were shapes as I continued to wedge the door open. I tried to focus, but instead, little white spots floated in front of me. Then, everything went dark.

I woke up to light dancing along my eyelids. The room was brightly lit, torches flickering along the stone walls. For a moment, a spark of hope flared within me, maybe I was somewhere else, somewhere safer than the Ivy Castle. But before I let myself get carried away, I let my other senses take in the environment.

The air was thick with the musty, moldy scent of the prison, and the silence was suffocating, broken only by the faint echoes of my own breath. I was still here, still trapped in my cell. But something was different.

Instead of lying on the cold stone floor where I had passed out, I felt something soft beneath me. My fingers brushed against the fabric under me, it was smooth, almost velvety to the touch. It had to be some kind of fur blanket. And when I pushed myself up to sit, I realized I was on a cot. My bare bedding had been replaced with a thin mattress.

I shot up, heart racing, to make sure I wasn't dreaming. As the blood rushed to my head from the sudden movement, the searing pain that had once pulsed in my face hit me. But then I realized, it was gone.

I raised my fingers to my face, gently exploring the smooth skin. No blood. No open gashes. Just soft, flawless skin. I trailed my fingers down to my neck, feeling the cold iron collar still in place and my pendant gone. Someone had healed me. Someone had put me on a warm, fur-lined blanket, on an actual mattress.

I looked down at myself, only to find I was dressed in a clean, white shirt, so large it could have passed for a dress. But why? And who? Who would care enough to make me comfortable?

Reed.

The thought hit me like a jolt of electricity, and I scrambled to my feet. My pulse quickened as I rushed to the bars separating my cell from Reed's. In the brighter light of the newly lit prison, I could see that his cell was empty.

The memories of what had happened before I blacked out began to replay in my mind, each one more vivid than the last, and bile crawled up my throat. Orrin's assault. His death, at Reed's hands. The other two guards. I remembered him pinned to the floor, and now? Now he was gone.

My heart pounded in my chest as the crushing reality settled in. There was no way Reed could have survived after what he did.

"Reed..." I whimpered, my voice barely a whisper, before sinking to the floor, overwhelmed.

"He's alive." A voice cut through the silence, and I jolted back, startled. "I did not mean to frighten you, miss," the voice added, its tone gentle yet firm.

I blinked, struggling to focus as my eyes landed on the figure before me. His green and black leathers were unmistakable, an Ivy Guard. Probably Orrin's replacement.

"Who are you?" I asked, though it seemed pretty clear who he was.

"My name is Lars. I've been assigned to you until the king returns."

I studied his sunken, tired face, unsure if he was one of the guards who had attacked Reed. I hadn't gotten a good look at either of them during the fight, but this blonde guard before me seemed to be the right height.

"Where is he?" I asked, urgency in my voice as I rushed to the front of my cell, where Lars stood on the other side of the iron door.

"We took the body—"

"Not Orrin," I hissed, the taste of his name bitter in my mouth. "Where's Reed? What did you do with him?"

Lars stepped closer, and his expression faltered. My heart sank before he could even speak. Reed was either dead or being tortured, and it was my fault. I knew I wasn't responsible for Orrin's actions, Reed had assured me of that, but if I hadn't tried to fight Orrin off, if I had just let him get it over with when we were in my cell, then Reed never would have come storming down those steps crashing into him. He might have still intervened when he found me underneath Orrin's vile body in my cell, but at least the other guard would have been there, perhaps stopping it before Reed took matters into his own hands. There were so many ways it could have played out, but losing Reed after all of it was the worst possible outcome.

"He was just another prisoner," Lars said nonchalantly, brushing a hand through his short blonde hair. "A thief. Why do you care?"

"He is my friend!" I spat, grabbing at the bars, my fingers closing around the cold metal. I forgot for a moment that they were made of iron, until the searing pain in my palms brought me back to reality. I yanked my hands away, a hiss escaping my teeth. "You said he was alive right?"

"For now," Lars said, his voice flat. "Although, I don't think you'll be seeing him again."

Tears stung at the corners of my eyes, though I quickly blinked them away. My face no longer ached, and the thought of it, the absence of pain, reminded me of one question I still needed answered: who healed me? But that would have to wait. For now, I needed to know what happened to Reed. He had been the only one to show me any warmth here, and now he was in their hands.

"He saved me," I pleaded, my voice breaking. "I know I don't deserve any kindness here, but he does. Please, don't hurt him."

Lars raised an eyebrow. "You really care for him? That dirty thief?"

Of course I did. Reed was the only one keeping me going through this nightmare. My fate was sealed, but I clung to the hope that he would escape when Hayden came for me. He had been so close to regaining his freedom, and now I had no idea where he was being kept or for how long.

"He's a good person. Better than most I know." I wiped my tears and held my head high, the truth clear in every word.

Lars shook his head, a small grin of amusement curling at the corner of his mouth, erasing any trace of confusion. "I knew it was a bad idea to place him here alongside you. Showing you a shred of kindness, probably filling your head with ideas of hope that your circumstances might change."

"I don't want my circumstances to change," I said, finding my resolve again. I stood my ground, meeting his eyes. "I want to pay the life debt, and I'm happy to do so. It's the king who's dragging his feet to make good on that debt."

"So you wish to die then hmm? No self-preservation left in you?" Lars challenged, sounding almost upset with my statement.

I was utterly fed up with the whole situation. When I agreed to come, I thought it would be over as soon as I set foot on the Ivy Isle. I had been ready to have my throat slit and leave this world to face Theodon's judgment, my debt paid and Hayden safe. But it wasn't that simple. The king was engaging in some strange, yet unsuccessful experiments. Every day, the guilt of my actions was tormenting me. I had narrowly escaped rape and lost my only friend here in the process. I was truly done with it all. Why would I want to go on living when each day brought more pain? I had long lost the will to live; death seemed to be the easier choice at this point. Reed was the only thing keeping me going, that and the hope he would make it out of this place. But now what? Why continue on?

"I wish Orrin would have just killed me," I muttered, not realizing I had spoken the words out loud instead of just thinking them amidst my swirling thoughts as I slumped to the floor. I guess it didn't matter anymore.

Lars expression shifted as his jaw tightened, "You really regard your life that little that you wish it would have ended at the hands of that filthy rapist?"

I couldn't help it. I really just wished it was all done and over with. I knew that as long as I was still alive, with the life debt still hanging over me, I would be at the mercy of the Ivy King and every guard in this place. Their little plaything.

I remained unmoving, not sensing any real effort to do anything else. I was broken. The assault, Reed, my new guard who could be just as bad as Orrin, what was the point anymore?

"Yes," I answered dryly. "I know the only reason my wounds were healed, is so that I could be alive and intact when the king returned to do whatever he has planned for me."

"No," Lars snapped, bending down to meet me at eye level. "You were healed because that thief begged me to help you."

I blinked in confusion, then looked up to meet Lars's gaze. "You healed me? Why?"

Why would the begs and pleas of a *dirty thief*, as he put it, sway him to help me? Healing another fae takes an immense amount of energy and physical pain. It didn't make sense.

"Because he probably saw the value in your life that you have clearly forgotten, Princess."

"It's not my life I'm worried about," I replied, taking a deep breath. "I'm worried about Reed's. Please, don't let him die."

I watched as Lars stood up, his green and black leathers straightening with the motion. I wasn't sure how high up in the ranks this guard was, but I hoped he could do something. Anything. He seemed kinder than Orrin, though that wasn't saying much. But he stayed and listened to my pleas.

"I'll see what I can do," Lars nodded, then began to ascend the stairs, taking a torch with him.

"Please don't take the light," I said, my voice pathetically weak. I had no right to make demands after he'd healed me, but being alone in the dark was the last thing I wanted.

"I wasn't taking the torch," Lars replied, taking a small step back toward my cell. "I was going to light the rest along the stairs, give this place some proper light and warmth. Just as I furnished your cell with a proper mattress and blanket, Princess."

"Why?"

"Because you are not an animal, and although Orrin may have seen you as such, I do not."

"Thank you."

"You're welcome." Lars turned and headed back up the stone steps, igniting torches along the way until the room was bathed in a warm light.

21

"Get up," a voice called from my cell door. "It's time to make some use of you."

I turned over in my cot, the fur blanket keeping me warmer than I'd expected, and gazed at the figure through the bars. It was Lars, the guard who had healed me. My new watchdog.

"Sleep well?" he asked as he began unlocking the door to my cell.

Truthfully, I hadn't slept well, not at all. Nightmares plagued my dreams, and this time, they were filled with Orrin and the horrors that had occurred in this very cell. I was sure my tired eyes would give me away, but I didn't want to have a conversation I wasn't ready for. "Like a babe," was all I managed to say.

The door to my cell creaked open and Lars stepped into the threshold, extending a hand to me. "Up we go."

I hesitated, recalling his words: "make some use of you." Was the king back? Was it time for another little experiment? I stared at his hand for a moment before swatting it away and using the cot as leverage to stand without his help.

"Where are we going?" I asked, more wary now.

"Well, with Reed unable to do his daily chores, it seems we need an extra hand in the kitchen."

My ears perked up at the mention of the kitchen. I was going to leave the cell, and on kitchen duty, no less. Maybe I'd get to cook or bake. Or maybe I'd just be washing dishes. Honestly, I didn't care as long as I got to see something other than these four walls. But as my excitement to get out grew, I was reminded of how I had ended up in this position. *Reed unable to do his daily chores.* Did that mean he was dead? Or still locked away? I swallowed the lump in my throat, preparing to ask, but before I could speak, Lars quickly interrupted.

"He's alive," he said, as if reading my mind. "I should've led with that." He started to escort me out of the cell, no chain or leash in sight.

Alive. Reed was *alive.* For how much longer, who knew? But today, he was alive, and I was about to be granted access to parts of the castle I never thought I'd see. As happy as I was to be put on kitchen duty, another thought tugged at my mind. Maybe I could find where Reed was being kept in the castle. It was risky, but what did I have to lose? We reached the top of the stairs, and I had to ask. "Where is he?"

"Before you get any ideas," Lars said, turning to face me. "He's locked away where you won't find him. So, under no circumstances should you try to go on some rescue mission."

Of course, he knew exactly what I had planned. I felt like a child being scolded by my parents, their disappointment evident in their eyes whenever I misbehaved. That was exactly how Lars looked at me now. His green eyes flashed with a challenge, or a threat, as if warning me to obey his orders. He had already shown me some kindness, so perhaps he could be reasoned with as well.

"Can I just see him at least?"

"I'm afraid not." Lars's tone was almost regretful. "To be honest, not many of the other guards thought it was wise that I let you out to help in the kitchen."

"Why did you then?" I asked, my curiosity piqued despite myself.

Lars sighed deeply, his nose whistling as he exhaled in thought. "There's no sense in keeping you locked away while the king is absent, especially since we can use all the extra help we can get right now."

I hadn't realized until that moment how much Lars might be sticking his neck out for me by letting me roam free. Even if it was under the guise of needing the extra pair of hands. While I was still frustrated that he wouldn't let me see Reed, I still did not understand why he was choosing to help me. The reasonable part of me knew there was little to be gained by pressing him further, so I simply nodded to show I was willing to let the matter rest.

"Follow me," he said, leading the way.

I followed him up the stairs, my heart pounding faster with every step as memories of Orrin clawed their way back and reminded me of what had almost happened on these very stone steps. I squeezed my eyes shut, holding my breath as I climbed, forcing myself upward until the air seemed to widen around me. At last, the space opened, and I reached the landing. I was free of that hell, at least for now.

Lars guided me through the Ivy Castle. As we continued down the hall, my eyes squinted from the light cascading in through the windows. I had forgotten how bright and beautiful the sun could be, especially after spending what felt like weeks in a dark prison with only a few torches to light the space. Still, nothing could compare to the natural light of the sun. Honestly, I could have just stood at the window, basking in the warmth of the sun all day, but Lars didn't stop. He just continued moving a few feet ahead. He didn't tug or pull me along. Instead, he allowed me to walk freely behind him, fully trusting me, though I caught him a time or two using the reflection from the windows to confirm I was keeping in step and wasn't going to cause him any trouble. So maybe not fully trusting me, but still, it was nice not to be grabbed or pushed around.

Even if I did find my one shot to escape, I had nowhere to go. If Ivy was anything like Ember, there were probably multiple docks surrounding the Isle, two at the very least. I was still so new to this place. I didn't know where anything was, no towns, no idea which way led to the forest. I'd be wandering aimlessly until I was caught again. No, I needed to stay here to get this debt done and over with. I'd confessed as much to Lars, so perhaps that's why he didn't feel the need to keep his eyes on me at all times as we navigated the castle. I suppose he could have thought I was lying, but then again, I'm sure he was smart enough to know that if I tried anything, he could easily overpower me with his earth magic or his sheer brute strength.

The castle looked just as worn and unkempt in the daylight as it had the dark night I'd first arrived. We passed through what appeared to be a ballroom, but the roots and vines creeping over the walls gave it the feel of a forgotten place, much like the main hall and throne room I'd seen before. The ballroom back home was the centerpiece of the Ember Palace, always alive with music and grandeur. Here, it felt as though life had drained from the room long ago. Sparse furniture, covered in dust, revealed glimpses of green and silver embroidery peeking from the cushions, like the room hadn't entirely given up, but the king had. A small piano in the corner hinted that this place was once filled with music, but now it sat neglected and abandoned. King Caraway, it seemed, had stopped hosting his court or anyone else for grand gatherings long ago.

I couldn't help but compare everything here to the Ember Palace. Our grand halls were always filled with laughter and warmth, brimming with guests, parties, and events. It was a place that never knew stillness, forever bustling with life.

I must have slowed my pace as I took it all in, wondering how Prince Hawthorne had grown up in such a dreary place. I had always imagined the Ivy Castle to be lush and vibrant, filled with flowers and fragrant scents. But what I saw before me was more ruin than beauty.

"Keep up," Lars called back, pausing at a doorframe, waiting for me to finish absorbing the sight of the ballroom.

"Why does everything look so sad and dead here?" I asked, still gazing at the corners of the room, unable to shake the oppressive feeling that clung to the air.

Lars leaned against the doorframe, letting me take a few more moments to study the room. "A lot of the Isle is still as vibrant as ever," he said, his voice quiet as he folded his arms across his chest, the green and black leather creaking slightly. "But the Isle is sick. Much like I suspect yours is."

Another confirmation that it wasn't just our Isle beginning to fade.

"What's causing it?" I asked, my fingers brushing over the green velvet of a sofa that looked like it hadn't been used in years.

"Nobody knows," Lars said, shifting his weight. "King Caraway has some ideas, though. It's become an obsession of his lately, finding a way to stop it."

No wonder he let his home fall into disrepair. It seemed that King Caraway had focused all his attention on saving his Isle, forgetting everything else. A twinge of something, regret, maybe, tightened in my chest at the thought. Did that mean he was a good king after all? Was everything he did part of a greater plan to save the Isle, and ultimately his people? Could whatever remedy he sought fix my home as well?

"Does it have anything to do with me or the star fragment, and why he's gone?" I asked, my curiosity getting the better of me.

"I've said too much already, especially to a foreign enemy." Lars straightened, his posture stiffening as he resumed the role of the ever-watchful guard.

"I'll be dead soon," I said with a small laugh. "Who am I going to tell?"

Lars didn't answer immediately. "It is not my place to talk about such things," he said, his voice taking on a more official tone. "Just know that whatever the Ivy King is doing, it's to save his Isle, to save his people from starvation."

Lars's words replayed in my mind. To save *his* people, *his* Isle. I could understand the reasoning behind it as I was sure my own parents would do whatever was necessary to save our people, but I still couldn't ignore the truth. King Caraway's actions were evil, no matter how noble his intentions might have seemed. He allowed Orrin to guard me, fully aware of what that monster was capable of. He left me to rot in a cold, dark cell, showing no concern for my suffering, as if I were nothing more than a pawn in his grand scheme. Yes, his goal might have been for the greater good, but the way he went about it was unforgivable. It was a cruelty wrapped in the guise of nobility. It was clear that Lars was no better; he remained loyal to his king, regardless of who endured the consequences.

"Take me to the kitchens," I demanded, eager to end the conversation. The thoughts swirling in my head were making it difficult to focus.

Without a word, Lars moved forward, his boots clicking softly as he passed through the doorframe. I followed, the sound of my footsteps muffled against the cold stone.

As we made our way down another musty hallway, Lars opened a pair of wooden double doors, revealing a kitchen. I hadn't expected much, considering the state of the rest of the castle, but this kitchen wasn't half bad. It wasn't as elegant as the one back at the Ember Palace, but it was functional, more than I could say for the rest of the place. I wasn't sure what task awaited me, but I knew one thing for sure: I wanted to cook or bake. The castle might be mostly empty, but I assumed the food would be for the Ivy Guards scattered around the grounds. I didn't care. I just wanted to get my hands dirty in flour and spices.

My eyes swept across the space, assessing it. Vines clung to the countertops, but there were clear patches where cutting boards and kitchen tools could be placed. The cupboards lining the walls were a hopeful sign. Maybe they were stocked with fresh ingredients, a contrast to the aging decay that surrounded us. A large oven was already warming, and in the corner, a water basin was stacked high with dirty dishes, which I hoped wouldn't be my responsibility to clean.

The last thing I noticed was the two figures hard at work in the kitchen. A female was skinning a rabbit, her movements quick and practiced, while a male chopped what looked like fresh vegetables.

The female, older than me with dark hair that was beginning to gray, looked up from her task. A strand of hair fell over her face, and she paused, her gaze shifting between Lars and me. "This her?" she asked, her voice laced with curiosity.

"Yes," Lars answered, ushering me further into the room. "This is Myrtle and her husband Bentley, the head cooks here at Ivy Castle. Well, I guess the only cooks at the Ivy Castle."

"Hello, my name's Eli," I said, my gaze still drifting around the kitchen.

"Not just Eli, Princess Eliane, correct?" Myrtle asked, pausing as she dropped the rabbit carcass onto the cutting board.

"Yes," I replied softly, already sensing the unspoken thoughts swirling between them.

"Ever been in a kitchen before, dear?" Myrtle asked as she moved closer to where Lars had led me.

Though she looked a bit older, there was still a quiet beauty that lingered on her face. She had only a few wrinkles, mostly smile lines, on her otherwise ivory complexion, and her eyes were a striking shade of blue. She wore a green kitchen dress that looked well-worn, covered in stains, with fresh blood on the apron, which I assumed was from the rabbit she was working on. The dress fit her well, so I knew that despite the king's cruelty, the servants were at least well cared for. Overall, she seemed inviting and kind, but I knew better than to make assumptions just yet.

"Probably to complain about the food not being perfect enough," Bentley snorted, not even bothering to look up from chopping a carrot.

Bentley, on the other hand, seemed cold and distant. He wore a simple green outfit made of cotton, though it was less cared for than Myrtle's, with many holes and loose threads fraying at the edges, giving me a glimpse of the skin beneath his shirt and the round swell of his bulging belly. His hair, well, what was left of it, was black, blending with his darker skin. I wondered if his hair loss was natural or a result of years of grumpiness and stress from being one of the last two cooks left to serve the entire castle, or what was left of it anyway.

I could've easily resented his assumption, but I didn't. I didn't know how to explain the circumstances of my life without sounding like I was fishing for sympathy, so I simply let it go. Instead, I moved to where Bentley was chopping away at the carrots, hoping my next words wouldn't offend him.

"You're cutting those too big," I said, watching as piece after piece fell to the board.

"What do you mean?" Bentley sneered, his balding head gleaming under the sunlight streaming through the windows, sunlight I had desperately missed.

"Considering the ingredients you're working with," I continued, gesturing toward the potatoes, onions, celery, and corn lined up on the counter, "It looks like you're preparing a rabbit stew?"

"What of it?" he replied, venom edging his voice.

"Well, if you keep cutting the carrots as large as you are, they won't cook as quickly as the rest of the ingredients. They'll stay hard while everything else softens." I reached for a knife, sensing Bentley's unease at my approach. "May I?"

Reluctantly, Bentley stepped aside, giving me space. I sliced the remaining carrots into small, even pieces before reaching for a potato. "And if you cut these like this," I said as I angled the knife down the middle of a spud, "they'll cook faster than if they're left whole."

It felt so good to be in a kitchen again, doing something, anything. The smell of fresh ingredients, spices, and herbs filled the air. For once, I didn't mind the scent of dead rabbits that lay scattered across the counter.

"Well, looks like she knows her way around the kitchen after all," Lars said with a smirk, his gaze narrowing at Bentley.

"It seems so," Myrtle added, returning to her task of skinning the rabbit.

Lars nodded and turned toward the double doors. "Well, it seems you three will get along quite well," he said, his voice carrying an edge of finality. "I have a few things to take care of. I'll be back later to collect you, Princess. Please, no funny business." He gave a slight bow of his head before departing.

"Did you spend much time in the kitchen at your palace?" Myrtle asked as she expertly sliced the rabbit meat into neat, even pieces.

"I did," I replied, my voice perhaps a bit too enthusiastic. "I loved it! Baking was my specialty."

"How are you at doing dishes?" Bentley muttered while he adjusted his cuts, following my instructions with surprising accuracy.

"I can do that if needed," I said, forcing a small smile despite the disappointment I felt.

"It's needed," Bentley groaned.

Myrtle handed me a worn apron; its edges frayed from years of use. I tied it around my waist, the fabric cinching my shirt in the middle and giving it more of a dress shape. With that, I was ready to tackle whatever task came next.

Doing dishes was my least favorite part of kitchen duty, the task monotonous, as a tinge of envy hit me each time I cleaned a plate or glass that came straight from the dining room where I should have had a seat. But no, I was in the back cleaning up the mess, and though I always appreciated my time away from the confines of my room, it still stung. But as I dipped my hands into the warm, soapy water, I found that old thoughts of jealousy began to fall away.

The soap had a pleasant lavender scent that filled the air, so comforting that I almost wanted to hop into the basin myself and scrub away the grime.

Between each dish, I discreetly ran the bar of soap over my arms and neck, washing away the dirt and feeling the tension in my body ease just a bit. The lingering traces of lavender on my skin gave me a sense of cleanliness I hadn't felt in far too long. I began to splash water on my face to clear remnants of the dried blood that probably still stained my skin, my cheeks began to burn at the thought of how I must have appeared. I watched as the clear droplets fell into the basin, the coolness refreshing against my skin. The water was slightly soapy, but there was no blood in sight. *That couldn't be right.* I scrambled to pick up a polished spoon, catching my distorted reflection looking back at me. I looked far from the princess I once was, but as I studied my reflection, there was no blood in sight. Not only had Lars healed my wounds, but he had also taken the time to clean the blood from my face. It was a small gesture and another unexpected act of kindness from the guard.

Bentley and Myrtle finished preparing the rabbit stew. The scent was heavenly, and my stomach betrayed me with a loud grumble. I realized, with shock, that I hadn't eaten in almost two days.

Myrtle handed me a raw carrot. "I can hear your belly from here. What have they been feeding you?"

"Scraps from what I assume were the leftovers of the meals you two have prepared," I replied, biting into the fresh carrot. The taste burst in my mouth, and I couldn't help but let out a small moan. Something so fresh hadn't touched my lips in so long. Myrtle gave me a small smile at my reaction, and I quietly appreciated her kindness.

I continued with the dishes, as more began to pile up after the lunch preparations were done. Though my opinion on dish duty hadn't changed, I was happy to do it. Being here was better than being back down there I thought as I decided to take extra long with this last batch.

I watched and helped wherever I could as the stew cooked over the span of a few hours, I even helped meal prep for the dinner tonight, eager to stay busy.

When the stew was finally done, I watched as Myrtle scooped a ladle of it into a bowl before setting it before me at the counter I was now seated at.

Myrtle placed her hand gently on my shoulder. "We have one rule in this kitchen: whoever made the meal eats first."

"But I didn't cook the stew," I said, confused.

"No," Myrtle smiled softly, "but you did a fine job with those dishes, now eat up."

I did as she instructed, diving into the meal like I hadn't eaten in days. It was a little less flavorful than the way I made it back home, but it was still delicious. I didn't mind the simplicity. It was food, and it kept my mind from wandering.

"So," I began, trying to break the silence, "how long have you two been working at Ivy Castle?"

"Too long," Bentley grunted.

Myrtle chuckled. "We've been the castle cooks for about sixty years now. This is where Bentley and I actually met." She smiled at him warmly, and he returned a half-smile, his eyes softening with affection. "He was terrible when he first started. In fact, he wasn't supposed to be stationed in the kitchens at all."

"Where were you originally placed?" I asked, intrigued by their story.

"I was the king's personal taste tester," Bentley said quickly, his voice filled with irritation. "It was a highly coveted position, an honor... or at least, that's what they called it."

We didn't have a position like that at our palace, but I'd heard that a few fae families back home still kept someone in that role. "That sounds like a dangerous job," I remarked.

"Not really," Bentley said with a casual shrug. "It's a thankless expendable job. It's technically only dangerous once if you happen to have that one wrong bite. Though I'm sure you understand given your royal blood, no one in their right mind would ever dare poison a king. The consequences would be too severe." Bentley shot a loving glare at his wife, and it seemed as though his hard exterior was slowly melting the longer he gazed at her. "Though the silver lining was that I got to enjoy the first bite of every meal Myrtle made. I fell in love with her cooking before I even laid eyes on her."

Myrtle and Bentley exchanged a look, their smiles full of nostalgia. "After a year of sampling the king's food, he finally demanded to see the fae behind it all."

"The day I mustered up the courage to step into the kitchen, I never expected to be met with such a vision of loveliness." Bentley continued, his voice soft with affection, and I was starting to see a different side of him. "It was far beneath my status to mingle with someone like her, a mere kitchen maid. But somehow, I couldn't stay away."

"So how did you end up switching roles?" I leaned forward on my stool, eager to hear more.

"I dropped my status and took a job in the kitchen," Bentley said, his face softening as he looked at Myrtle before his hardness crept back into his tone. "The king was furious, but overall, he understood." He brought Myrtle's hand to his lips, pressing a small, affectionate kiss to her knuckles.

He might have been grumpy, but I could tell he was a romantic at heart. Their love had clearly stood the test of time, and it still sparkled in their eyes.

"The best way to a male's heart is through his stomach, they say," Myrtle added with a playful smile. "That's certainly true in Bentley's case."

"Caraway must have been generous to let you drop rank."

"Oh, no," Myrtle said quickly, "it was King Fern, Caraway's father. It wasn't for another few years until Caraway took the throne. I doubt things would have played out the same way if Caraway had been king at the time."

"Is he a cruel ruler?" I asked, my voice dropping to a whisper as I tried to gauge their opinions. I had my suspicions about King Caraway, but I needed to know more.

"We do not speak ill of the Ivy King," Bentley said sharply, his brows furrowing.

"Prince Hawthorne gives us hope—" Myrtle began, before Bentley interrupted her.

"And he's dead, remember?"

There was a pause of silence as the two of them looked at me, their expressions turning serious. Mentioning their prince seemed to have reminded them of why I was here in the first place. To them, my brother was the one who had murdered Hawthorne, though I suppose I was guilty by association.

From what I knew of Hawthorne, he wasn't like his father. He may have been a flirt, but overall, he had seemed kind and nothing like his cruel father. The word "hope" echoed in my ears, making me believe that they, too, disagreed with the current king's way of ruling and were eager for a new reign.

"I'm sorry," I said softly, "about your prince. He was kind to me, and he didn't deserve to die."

The two shared a brief, meaningful look before Myrtle cleared her throat. "It is not your fault, my dear. Best to move on."

I studied her face, looking for any sign of sadness, but instead, there was only worry. Was she afraid of what would happen if Caraway held control of the Isle? I shook my head, reminding myself I had no business involving myself in their struggles. I couldn't change the fate of their Isle, and when Caraway returned and learned about Orrin, I was certain my time would be up.

Once we all finished our stew, I collected the bowls and immediately started scrubbing them beneath the water, thankful for the task. Myrtle and Bentley moved around the kitchen, preparing trays filled with bowls of stew, ready to be served. My job here was done, the dishes were clean, and I figured it was as good a time as any to ask about dessert.

"Myrtle," I whispered, trying not to sound too eager. "If you'd like, I can get dessert ready?" I had so many ideas. Maybe a simple fruit dish or even a custard, but I didn't want to overstep. It was her kitchen, after all, and I was still the guest.

"No," Bentley's voice cut me off, sharp and irritated as he picked up a tray.

"Bentley, be nice," Myrtle scolded, "and go take that tray to the guards."

Bentley muttered something under his breath as he left the kitchen. I couldn't help but notice how different he was from Myrtle. Where she was so warm and welcoming, he was so cold and distant.

"Don't mind him," Myrtle said with a gentle smile, "he's just a grumpy old fae."

"It's alright." I forced a smile. I wasn't a guest, after all, I was a prisoner. It made sense he wouldn't like me, and I couldn't blame him. Still, I wanted to stay and be useful. "So," I started again, trying not to sound too desperate, "can I get dessert started?"

Myrtle's face shifted, her smile dropping a little. She shook her head and picked up a tray. "Perhaps another time, Princess. For now, I think you're all done here. You may be relieved. I'll let Lars know."

Relieved? No, I couldn't be done, not yet. Did she think I'd rather be back in that dark, cold cell? I couldn't go back there, not yet at least. I needed to stay busy, to keep my mind from spiraling back to Orrin and the still too fresh events of what happened down there. Not only that, but I needed a distraction from the thought of Reed, of what they might be doing to him, of how much pain he must be in. No, I wasn't ready. I needed another task.

"I can sweep!" I blurted, grabbing a broom from the corner. "Or I can wipe down the counters." I snatched a rag, my hands shaking as I moved, barely aware of what I was doing. My body was acting on its own, driven by some frantic need to stay in motion.

"Princess," Myrtle's voice was gentle as I continued to clean, scrubbing at the counter, my heart racing. "It's okay."

I didn't dare look up. I was afraid if I did, I'd see Lars standing in the doorway, waiting to take me back to my cell. So I kept working, pretending like the frenzy in my chest didn't exist, like the anxiety didn't feel like it was going to tear me apart.

Suddenly, I felt warm hands on my shoulders, steadying me, grounding me. Myrtle. I froze, the broom and rag still in my hand as I tried to calm my racing thoughts.

"Princess," she said quietly. "It's okay."

I couldn't stop the trembling, couldn't stop the emotions threatening to spill over. Tears pricked at the corners of my eyes. "Please," I whispered, my voice breaking. "I just need to do something." I begged as a tear slipped down my cheek.

Myrtle's voice dropped low. "Princess, what..." She paused, glancing over her shoulder. "What happened in that cell?"

More tears welled up in my eyes, and I let my gaze fall to the ground. I didn't want to answer her. I didn't want to think about it, let alone say it out loud.

"I know Orrin was your guard, and I also know there was an altercation, but..." I watched her throat move as she swallowed hard. "Did he hurt you?"

An uncomfortable silence stretched between us, an unspoken understanding hanging in the air. I could feel Myrtle's patience, her quiet kindness, as she gave my shoulder a gentle squeeze. When she finally released me, she handed me a tissue. She didn't say another word about it, though I knew she must've understood.

"How are you at organizing spice racks?" she asked, her tone shifting, breaking the silence.

"Spice racks?" I asked, my voice still shaky.

"It's a tedious job," she said with a small smile. "It could take a while. Do you think you can handle it?"

I nodded, relief flooding through me. It was a task, a simple one, but it was something. "I can."

"Good," Myrtle said, nodding. She stepped back and picked up the tray of bowls filled with stew. "I'll leave you to it, and I want it perfect, so don't rush. Take your time."

"Myrtle," I whispered before I could stop myself. She paused in the doorway, glancing back at me.

"Yes?"

"Thank you."

She nodded, a shared understanding passing between us. Then she was gone. I was grateful she didn't ask for more details. I wanted to erase those memories, and keeping busy was the only thing that helped. I couldn't stay here forever though. Eventually, Lars would march me back down those steps to that horrid cell, to the memories I couldn't shake. But for now, I had a task. Something to keep me busy. Something to keep my mind from unraveling. And that was enough for now.

Fortunately, Myrtle was able to give me task after task after serving the lunch, keeping me busy well into the evening. After I helped get things ready for dinner, Lars came back for me and it was time to face reality yet again.

We moved through the castle in silence, Lars leading the way, my footsteps trailing behind his. With every step, I could feel my heart pounding harder and faster, each turn in the hallway causing a hitch in my breath. Lars didn't look back, and I was grateful for that. I couldn't let him see the panic slowly creeping up inside me. As we reached the door to the prison cells, I took in a shaky breath, the anticipation of what was coming settling over me.

I just needed to breathe. Remembering Reed's words, I inhaled through my nose and exhaled through my mouth, calming myself before descending into the cold, dark cage that waited below.

The door swung open, and the room was still brightly lit, the flickering torchlight casting long shadows along the walls. Lars held the door open as he instructed me to take the lead. The words barely registered, muffled by the haze of my own thoughts, but I nodded anyway and took a deep breath, determined to hold it until I reached the bottom of the steps. Each step felt heavier than the last, but I kept moving slowly, carefully, focusing on maintaining control.

I'd have to move faster if I was going to make it all the way down without releasing my breath. Deciding it was better to get it over with quickly, I quickened my pace. Halfway down, I tripped. No, I didn't trip; I slipped, and in the next instant, I found myself sprawled on the steps, my body jarred from the fall.

I looked up, the shock still reverberating through me, and saw Lars moving toward me quickly, his face tightening with concern. That's when I saw what I'd slipped on, it was a small pool of blood of my own blood on the steps that hadn't dried yet, still glistening like gold in the torchlight.

A wave of emotions hit me all at once, intense and overwhelming, but it wasn't until I felt Lars' hand move toward me that I realized I was still holding my breath. The floodgates broke open then. I exhaled sharply, the scream escaping before I could stop it.

"Don't touch me!" I shouted, my heart pounding as memories I wasn't ready to face surged up. Memories of what had almost happened, right where I was now sitting.

Lars pulled back immediately, his voice soft and apologetic. "I'm sorry."

I could see the genuine remorse in his eyes, but the sudden contact triggered something deep inside me. Tears and panic began to overwhelm me, my breath coming in frantic gasps. I couldn't do this. No amount of breathing exercises would help. I was trapped, frozen in place.

"I can't..." My voice trembled, the words a mere whimper, barely audible.

Lars knelt beside me, his presence steady despite the chaos inside me. "If you let me, I can carry you the rest of the way."

The suggestion hit harder than I expected. "No!" I barked, the panic turning to frustration. It wasn't just the idea of being touched by him that scared me, but the fact that, while Lars was kinder than Orrin, I still did not know this male or what he could be capable of. But I couldn't stay down here either, especially on these very steps. Not tonight, not when it was all still too fresh. My chest tightened as the walls, the steps, everything felt suffocating, like the past was closing in on me.

"Please, just take me somewhere else, anywhere else. Just for tonight. Reed said there was another prison in the castle?" My voice cracked, the plea escaping in a rush. My body refused to cooperate, like a foreign thing I couldn't control. "You don't even have to put me near his cell or you can even just switch us, but please don't make me go back down there!"

Lars paused, his eyes softening with understanding. "Okay," he said, the word unwavering. "But you'll need to will your body to move." He crouched down beside me, close enough that I could feel the warmth of his presence. "Or, with your permission, I can carry you."

I didn't hesitate. I couldn't. I nodded, the tears blurring my vision, but I managed a fragile whisper. "Okay."

I took one last, deep breath, steeling myself for the contact that was coming. I closed my eyes, not daring to look, and before I knew it, I was in Lars' arms. His grip was unyielding but careful, as if afraid I might break. He lifted me effortlessly, and I kept my eyes shut, my panic beginning to flood back in as I had no idea where we were going. I tried to stay calm, focusing on the steady rhythm of his heartbeat, letting my pulse gradually sync with his.

We moved up the steps, the world outside my closed eyelids a blur. My breathing gradually steadied, syncing with the steady thud of his chest. I imagined I was in Reed's arms instead, his familiar embrace grounding me, helping me cling to whatever fragments of reality I still had left, even if that reality was now bleak.

I took another deep breath, and for a moment, I let my mind wander. A faint, almost imperceptible trace of mint seemed to fill my nostrils. I could have sworn it was Reed's scent, lingering in the air. I never thought that a smell, real or imagined, could offer such comfort, but it did. Thoughts of Reed, his presence, even just the memory of his scent, were all that kept me tethered.

Then, the creak of a door breaking open slowly pulled me back to the present, reminding me that, no matter how much I wished to escape, I was still far from where I wanted to be.

"We're here," Lars said, his voice calm and reassuring as we entered a warm room.

I slowly opened my eyes, squinting against the unfamiliar surroundings. This wasn't the cold, stone-walled prison I'd expected to find myself in. No, it was something far different, far more lavish. The room was warm, welcoming, and filled with light. Gone were the dark, damp vines that crept along the castle's walls. Instead, the space felt almost lived-in, in a way that didn't evoke fear.

I scanned the room, taking it all in. A large green leather couch sat near a lit fireplace, its flames dancing brightly against the evening chill. A large wooden table stood in the corner, surrounded by matching chairs that complemented the rich green of the couch. Opposite, across from me, was a large, well-made bed with a tidy, inviting arrangement of green linens.

"I don't understand," I muttered as I stared at the unfamiliar room. My panic flared again. Had Lars brought me here for another reason, something darker? "Is this—?"

"No," Lars interrupted. "This is not my room. It's yours for the night. I'll stand guard outside. No one will come in, and no one will know you're here. It'll be our little secret."

"Whose room is this?" I asked, my eyes scanning the space desperately, as though I might find some clue to explain the gesture.

"It's a guest room here in the castle," Lars said matter-of-factly. "It's currently vacant. I've been using it from time to time to get away from the other guards for the past few days since the king's been gone."

Lars lowered me to the floor, and I stood, my legs shaky but functional once again, as I walked further into the space, taking it all in. I turned back toward Lars, still in shock. "Why?" It was all I could manage, my voice barely a whisper as I searched his face for an answer.

Lars met my gaze without hesitation. "You've been through enough. And with the king due to return soon, I don't know how much more kindness will be shown to you. Hopefully, this will do for now."

His words hit me harder than I expected, brutal in their truth. I was on borrowed time, and everyone knew it. This small act of kindness might be all I'd get before everything ended.

"Thank you."

Lars nodded and turned to leave. "Get some sleep, Princess."

With that, he was gone, and the door clicked shut behind him, leaving me alone in the warmth of the room. Alone and safe for the night.

I slid beneath the cotton covers of the large bed, the softness a stark contrast to the cold stone of my cell. With each breath, I sank deeper into the mattress. The fabric felt warm against my skin, no doubt from the roaring fire in the room. I had almost forgotten the feeling of warmth, the illusion of safety. Yet I wasn't safe, not even close, as my thoughts drifted restlessly and sleep refused to come. After a few minutes, I couldn't stay still any longer. I untucked myself and began pacing the length of the room, my footsteps muffled by the thick carpet beneath me.

The space was lavish, more than any ordinary guest room should be. It seemed almost as grand as my own chambers, or Hayden's, with only a few personal touches missing. The room felt too fancy for a typical guest room. I wondered if it was meant for relatives of the Ivy King or perhaps kept for his lovers or paramours. It certainly seemed elegant enough, especially when compared to the rest of the castle.

As I continued to look around, I spotted a sliver of glass peeking behind a green velvet curtain. A window. I parted the fabric and stared into the starry night sky. It was dark outside, and hard to see anything below, but still, the window seemed to scream freedom. I was alone, with only Lars aware I was no longer in my cell. The ground seemed far, but I was sure I could fashion something from the bed sheets to climb down. It wasn't as if I hadn't tried sneaking out of the palace and safe house before. It would be so easy to leave, find my way to the docks, and wait for Hayden's rescue.

Hayden.

No. I couldn't leave. That was the very reason I was here, to spare Hayden from paying the price for my actions. I stepped back from the window, watching the small flicker of hope sputter out. No, I had to stay. I had to see this through. The king would be done with me soon. Maybe once he returned, everything would come to an end. For now, I just needed to calm my racing mind and find a way to distract myself.

As I walked lap after lap, my eyes drifted toward the large wooden wardrobe in the corner. The intricate carvings along its surface caught my attention, vines twisting and curling over the wood, delicate flowers blooming within them. Flowers I didn't recognize, flowers that seemed native only to the Ivy Isle.

I traced my fingers over the designs, following the vines until my hand landed on a flower-shaped knob. Curiosity tugged at me, and I opened the wardrobe door. I expected it to be empty, but instead, I found clothing.

Elegant, meticulously crafted garments that hung in neat rows. My fingers brushed over the fabrics, velvet, cotton, leather, each material distinct, each garment far more beautiful than anything I'd ever worn.

The clothing was all in shades of green and black, the colors of the Ivy Isle. But these garments were different from the guards' uniforms. There was something more to them, thick silver threads woven into the designs, glinting under the low light of the room.

I pulled a coat from the rack, my fingers brushing against the soft material. Something about the style felt familiar, but I couldn't quite place it. My eyes roamed over the remaining clothes, and then it clicked.

Prince Hawthorne.

The coat I held in my hands was nearly identical to one Hawthorne had worn, silver woven into the fabric in the same intricate patterns. I stared at the clothes, the realization settling into the pit of my stomach like a stone. The silver, the style, the designs.

I looked around the room once more, and the truth crashed over me. This wasn't just any guest room. This was *his* room. Prince Hawthorne's room. And now, his murderer was going to sleep in his bed.

My insides twisted at the thought, and suddenly, my cell was starting to look more and more appealing again. Lars had already gone out of his way to make me comfortable here, so I couldn't object now, not after I'd made such a big deal of it. Unless this was some cruel reminder of why I was here in the first place. Either way, I would have to stay. But sleeping in this bed, in *his* bed, felt too morbid.

Quickly, I hung the coat back up and shut the wardrobe door, as if closing it could somehow seal away my discomfort. My eyes shifted to the leather couch in front of the fireplace. That would be my bed for the night. It was still far more comfortable than I deserved, but better than shamelessly lying in Hawthorne's bed.

The couch was already made up with throw pillows and a thin blanket that seemed more decorative than functional. But it would have to do. Curling up on the couch, I pulled my legs into my chest, instinctively trying to make myself small. Despite how large the couch was, I wished I could just vanish into it. I turned my face toward the dancing flames in the fireplace, letting the warmth soak into my skin as thoughts of home filled my mind. The heat of the room felt so familiar, yet so distant. I closed my eyes and let my mind drift back to the Ember Palace. I was there, in my own room, tucked away in my own bed. For once, I didn't mind being locked in, because it meant I was safe. The crackle of the embers rocked me to sleep like a lullaby, and soon my mind relaxed, and sleep finally found me.

"Scream for me, princess," Orrin's voice snarled in my ear.

I opened my eyes.

I wasn't on the couch. I wasn't in the warmth of that room. No. I was back there, trapped under him, pinned beneath his heavy, overpowering body, unable to move. *No, no, no. This couldn't be happening.* I was still in that room, I never left. The warmth, the kindness, the bed, it all felt too good to be real. My mind had to have created them, a shield to protect me from the horrors I knew were coming. The kitchen, Lars, the prince's quarters, they were nothing but an illusion, a fleeting fantasy. I was still trapped under Orrin's suffocating grip, waiting for the pain I knew he was about to inflict.

"Reed!" I screamed, desperate. *Please, come for me. Please, make this stop.* He would come down the steps like before, just like in my mind. He would save me.

"Reed!" I cried again, but no one came. No one answered.

I could feel Orrin moving closer, his body pressing down on me with a terrible, crushing weight. My body trembled with fear, helplessness, and dread. He positioned himself at my back, pressing into my spine, his breath hot and foul against my ear.

"Reed," I whimpered, my voice barely audible, broken by the terror clawing at my throat.

Then, from the darkness, a voice called out to me.

"Princess?"

The voice sounded familiar, its echo growing louder in my ears, as if it were shouting at me, getting closer and closer.

"Wake up!"

I closed my eyes tight, the pressure of Orrin's weight still digging into my flesh. My body shook under him, but it wasn't me controlling it. It was as if a phantom was pushing and pulling on my shoulders.

"Eli, it's a dream, you have to wake up!" the voice called again. No—not one voice, but two. One male. One female. A female's voice I recognized from her haunting hums.

I forced my eyes open, and suddenly I was no longer on the cold, stone steps of the prison. Instead, I was back on the leather couch in Hawthorne's room. I blinked, confused, as a dark figure loomed over me. Its hands gripped my shoulders. My instincts kicked in, and I twisted out of its hold, pushing with all my strength. My fist connected with the figure's face, and I heard a sickening crack.

"Get away from me!" I screamed, scrambling off the couch.

"It's just me," the figure said, a pained voice muffled as it pressed a hand to his nose where I had hit him. "It's Lars. I heard you screaming. Are you alright?"

The blurriness in my eyes began to fade, and as I focused, I saw Lars standing there, his hand still covering his nose. It was just Lars, but no female, in sight. "I am so sorry, I thought... I thought you were someone else."

"It's okay," Lars reassured me, his voice gentle despite the fact that I had just hit him. He offered me his hand. "You were just having a bad dream, that's all."

I didn't take it, still not trusting this male, as I pushed myself up to my feet. Still disoriented, I glanced around, noticing I had fallen off the couch in my panic, my legs unsteady beneath me.

"Why were you on the sofa and not in the bed?" Lars asked, sitting back down, his hand still holding his nose in place.

"This is Hawthorne's room, isn't it?"

After a moment, Lars nodded. "Yes."

"It just felt wrong sleeping in a dead prince's bed."

I wondered if he felt any shame in it, staying here in his prince's room without remorse. "How do you do it without the guilt?" I asked, my tone laced with a hint of disgust and anger.

Lars just stared at me as his hand fell from his nose, and I was relieved to see no blood as his face twisted in confusion. "Do you really think I am some heartless creature who cared nothing for my prince?"

"I don't think anything," I spat. "I don't even know you or what you're capable of. I don't know where your true loyalties lie, if you so easily dismiss the death of your prince and moved into his room, a room that is still filled with his belongings, might I add!"

I don't know why I was so passionate about this, why I was defending a dead prince, one that I killed no less, but this whole thing bothered me.

"We all grieve differently, Princess." Lars scolded. "Hawthorne was a friend of mine. I served as his personal guard when the occasion called for it, and I'm certain he wouldn't have any issue with me lodging here." He took a slow breath. "Since the news of his passing, there hasn't been a second that goes by when I don't think about how things would have played out differently if I had accompanied him on his trip to Ember Isle, if I could have been there to protect him, to intervene somehow. But no, I was stuck here, bound to my usual duties." His eyes clenched shut as if the weight of his guilt crushed him. "He was more than just my prince. He was my friend. And if it's between me taking this room or one of the other brute guards, then I'm sure I'd have his blessing."

There was sincerity in his words, and I didn't even consider his and Hawthorne's relationship and the fact that he was, indeed, mourning the loss of his prince. Now I was the one who felt guilty. Maybe Lars was exactly the kind of male he presented himself to be. Honorable.

"I'm so sorry, I didn't mean to presume," I whispered, feeling awful.

"It's fine, I'm sure I would have assumed the same if I was in your position."

I nodded. "I'm sorry about your nose, too."

"Don't worry, it will heal quickly." He smiled slightly, though it was strained. "Nice right hook, though."

I couldn't help the small chuckle that escaped me, though I wasn't sure whether I should be proud or ashamed of myself.

"What exactly did you hear?" I asked, hoping he hadn't seen the worst of my nightmare.

"You were calling for Reed," Lars replied, guiding me back to the couch. "You were thrashing around a lot too. Did you have a night terror about Orrin?"

Orrin. I winced when I heard his name. Just the thought of him made my skin crawl. I nodded, feeling my hands tremble again, my gaze dropping. "I was back on those steps, right before Reed intervened."

Lars reached out, his hand hovering over mine as if unsure whether to touch me. I could see the hesitation in his eyes, and I appreciated his restraint. I wasn't ready for that yet.

"He's dead, Eli," Lars said softly, sitting next to me. "He can't hurt you anymore."

I swallowed hard, the words sinking in, but not easing the pain. "If I could just see Reed, even just to thank him again…" I trailed off, looking up at Lars with desperation.

Lars studied me for a moment before he finally said, "I am sorry, but you can't. But the next time I do my rounds on that side of the castle, I will let him know of your appreciation."

I knew there was no way I could convince Lars to let me see him, but I had to give it a shot. At least he said he would pass the message along, which I was sure was something no other guard would bother to do.

He rose to his feet, glancing back at me. "Now, I think it's time for you to try and get some sleep."

He turned to leave, but I caught his sleeve.

"Can you just stay in the room? Just until I fall back asleep?"

Lars hesitated, then nodded. "Of course." He pulled one of the matching chairs from the table and dragged it closer to the couch. It scraped against the floor softly. "I'll stay right here."

"Thank you," I whispered, his presence offering me some comfort. I wrapped the blanket around my shoulders, trying to gather my scattered thoughts. "I know I already asked, but why are you doing this? Why bother to show me any kindness?"

"I already told you, you've been through enough, and I don't want you leaving this place thinking all Ivy fae are villains."

"Leave this place?" The words came out flat. "You mean when I leave this world? When I die?"

"No," he said firmly, without hesitation.

"But the debt," I began, but he quickly cut me off.

"My king is not superstitious, and if he can truly accomplish his task..." He paused, like he realized he might have said too much again.

I knew there was more to this, but I couldn't figure out what. And what about Theodon and the law? The thought of my Isle being punished because the king wanted to experiment with me, instead of just finishing what he needed to do, made my stomach tighten.

"Lars," I said softly, "why are you loyal to your king?"

"Because he is my king. Why wouldn't I show him loyalty?"

"Just because someone wears a crown, or was born into a royal bloodline, doesn't mean they deserve loyalty," I said with a bitter tone in my voice. "I'm a princess, Lars. For years, my family and

I lied to our people. If they chose not to be loyal to us after that, I would understand. Loyalty is earned, not given."

Lars stared at me, as if trying to find the right words. "I understand what you're saying," he began slowly, "but I think you're missing something important. Loyalty isn't just about trust or who's earned it through actions. There's more to it than that."

"Like what?" I argued.

"My king, your king, and all the rulers who came before them weren't just given a crown because of bloodline alone. They were chosen by Theodon's gifts, by the elements, to lead and protect us. That's why King Caraway holds the throne, and why we owe him our loyalty. It's not about whether he's perfect, or whether the crown feels deserved by anyone's standards. It's about the role he's been given in this life, a role that comes with so many responsibilities. My king may not be beloved by all, but without him, and those who came before him, everything could crumble without that guidance, that structure."

I frowned, still conflicted. "That doesn't mean there aren't flaws. What if the leader doesn't act with everyone's best interests in mind? What if it's all false promises and power plays?"

I watched him run a hand through his hair, the motion slow and deliberate. "And how was hiding you, the keeper of the Ember, from the kingdom and lying to your people not a false promise? Not just a power play to make sure a male ended up on the throne, hmm?"

I didn't answer, not because I couldn't, but because he was right. Even though Hayden truly held the Ember, or most of it at least, how was lying to our kingdom, to our people, any more justifiable? Any more morally right?

Lars met my gaze. "Leadership isn't about perfection; it's about stability. What my king is doing... it's for the greater good," he said, his words filled with conviction. "I have to believe that. I have to believe we're putting our people first. And truly, I am sorry you got swept into all this, especially since it was your brother who murdered my prince, not you. But we have to think of the good of the many before the few."

I could feel the knot in my chest tighten, but I simply nodded, unsure if I could say anything else that would make a difference. Maybe there was no hope of getting through to him, but still, I found myself wanting his company. I would have preferred it to be Reed, but Lars would do. He might have blind loyalty to his king, but at least he was kind, which only made me wonder more about who he really was.

His words echoed through my mind. Maybe blind loyalty is just that. Blind. But perhaps it's also a part of the balance that kept everyone standing. It made me wonder if perhaps Branton had blind loyalty to my father. I couldn't recall my father ever making Branton do anything immoral, but maybe I only thought that because he was my father. Or maybe it was because, truthfully, I never knew the decisions my father made, at least not the important ones. I was never meant to sit on the throne and was always shut out when it came to political matters, things that, honestly, I was thankful for. But now, it made me wonder what was really going on in some of those meetings my parents held.

Lars was right about one thing though: ruling was a huge responsibility, and with that role, you couldn't possibly please everyone.

Branton had been Captain of the Guard throughout my father's reign for so many years, but how much did I truly know about him and his personal opinions? What had made him join the Ember Guard? After years of loyalty, did he even have the power to challenge my father, or was expressing himself in such a way forbidden? Had his role come at the cost of his own beliefs?

The questions swirled in my mind, each one leading to more confusion. I glanced back at Lars. He was loyal to his king, but I couldn't help but wonder: What did that loyalty cost him? What was he sacrificing for the stability he so believed in?

"Lars?" I whispered again, my voice softer this time.

"Yeah?"

"Why did you want to join the Ivy Guard?"

He seemed to think for a moment before responding, his voice steady. "I wanted to help people. Protect them. That's what Ivy Guards do."

"Not all of them," I muttered under my breath, though I knew he'd caught it.

Lars' expression hardened, and I saw the subtle shift in his eyes. "He should have never had a place amongst the Guard," he said, his voice low but tinged with a sort of fury. "Orrin could be cruel and reckless, and while I tell myself that King Caraway acts for the good of the Isle, for the good of his people, I can't ignore the fact that he kept Orrin close for so long. You don't put a male like that at your side unless part of you sees something in him… maybe even something familiar. Cut from the same cloth, as some say," Lars said, his voice trailing off like he hadn't meant to say that last part out loud.

I couldn't help but feel a strange sense of comfort in his words. Even though Lars remained loyal to his king, his moral compass was still intact. He knew what Orrin had done was horrible, and unlike Caraway, Lars still had the ability to see the difference between right and wrong.

"How old were you when you knew you wanted to join the Guard?"

He looked at me then, an edge of irritation creeping into his voice. "Shouldn't you be getting some sleep?"

I hesitated, then shrugged. "Normally, Reed would talk to me as I fell asleep," I said. "The sooner you start, the sooner my mind will drift off," I added, doing my best to keep the bitterness out of my voice.

Lars didn't reply right away. But after a beat, I could see the tension easing from his posture, the silence stretching between us not quite as heavy as before. Maybe, just maybe, he would answer.

"I knew I wanted to help people when I was about six or seven years old." His voice was steady, but I couldn't help but feel a strange pain in the words.

That sounded so young to already have your mind set on something so serious, but then again, when I was that age, I wanted to be a famous singer and dancer, someone adored and admired, someone whose talent captivated audiences in the theaters back home. I used to watch them when I was very young with wide eyes, dreaming of the spotlight, the attention, the praise. The only problem was, I couldn't sing or dance, so I let my mind set its sights on other dreams. But Lars, he stuck to it. He knew he wanted to be a guard and he followed through.

My chest tightened as a thought swirled through my mind. If Lars had known he wanted to be a guard from such a young age, what had he seen? What horrors had shaped his need to protect, to serve, and to fight?

"That's very young to decide your future," I said, my voice tentative. I tried to keep the words light, hoping his decision had come from something positive, like maybe seeing the glory and the respect that came with being a guard was what inspired his decision. Not from some dark place, not from needing protection himself.

Lars hesitated before answering, his voice trailing off, "Yes, well..."

There was more to his story, and I wasn't sure if he wanted to share. I had no right to pry, but I desperately wanted to know. I wanted to know what had shaped him, what had made him who he was. I wanted to know if he understood the panic I felt, the fear that gripped my chest, because maybe he had felt it too at some point in his life. Maybe that was why he was being kind to me.

"You don't have to talk about it," I said. "But if you want to, I'm a great listener."

My thoughts drifted to Reed, to how many nights he had listened to me without judgment, how he had comforted me when I was lost in my own fear. Reed always knew how to keep my spirit alive, how to fill me with hope, even in the darkest of times. Maybe I could offer Lars something similar. Some sort of comfort and understanding, even if it wasn't much.

"Hearing my story won't change or improve your own situation," Lars said plainly. "Best to leave scars from the past behind us."

"I wasn't asking you to tell me because I thought I could use the information to manipulate you or my circumstances. I'm very aware of what my fate is. I just thought, maybe, if you wanted somebody to talk to, someone who wouldn't judge you for it..." I wasn't sure how to continue. In a small way, I did want him to trust me, because maybe with that, I could see Reed. But the more I thought about it, the more I realized I really just wanted to hear him out. "Never mind, I shouldn't pry. Seems I forgot my place."

"Your place?"

"Look, I'm not unaware that the treatment I've received since you became my guard is not the usual way things go between a prisoner and a guard," I explained. "So, I understand if I crossed some sort of boundary. I won't bring it up again. Goodnight." I turned away from him on the couch.

There was a long silence, only the sound of the cracking logs in the fire filling the space. Though the sound brought me comfort, I still felt like I was somehow rejected. It wasn't so different from how my whole life had been, I suppose—filled with loneliness, and aside from Hay, there was never an opportunity for someone to open up to me, nor for me to do the same. I was used to comforting myself through most bad nights, and I had hoped I could use that skill for Lars. Guard or not, at least he seemed to truly want to help others.

"Princess?" Lars whispered. "Why do you want to know? How does my past help you? What do you get out of it?"

"Nothing. It helps nothing. But I know how holding things in can cause resentment until your emotions consume you. Sometimes, it's nice to know there's someone there who can listen and lighten your load." I turned, facing Lars again, who was looking deep into the flames as if the answer would dance there, in the fire, to reveal my motives. "I can't tell you how many times I've wished I had someone who would simply listen to my problems, not trying to fix them, but just listen, just so they wouldn't consume me from the inside out."

Lars' gaze shifted from the flames and locked onto mine. "You didn't have anyone to talk to?"

I simply shook my head, not wanting to explain my own sad story when I was trying to focus on his. "Like I said, I'm a good listener, and I understand how important it is to have someone who can do just that."

There was a long pause, and I could see it in Lars' eyes. He was caught in some internal battle, torn between whether to open up or simply command me to go to sleep. I watched him carefully, waiting to see which path he would choose, silently hoping it would be the former.

"I wanted to be someone like the guards I looked up to, the guards who…" He paused, taking in a deep, shaky breath. "The guards who always protected me."

His voice cracked just slightly, and I could hear the pain woven into it. It wasn't just a story about admiration anymore. This was personal. Something had happened to him, something that had shaped him in ways I hadn't yet understood. And even though I'd given him the choice, the option to keep it to himself, he had chosen to open up, to share this part of himself with me.

It was a vulnerable thing, and I wasn't sure if I was ready to hear the rest, but I knew I wanted to. I couldn't just ignore the trust he was giving me.

"You can tell me, if you want," I offered gently, trying to keep my voice steady, to reassure him that whatever it was, I would simply listen.

He looked at me then, the flicker of something darker crossing his face before he made a forceful looking smirk. "I don't talk about it much," he muttered. "But if having me talk to you will help you to actually sleep, I guess I might as well."

There was a hint of sarcasm in his tone, but I could still hear the pain lurking beneath. He scooted his chair closer to the couch and the movement felt almost like a secret, like whatever he was about to say was something too fragile to share with anyone else, yet he was trusting me with it. From the way he spoke, I doubted many others in the castle knew this side of him.

He started, his voice softer now, "When I was younger, my father wasn't the kindest to me."

I could see a shift in his gaze as he continued. "I was a handful," he went on, "and he just didn't know what to do with me. He wasn't ready to be a father, not really. When I was about five, being a parent was kind of... thrust upon him. He had no idea what he was doing, and I couldn't fault him for that." He paused for a moment, and I could see him trying to piece his thoughts together. "He was doing his best, but that didn't stop him from lashing out on me from time to time. Still I did not blame him, it was not his fault."

I held my breath as his face twisted with pain, something dark and broken slipping past the cracks in his usual controlled demeanor. "Sometimes it was just yelling or locking me in my room," he continued, voice almost lost. "But other times..." He stopped. The words stuck in his throat, and I could see how hard it was for him to go on. "Other times, he would use more physical methods to punish me."

His body tensed as if the memories were too much to bear. I wanted to say something, anything, to make it better, but I couldn't. Words felt so small in the face of what he had lived through.

He paused, and I could see the storm in his eyes. "You said you didn't blame him?" I asked, needing to understand. Why would he forgive someone who hurt him so much?

"No," he said quietly. "He always tried his best. He was a good father, in his own way. I knew he loved me, he just... had a hard time showing it."

I didn't know what to say. I'd always hated how my parents handled my existence, how they kept me hidden away, but they'd never resorted to physical punishment. They hadn't treated me the way his father had treated him. For that, at least, I was thankful.

"You said you look up to the guards?" I asked, wanting to know how that part of the story factored in.

His gaze softened slightly, and I could tell that, even after all these years, the memories of the guards still held a place in his heart. "Yes," he said, his voice quieter now, as if remembering a different time. "I had an uncle and a few of his friends who worked for the king when I was younger. I spent a lot of time here in the castle. The guards, they always protected me. On those days when my father's mind was slipping, when his emotions ran wild with rage, my uncle and the guards stepped in. They would talk to my father, make him see what he was doing wasn't right, even if I was the one who caused it. Even when it was my fault he lashed out."

I could hear the faint shake in his voice, the emotion threatening to crack through. Without thinking, I reached out, my hand brushing his, offering some comfort. His eyes met mine, confusion flickering there, as he probably didn't expect my touch. I couldn't stand seeing him like this. He wasn't like the others; there was something more to him.

"It's never the child's fault," I said, my eyes locking on his, trying to make him believe it, to believe me.

He didn't respond right away. Instead, he slid his hand away from mine, withdrawing as if my comfort was something he didn't want or need.

"It didn't matter," he continued, his voice distant again, but I could still hear the quiet ache in it. "My father always apologized after, and I knew he felt horrible for what he'd done. But the wounds... the wounds of his rage, they still lingered." He paused, his eyes focused on some faraway place. "Somehow, the king's guards always got my father to see reason. And I respected them for that. They protected me, a child they hardly knew, and they welcomed me into this castle. From that moment on, I knew I wanted to help others. I wanted to make sure no child ever had to suffer, whether it was from physical pain or something else. I knew I had to do something to protect them, to be there when no one else was."

I nodded, understanding. "Is that why you stay loyal to the king? Do you truly believe that whatever mission he's on is for the greater good? For everyone's protection?"

"Yes," he said firmly. But it sounded like he was trying to convince himself as much as he was trying to convince me.

The silence stretched until, finally, I broke it, my voice dryer than I intended. "Well, then I hope you're right."

The words felt empty as soon as I said them. I knew he wasn't right. The fairytale of someone thinking their purpose was divinely ordained, that they were meant to save everyone? It was a dangerous illusion. It was a story that only ever ended in war and bloodshed. I could already imagine Theodon's growing rage at whatever Caraway was planning.

But none of that truly mattered, did it? I was just Eli—the powerless princess, a mere pawn in a game I helped write the rules for. In the grand scheme of things, I was nothing. When the Ivy King inevitably failed, I just hoped Lars wouldn't blame himself. I hoped he wouldn't feel responsible for believing in the empty promises of a wretched king.

"Me too," he said quietly, though I could hear doubt creeping into his tone.

My eyes began to grow heavy, and I wasn't sure if it was from truly being tired or from the utter exhaustion of hearing the pain in Lars's past. Either way, I didn't want to talk anymore. His mind was made up on following Caraway blindly, and I just didn't have the energy to tell him how wrong he most likely was.

"I'm tired," I said as I shifted on the couch, turning my back to where Lars sat in the chair.

"Good," he said, "I'll stay right here until you fall asleep."

"Goodnight, Lars."

"Goodnight, Princess."

24

The next few days seemed to fly by. Every day, Lars would escort me to the kitchens in the morning, and he'd come collect me in the evening, letting me stay in Hawthorne's room each night. He knew I still wasn't ready to face my cell again, and though I knew it wouldn't last much longer, I was thankful for his kindness. He hadn't opened up to me as deeply as he did that first night, but still, he offered polite and casual conversation. He still rushed into the room at night, finding me on the couch in front of the fire when I inevitably had a nightmare, whether it was about Hawthorne, Reed, or Orrin. I still couldn't bring myself to sleep in the bed, but it seemed to do little to stop the nightmares.

Lars was a male of few words, but there was a sort of cordial friendship growing between us. Not only was I making headway there, but I also seemed to be winning Bentley and Myrtle over. Something told me that maybe Myrtle had told Bentley about my little episode, and perhaps that was why he was being so much kinder to me. Still, neither of them ever treated me with pity. The last thing I needed was their sympathy when, in reality, the only thing that could keep my head clear and my body moving was a bit of routine and normalcy.

I continued to help around the kitchen, and was even given a few simple green cotton dresses, just like Myrtle's, signaling my temporary role as a kitchen maid. Something told me the dresses came straight from Myrtle's personal wardrobe. I knew Myrtle liked me from the start, but the small trust I was earning from Bentley felt like the biggest victory. In fact, they both agreed I could make the dessert. All these small wins began to lift my spirits, though my mind still wandered back to Reed. I asked Lars daily for updates, desperate for any news, but all Lars ever told me was that Reed was still alive and locked away, at least until the king returned to decide what to do with him. That news was less comforting than I think he thought it sounded. I just hoped he wasn't in any pain and that his spirit hadn't been broken.

"Princess," a feminine voice cut through my thoughts.

"Sorry, Myrtle," I said, shaken back to the present. "What did you say?"

"I asked if you had everything you needed to make the dessert you planned, Princess."

"I think so," I said, continuing to scan the ingredients before me. "And I told you, please call me Eli."

"Do you think that's wise? What if she poisons the guards?" Bentley grumbled, though it sounded more lighthearted than actual disdain.

"Well, luckily for us, we're fresh out of poison on our spice rack," Myrtle winked at me, grabbing a few mixing bowls.

"I meant, dear wife," Bentley stared me down, his eyes filled with judgment, "How can we trust that whatever she whips up won't be foul?"

His lack of faith in my abilities only fueled my determination to make the most decadent dessert he had ever tasted. This was my chance to prove him wrong. I rolled up my sleeves and began taking inventory of the ingredients at my disposal: butter, flour, and eggs. I felt the rush of muscle memory kick in as I measured and prepared the components for the dessert I had in mind.

"Do you have any more fresh vanilla bean?" I asked, my hands already in motion, gathering ingredients with practiced ease.

"We're all out," Bentley muttered, not looking up from his task.

"We have ground hazelnut?" Myrtle offered.

"Perfect. How about cinnamon?" I asked, already feeling the creative spark ignite.

"By the bark," Myrtle replied, handing me the cinnamon.

I got to work, mixing and measuring with a surety that came from years of practice. I knew exactly what I wanted to make, and there was no need for a recipe. My movements were fluid as I moved around the kitchen, scavenging for more ingredients to add to what would soon be a trust-winning dessert. I didn't even notice Myrtle and Bentley had perched themselves on stools to watch me, but I didn't care. This was one thing I knew I was good at.

"Baking pan?" I called out, my arm still whisking the batter together.

Myrtle smiled and placed a cake pan on the counter. I poured the batter into the pan and shook it gently to level the contents, making sure it was even and smooth. With a steady hand, I placed the pan into the oven and immediately turned my attention to the frosting.

The kitchen, though sparse, still had what I needed, sugar and cream, perfect for making a whipped cream frosting with a touch of cinnamon. The two fae continued to observe me as I stirred the mixture vigorously. My arm began to cramp from the effort, but I pushed through. I had something to prove here, and I wasn't going to stop until I had created something spectacular. Finally, the frosting thickened and became smooth. I placed it in the cooler to set until the cake was ready.

"Well," Myrtle said proudly, watching me work, "It seems you weren't lying when you said you spent a lot of time in the kitchens. You look like a regular pastry chef."

"Let's not get ahead of ourselves," Bentley said. "We still need to taste it before we start declaring her with such a title."

"You will eat those words, Bentley! Just you wait."

"Well, let's hope it tastes as good as it smells."

I got started on the dishes while Myrtle and Bentley prepared dinner, still not trusting me with that meal just yet. Though, I was sure after they tried my creation, it would only be a matter of time before they let me take the reins on the main course as well.

When the timer went off, I sprang into action, making sure the cake had cooled enough before I began frosting it. I glanced back at Myrtle and Bentley as they continued preparing dinner, but I couldn't help noticing Bentley's eyes growing wider each time he glanced at the cake or caught a whiff of its sweet scent. I couldn't wait for him to try it. Oddly enough, his approval was the one I craved most, and I was sure I would earn it.

Once the cake had cooled and the frosting was evenly spread, I found a few fresh apples, sliced them, and used them to garnish the top, dusting the plate lightly with cinnamon and sugar. I cut a slice for each of them and set the plate down in front of them both, eager to hear their thoughts.

"Go ahead, give it a try," I urged.

I placed a slice on my own plate as well but didn't touch it. Instead, I watched as Bentley slid Myrtle's plate in front of him and took a bite.

"Bentley!" Myrtle scolded.

"Sorry, dear," he said through a chew. "Old habits die hard. Had to make sure it truly wasn't poisoned."

"And?" Myrtle crossed her arms.

Bentley sat still for a moment, and I hoped he realized I had not in fact poisoned him. Then a smile tugged at his lips. "Maybe just a few more bites… you know, just to be sure," he teased.

Myrtle rolled her eyes and promptly grabbed his slice, taking a bite.

My heart pounded in my chest, and I bit my lip, waiting for their verdict.

"Well?" I asked, unable to hold back any longer.

"I apologize for having any doubt in your abilities," he finally said as he continued eating so quickly that I thought he might choke. "What is this dessert?" Bentley asked, taking bite after bite.

"It's cinnamon and hazelnut cake, or as we call it on Ember, Cinder's Delight, I used to make it all the time back home."

"Well done, Eli," Myrtle added, her smile warm and approving. "I dare say you may have out-baked me."

It felt good to know I was still good at something, that I wasn't completely broken or worthless after what happened in the cell. I could still bring a smile to someone's face. "Thank you," I said, continuing to cut up the cake and disperse it onto smaller plates. I set aside two pieces, one for Lars and the other for Reed. I hoped that after Lars took a bite, it would put him in a good enough mood and he would deliver a slice to Reed wherever he was. In that moment, I remembered Reed had mentioned that some of his chores were in the kitchen.

"Myrtle," I asked quietly, realizing I never even thought to ask, "Do you know what happened to Reed? Have you heard anything?"

"Reed?" Myrtle looked confused.

"He's another prisoner here," I explained. "He said he spent some time in the kitchens. I thought maybe you might know where he is."

"That shaggy-haired boy who helped out about a week ago?" Bentley cut in. "My wife was gone most of the day, but I saw him. A good lad."

"Is he okay?" I pressed, hoping he knew something, anything.

"I haven't seen him since that day. Why? Something happen?" Bentley's tone shifted, his brows furrowing with concern.

I didn't want to delve into what had led to Reed's disappearance. The time spent in the kitchen had almost made me forget the dark events had taken place, what had happened, and what might still happen. This moment, surrounded by Myrtle and Bentley's warmth, had been a welcome distraction.

"He was just moved to another part of the castle, so I was just hoping he was alright."

"I'm sure he is," Bentley said, offering a small smile that almost caught me off guard.

I nodded, not wanting to press them any further about information they likely had no knowledge of. Instead, I let my mind be distracted again as I began to clean up our plates, needing to focus on something else.

As I dried the last dish, Myrtle and Bentley continued talking. They shared a bit more about their lives, their daughter, and their years serving in the Ivy King's castle.

"So, does she work in the castle too?"

"She did for a while," Myrtle said with a sigh as she stacked the freshly cleaned plates. "But she's flown the coup. She owns a small dress shop on the west side of Forsythia now."

"Owning a business in the capital city of the Ivy Isle must be something you two are very proud of," I said, trying to lift her spirits.

"Oh, we are, but we miss her, is all. She's so busy designing and handcrafting her dresses that we don't get to see her as often as we'd hoped."

A tear slipped down her cheek, and she quickly wiped it away, though she didn't try to hide the emotion. I understood that feeling of loss, the ache that came with being separated from someone you loved.

"Well, I'm sure she misses you both dreadfully," I said softly, offering Myrtle a warm smile. "And I'm certain her dresses must be lovely. If I were here under different circumstances, I would love to wear one for my kingdom."

My words seemed to lift Myrtle's spirits. The smile that spread across her face assured me that I'd said the right thing. Despite everything, I was still a princess, and I knew hearing that a member of the royal fae had an interest in her daughter's creations would bring her joy.

Bentley, to my surprise, added, "We do have one of her earlier designs back in our quarters. It's about your size. I'm sure Laurel would love for you to have it."

I blinked, a little taken aback. "I would love that, but I doubt it would be proper for a prisoner to wear such a thing."

Considering the little time I likely had left in this world, would it really matter if I wore a beautiful dress or not? They'd allowed me to keep my ruby dress when I arrived, though perhaps it was more of a punishment, a constant reminder of my fall from grace.

Myrtle made a disapproving sound and waved Bentley away. "Go fetch it for her, dear."

Bentley nodded and turned to leave, but as the door swung open, he froze. Standing in the doorway was Lars, and I knew at once my time in the kitchens for the day was coming to an end.

"Pardon me, sir," Bentley said, offering a half bow to Lars. "I was just fetching something for Eli here."

Lars stepped into the room, his towering frame pushing Bentley aside with little effort. "It will have to wait until tomorrow," Lars said, his voice resolute. "For now, I must return her to her cell."

It was still our little secret that he was actually letting me stay in Hawthorne's room, though something told me Myrtle and Bentley wouldn't be angry that a prisoner was receiving such luxuries. No, they seemed more like friends now.

"I need to serve dinner," I said softly, hoping Lars would let me stay just a little longer.

"Myrtle and Bentley will take care of that. For now, I need to get you back to your cell." Lars glanced over my shoulder, where the two slices of cake I had saved still sat on the counter. "Did they finally let you do a little cooking?" he said as he picked up a plate, giving it a smell.

"Yes," I said, trying to sound sweet. "One of those slices is for you, to thank you for all your kindness."

"And the other?" Lars lifted a brow, clearly questioning me.

"I was hoping you could take it to Reed," I added, offering him a hopeful smile.

"He murdered a guard, Princess, murderers don't get cake."

"Please," I begged again. "You don't have to say it's from me. Just deliver it with his regular meal. I owe him so much more, but for now, this is all I can give him. Please, Lars."

"You're okay with the fact that he's a thief *and* a murderer?"

"I've done worse," I admitted, shrugging. What Reed had done, he did to save me. In contrast, I had killed the prince out of stupidity and recklessness. "He's a good person, and you know it."

Lars looked at the plate with a reluctant sigh. "Fine, but you tell no one."

I nodded quickly. Who would I even tell? "Thank you."

"I will come back for it and deliver it once you are all locked away."

I looked at Myrtle and Bentley, but they didn't seem distraught by his words. Something told me they possibly already knew about my other sleeping arrangements.

"You be sure to bring her back tomorrow," Myrtle started. "She's in charge of lunch."

My face lit up at her words. "Really?" I asked, still not believing it.

"Really," Bentley answered for her.

It felt good to be recognized for my talents and to know that they still enjoyed my presence here. Something inside me warmed, as if they truly wanted me around. Despite being a prisoner, I was useful and had purpose.

"I'll be sure to bring her back bright and early," Lars said before ushering me out of the room.

As he guided me back to my room, the walk felt unreal, as if I was experiencing true happiness, but with every step, it started to fade as I thought of Reed yet again. I had done so many wrong things and was being rewarded, yet Reed was suffering somewhere in the castle. I wasn't sure how much longer it would be until the king returned, so I needed to try one more time.

"Lars," I said before he shut the door of Hawthorne's room. "You promise you will deliver him the cake?" I asked.

"I said I would," he said dryly. "Now go to bed while you still have the luxury of staying here."

"Caraway is returning soon, isn't he?" I asked, already knowing the answer.

"Most likely, yes."

"Then please let me see him. Please, let me see Reed!" I pleaded.

"I already told you, Princess, you cannot."

Anger began to boil inside of me and I couldn't contain it anymore. "Why?" I shouted as I shoved him back without thinking.

I didn't know what came over me, a powerless nothing who had just assaulted a guard who possessed earth magic. Not that it would matter, considering he was three times my size and could probably snap me like a twig with his strength alone. Logic completely vanished as I shoved him again. "Why can't I just see him? Just talk to him!" I shouted, tears pricking at my eyes.

"Princess," Lars said firmly as he held my arms down, immobilizing me. "You're making a scene! Do you want the other guards to know what I've been letting you do? Where I've been letting you stay?"

"I don't care!" I shouted as he shoved me into the room, closing the door behind us.

I knew it was unwise what I was doing and that I could get Lars in a lot of trouble if anyone found out, but I had to do something. If Caraway was due back any day, that meant Reed would most likely be dead soon. I just needed to see him, needed to tell him how sorry I was and that this was all my fault. I couldn't let that night, that horrific event, be the last memories I had with him.

My whole body began to shake. I went from being the happiest I had been in a while in that kitchen, straight back to the emotional mess I was. The mess that Reed saw past and talked me through. I needed to see him. I needed him, and Lars just didn't understand.

"Please," I said as I slumped to the floor, rocking myself back and forth. "Please don't let him die, not because of me." My tears flooded out now, and there was no stopping it.

"Princess," I heard Lars's voice closer to me now.

Looking up, I realized Lars had lowered himself to the floor with me, his hands holding my shoulders to stop my rocking.

"Please," I said one more time.

Lars' gaze shifted to something softer, something that looked like regret. "Does he mean that much to you?" he asked. "This stranger you only knew for a few weeks."

Hearing him say it out loud made it sound more absurd than it was. But the fact was, yes, Reed did mean that much to me. The night he eased my nightmares, the day he told me about the sun, but most importantly, the night he saved me from Orrin. I wasn't going to try to explain it to Lars; he wouldn't understand. So, instead, I just offered him the simple truth.

"Yes," I said. "Yes, he does."

There was a long silence between us, and I could see so many thoughts running through Lars' head. But finally, those eyes that were filled with confusion turned into something soft and understanding.

"Alright, I will see what I can do, but first I need you to dry your tears and get some sleep. Can you do that?"

I nodded as Lars helped me up from the floor and guided me toward the couch.

"You promise?" I asked as I wiped a tear away.

"Yes, now please get some rest and no more tears, alright?"

"Alright."

And with that, Lars left the room, and I was once again alone. I wasn't sure if Lars was telling the truth or if he only said that to get me to calm down, but I held onto the hope that he was being sincere. I needed to cling to that belief if I was going to make it through the night. It was out of my control now, and I just had to hope Lars was as honorable as he had presented himself to be.

Somehow, I had made it through the whole night without a single nightmare. I wasn't sure if it was because of the happiness yesterday's kitchen adventures had brought me, or the fact that Lars had told me he would try to find a way for me to see Reed today. Either way, I was thankful for the rest.

I looked out the window, and from the position of the sun, it seemed to be about ten in the morning. I guessed Lars had let me sleep in. I couldn't be mad at him; I truly did need the rest. But now that I was awake and I was ready to get to work.

I changed into one of the green cotton dresses and prepared myself for the day ahead. I was going to make lunch and, hopefully, see Reed. At least that was the plan.

Soon, Lars softly knocked on the door, ready to escort me to the kitchens. My emotions were all over the place. I wasn't sure when Lars would be able to take me to wherever in the castle Reed was being locked away, but I hoped I could keep my mind occupied until then.

We arrived at the kitchens, but before opening the door, Lars stopped me. "I said I would try, alright? I can't promise anything."

I nodded, a small smile of hope blooming on my face. But it was quickly followed by a glaze over my eyes, tears beginning to form again. I wasn't sure if it was from the happiness of seeing Reed later or from the sadness and doubt that this was just a false hope and Lars wouldn't be able to follow through.

"I said no more tears, Princess. Remember?" Lars said, wiping away a stray tear.

I nodded. "Just try, alright?"

"I will."

And with that, he turned on his heel and disappeared down the hall, leaving me alone to get ahold of myself before I entered the kitchen.

As soon as I stepped through the door, I was greeted by Myrtle and Bentley's warm smiles, and the sight of them instantly warmed my heart.

"Good to have you back, Eli," Myrtle said, her arms opening for a hug.

I let myself be enveloped in her warm embrace, the kindness of her touch soothing my nerves. In this kitchen, I felt at peace again.

"Alright, you emotional female saps," Bentley muttered, his voice playful, "this lunch isn't going to cook itself."

I smiled but couldn't resist adding, "I have some ideas if you haven't already prepped the meal."

"What do you need?" Myrtle asked, her eyebrow raised with interest.

"Just some quails and the fixings for a salad."

Myrtle nodded. "That should be easy enough. Quail are practically everywhere on this Isle, though I'd wager the guards might be getting tired of it."

"That's because they've never had quail the way the Ember fae cook it," I said, my voice filled with confidence.

Bentley chuckled and left the kitchen, likely to fetch birds I needed for the meal.

Over the next hour, Myrtle helped me gather fresh lettuce, radishes, cucumbers, and both red and green peppers, perfect for the salad. "Do you have any pre-made dressing?" I asked as I began slicing lemons on the counter.

"What flavor?" Myrtle asked, rifling through the cabinet.

"Balsamic would work nicely," I replied, mixing the lemon slices with a handful of shredded mint leaves.

"What exactly are you making?" Myrtle asked, passing me a bottle of balsamic dressing.

"Quail Fattoush Salad. It was always a favorite back home." I added the dressing to a bowl, mixing in a bit of lemon juice and mint.

"Can't say I've ever had it," Myrtle said, watching me with curiosity.

"You'll love it!" I said with more enthusiasm than I intended. I had no doubt that this dish would win them over just like my dessert.

I focused on the dressing as Myrtle continued chopping vegetables for the salad. The kitchen hummed with our quiet work, the ingredients coming together smoothly, when the kitchen door suddenly creaked open.

"Were you able to get the quail, Bent—"I stopped mid-sentence, my gaze snapping to the doorway.

It wasn't Bentley standing there with an arm full of quail, it was Reed.

"Hey, Sparks," Reed greeted, a half-smile tugging at his lips.

Without thinking, I bolted from behind the counter, nearly knocking the bowl of dressing over in my haste. I launched myself at Reed, my arms wrapping around his neck, not even feeling the burn from his iron collar in my excitement.

"Miss me?" he asked with a small chuckle, his arms wrapping around me in return.

I pulled back slightly to meet his eyes, disbelief still lingering in mine. "You're here?" My voice was barely above a whisper, still in shock that he was standing there, right in front of me. "How? What happened?" I didn't even wait for him to answer, I just held him, realizing this was the first real embrace I had ever shared with him.

I couldn't speak for a few moments. I thought I would only get to see him through bars in whatever cell he was being kept in, I had no idea I would get to be with him like this. I was so lost in the relief of his presence, that I realized I hadn't let go of him. Slowly, I released him from my tight embrace and stepped back, my eyes scanning his body to confirm that he was fine, no cuts, no bruises, just Reed. "How?" I asked, still dumbfounded, struggling to understand how or why he was here in the same kitchen as me.

"Lars said I was needed on kitchen duty today," Reed replied, flashing me a smile that warmed my heart. "But it looks like you've got it all under control."

I took a deep breath, watching as Reed stood there, alive, unscathed, and smiling, and it felt like I could breathe again. My gaze flicked toward the door, ready to thank Lars, but he was already gone. I assumed he wanted to give us time alone, especially after the scene I had made about begging to see him, but that hardly mattered now because Reed was here, and I could focus on nothing else.

I scanned him again to be sure, my worry simmering just beneath the surface, and then, unable to hold it in any longer, I pulled him close. "No," I whispered into his ear, "I meant how are you completely fine? You killed a member of the Ivy Guard. I thought, I thought..." I couldn't finish the sentence, the words choking in my throat, too much fear and uncertainty clouding my mind.

Reed exhaled deeply, his voice soft and steady as he spoke. "They can't do anything final until the king returns." He said it with a casual shrug, like his life wasn't hanging in the balance. "Besides, Orrin was a dick. He had it coming."

I shushed him quickly, glancing over my shoulder to make sure Myrtle hadn't overheard. She was still busy mixing the greens into the salad. I pulled Reed toward the far corner of the room, lowering my voice even further. "Did they hurt you?" I hesitated, unsure if I really wanted to know the answer. But the unknown gnawed at me, maybe torture couldn't be authorized without the king's consent, maybe I was hoping for a reason to believe he was truly unharmed.

Reed's eyes darkened for a moment, his voice low as he replied, "Yes." He reached for my hands, holding them gently, his thumb brushing small circles against the back of my hand. "Can we talk about this later?"

I hesitated, my heart racing as the urgency of his request sank in. "Where?" I asked, not knowing where we could speak privately, away from prying ears.

"I know a place," Reed said, squeezing my hands gently, "but not now. We can slip away after we finish in here. Trust me."

I nodded, feeling the warmth of his palms in mine, the tension in my body easing slightly with each passing second. My shoulders relaxed as his thumb continued its soothing motion, and I allowed myself to be comforted by his presence. That was, until Myrtle's voice broke through.

"Enough of that, you two!" she called, sending us both a playful glare. "Use those hands for something useful and help me with this lunch!"

Reed's smile mirrored my own, an unspoken understanding passing between us. Without another word, we unclasped our hands and returned to the task at hand while Reed assisted me.

Later, Bentley returned with two large baskets of fresh quail, ready to be de-feathered and cleaned. I wasn't sure when it had happened, but somehow, in this kitchen, I had slipped into Myrtle's role as the head of the operation. Reed, Bentley and Myrtle moved at my direction, following my orders with ease. It felt natural, like a rhythm I'd stepped into without thinking. I had done this so many times before back home in Kalynda's absence, leading the kitchen, commanding attention, keeping everything in motion. It felt familiar, almost like home.

And for the first time since I'd been thrown into this chaotic world, I felt like I belonged.

I glanced over at the quail roasting slowly over the hearth. It was coming along perfectly. Quail cooked quickly, but I'd suggested a slow roast to really lock in the flavor of the spices rubbed into the bird. Bentley and Myrtle had been reluctant at first, concerned about the time it would take, but now I could see they didn't mind. It gave them more time to chat, sharing stories about Myrtle's courtship and Bentley's proposal. Those two were the very definition of enduring love.

While I often caught Bentley staring at Myrtle with longing, I couldn't help but glance at Reed from time to time. There was something different about him now. Maybe it was that his absence made me realize just how much I needed his company. Or maybe it was the fact that, if he hadn't been there that day, if he hadn't acted, who knows how far Orrin would have gone. He protected me when I needed someone, and I would never forget that. My mind was consumed by him entirely and sometimes, I even wondered if he was too good to be true and if I had imagined him, imagined the person I needed during my darkest moments. I didn't realize how much his presence had actually affected me until he was gone. But this was real. He was here, and it felt like everything had reset. A small smile tugged at my lips as I watched Reed, perhaps a little longer than I intended. When he caught my gaze, a faint smile spread across his face, and I quickly turned away, trying to focus on finishing the meal; anything to keep myself busy and to stop thinking about Reed this way.

As the meal came together, I let myself enjoy the comfort of the kitchen, of being with people who, in such a short time, had become incredibly important to me. It was foolish to get too attached to anybody with Theodon's judgment looming over me, but for now, I needed this sense of peace, this feeling of being needed. It was a balm for my soul, something I wasn't ready to let go of.

"So, Reed, was it?" Myrtle purred. "How did you two meet?" She waggled her fingers between the two of us, a mischievous smile tugging at her lips. My cheeks flushed with warmth, and I prayed it wasn't as visible as it felt.

"Yes, ma'am," Reed spoke up, saving me from the embarrassment of explaining how he had found me hungover and alone in the desert, only to offer me more liquor and watch me hurl my guts out right in front of him. "We met back on the Ember Isle, while I was roaming, well, rather running away in one of the desert oases."

"Odd place for a princess and a thief to meet, wouldn't you say, Reed?" Bentley chimed in, his tone dripping with skepticism as he crossed his arms over his chest.

I bristled at Bentley's words, hating that they saw Reed as nothing but a lowly thief. "He was only trying to feed his family back home," I said, standing up from my stool, as I came to his defense. "We met when he was trying to escape the cruelty of the Ivy King." I knew I shouldn't be speaking ill of the king in front of these fae, but the truth had to be told. "He was trying to escape, but the Ivy Guards caught him while arresting my brother."

I could feel the heat in my face as the conversation grew more tense. I wasn't sure what came over me, but I couldn't stop myself from defending Reed, just as he had defended me.

"And why were *you* out there?" Bentley asked, his voice laced with that same disdain.

"I..." I stopped myself, trying to recall what lies I'd told to the king and what I'd told Reed. "I just wanted to be there for my brother on his big day." I let out a huff, hoping it was a satisfactory answer. At least it was technically true. I had wanted to be there for Hay.

"And now you two are here," Myrtle mused, her eyes twinkling with amusement. "Both prisoners of the Ivy King. Maybe it was fate."

Fate? Fate wanted us to go through all of this pain and suffering? If this was fate, it had a twisted sense of humor. Two fae marked for death, bound by the cruelty of the Ivy King. No happy ending awaited us. This was not how any story was supposed to go. And yet, I couldn't help but wonder, when did I start thinking of Reed and I as an 'us?'

I glanced at Reed out of the corner of my eye, and there was that same smile, small but knowing. It was like Myrtle could see something I wasn't ready to acknowledge, and it made my stomach tighten.

I shook my head, forcing myself to focus. "I need to check on the quail," I said stiffly. I turned on my heel and hurried away from the table, not waiting for a response.

I spent a few minutes at the roasting quail, poking at it aimlessly, pretending to be busy as the heat of my face slowly subsided. By the time I returned to the table, the conversation had thankfully shifted to something else. *Thank the stars.*

It seemed drinks had become the new topic of choice, and a glass of red wine was now set out for all four of us.

"Drink up," Bentley said, raising his glass with a grin. "We've all worked hard today. Once lunch is ready, we can have another round. Cheers." He and Myrtle clinked their glasses and drained them in one go.

"Cheers," I echoed, lifting my glass to meet Reed's. Our eyes met, and then, in perfect unison, we both brought our glasses to our lips. I couldn't seem to pull my gaze away from his mouth, watching his lips part slightly as he swallowed, the crimson wine staining them in the most captivating way. My pulse quickened, and a wave of warmth rushed through me, though whether it was from the wine or something else, I wasn't sure.

I felt dizzy, caught in the pull of the moment, and then I lost my grip on the glass. The wine spilled down my chin and splashed onto my dress. *Great.*

Reed's eyes opened as he finished his wine and took in my red stained chin and dress, a small laugh escaping his lips. Those same lips I was just staring at moments ago like a fae in a trance. *What the hell was happening to me?*

"Forget how to swallow," Reed said in a voice that sounded a bit huskier than usual.

"W-What?" I stammered as I took in his words, a phrase I was sure he carefully crafted. *Did he see me staring?*

"Your wine, it's all over you," Reed laughed again clearly enjoying himself at my expense.

"Oh dear," Myrtle said, rubbing her hands on the material-soaked wine. "Luckily this dress was already on its last leg before your wine got to it. All for the best I suppose."

"Do you know where I could get a fresh one?" I hesitantly asked hoping that as a prisoner I wasn't being too demanding on wanting clean clothes.

"Even better!" Myrtle said with so much excitement in her voice it almost knocked me off my stool. "Follow me!"

Myrtle led me down the hall while Reed and Bentley remained behind in the kitchens. This section of the castle was surprisingly brighter than the rest, with sunlight filtering through high windows, casting long shadows on the worn stone floor. Only a few stray vines crept up the walls, their tendrils twisting lazily around the stone as if the castle had surrendered to nature's slow takeover.

"Why are there so many vines and roots within the castle walls?" I asked, the question finally escaping my lips after days of quiet curiosity.

"Oh, it's been this way for ages," Myrtle answered casually, "King Caraway is hardly ever here, and for years now, his attention has been elsewhere." Her words lingered in the air, as if they contained more than she was willing to say.

I raised an eyebrow. "What about the servants? Surely, they'd keep the place clean."

Myrtle shrugged slightly, "The king has many subjects, but very few servants within the castle itself. Every year, our numbers dwindle. People come and go, but the staff..." she trailed off, shaking her head. "It's been like this for as long as I can remember."

"Why?" I asked before I could think better of it. I hoped I wasn't crossing a line.

Myrtle didn't seem offended, but the quiet sincerity in her voice made me feel as though I had hit on something deeper. "I don't really know, to be honest."

That only made me more curious. From my few encounters with Caraway, he seemed to be slipping from reality. His obsession with some form of world domination disguised as peace was clearly his main focus. Maybe it was for the best that so few had witnessed his descent into madness. But, if he wasn't even present half the time, did that mean the burden of ruling had fallen to Hawthorne in Caraway's absence? The thought made my stomach drop. Hawthorne might have been this Isle's only hope if Caraway continued to spiral, and I had taken that hope away. I shoved the thought aside, knowing the past couldn't be undone, and turned my focus to the present as we reached a door at the end of the hall.

She opened it, and the room inside was an unexpected contrast to the dark, looming corridors of the rest of the castle. Myrtle's chambers were soft, charming, almost whimsical. The room was filled with delicate animal figurines on various shelves and tables, each one carefully arranged. Bright colors adorned the walls, and the atmosphere felt light, even peaceful. It was as if Myrtle had created a little sanctuary within the imposing stone walls of the castle.

Her bed was the centerpiece, a large mass of pink fabric that looked like something straight out of a fairy tale. It resembled a cupcake, layers of lace and satin piled high, and I couldn't help but smile at the thought of Bentley, curled up in all that pink fluff.

"Here we are," Myrtle said, as she rummaged through her wardrobe. "This is the gown we told you about."

She pulled it out, holding it up proudly. I took a step closer, my breath catching as I gazed at the dress. It was nothing like the light and thin made gowns I was used to back home, but it was magnificent in its own right. The fabric shimmered with a subtle, almost ethereal glow. The sleeves were white, puffing out dramatically at the shoulders and again at the elbows, the shape held in place by golden cuffs that glinted in the light. A soft pink fabric met the sleeves, forming a bodice that was embroidered with delicate golden leaves. The skirt fell gracefully to the floor, the same pink fabric cascading down in smooth folds, with more gold leaves placed along beaded vines all along the skirt. "It's beautiful," I whispered, unable to tear my eyes away. "Your daughter is a wonderful designer," I said, my voice full of admiration.

Myrtle laughed softly, a note of pride in her tone as she held the dress against my body. "Oh, I know. She has a gift."

I looked down at the gown she held in front of me. "Looks like it should fit you perfectly."

I glanced down at myself, my stomach twisting. Even though I had been cleaned up a few nights ago, after blood had stained my skin and clothes, I could feel the grime building up again. I was only able to scrub here and there while on dish duty, but I still felt unclean. The thought of slipping into such a pristine gown, with dirt and wear still clinging to my skin, made me uneasy. "Myrtle," I said hesitantly. "Would it be alright if I cleaned myself up before changing? I'll be really quick, I promise."

"Of course," she said warmly. "I'll get a bath drawn for you. It'll only take a moment."

I had only planned to scrub my skin quickly with a washcloth, but now that she had offered a bath, I couldn't refuse. "As long as it's not too much trouble."

"Not at all. Wait here, I'll get everything ready."

Myrtle moved quickly, and before I knew it, a steaming hot bath had been filled to the brim. The air in the room was heavy with the scent of floral soaps and oils, all carefully arranged around the tub. I assumed Myrtle had left them out for me. With her back in the kitchen finishing up lunch, I had the entire room to myself.

I let my wine-stained dress shimmy down my shoulders until it pooled at my feet on the floor. I dipped a toe into the water, testing its warmth, and was met with an immediate wave of relief. It felt incredible. My body, worn from, well everything, seemed to ache less with every passing second in the water. I couldn't resist it any longer and I sank into the bath, allowing the heat to envelop me, and instantly, I felt the tension in my muscles begin to melt away.

The soaps and oils Myrtle had left out smelled divine. One fragrance was a blend of roses and honey, soft and sweet, while the other was a calming mix of chamomile and lavender. I lathered both into my hair and skin, hoping it would be enough to wash away the lingering smell of my prison cell I was sure had embedded itself into my flesh despite the last few nights being in Hawthorne's room.

What had started as a quick bath turned into a stolen moment of peace. No one came looking for me, and I figured my absence from the kitchen was still acceptable. I leaned my head back against the cool porcelain, letting my heavy eyelids drift closed. Everything felt calm and peaceful until I heard someone call my name.

The door to the bathing room flew open with a loud creak, causing my eyes to snap wide with panic. My blood ran cold, my heart skipped a beat, and before I could fully react, I instinctively covered my chest with my arms. My face burned with embarrassment as I realized who it was. Reed. His jaw hung open in shock, his body frozen in place as his eyes widened, taking in the unexpected sight of me.

"Uh—" Reed stuttered, his eyes snapping to the floor as he quickly turned away. "I'm sorry, Sparks. Myrtle sent me to check in on you. I'd been knocking and calling your name, but you didn't answer. I thought maybe… maybe you had drowned." He said lightheartedly, but there was a glimmer of concern in his tone.

He'd been calling for me? How long had I been asleep in the tub?

"I'm okay," I said, my voice shaking from the lingering embarrassment. I kept my arms crossed over my chest, trying to sink lower into the water. "I didn't even realize I'd fallen asleep." I felt a subtle ache in my neck, a reminder that I must have nodded off with my head against the iron collar that still held me captive.

"I'll leave you to it, then," Reed said, his back still turned as he started to leave the room.

"Wait," I called out before he could go. "Could you bring me the pink and white dress from Myrtle's bed? Just keep your eyes closed when you come back in."

"How am I supposed to hand it to you with my eyes closed?" Reed teased.

He wasn't wrong. I grabbed a washcloth and draped it over my front, making sure my bottom half remained hidden beneath the soapy water, though when I looked down, the water seemed more clouded with dirt and grime than with soap, which only made me feel more embarrassed as I stared at my own filth. "I'm covered now, so it should be fine," I replied, my voice still shaky from the awkwardness.

Reed turned back to me, slowly lifting his eyelids. I could see his face redden, mirroring the warmth that had spread through my own body. His eyes lingered on me, and I swallowed hard, feeling the tight coil of tension growing between us. Reed's chest rose and fell, his breath slightly uneven as his eyes roamed my covered body.

I cleared my throat, desperate to break the awkward silence. "Um, the dress?" I breathed, my voice barely above a whisper.

"Yes," Reed replied quickly, turning and disappearing into the other room to retrieve the gown.

He returned soon after, his gaze lingering just a bit longer than necessary on me as he placed the dress on a nearby bench. "I'll wait for you out in the hall so you can get dressed," he said, his voice tight.

I hurriedly dried off, my skin still warm from the bath, and slipped into the dress. Myrtle was right, it fit like a glove. The gown hugged my body perfectly, accentuating every curve. The only problem, as always, were the laces at the back. What was it about me and these damned laces? I tugged at them, trying to tie them tight enough, but the task proved more difficult than I'd anticipated. Frustration bubbled up as I struggled, and before I could get too worked up, I gave up on the last few and would just have to let Myrtle finish them for me later. I tore a scrap from my wine-stained dress and placed it under my collar. The dry fabric eased the sting immediately, and with that, I felt ready to go.

"Shall we?" I asked, stepping into the hall and joining Reed.

"After you," Reed motioned for me to take the lead, as if I knew my way around this castle. I started to move, but Reed suddenly stopped me, "Wait!"

"What?"

"You can't walk around this castle with your dress half-tied and your back exposed!" Reed scolded.

I sighed, fighting the urge to roll my eyes. "I was just wearing an old, thin cotton dress. I'm sure I was showing more skin then than I am now."

"Hold on," he said, and before I could respond, he was behind me in an instant. His warm fingers lightly grazed my back as he gathered my damp hair, careful not to touch my iron collar as he draped my hair over my shoulder, allowing him better access to my back as he began to lace up my dress.

I felt a jolt of electricity race through me at the sensation of his fingers brushing against my skin. My eyes fluttered closed for a moment, and I couldn't stop the soft shiver that ran down my spine. His touch was light, almost tentative, yet each brush sent a wave of heat through my body. I felt myself arch into him instinctively, my skin tingling where his fingers lingered. It was too intimate for something so simple as lacing up a dress.

A fire stirred low in my belly and I began to wish I hadn't laced the dress up as much as I had, wanting to stay in this moment just a little longer, to let the sensation linger. My thoughts began to scatter, and for a brief moment, I was transported back to that night in the Ember Palace. Hawthorne had laced me up then, though I'd been drunk at the time. And just like then, my body responded to his touch causing a strange fluttering in my chest.

Was it just the sensation of being laced up that stirred something inside me? Maybe that was my version of foreplay? I wasn't exactly an expert, but I knew it felt good. It was strange, maybe even a little embarrassing, but something inside me craved that kind of closeness.

"All done," Reed said, his voice almost a whisper as his fingers brushed down the now-fully tied bodice, sending one final spark of heat through me.

"Thank you," I said softly, my voice slipping out smoother and sultrier than I was used to as I turned to face him, twisting my hair so it fell back down along my shoulders.

I watched as Reed's eyes scanned me in my new gown. However, I noticed his gaze linger a little too long on my chest, his eyes widening and his nostrils flaring. I looked down and realized the spot where my damp hair had hung had made the fabric of my dress transparent, the outline of my hardened nipple clearly visible beneath it.

Instinctively, I knew I should cover up or turn away, but I didn't. I realized I wanted him to look,. Even though I felt unbothered, I noticed how red Reed's face had become, and it only seemed to deepen by the minute. I decided to place my hair back in front of me, sparing him the distraction or embarrassment, and watched as he blinked rapidly, only just realizing he'd been staring.

"I'm sorry," he muttered, his gaze dropping to the floor.

"It's alright," I replied with a half-smile, not wanting him to feel ashamed. I knew I wasn't. "Are you ready?"

Reed nodded, and we headed down the hallway. A small grin stayed on my face, knowing Reed had seen me, and from the look on his face, it seemed he liked what he saw. Not to mention the slight bulge in his pants that I noticed before I myself had to redirect my gaze. There was something oddly satisfying about this whole thing.

When we returned to the kitchen, the scent of freshly prepared food immediately greeted me. Myrtle had already arranged everything just as I'd instructed, the dishes artfully laid out on the counter, each one looking more perfect than the last. I stood for a moment, taking it all in, not just with my eyes, but my nose, inhaling the rich aroma of the roasted meats, the tang of the salad dressing, and the subtle spices from the bread. I felt a deep sense of accomplishment well up inside me.

"Here," Bentley said, pushing a plate my way with a small grin. "Remember, we eat first."

I nodded quickly, pulling the plate closer as Bentley placed another one in front of Reed and Myrtle. I tried to steady my breathing as excitement bubbled up inside me. I couldn't wait for Reed to taste the food, but I was also nervous. I knew the meal had to be better than whatever slop they served him in his cell, but that didn't make me feel any less vulnerable. I wanted his approval more than I cared to admit.

Reed didn't waste any time digging in. His eyes closed for a brief moment as he chewed, savoring the bite.

"Wow," he muttered, a faint smile tugging at his lips. "This is amazing."

Heat rose to my face at his praise. I quickly took a bite myself, trying to steady the sudden flutter in my stomach. I wasn't one to boast, but damn, we had nailed this meal. The meat was tender, perfectly seasoned, and the salad dressing, just the right amount of tartness, tied everything together beautifully. I could almost hear Kalynda's voice in my head, telling me I'd done well. She would've been proud.

Bentley and Myrtle took the other plates to distribute to the guards on duty, while Reed and I were left alone in the kitchen. I wondered briefly how the guards felt about us walking around so freely. I could practically feel the unease in the air, as if they would suddenly come rushing in to restore order. Unless Lars was there to back up his decision, I knew the other guards would be suspicious of two prisoners roaming the castle without supervision.

Reed and I ate in a strange silence, the clinking of silverware the only sound between us. I wanted to ask him about what had happened after he'd been dragged away. What had he endured, but he'd said he knew a place where we could talk. A place where we wouldn't have to worry about the guards. But where? And how? There was no way he could mean somewhere inside the castle without risking exposure.

"Thanks by the way," Reed said suddenly, breaking the silence. "For the cake."

I blinked, momentarily confused, before remembering. I'd asked Lars to deliver him a piece of cake. I was glad to hear that Lars had kept his word on that, as well as allowing me to actually see Reed. Though seeing him this way, free from behind bars was still too surreal.

"I'm glad it made its way to you," I replied with a small smile.

"Lars isn't so bad. He's a lot nicer than some of these other pricks."

I raised an eyebrow, a smirk tugging at my lips. "I've come to think of him as a decent male, too. For a guard that is."

There was an odd shift between us, a kind of quiet understanding. Maybe it was because, for the first time, we were truly alone, no guards, no bars, just the two of us. It felt like a small slice of freedom.

I found myself watching Reed more intently, studying the way he moved, the way his fingers gently pressed against his plate as he finished the last bite. His features, those strong, sharp lines, even his scar, were even more striking now that I had the chance to see him without the usual constraints of the prison bars. His hair, salt-and-pepper, like the first signs of a storm on the horizon, seemed to highlight the hardness of his jaw and the intensity of his eyes. I had noticed these things before, but now, I couldn't look away.

Reed's gaze met mine, and the moment hung in the air between us like something delicate. I didn't know what to say. My heart was beating faster than it should have been, and I suddenly felt very aware of how small the space was between us.

"So," I said, breaking the moment and trying to gather my thoughts. "You said you'd explain what happened and that you know a place?"

Reed flashed me a grin, as he took my empty plate and began to wash it in the sink, moving with the easy confidence of someone who knew exactly what he was doing. "Yes," he said slowly. "But not yet."

"Not yet?" I repeated, my voice tinged with frustration. Had he forgotten we were still prisoners? "Where exactly is this place?" I asked, a hint of suspicion creeping into my voice.

Reed dried his hands on a towel before turning to me, his expression suddenly more serious, though there was still a playful edge to his eyes. "It's a surprise. Trust me, you'll like it. But you'll have to be patient."

"And what are we supposed to do when the guards come to get us?" I asked, crossing my arms over my chest. "Or when Myrtle and Bentley come back to find the kitchen empty?" I didn't want to doubt him, but something about this situation felt too dangerous.

Reed's smile returned, this time with a touch of mischief. "While you were bathing, I spoke to Myrtle and Bentley. They're going to cover for us for a bit. Just long enough for us to talk in private with an added bonus."

I stared at him for a moment, processing his words. *A bonus?* What did he mean by that? I couldn't help but feel a little excited, but also a little scared.

"What kind of bonus?"

"You'll just have to wait and see. Just trust me."

I hesitated, then nodded. "Fine, but it better be worth it," I teased.

Reed chuckled. "It will be. Now sit back and relax. You did all the cooking and prepping, and the least I can do is clean up."

I did as he instructed and poured myself another glass of wine, the rich red liquid sliding smoothly into the glass. As I took a sip, I couldn't help but notice the way Reed moved, his every gesture fluid and confident. It was strange how much I noticed about him now; how much he had come to mean to me.

I wasn't sure if it was the wine, or if something else was happening, but I could no longer deny the attraction I felt toward him. Reed was beautiful, there was no other way to describe it. Not only was he beautiful on the outside, but he was beautiful on the inside as well. He was good all the way to his core, someone who deserved better than this place.

I watched him as he finished cleaning, my heart giving a small, painful squeeze. When Hayden came for me, I would make sure Reed went in my place. He didn't belong here. I couldn't leave with him, my fate was already sealed, but Reed could be free. And I would make sure that happened.

I switched from wine to water, hoping the cool liquid would clear my head. Reed and I continued cleaning the kitchen, dusting every nook and cranny. Neither of us was eager for the day's work to end, knowing where we would both end up once the chores were finished. Myrtle and Bentley checked in a few times, each visit bringing a new mundane task: take stock of the food, organize plates and bowls by color and size, polish every inch of the silverware. Eventually, Myrtle muttered something about needing to inventory the livestock with Bentley. I was thankful for the tasks, and I was sure Reed was too. They kept us busy for a few hours and gave me time to talk to Reed just like we used to in the cells.

I knew he wasn't ready to talk about what happened after the guards took him away, so I didn't press him. Instead, I focused on lighter subjects like stories from home and the trouble we got into when we were younger. I even told him about Lars and the unexpected kindness he had shown me since becoming my guard. Reed seemed surprised, maybe even a little upset that I spoke so highly of him. I wasn't sure if he was angry that I was sort of befriending an Ivy Guard, or if he felt like he was being replaced as my tether in this nightmare of an Isle.

"It's just nice to have someone on my side, I suppose. Someone who doesn't see me as the enemy."

"Is he, though?" Reed asked. "He is still a guard. Don't mistake his kindness for any shred of loyalty to you. That's not how these guards work."

I didn't want to argue. I still didn't know what kind of pain the other guards might have inflicted on Reed, and I truly hoped that Lars wasn't one of them.

"Lars..." I began, searching for the right words. "Lars wasn't one of the guards who hurt you, was he?"

"No," Reed answered quickly. "You are not wrong that he is different from the others, but don't for a second let your guard down. Not here. You don't know where his morals and duties truly lie."

"But if it weren't for Lars, you would still be locked away," I said, hoping Reed was wrong about him. I couldn't lose another friend here, not when Reed would surely be locked up again.

"Just keep him at arm's length, alright?"

I nodded, and we let the conversation end there as we returned to our work, trying once again to keep the conversation light and optimistic.

I stared out the window, watching the sunlight filter through the thick branches of the trees. Though the branches blocked most of the sun's enchanting glow, it was still better than nothing. The sky had deepened to a soft amber, and I wondered if I might stay in the kitchen a little longer to help prepare dinner. Maybe I could beg Lars to let me and Reed stay, anything to keep Reed from having to return to wherever they had him locked away.

Lars had been kind enough to let me sleep in Hawthorne's room, but I knew that kindness had limits. I couldn't rely on it again. I'd have to swallow my fears, try to erase the dark memories of the cells, and move forward eventually, but maybe he could spare a little more kindness and let Reed and I stay here a little while longer.

"Well, I think we did a damn good job here," Reed said as he washed his hands. "Now, are you ready for the surprise?"

"Yes!"

Reed extended his hand, and without hesitation, I took it. The warmth of his skin instantly seeped into mine, but it did little to quell the shivers that ran through my body. I wasn't sure when Reed had shifted from stranger to friend to something more, but I welcomed it and I hoped, perhaps, he felt the same.

We left through the back door, our hands still intertwined. Just beside the door was a spiraling staircase, the stones worn smooth from years of use. It looked like it led to some sort of landing.

"Can you climb?" Reed asked gently.

My body had endured more than its fair share of strain, but I hadn't fully realized how much strength I was starting to regain over the past few days. Between staying active and eating properly, I was beginning to feel like myself again. I also knew some of that had to do with when Lars healed me. He could have easily transferred just enough power to close the wounds, but I didn't realize how deeply I could feel the healing beneath my skin. He must have given me more than I realized, not just to fix my broken nose and the gashes on my face. I'd need to remember to thank him for that.

"I'm fine," I nodded and followed him up the stone staircase, each step echoing in the silence.

The ascent was steeper than I expected, and my breath grew heavy, but I kept moving. I was outside, and nothing felt more freeing than the fresh air. I could climb a mountain if it meant escaping the suffocating walls of the castle.

"Are you sure no one will see us?" I asked between breaths.

"I'm sure, Myrtle said the guards don't patrol this area."

His certainty reassured me, though I couldn't help but wonder how he'd found this place. Or where we were headed. I kept my eyes on the stairs as I climbed, but when I finally looked up again, Reed had vanished.

"Reed?" I whispered.

"I'm here," he called back, poking his head around the corner at the top. "This is as far as we need to go."

I joined him on the landing, my eyes immediately drawn to the breathtaking view before me. The treetops stretched out below us, and beyond them, the Isle seemed to go on forever, bathed in a warm, golden light. It was so beautiful that my throat tightened, and I felt tears prick at the corners of my eyes.

"How did you find this place?" I whispered, my voice filled with awe.

Reed took a step closer, his expression soft. "I was sent here to scrub some stone on my first day. I thought they'd brought me up to toss me off the edge, but instead, I just cleaned. It wasn't easy, but the view made it worth it."

"It's incredible."

Reed grinned, his eyes bright as he nudged my shoulder. "It's private, too. Now look straight ahead."

I did as he suggested, and then I saw it, the perfect view of the sunset, with no trees to block the sun's descent. I had caught glimpses of the sun through the kitchen windows, soaking in the warmth of its rays as they filtered through the trees, but nothing compared to this. Being outside, in the open, bathed in its presence felt entirely different. The sky was a riot of oranges and pinks, and as the colors deepened, tears I hadn't even realized I was holding back began to fall.

"I thought it would be the perfect place to watch the sunset," Reed said softly, his voice a tender warmth against the chill in the air. His hand brushed mine, and I let my fingers curl into his.

I stared at the sky, the colors shifting as the sun dipped lower. "Thank you," I said, my voice barely above a whisper as I turned to face him.

"Why are you crying?" he asked reaching out to catch a tear that had escaped. "Was the climb too much?"

"No," I whispered quickly, stopping him before he could misinterpret. "I… I just missed this. The sun, the fresh air, the feeling of freedom. It's been so long since I've felt this alive."

He said nothing, but his arms wrapped around me in a warm embrace. I melted into him, letting his presence anchor me as my body relaxed against his. For a long moment, neither of us moved, just existing in that quiet space. A moment that could disappear at any second.

When I finally pulled away, Reed guided me to sit beside him on the ledge. Our hands remained intertwined, and I could feel his steady warmth against the cold air.

"So…" I began, hesitant, knowing the question I had to ask. "What happened after you killed Orrin?"

Reed took a slow breath, his expression darkening. "I was brought in for questioning. I'll spare you the gruesome details, but it wasn't pleasant. The guards seemed to think I did it for justice, for the crew he had executed on the king's orders. They thought I was restoring balance."

"I'm sorry," I whispered, guilt rising in my chest.

Reed's face hardened, a flash of anger in his eyes. "Don't apologize. You have nothing to feel sorry for. Orrin got what he deserved."

"But you didn't deserve to be hurt because of me. You did nothing wrong."

"I would take everything they did to me a hundred times over if it meant ending that bastard's life," Reed's voice softened, a quiet sincerity in his words. "You're innocent, Eli. You're here to repay a debt your brother owed. Nothing that's happened to you has been fair."

I looked away, my gaze drifting down to the long drop below us. Guilt gnawed at my insides. Reed still thought of me as innocent, but he didn't know the truth. He didn't know I was the one who'd killed Prince Hawthorne. I'd made a mistake, a mistake that would haunt me for the rest of my life. I had to tell him. But I feared it would change everything between us. He had been the one person who understood me, who had shown me nothing but kindness. If I lost him, I didn't know what I would do.

"Reed," I said, my voice trembling as my heart raced. "I haven't been honest with you."

"What do you mean?" His brow furrowed in confusion.

"I… I'm a bad person," I began, but he cut me off.

"No, you're not," Reed interjected quickly, his eyes narrowing. "You're just dealing with survivor's guilt. Orrin—"

"It's not about Orrin," I snapped louder than I intended. My heart pounded in my chest, and the words burst out before I could stop them. "I killed Prince Hawthorne."

The silence that followed felt like it stretched on forever. I watched Reed's face for any sign of judgment, any hint of disgust. But all I saw was confusion. A quiet, intense kind of confusion.

"I thought it was your brother," Reed said slowly, piecing it together. "He was the one who went on the hunt, right? He's the one who shot the prince?"

"No," I said, my breath hitching as I unclasped our hands. "Hayden was too hungover that morning, so I went out to do the royal hunt for him. It was my chance to prove I was worth something to my kingdom. But that morning, I was sick too, that's why I accused you of drugging the gin." I paused, trying to steady my shaking hands. "Because I saw a stag. Or I thought I did and I released the arrow. When I got closer… I realized my mistake. I don't know what happened, but I can't stop thinking about it. I can't stop feeling the guilt."

Reed said nothing at first, his eyes searching mine. His hand hovered near my own, as if unsure whether to touch me, but his words were steady.

"Eli," he said gently, "you didn't mean to. It was an accident." His hand finally settled on my shoulder, offering warmth that I didn't deserve.

"No," I shook my head, pulling away from his touch. "I killed him, Reed. I killed an innocent person. I hear the sound of the arrow hitting him every night in my dreams. It haunts me." My voice broke, and the tears spilled freely now.

"That's why you have the night terrors?" Reed asked softly.

"Yes, I can't un-see all of that blood, the pain I caused." I whispered, the burden of my guilt suffocating me. "I don't deserve any kindness. The longer I live, the heavier it gets. I just want it to end. I want it to be over." I didn't mean to confess that last part out loud, but there was no taking it back now.

Reed's arm tightened around me, pulling me into his embrace. "It was an accident, Eli. You didn't mean to. I'm sure of that. And I'm sure of something else, you have no evil in you, not one ounce of it, do you hear me?"

"It doesn't change what happened," I whimpered against his chest. "He's dead because of me. This whole kingdom lost its heir, their future, because of me. And I don't even know what the king wants from me. Whatever it is, I seem to be failing at that too."

"Stop," Reed said, his voice fierce now. "Look at me. You'll keep fighting. Do you hear me? You'll keep fighting for your life."

I looked into his silver-gray eyes, and for the first time in what felt like forever, I saw something other than pity, something like hope. "When the king gets what he whatever it is he wants from you, you won't give up. Do you understand? Accidents happen all the time. Maybe it was my fault for giving you that drink. Blame me if you need to. But please, Eli, don't blame yourself." His voice softened. "You deserve to live, just like everyone else."

I swallowed, my chest tight with emotion. Reed was right. Things happened, sometimes without explanation. But that was no excuse to give up. I had to keep going. For myself. Only Theodon could judge me in the end. Reed didn't seem to think I was a bad person, so why was I judging myself so harshly? Maybe I needed to hear those words of validation, words of comfort.

Reed continued to hold me in his strong arms, with a gentleness that was almost too much to bear. It was soft, delicate, but I needed more. I wrapped my arms tightly around his torso, pressing myself against him as if to anchor myself in the moment. He was my tether, and he understood. His embrace tightened, the need in his grip consuming me.

Time stood still. I had no idea if we'd been like this for minutes, hours, or days. All I knew was that I needed this, needed him. The magnitude of everything, the danger, the fear, it all felt distant in his arms. But my body, desperate for rest, forced me to pull away. I knew if I didn't, I'd fall asleep right there, with my heart beating in sync with his.

A sharp breeze stung my tear-streaked face, and I winced slightly, the cold air snapping me back to reality. Before I could fully register the sensation, Reed's warm fingers gently brushed against my cheek, wiping away the last of my salty tears. His hand lingered there for a moment, and I wasn't ready to let go of the warmth. Without thinking, I grabbed his wrist, holding him close, unwilling to let the sensation slip away.

Reed didn't pull back. Instead, his fingers, heated and tender, trailed down my cheek, lingering on my parted lips. My heart began to race, and I could feel his pulse beneath my skin, thumping in time with my own. His touch was slow, deliberate, and it was clear neither of us could deny the magnetic pull between us.

"Reed," I breathed, the word escaping me in a rush of air.

"Eli," he murmured in return, his gaze burning into mine, a fire kindled deep in his eyes. I could feel the heat spreading through my chest, up my neck, a rush of warmth that pooled in the pit of my stomach.

I leaned forward, drawn to him, and he did the same. His hand slid to my waist, holding me with a confidence that made my head spin. Our faces were so close now that I could feel the heat of his breath mingling with mine. The scent of mint clung to the air around us, familiar and intoxicating.

I wanted this. More than anything, I wanted this. And if I was going to die, I swore it wouldn't be before I had a chance to feel this with Reed.

His grip on my hip tightened, our lips were just inches apart and my body moved forward before I could stop it. My lips began to tremble as I leaned in closer. But before I could close the distance, a voice shouted from behind us, snapping me out of the moment.

"Hey!" The angry voice was sharp and commanding. "What the hell do you two think you're doing up here?"

Reed and I jerked apart, and I craned my neck to see an Ivy Guard standing on the landing, his eyes narrowed in suspicion. We were caught. And unlike Lars, I doubted this guard would be so willing to listen to reason.

"We were just doing some cleaning," Reed said quickly, positioning himself between me and the guard, his posture protective. "We lost track of time."

"Who sanctioned this?" The guard demanded, his hand resting on the hilt of his sword, fingers twitching with impatience.

I stood up quickly, hiding behind Reed. My heart raced, and for a moment, I wasn't sure whether I was more afraid of getting caught or getting Reed into trouble. But I had to say something. I had to cover for us. "Lars sent us up here," I said, my voice shaking slightly. " He'll explain everything." I hoped the guard would take the bait, and I prayed that Lars would cover for us. He was the only rational guard I'd encountered here. Sure, he'd be pissed about the lie, but I'd take his wrath over this guard's any day.

The guard's brow furrowed. "Who's Lars?"

"He must be new if he doesn't know Lars," Reed muttered low so only I could hear.

"He took over for Orrin," I added quickly, my mind racing. "He's the one in charge now."

"Still don't know him, but if he was on the prison watch shift, he's gone." The guard said firmly.

"Gone?" I whispered, my stomach sinking.

"Yeah. He likely went to meet the king at the northern docks earlier today. Should be back at the castle soon."

Caraway was back? *No, no, no. This couldn't be happening.* If he was due to be back soon, there must be a closer private docking area. What did it mean for me? For Reed? If the king had returned, he would have the authority to issue an execution order. Reed could die for killing one of his guards, and I wouldn't be able to stop it.

"What do you mean, he's back?" Reed asked, his voice a little too calm, almost too confident for someone speaking to a guard.

"He came back early," the guard explained, his tone cool. "He'll probably want her waiting in the interrogation room. So you can either come quietly, or I'll be forced to do this the unpleasant way." He unsheathed his sword with a sharp metallic sound.

"She'll go quietly," Reed said, speaking for me, his voice rigid. "Just put the sword away, and we'll both go."

"You're the one who killed that guard, aren't you?" The guard took a step forward, his sword raised threateningly. "Orrin, wasn't it?"

"Just put it away," Reed said calmly, his eyes never leaving the guard. "It's up to the Ivy King to punish me and decide my fate, not you."

The guard didn't seem to care about Reed's words. He continued to advance, his sword gleaming in the dim light. It was clear he wasn't going to listen, and I could see the tension in Reed's shoulders, the readiness in his stance.

"We'll go peacefully," I said, stepping forward, trying to buy us time as I moved towards the stairs.

"You killed one of my own," the guard spat, voice dripping with venom. "I doubt the king will care too much. Besides, he just wants the girl. You? You've been forgotten. Nobody cares what happens to you."

Before I could react, the guard raised his sword, ready to strike Reed. My heart stopped.

I couldn't let him do this..

"Eli!" Reed shouted in panic, his voice breaking as he reached for me.

I didn't think. I couldn't think. My body reacted before my mind could catch up, throwing itself in front of him, a desperate shield against the blow. The strike sliced through the air, so close I could feel the rush of it, but I didn't flinch. My heart slammed in my chest at the thought of Reed dying in cold blood right there, in front of me. It was unbearable. It couldn't end like this. Not while there was still a chance, a way out.

Everything around me became a blur. I felt vines begin to curl around me. The guard must have used his magic to avoid spilling my blood or the king would surely punish him. At least I was untouchable for now.

"Reed, run!" I managed to shout, my voice desperate.

"What the hell?" the guard muttered under his breath. I didn't waste any more time; I hoped Reed was making his escape.

As the vines began to retract, I turned to see where Reed had gone. But before I could fully process anything, something hard struck the back of my head. My vision blurred, everything spinning out of control. I staggered, my knees giving out as I fell to the stone ground. Pain exploded in my body, and all I could do was pray that Reed had gotten away.

And then, darkness swallowed me whole, leaving me numb.

My head throbbed, a steady pulse beneath my skull, as my eyes fluttered open. The air was heavy with an unsettling stillness, and the faint flicker of flames danced in the corners of my vision. I squeezed my eyes shut, letting them adjust to the harsh light, a sharp sting lingering behind my eyelids.

"Finally awake," a voice purred, low and familiar. It was King Caraway.

I blinked, trying to focus. How long had I been unconscious? It felt like an eternity, yet the moment I opened my eyes, I knew exactly where I was. The interrogation chamber. Cold stone walls, flickering torches, and the unmistakable scent of sweat and metal. I couldn't remember the last thing that happened, but the fear gnawing at my gut told me it hadn't ended well.

"Where's Reed?" I croaked, my voice barely more than a rasp. My throat was raw, every breath like sandpaper against my lungs. I had to force the words out, and they came with a burning sensation that made me wince.

"I wouldn't worry about him," he hissed. "He's been put back in his place and dealt with."

His words sank in slowly, but they didn't bring me any comfort. I tried to push myself upright, but the chains around my wrists clinked, holding me in place.

"How are you feeling?" The king's question felt almost casual, as if it weren't a prelude to something far worse.

How was I feeling? My muscles ached, and a hollow emptiness weighed down on me. My body felt weak and drained. The lingering ache in my skull told me I'd been struck, but that didn't explain why I felt so empty.

"What did you do to me?" I managed, but my voice trembled with something that sounded a lot like fear.

He didn't answer right away. Instead, he turned, his boots scraping against the stone floor as he moved to a nearby table. I followed his movements, watching as he laid out a series of instruments, familiar knives and the star fragment.

"Every time you woke up," he began, his tone cold, "I had Grove," he gestured to the guard in the corner of the room, a male I didn't recognize, "sedate you to keep you calm. Can't have you using your magic while your collar was off, now can we?"

I moved my neck from side to side searching for the sting of the collar against my skin, a small pain I had gotten used to thanks to the fabric I hid beneath it. It was gone.

I kept my eyes locked on the king, watching as he picked up a dagger from the table. The blade gleamed, ancient and etched with strange symbols, its shape far different from the one he'd used before.

"Still checking to see if my blood shimmers?" I asked, forcing the words out with sarcasm that tasted bitter in my mouth. I shouldn't have said it, but I couldn't stop myself.

He chuckled darkly. "I already checked while you were unconscious," he said. "This…" he trailed off as he examined the dagger in his hand, "is for something else entirely."

Before I could brace myself, he slashed down the front of my dress, moving with unnerving speed. The fabric tore easily beneath the blade, Myrtle's gift now ruined, the edges of it hanging in tatters.

My breath caught. The king had promised before that he wouldn't touch me, but had something changed? Was my refusal to break finally driving him to lash out, to punish me with my own body?

I closed my eyes tightly, trying to block out the sight of him. I imagined myself somewhere else, somewhere warm. Reed's arms around me, his steady breath against my neck as we watched the sunset together. The sky was painted in hues of pink and orange, soft and peaceful.

I wasn't here. This wasn't happening.

But then, something sharp and agonizing sliced across my skin, pulling me back into the nightmare. My eyes snapped open as the pain flared across my chest, a searing line where the king had driven the dagger between my breasts.

"What are you doing?" I screamed, my body jerking, instinctively trying to writhe away from the agony. The blood, warm and sticky, pooled beneath me, slick and shimmering in the dim light.

"Hold still," he ordered, his voice dangerously calm. "This can be a clean cut unless you want me to accidentally take something more from you."

I forced my chin down, desperate to see what he was doing. Blood began to trickle down my sides, soaking into the ruined fabric of my dress. The sharp tang of it filled my nostrils, mingling with the stale, oppressive air. I was drowning in it.

"Please," I gasped, my chest rising and falling in frantic breaths. "Stop this. Please."

Just when I thought the pain couldn't get any worse, the king's cold fingers slid into the fresh cut, as if he were carefully peeling open my skin. The flesh tugged and ripped wider under his touch, causing nothing but searing pain to radiate through my entire body. The burning agony was relentless and I couldn't stop myself from screaming as tears began to fall faster than I could stop them. My voice was raw, desperate, but the king didn't flinch. His gaze stayed fixed on the wound, as though the sound of my suffering was nothing more than background noise.

I turned my head, eyes searching for the guard in the corner; his face was a stone mask, completely unmoving. If Lars had been here then maybe I would have had a chance. But where was he? Now I was at this new guard's mercy, and it was clear no help would come from him. "Why are you doing this?" I gasped, each word dragging out from my chest like thorns. "What do you want from me?"

"All in good time," he replied, his voice smooth and unbothered. He was unmoved by my pain, my tears, my fear.

When he finally removed his fingers from the gash, I could barely breathe. He reached for the star fragment, his movements precise, almost reverent and the stone seemed to gleam in the dim light.

"No paste this time?" I snarled through clenched teeth, the anger burning hotter than the pain. I still had no answers as to why he was doing this or what he was hoping to achieve. "Just kill me and get it over with!" I begged.

Caraway didn't answer. He only looked at me with a glimmer of amusement in his eyes. "*Shhh*," he said softly, as if I were a child throwing a tantrum.

He pressed the star fragment directly into the center of my chest, pushing it into the gaping wound. The coldness settled on my skin, seeping deep into me as if it were trying to merge with my very bones. Then, in an instant, the coldness transformed into scalding heat. The pain began to surge through my every nerve.

"Can you feel it?" he asked.

"It burns!" I screamed, unable to stop myself. It felt like every ounce of the little magic I had in my body was being pulled toward the open wound, as though the star was siphoning it all away, draining me dry. The world blurred around me, and the raw heat in my chest made my skin feel like it was on fire.

The king stepped back, watching me writhe in agony beneath the chains that bound me. My body bucked helplessly, every muscle screaming, but the pain was different now. The more the magic flowed, the more I felt myself unraveling, pieces of me slipping away with each pulse.

How much time had passed? It was impossible to tell. One moment, I was burning, writhing, and the next, the pain dulled. The searing fire that had consumed me seemed to fade, replaced by an eerie numbness. My body went still, the blood still dripping down my chest, but it was muted now, the shimmer less vibrant. I could still feel the faintest tingling of magic, but it was weak.

Caraway moved quickly, taking the star fragment from my chest with a careful, almost tender motion, as if he were handling something precious. His hand closed around it, and then, just as swiftly, he moved it out of my sight, carrying it to another part of the room.

I lay there, dazed, unable to speak, the world spinning around me. My eyes fixed on the ceiling, the cold stone above, and my thoughts wandered. Home. Family. Reed.

I wasn't sure what that star fragment did, but I had a hunch. It had drained the small traces of magic I had in my body. Already I could feel my body slowly replenishing it, but with such a small amount I possessed, I doubted it would be enough to even heal me no matter how slowly the process.

Was that what he wanted? My small bit of magic? The Ember he thought I possessed? Either way he wouldn't be able to get what he wanted from me. I was the powerless princess. The almost human Pyronia. I was sure my purpose and use to the Ivy King had been served and only death awaited me now.

I knew Hayden was still coming for me. But when he came, he would find only my lifeless body. He would never know my plan for him to take Reed in my place, to take him somewhere safe while I accepted my punishment. I would never have the chance to explain, never see Reed free.

Yes, Hayden would come to Ivy Isle, but he'd arrive too late it would break him, and I could only hope he wouldn't do something rash by seeking revenge.

A loud clatter shattered the silence, snapping me from my dazed thoughts. My eyes darted around the room, frantic, searching for the source. The Ivy King had overturned the entire table, sending metal instruments scattering across the stone floor. The room seemed to vibrate with his fury. I could almost feel the heat of his wrath radiating off him.

"Your Highness?" Grove's voice trembled, hesitant as he tried to find the cause of his king's rage.

"It didn't work!" Caraway's voice cracked like thunder. "I did everything right, down to the letter," he muttered to himself, as though trying to convince his own mind.

Hearing his words only confirmed my suspicions. He was after the Ember, and somehow, he believed the star was the key to unlocking it. But the Ember wasn't with me, and now I was more certain than ever that no trace of it ever remained inside me.

Caraway's furious steps echoed through the room and before I could even react, the back of his hand crashed across my face, the sting sharp and immediate. "Where is it?" His voice was low, but it vibrated with such intensity that I could feel the heat of his breath against my skin. His face loomed dangerously close, and I could taste the bitterness of his rage in the air. "Are you, or are you not, the firstborn heir to the Pyronia line?"

"I am," I forced the words out, my voice trembling, hoping that truth would be enough to satisfy him.

"Then where is it?" He snarled, his hand gripping the gash on my chest, reigniting the fire of pain. "Where is your Ember?"

"I don't know," I gasped, squirming beneath his touch, trying to pull away as the gripping pain flared beneath his touch. "What do you even want with it?"

The king didn't answer. His eyes, cold and calculating, never left me as he withdrew his hand from the wound. With the other, he gripped the hilt of an ancient dagger.

Just when I thought he might be done with me, I felt a sharp, cold slice across my stomach. The excruciating pain hit like a sudden storm as pain crashed like waves through my entire being. Every nerve of my body was alert as I felt the warmth of blood began to pool beneath my skirt, this cut hurting far more than the gash in my chest. I couldn't see the wound, but the sensation was so much worse. It felt as though my insides might spill out of me. The pain continued to pulse through my body, so intense that I couldn't scream, couldn't even make a sound. I couldn't cry. I couldn't fight back. I could only feel the blood seeping beneath me, mixing with the searing ache.

"Take her back down to her cell," the king's voice broke through my haze. "Do not put on the collar. I need her to heal, but at least she can suffer a bit longer."

Grove's rough hands grabbed me, lifting me over his shoulder. My blood soaked into the leather of his tunic as my vision began to blur. Each step he took down the stone staircase was familiar, though I could hardly focus on anything but the pulsing pain. I was back in my cell and when Grove departed, leaving all but one torch lit. I was all alone.

Iron collar or not, I knew there was no healing from wounds like these, not in this state. Not when the king basically drained me of all of the little magic I had. It could never replenish quick enough. I'd bleed out slowly, my life extinguishing in this cell. But Hayden would finally be safe. The Ivy King would have his vengeance, my life debt complete, and it would all be over I told Reed that I would fight to survive. But now? I was just too tired, and the pain was too much. I just couldn't anymore. I used the little strength I had and crawled into the familiar dark corner of my cage as I welcomed the peace that came with death. Ready to hear that melodic humming I heard before. Ready for it all to end.

Through my slips of consciousness, I heard the creak of the iron-barred door stir next to me. Someone else was in the cell beside mine. At least, I thought so, unless I was truly delirious and imagining it.

"Sparks?" A gentle voice whispered.

The sound of Reed's voice sent a calming wave through my entire body. I couldn't move to confirm whether he had been hurt, but hearing him was enough. He was alive. This was my chance to tell him about Hayden's plan.

"Reed?" I groaned, barely able to shift my head toward his direction, still lying in the furthest corner of my cell, my back turned to him.

"Yeah," Reed answered, his voice soft, almost tender. "I'm here. Are you okay?"

"I don't think so," I rasped, a cough rattling in my chest, the strain on my muscles sending a jolt of pain to my core.

"What did the Ivy King do?" Reed's voice took on an urgent, almost desperate tone. "Did he finally tell you what he was searching for?"

"He wants the Ember," I said, leaving out the gruesome details of the torture. I didn't want Reed to have to picture that. "But whatever he tried to do to extract it, it didn't work."

"Why?"

Because I don't have the Ember, I never did, I thought to myself. Slowly, I could feel myself slipping away. I was dying, and I knew it. I needed to tell Reed the truth before everything went silent, before the end came for me. If Hayden was still trying to save me, he needed to know everything, everything that might give him a chance to stop the king.

"Reed," I began, but another fit of coughs seized me, my body rolling into the light. "Reed, I—"

"Eli!" Reed gasped. "What happened to you?"

Without the shadows of my corner, I knew Reed could see the bloody rags that clung to my shredded body. I didn't care that my bare chest was exposed, not that you could see much of it through the blood and grime caked onto my chest and stomach from the cell floor.

"It doesn't matter," I said, struggling to speak.

"Who did this to you?" Reed demanded.

"The king," was all I could manage.

"*He* did this?"

I groaned in response, a strangled breath escaping my lungs with a cough.

"That motherfucker," Reed spat, his voice seething with rage. "But why?" he asked frantically, "And why aren't you healing? You're…you're free of your collar!"

This was it. The opening I needed. My muscles screamed in protest as I dragged my battered body as far as I could across the floor, inching toward Reed's cell. "I lied," I gasped, pain lacing my words. "I don't have the Ember. Hayden does."

Tears stung my eyes, but I couldn't stop. "I was born a twin, and because of that, my magic was weak, almost nonexistent. No one expected me to survive. But I did."

"But the life debt?"

"The Ivy King demanded the life of the firstborn," I continued, my voice strained. "And that was me. But I wasn't the one the Ember chose."

There was a long silence before Reed finally spoke again, "Eli, listen to me," Reed urged, his voice intense, a note of desperation threading through it. "You need to pull every ounce of magic you have left and heal yourself before it's too late."

"I can't, even healing a small cut takes a long time. The magic in my blood can't heal wounds like these."

"But that day in the oasis," Reed said, his voice faltering. "I saw *your* magic."

"It was my pendant," I interrupted quickly, knowing I had to get to the point. "Reed, listen to me. Hayden is coming for me by the next full moon." I coughed, struggling to catch my breath. "I don't know exactly when that is, but when he does, I need you to go with him. He'll keep you safe. He'll take you wherever you need to go. And then, you have to tell him what the king's plans are, how he's trying to steal the Ember."

"You will tell him yourself," Reed insisted. "If you can get a little closer, I can heal you."

I looked up, meeting Reed's eyes. There was no question in his face, he would do anything, give everything to heal me. But *his* iron collar was still on.

"Your collar," I whispered, barely able to speak. "Please, promise me you'll escape when Hayden arrives."

Reed's features twisted into something fierce. "Stop it," he said, his voice calm but undercut with what sounded like rage. "Guards!" he shouted. "You promised you'd fight to live. I need you to do that now, okay?" His eyes glistened with unshed tears, mirroring my own. "Guards!" he yelled again, his voice cracking.

And then I heard the heavy door at the top of the steps slam open.

"What the hell is going on down here?" I heard Grove's voice echo through the room.

"You need to heal her!" Reed's voice cracked, an edge of desperation beneath the command.

The guard stopped in his tracks, glancing me over. His eyes, hard and indifferent, assessed my battered form. Then, with a dismissive shrug, he muttered, "her collar is off, per King Caraway's orders. She can heal herself."

"She's too weak!" Reed's voice rose. "You need to do it, or she's going to die. And then what will the king say, huh?" He sounded frantic now, a raw edge of panic seeping into his words. "He still needs her. Don't you get that? Do you want to be the one the king blames when she perishes?"

Grove snorted, a cruel laugh escaping him. "Do you know how much of my energy it would take to heal all of that?" He gestured at my ravaged body with a flick of his wrist. "I was in that room. I saw everything the king did to her." The guard took a step back, starting to walk away. "She's the Ember Princess, and with a family like hers? A few more hours, and she'll be as good as new."

I lay there, struggling to hold onto consciousness, my thoughts swirling in a fog of pain. His words settled heavily in my chest, but I didn't have the strength to argue. My body, broken and battered, had nothing left to give. I could feel my life slipping away, like sand through my fingers.

I considered revealing the truth to him, but the risk was too great. The Ivy King would have to believe that the magic he drained from me was too much for my body to replenish in time to heal fully. That had to be the story. Let him think he was the one who made the fatal mistake. Let him believe he'd lost the one piece in his game that mattered most.

"Then take off my collar and I'll do it!" Reed's voice exploded suddenly as the guard continued his retreat up the stone stairs. "Unlock this goddamn door, and let me go to her. Now!"

The authority in his voice was so commanding that, for a brief moment, I might have obeyed him myself.

"Get Lars," I groaned, my throat raw and dry from the effort. It was a half-hearted plea, but it was the only thing I could think to say.

"Who?" Grove asked, a hint of confusion in his voice.

Maybe he was new as well and didn't know Lars. It felt like the last bit of hope I had was slipping away.

Despite the flickering torch still casting its weak light across the damp stone walls, my vision was growing darker, blurring around the edges. My limbs felt as though they were made of lead, heavy and unresponsive. Even if Reed somehow managed to convince the guard to remove his collar, the flow of magic in his blood would take time to adjust, time I simply didn't have. Who knew where Lars was stationed, and with the king back, I couldn't count on him for help. My senses screamed at me that I was running out of time.

The world around me faded to muffled echoes, like I was submerged underwater. Shapes blurred and twisted before my eyes. But then, out of the haze, I felt something.

A warm solid, comforting presence shifted me, pulling me into a lap. I could feel strong, familiar hands brushing over my body with delicate care, sending waves of energy coursing through me. A pulse of magic wrapped around my aching form, slowly stitching together the damage done by the king's cruelty. It was slow at first, but it was enough to keep me tethered to the world, to give me something to hold onto.

I tried to focus my blurry vision, but it took all my effort just to stay awake. The warmth of the body cradling me, the way his hands moved over my chest with a tenderness that cut through my fog, told me everything I needed to know. It had to be Reed.

Somehow, he'd convinced the guard to remove his collar, and now here he was, kneeling beside me in the cell, his magic flowing fiercely through me, almost overwhelming in its intensity. My body trembled as the pain began to dull, the worst of it starting to fade into nothingness. My vision began to sharpen, the edges of the world pulling back into focus. My breath came easier, and for the first time in what felt like ages, I could think clearly.

And when I finally managed to focus fully, there he was. *Reed*. His face, tense with concern, hovered above me, his brow furrowed in concentration. He didn't speak; he didn't need to. His touch was everything I needed, everything I had been waiting for. With each pulse of his magic, the darkness in my mind receded, and I found the strength to cling to the fragile thread of life that still remained.

I didn't know how much time I had left, but for the first time in what felt like an eternity, I believed I might make it through.

My wounds had completely healed, but as I tried to move, Reed's weakened body slumped to the cold, hard floor, leaving me still partially draped across his lap.

"Reed?" I shook him frantically, panic flooding my chest. His body was so still, too still. He had pushed himself beyond his limits, and now, I was terrified it was too late. "Reed," I whimpered, my voice barely above a breath, "Please wake up, please!"

His skin was ghostly pale, and he lay motionless on the cold floor of my cell. But then, I noticed the faint rise and fall of his chest. *He's still breathing*, I thought, a wave of fragile relief sweeping through me. He was alive, but barely. And he needed help.

"Please," I begged, turning to the guard who was staring down at Reed with an expression I couldn't quite decipher. Was it horror? Sympathy? No, that was impossible. He didn't care about a prisoner. But I had to try. I had to do something. "Please help him. He needs water and fresh air."

"Fresh air?" Grove's voice was hoarse with confusion, as though my request didn't make sense to him.

"He's from the Isle of Gust," I explained quickly. "The breeze, the fresh air, mixed with something in his stomach, it'll help him regain his strength." Reed couldn't die, not after everything he'd done for me. Not now, when Hayden was coming any day with the chance of freedom; Reed's ticket out of here.

I glanced down at Reed again, my heart sinking. His breathing, which had been slow, became erratic. His chest heaved in desperate gasps, and I felt the blood drain from my face. I watched in horror as his body began to convulse violently, as though it were vibrating under some unseen force.

"Reed?" I whispered, my lips trembling as I hovered helplessly over him. "What's happening to him?"

I screamed, my voice cracking with fear, "What's happening to him?!" I turned to Grove, hoping for some kind of answer, anything to make sense of the nightmare unfolding before me. I had never seen anyone drained this badly after healing another. How could this be happening? Was this the toll healing had taken on him when I was so close to death?

"I don't know, I've never seen something like this before," Grove murmured.

Without warning, Grove stepped into the cell, his heavy boots scuffing on the stone floor. He moved swiftly, scooping Reed's limp body into his arms with an ease that only highlighted how fragile Reed had become. He tossed Reed effortlessly over his shoulder like a sack of flour, as if Reed weighed nothing at all.

Everything happened so quickly, I couldn't even process it. One moment, Reed was in my arms, and the next, nothing. I was left locked in the cold, empty cell, staring at the spot where Reed had been.

"Where are you taking him?" I screamed, my voice hoarse with terror. "Please don't hurt him!"

Grove said nothing. He didn't even spare me a glance as he carried Reed's body up the steps. Reed's body twitched, his limbs jerking uncontrollably, his breath ragged and strained. In the flickering torchlight, I watched in utter confusion as his body seemed to warp, shifting between what looked like different ages. The changes came so fast, speeding up and slowing down, back and forth, like time itself was fighting to decide which direction to take.

The reality crashed over me in waves. Something was very wrong.

I watched helplessly as Grove carried Reed away, the violent convulsions wracking his body growing worse with each step. And then, the terrible, undeniable truth slammed into me. Grove wasn't taking him to safety. He was taking him to the king. The king would kill him, he would kill us both.

The terror I felt was suffocating, and the guilt that consumed me was unbearable. I should have never let Reed heal me. I should have known how much it would take out of him. I should have been stronger.

My thoughts tumbled over each other, all too fast, all too heavy. It was my fault. Reed was dying because of me. And now, because I couldn't give the king what he wanted, I would die too.

Hours dragged on, each one stretching into the next like an eternity. Still, there was no sign of Reed's return. *Please be okay,* I repeated to myself, the words a silent mantra in my mind. Every time the stillness in the cell grew, my anxiety did, too. The silence was suffocating, a heavy weight pressing down on me. There were no guards making their usual rounds, no clinking of keys or boots echoing along the stone corridors. It was just me, alone in a cold, dark space that had already carved itself into my memories, a place I knew would haunt me for the rest of my life, however long that was.

I hated this place. I hated this Isle. I hated Caraway. He was clearly after the Ember, and now, I was certain he suspected I'd lied and must have realized that Hayden was the one with the power. Law or no law, once he was done with me, he'd turn his attention to Hayden. This whole thing was so much bigger than how it all started and there was nothing that would stop him from doing whatever it took to get to the Ember. No one was safe.

Reed had been right. I needed to fight for my life. I needed to warn my parents about the Ivy King's plans, and maybe they would know more about how he had gotten hold of something capable of draining a fae of their power, or worse, their elemental gift. It was crystal clear that he wanted the Ember, but I still couldn't grasp his ultimate goal.

The sound of keys jangled in the distance, the unmistakable clink of metal against metal, followed by the echo of boots descending the stone stairs. My heart thudded in my chest, the sound sharp and rapid. Was it Grove? Was he coming to bring Reed back, to lock him away once more? Was Reed already dead? Or was it Caraway, coming to finish me off, to interrogate me again and break me further?

I strained my ears, trying to decipher the sounds. The footsteps grew closer, but when the figure came into view, I froze in disbelief.

"Lars?" For a brief moment, I wondered if my mind was playing tricks on me, conjuring up illusions. But no, it was him, it was definitely Lars.

"*Shhh,*" he whispered urgently, cutting off any further questions before they could escape my lips. He hurried toward me, unlocking my cell door with a practiced motion, his eyes scanning the stairs behind him before fixing on me. "We don't have much time. We need to hurry." Lars finished as he threw a dark hooded cloak my way.

It landed on the floor, my muscles refusing to move. My body was frozen, a wave of anger and relief crashing over me. I was furious that he had gone to greet the Caraway without even telling me, leaving me at the mercy of the other guards. Some part of me truly believed that if Lars had stayed, things with Caraway would not have gone as far as they did. And yet, there was a quiet relief curling in my chest at the sight of him, the simple fact that he was alright. I had feared his absence meant that Caraway had discovered that, under Lars' watch, I had been allowed to move freely about the castle and had even been freed from my cell. But he looked unharmed. And now, he was letting me out again—unless it was to bring me to the king for another round of punishment and pain.

"Wait, what's going on?" I asked and picked up the cloak still unable to comprehend his words. I took a small step back, my hand instinctively curling into a fist, just in case. The thought of returning to that interrogation chamber, the pain, I couldn't bear it.

I pulled the cloak over my body, only now realizing my dress was still cut down the middle, leaving much exposed. My face became heated at the thought of what Lars could see.

Lars paused, his gaze softening. He took a careful step closer, his voice calm, almost soothing, as though he feared startling me. "I'm not here to hurt you, Eli," he said, his words sincere, tinged with an urgency that struck deep in my chest. "I promise. But we don't have much time. We need to leave now."

"Where's Reed?" My voice was raw, desperate. "Did they… did they kill him?"

"No," Lars answered quickly. He stepped further into the cell, his hand reaching for mine with a gentleness that surprised me. "He's alive. He's locked up in a cell in another part of the castle. He was delirious when they brought him in, so the king hasn't had a chance to question him yet. But…" He hesitated, glancing down for a moment, as though choosing his words carefully. "He did mention something in his haze. Something about your brother. And the full moon?"

The words hit me like a blow to the stomach. Oh no. Reed had said something. And if Reed had said it, Lars must know. And if Lars knew, that meant the king likely knew, too.

"Listen," Lars continued, his voice growing more insistent. "If what Reed said is true, you need to go. The full moon is in two days. You need to be at the southern docks by then, that's likely where he will be making port if he's coming from your home. When he arrives, you have to go with him."

Two days. Two days, and I could leave this nightmare behind me. The thought was almost too much to process. I would be free. I could escape all of this.

There was still so much I didn't understand. Why was Lars doing this? What did he want? Was this some kind of trap? Had he really turned against the king? Or was I just a pawn in a larger game, meant to lead them to Hayden, so they could take him, too?

I studied Lars's face, searching for any sign of deception. But all I saw was sincerity, a deep, unwavering resolve. Even as an Ivy Guard, he had been kind to me. He had helped me, helped Reed. There was no sign of malice in his expression, so maybe I could trust him.

"Why?" I asked, my voice shaking. "Why are you helping me?"

Lars exhaled, his gaze dropping to the floor for a moment, as though considering the question. "If you stay," he said, his voice heavy with regret, "the king will either kill you, or use you as leverage. He'll break you again and again, until you're nothing. He'll use you to get what he wants, Princess. And with everything you've already suffered? No one should have to endure that." His face twisted, pain flashing across his features. "I won't stand by and watch him destroy you and himself in the process. I can't."

The words settled over me like a cold shadow. It was the first time someone had spoken of the king's actions with such raw truth.

I swallowed, my throat dry, my chest tightening. "But why should you care?" I shot back, the bitterness rising again. "Aren't you supposed to be loyal to him? You swore an oath to serve the Ivy King."

Lars's jaw clenched, his eyes flashing with something I couldn't quite place. "I did," he said quietly. "But the Ivy King..." He trailed off, as if the words were too heavy to speak. He let out a breath, a faint tremor in his voice. "He's not the same and I don't recognize him anymore. He's consumed by power and each day, he loses more of himself and who he used to be. I can't stand by and watch him destroy everything he touches. He is slipping, Eli. He doesn't care about what he's becoming, about the lives he's ruining. He will continue to hurt you then he'll kill you. That's what he does to things he no longer has use for."

Lars held out his hand then, his palm open, a silent plea in his eyes. "Now, please. Come with me." The words hung in the air and I didn't know what to make of them, of him. But what I did know was that I had to make a choice. If I stayed, I would die. Or worse, I would be used as a pawn in Caraway's twisted game. If I left, I could at least fight for my life.

And I wasn't going to let the king win.

"Alright," I said, my voice steady despite the storm inside me. I reached out and took Lars's hand. "I'll go. But you have to release Reed, too. I won't leave him behind." I proclaimed, leaving no room for argument as I started towards the steps.

Every step I took was a mixture of fear and hope, my heart pounding with every footfall. *This is it,* I told myself. *I'm leaving. I'm finally leaving, and Reed was coming with us.*

"So you are going to get him right?" I asked as I continued to follow behind Lar's sure and steady footsteps until we reached the top.

"Princess," Lars huffed, "we simply do not have time." His jaw was set in a firm line, his hands twitching at his sides like he was fighting an internal battle.

"He saved me, twice now," I argued, "and this is how I am going to repay him? Leaving him here to rot or be torn apart by the king?

You said it yourself, the king discards those who are no longer useful to him."

He had to see that right? How can he be so angry about how I was treated yet he couldn't care less about what happened to Reed. Someone who shouldn't have been here in the first place.

"We can't take him with us," Lars said, his voice commanding. "It's too risky. Now put that hood up and cover yourself."

My chest tightened at his words. Too risky? "I'm not leaving without him." The words came out before I could stop them. My hands curled into fists, my heart fighting against the rational voice in my head that told me Lars was right.

Lars halted and turned, his expression softening for just a moment, but his eyes remained hard. "We don't have time to argue, Eli. You need to come with me. I'm the one who knows the way. I'm the one who can get us out of here without anyone noticing. We need to move now," he snapped, his voice fierce and urgent.

I wanted to argue, wanted to scream at him that I wasn't going anywhere without Reed, but the urgency in his voice left no room for defiance. Without another word, Lars moved toward the hall. The castle around us was quiet, eerily so. There was no bustle of servants, no sound of distant conversations. It was as if the entire castle was holding its breath.

"Where is everybody?" I whispered as I followed him through the dim corridor.

Lars didn't answer right away. His eyes flicked over his shoulder, and a faint smile tugged at the corner of his lips. "I may or may not have put a sleeping draft in the wine at dinner," he said, a dark humor flashing in his eyes. "Had to make sure I had time to sneak you out."

As we continued down the hallway, my mind raced with the implications. The halls seemed to stretch on forever, more labyrinth than castle. The further we walked, the more the walls seemed alive, as though the vines were reaching for us, the roots growing deeper into the stone, taking hold reflecting the kings growing anger and hate.

Finally, Lars turned into the kitchen, and I felt a wave of warmth hit me as we stepped inside. The place was dimly lit by a few sputtering candles. Myrtle and Bentley were already there, waiting. Myrtle, her face a mixture of worry and relief, stepped forward without hesitation and wrapped her arms around me in a tight, almost desperate hug. I stiffened at first, but then I melted into her embrace, the comfort of her familiar scent and presence soothing the raw panic gnawing at me.

"Eli," she whispered, pulling away just enough to look into my eyes. "I heard what the king did. I'm so sorry." Myrtle's gaze drifted to where the cloak had opened, exposing the cut down the front of my dress. I watched as she gently closed the cloak again, hiding the painful reminder of what had happened.

I swallowed hard, my throat tight. What had been done to me, to Reed, was too much to speak of. I shook my head, as if denying it would make it go away.

"You will not remain in this castle a moment longer," Myrtle said, her voice rigid and full of quiet resolve. "Lars will escort you to the southern dock where I hear your brother will be waiting for you, yes?"

I nodded, overwhelmed with the kindness Myrtle and Bentley were showing me, knowing their aid in my escape could lead to their punishment or even death.

"When you reach the Forsythia city center, you'll need to look for my daughter's shop. "Lovely Laurel Designs." Myrtle continued, her voice calming me with its warmth. "She will give you anything else you may need for the journey. Just tell her you're a friend of mine, tell her my name. She'll help you."

I nodded, her words settling into me. Bentley stepped forward next, a quiet strength about him that made him stand out in the dim light of the kitchen. "I've arranged a horse for you," he said. "One of the Ivy Guard's own. When you reach Laurel's shop, she'll switch your horse with one of hers, something less noticeable, harder to trace. You'll need it when you make your way through the Ivy Forest."

"Thank you," I whispered, the enormity of their kindness washing over me.

I turned to Lars, my heart twisting. "I'm still not leaving without Reed."

Lars's expression hardened, but there was a flicker of something in his eyes that looked like regret. "We have been through this, we can't take him, Eli. It's too dangerous."

I felt tears welling up, hot and quick, burning my eyes. My breath hitched as I looked at Lars, pleading. "I can't leave him behind. I won't."

Lars hesitated, his jaw tightening. For a long moment, the only sound in the room was the quiet crackle of the fire in the hearth, and the beating of my heart, loud and frantic in my ears. And then, slowly, his face softened.

"Reed really means that much to you," Lars simply stated with sincerity.

I didn't say anything, letting the silence stretch between us, hoping it would speak for me. My lips turned down, and a lump formed in my throat, which I tried to swallow, clearing it as best I could.

"Fine," he muttered. "But if he slows us down—"

"He won't," I quickly answered.

With that, Lars turned, striding toward the door without a glance back. He was getting Reed, and everything would be okay.

Myrtle guided me out the back door and towards the horse Bentley had prepared. She added a bag to the horse's side, her face full of warmth when she gave me another embrace. "Be safe, Eli. You have a long road ahead of you."

Bentley reached into a small pouch at his side and handed me a small satchel of food to add to the bag. It was just simple provisions that might keep us alive on the journey ahead. "Stay strong," he said quietly.

I clasped the bag tightly, nodding in thanks. Myrtle kissed my forehead before pulling away, her eyes filled with sadness and hope.

"You will make it, Eli," she said softly.

I nodded, knowing in my heart that I would never forget this moment or their sacrifice.

The cold night air bit at my skin as Bentley and Myrtle waited with me outside. I gave the horse a few strokes along its silky ebony fur, silently thanking it for the escape it would assist in.

"Ready?" Bentley's voice broke the silence, low and steady, as he helped me onto the horse. The animal shifted under me, its muscles rippling with power.

Before I could respond, a sharp, urgent voice cut through the quiet. "Eli!"

I turned instinctively, and my heart nearly stopped.

Reed.

He came running toward me, his movements stumbling, as if every step cost him. He was wearing a torn, bloodied shirt, my blood I realized, but the sight of him, alive, moving toward me made everything else blur into the background. I didn't think, I didn't hesitate. I jumped off the horse and ran.

We collided in the middle of the yard, my arms wrapping around him so tightly that I almost feared I might crush him. But it didn't matter. I had to hold on.

"I was so worried about you," I whispered, my voice breaking, hot tears spilling from my eyes. My hands trembled as I cupped his face, brushing the strands of hair away from his forehead. "I thought I lost you."

Reed's smile was weak but genuine, and it made my heart ache. "I'm okay now. We need to hurry, Eli." His voice was rough, strained as he threw a bag towards Bentley to tie to the horse. "I don't know how much time we have," Reed continued, glancing nervously toward the castle. "When Lars went to free me, a few guards started waking up. He had to stay behind to distract them. Told me to get a head start, that he'd meet us at Laurel's shop as soon as he could. But if he's not there in a few hours, we need to go without him."

I could feel my pulse quicken. Lars was staying behind? That didn't sit well with me. What if something happened to him? But I couldn't let my fear hold me back now. Reed was free. He was with me. That was all that mattered.

Reed caught my hand gently, his touch grounding me. "We'll be okay, Eli," he said softly, reading my thoughts. "But we have to go. Now."

I nodded, swallowing my nerves, and allowed him to help me onto the horse. My heart fluttered in my chest as I slid in front of him, his body settling closely against mine. The warmth of him at my back felt like a lifeline in the frigid night air, and I couldn't help but lean back just a little, allowing myself to savor the moment of comfort before we were thrust into the unknown again.

Myrtle and Bentley stood in the shadows; their faces etched with worry but also determination.

"Take care of her, Reed," Myrtle said.

"I will," Reed promised, but I could see the same fear in his eyes that I felt in my chest.

Bentley nodded once, his face unreadable, and handed Reed the reins. "Go. Don't look back."

With that, we turned the horse toward the road, the steady clip-clop of its hooves echoing through the stillness. The castle behind us faded into the darkness, and as we rode through the grounds, I could feel the weight of the place lifting from my shoulders. But even as the castle disappeared, I knew we weren't free yet. Not by a long shot.

29

The cobblestone streets of Forsythia were eerily quiet, stretched out under the heavy blanket of night. Not a soul was in sight, just the soft hum of the wind and the occasional creak of the horse's saddle as we moved through the narrow, shadowed alleyways. The buildings towered over us, their jagged edges softened by time and neglect. Ivy clung to the stone like nature's last desperate attempt to reclaim what had been taken.

The air was colder than I had expected, biting into my skin, making me shiver. I pulled my arms tighter to my chest, but the chill still seeped through the fabric of my cloak.

Reed must have noticed as his arm wrapped around me, pulling me closer to his warmth. His touch was comforting, a welcome reprieve from the cold, and I leaned into him. His chest was solid against my back, steady in a way that made me feel grounded.

"Cold?" he murmured, his breath warm against my ear.

"A little," I admitted, my voice softer than I intended. My heart quickened, not from the fear of what we might face, but from the proximity between us. The way his body pressed against mine, the natural rhythm of our movement together, stirred something inside me. Something I hadn't expected.

"I've got you," Reed said, his voice steady, almost a vow. His breath tickled the back of my neck as he adjusted his grip, his hand sliding from my waist to rest lightly over my chest.

My heart began to pound in my throat. I closed my eyes for a moment, letting the warmth of his touch sink into my skin. Everything around us seemed to fall away until all that remained was the steady rhythm of the horse's hooves and the steady press of Reed's body against mine.

We rode in silence for a while, the city slipping by in a blur, but I couldn't deny the pull I felt toward him. I couldn't ignore how much easier this journey seemed with him at my side. His presence made everything feel a little less terrifying, as if, with him here, we could face whatever came next.

When we finally reached the dress shop, Reed urged the horse to a halt, the sound of hooves scraping against the cobblestone echoing into the night. The building stood quietly in front of us, its windows dark except for a dim light flickering behind the door.

"I'll go knock," Reed said, his voice calm and steady. "Stay on the horse."

I nodded, a knot of nervous energy tightening in my stomach. He pounded on the door, the sound sharp in the still night air. The door creaked open after a few moments, revealing a tall female with auburn hair. Her features were hard, her eyes sharp with a mix of anger and suspicion.

"What in the name of Theodon do you want?" she grumbled. "Shops closed!"

"Myrtle and Bentley sent us," Reed said, his tone unbothered as he gave a casual nod to me.

There were a few more words exchanged in hushed tones that I couldn't quite make out, but before I knew it, Laurel, was ushering us inside.

She gestured toward the fire and poured us both tea. Her home, nestled above the dress shop, was decorated in much the same style as Myrtle's room, filled with knick-knacks, soft pillows, and an obscene amount of pink.

"So, you're a friend of my parents," Laurel said, settling into a chair across from us, a wry smile tugging at her lips. "I just love how she volunteered me to help perfect strangers."

"I am so sorry," I began, feeling my stomach twist into knots. Here was another person who was risking punishment if Caraway found out she had aided us.

Laurel waved it off with a dismissive laugh. "I'm sorry, I'm just tired and cranky," she apologized, pouring herself another cup of tea. "So Reed explained you need a few items and a horse?"

"Yes," I said, glancing at Reed, silently thankful that he had already taken the lead in asking her for help. It was a relief not to have to burden her any more than necessary.

"I saw a large brown steed in the stables when I put the guard's horse in for the night. Could we have that one?" Reed asked, his voice smooth, almost like a demand.

"Of course," Laurel replied quickly, without hesitation. "And Reed, my parents... I know they told you to come here, but are they alright?" she asked, her focus completely on Reed. "The Ivy King isn't going to harm them, right?"

"No," Reed answered immediately. "They will be alright."

Truthfully, neither Reed nor I knew what would happen to Myrtle or Bentley if Caraway found out they had assisted us. Still, the worried look on Laurel's face softened as soon as Reed reassured her that her parents were safe. It was probably the small bit of information she needed in that moment before her thoughts and fears could spiral.

The warmth from the fire began to seep into my bones, making the weight of my cloak feel unbearable. I started to untie it, but Reed's hand stopped mine gently.

"Um, Eli," he said, his fingers brushing mine as they stopped me from undoing the cloak. "Your dress is still..." His voice trailed off as I realized what he meant. "Unless you had a chance to change it before leaving the castle?"

My dress, the one Laurel had designed, was still ripped and stained with blood, too much of my skin exposed. I felt a wave of embarrassment wash over me, especially with Laurel sitting right there, as well as now realizing that Reed must have seen and felt everything when he was healing me.

"Laurel," I asked hesitantly, my voice almost a whisper. "Do you have a change of clothes I could borrow?"

She chuckled softly, her eyes twinkling. "You're in a dress shop, remember?" she said, winking as she stood to fetch something.

Before she could leave, Reed spoke up again, a thoughtful frown on his face. "Maybe something more comfortable for sleeping? I was thinking maybe Eli could rest a few hours while we wait for Lars."

I opened my mouth to protest, but Reed cut me off before I could speak. "You need to sleep," he insisted softly. "It might be your only chance to sleep on an actual bed during this journey. I imagine we'll need to camp in the forest along the way to the southern docks."

I met his gaze, the heaviness of exhaustion pressing down on me. He was right. I was so tired. I nodded reluctantly. "Only if you rest too," I replied softly.

Laurel raised an eyebrow. "I have a guest room," she said, her tone light. "But there's only one bed."

Reed glanced at me, then back at Laurel. "I'll take the floor."

After we changed, Laurel led us down the hall of her home. The further we went, the colder it became.

"Sorry," Laurel said, offering a small smile. "There's no fireplace on this side of the house. The guest room is still a work in progress, but there are plenty of blankets on the bed for you."

We entered the small space, the bed dominating the room but the area itself was sparse, only the bed and a small desk in the corner. She wasn't kidding when she said it was a work in progress.

I climbed into the bed, sinking into the warmth of the blankets. Reed, started to make a bed for himself on the cold floor and I couldn't help but feel guilty. He didn't deserve that.

"Reed," I said softly, my voice barely above a whisper.

"Sparks?" he answered, pausing in his task.

"We can share the bed," I said, my heart fluttering in my chest. "It's alright."

"Are you sure?" he asked.

"Yes," I said. "I don't want to be alone."

Without another word, Reed slipped under the covers, his body warm next to mine. Our eyes met for a moment, something unspoken passing between us and the air in the room seemed to grow thicker, heavier.

I could feel Reed's body so close to mine, his warmth seeping into my skin. I shivered, but not from the cold.

His voice was soft, almost a whisper. "Your skin is like ice," he murmured, his breath warm against my skin.

"Can you warm me up?" I asked, feeling a spark of bravery.

Reed didn't hesitate. His arms wrapped around me, pulling me close. I finally allowed myself to relax, letting the heat of his body melt the chill from my bones. In his arms, for the first time in what felt like forever, I felt safe.

So many thoughts raced in my head. I knew we were still in danger, probably being hunted by the Ivy King right this moment, but this just felt right. I had to keep positive, we were both getting out of here. We would both be safe soon and far away from this place. The thought gave me peace, but it did not stop the flutter in my heart I was sure Reed could feel vibrating against his warm arm that held me tight. He was so calm. So relaxed, it made me remember how just hours ago he was drained and possibly dying.

"I've never been more scared in my life," I whispered, my voice tight with emotion just needing to say it out loud. "When I saw you... when you were convulsing on the floor after healing me."

Reed's heart began to race, his chest pulsating at my back. Was he unaware how close to death he was?

"What did you see?" he asked dryly.

I still wasn't sure, "You looked like death, like death was taking over your whole body, changing you into a shell of who you were." I closed my eyes tight trying to forget that thought as I turned my body around in his hold. "I thought I had lost you." I opened my eyes, the two of us now facing one another.

Reed's arms tightened around my lower back, pulling me even closer until out foreheads touched "I'm here, Eli. I'm not going anywhere."

The air between us crackled with electricity, thick and heavy with everything that had been building, unspoken and dangerous. Reed's hands were on me, his fingers shaking ever so slightly as they slid down my arms, pulling me closer. His eyes were dark, intense, searching mine as though he could see into my soul, read every fear, every desire.

I couldn't hold back anymore.

Without thinking, I leaned up, closing the small distance between us, and kissed him. At first, it was soft, tentative, the brush of lips hesitant but loaded with intention. But then I felt the heat, the ache. Everything that had been simmering between us for days, weeks, maybe even longer, exploded in an instant.

I pressed into him harder, desperate for more, and he responded instantly, deepening the kiss, his hand sliding to the back of my neck, pulling me into him like I was the air he needed to breathe. It was wild. Uncontrolled.

His mouth moved against mine with an urgency that sent a thrill of heat down my spine. His lips were warm, but there was a tenderness behind them too, as though he was afraid to hurt me, even as the kiss became more insistent, more passionate. His tongue brushed against mine, and the world around us disappeared. There was only him. Only us.

My hands roamed, tracing the hard planes of his chest, feeling the heat of his skin beneath the fabric. I couldn't get enough of him. I pulled him closer, my body aligning with his, every inch of me burning, craving. The kiss deepened, fevered now, every movement slow but filled with purpose, each touch making me feel like I was shattering and coming together all at once. His fingers slid to my face, cupping my cheek gently, but I could feel the tension in him, the way he was fighting to keep his control. It made me want to break it. I wanted him, wanted all of him.

I pulled back just slightly, breathless, our foreheads resting together as we both tried to steady our pounding hearts. His lips hovered over mine, still warm, still full of promise.

"I just had to." I started, but my voice faltered, caught in the rawness of the moment. I couldn't find the words. I didn't need to. He understood. And then his lips crashed into mine again.

Reed's lips were everywhere —on my mouth, my neck, my jaw —each touch sent a wave of heat through my veins, making me want more. I slid my hands up to his chest, then around his neck, being extra careful around his still locked iron collar as I pulled him into me. I needed him closer. I needed this to never end.

I tangled my fingers in his hair, tugging him to me as the kiss grew more desperate. His tongue brushed against mine, gentle at first, then harder, coaxing me, urging me to surrender to the kiss, to the moment. I couldn't hold back any longer. I pressed my body into his as I draped a leg over his thigh feeling every inch of him his warmth, his strength, the way he fit perfectly against me.

He groaned into the kiss, a low, hungry sound that made my stomach tighten with want.

He pulled me closer, his hands sliding down to my waist, lifting me slightly as if I were weightless. I wasn't sure how it happened, but suddenly I was on top of him as I straddled his waist, our lips still frantically connected.

I leaned back, feeling the hard evidence of his arousal pressing against me through his pants. I'd never gone this far with someone before, and honestly, I was nervous.

His body was clearly hungry for more, and the heat building between my legs told me my body wanted more, too. This wasn't how I had imagined it. On the run and in a stranger's home. But I had always pictured the person I'd share this experience with for the first time would be someone like him. Someone like Reed. It might be the only chance I'd get to experience this, depending on how the rescue mission played out.

I pushed my worries aside, letting my body take over. I began rocking my hips gently over his erection, unsure if I was doing it right. But the soft moans slipping from Reed's lips made me think I was.

"Sparks," he moaned, his hands finding their way to my hips, guiding me the way he wanted.

The friction between our bodies sent waves of heat through me, and I couldn't help but keep moving. Reed started matching my rhythm, and soon we were in sync, the pace quickening as I felt the familiar pull of a climax building.

I bent down, pressing my lips to his. I needed to feel him, needed more of him. The kiss deepened, hungry and desperate, as we both knew we wanted this. We needed this release.

Reed's fingers tangled in my hair as his thrusts over my panties became faster, harder, full of need.

"Should we take our clothes off?" he gasped, breathless.

I wanted to, and I wanted him, desperately. But not here, not now. How could I tell him I had never done this before? After I bled on the sheets, he'd surely know. I could feel my body trembling at the thought.

"Um…" I managed to choke out, my voice barely a whisper as my body stopped moving with his and I could feel myself begin to shake with nerves.

"We don't have to," Reed murmured as his hands slid up and down my arms, soothing my shaking skin. "We can stop now and just go to sleep."

His body stilled beneath mine, and I was relieved that he wasn't upset I didn't want to go further. But even with the layer of clothes between us, I still wanted this. It was a frantic, desperate need. I was so close and I could tell he was close too.

I rocked back against him, moaning softly, "I want to at least finish." My voice came out more sultry than I intended. "Just like this. Is that okay?" I asked, meeting Reed's wide eyes.

"I'll take you however you'll have me," Reed smirked, his hands on my hips again as he picked up his rhythm.

The sound of our harsh breaths filled the room as our bodies moved together. I closed my eyes, the pleasure intensifying with every movement. My pace quickened, and I could feel the climax building, spreading through me. I needed this. "Reed!" I gasped, my voice shaky. "Don't stop."

"I can't hold back any longer," Reed whimpered, his voice a mixture of pain and pleasure as his thrusts became more desperate.

I moaned, with one final twist of my hips. My body trembled as my climax washed over me, sending waves of heat and pleasure through every inch of me. I collapsed forward, my forehead resting against Reed's. I started to pull away, but Reed stopped me.

"Not yet," he pleaded, his voice raw.

It was then that I realized the warmth between us wasn't just mine. Reed had found his release too, and I could feel it soaking through our layers and into my panties.

"Okay," Reed said breathlessly, "I think I'm good now."

I slowly moved off of him, but he pulled me back into his chest, his heartbeat racing in time with mine. His lips found my neck, planting soft kisses along my skin, trailing up to my jawline.

"That's never happened before," he whispered into my ear, his warm breath sending a shiver through me.

"What do you mean?" I asked, genuinely curious. Was he a virgin, too? Was this kind of closeness as new to him as it was to me?

"I've never felt like that," he admitted, his voice husky. "Without actually being inside a female. Sorry if that's too blunt." He laughed softly, nervously.

"Me neither," I said with a yawn, trying to hide my exhaustion. It wasn't a lie I had never felt like this with a male before. The only release I'd ever known had come from my own hands, and even that was nothing like this.

Reed kissed my cheek softly. "You need to sleep, Eli," he murmured, his voice gentle. "And hopefully, after that, it'll be a peaceful one."

I felt a small laugh begin to build, but it was cut off by another yawn. Reeds slowing heartbeat began to dull my own, and as I closed my eyes, I fell asleep with a smile on my face.

We woke up in each other's arms, tangled in the warmth of the blankets, and I could feel Reed's steady breath against my neck. His fingers were lightly tracing patterns along my arm, and for a moment, I thought time had stopped. The world outside felt distant, muted, like we were the only two people left on the Isle. I never wanted to leave this moment. The quiet safety of his embrace, the feel of his chest rising and falling against mine.

But all good things were fleeting.

The door creaked open, and I startled, my heart jumping into my throat as Laurel stepped inside. Her presence was like a breath of fresh air in the room, though she didn't seem surprised to find us sleeping in each other's arms.

"Your friend never showed," she said softly. "It's already been a little over two hours edging on three now, I think its best that you continue on without him."

I shifted, reluctantly pulling away from Reed, who groaned in his sleep before blinking his eyes open. Lars never made it. Did the king wake up from the sleeping draft? Did he know Lars was assisting us? I didn't want to leave without Lars, especially since he was the only one who knew how to navigate the Isle. Reed and I had never done it before unless you count my being dragged behind a horse and even then, I wasn't sure if it was the same docks we needed to travel to now. We needed Lars, but we also needed to move.

"I've switched your horse. It's best you move quickly and under the cover of the night that still remains." Laurel said swiftly.

I nodded, my mind racing as I slowly sat up, my body still heavy with sleep. But the magnitude of what was ahead pressed on me, and the warm cocoon we'd been in began to unravel.

Reed and I got to our feet, stretching stiffly. I felt every muscle in my body groan, sore from the tension of the last few days, but the pull of the journey ahead overpowered it. I was thankful for the clothes Laurel had left for us, even if they looked more stylish than practical. But the boots and coats she added helped balance it out, offering the warmth and practicality we desperately needed. As I bent down to take off my boots and replace them with one of the pairs Laurel had provided, I hesitated, a pang of guilt settling in. These weren't even my boots, they were Adan's. A piece of home that had stayed with me. After losing my pendant, they were all I had left. And with no way of knowing if this plan would actually work or if I would ever make it back to Ember, I couldn't bring myself to let them go. I placed the new boots back on the floor and pulled mine on again. They were still a bit too big, but they would do.

Reed dressed quickly, slipping into a white tunic that clung to his broad shoulders, the soft fabric hugging his chest like it belonged there. Over it, he pulled on a green and silver leather vest that had intricate stitching around the edges, the colors blending together like the moss and leaves of the forest. He put on new pants as he discreetly threw out the ones he had ruined. His black pants fit snugly and he looked just like a warrior except for the iron collar. A warrior with a softness to him that was still unmistakable.

While I would have preferred to shower and clean myself up after the activities Reed and I engaged in just a few short hours ago, there was no time. I stepped into the dress Laurel had picked out for me. It was a simple thing, but with an elegance to it that made me feel both humbled and special. The fabric was a forest green color, soft like worn cotton, but the chestnut brown velvet overlay gave it a touch of luxury, with delicate lace at the collar and cuffs. I was thankful my iron collar was never put back on me or the whole ensemble would surely clash. I pulled the dress over my head, I realized how well it fit, not just in size, but in the way it made me feel ready for whatever came next. The sleeves were puffed slightly like her earlier designed dress I was gifted from Myrtle, and the skirt flowed around my legs as I moved. There was something regal about the way the velvet gleamed in the dim light. Hopefully I no longer looked like an escaped prisoner.

Reed caught my eye as I tied my wild copper hair back, his gaze lingering on me for a moment longer than necessary. I couldn't help the flush that spread across my cheeks.

"Ready?" he asked, his voice a little rough, though there was a hint of a smile on his lips.

"Let's go."

We moved outside, where the cold night air hit me immediately. The brown and white horse stood quietly in the distance, packed and ready to go. My eyes drifted to the bags we had gathered from Laurel. It held a few days worth of supplies for the road ahead. But as I turned to grab one, something caught my eye, two swords were strapped to the side of the pack that Reed had run out of the castle with.

I froze for a moment before turning to Reed. "Where did these come from?"

He met my gaze with a glint of mischief in his eyes. "I grabbed them from a sleeping guard when Lars let me out. Once a thief always a thief." He gave a wry smile. "Better to have some protection, just in case."

The realization hit me hard. Without Lars, not only did we not know the way to the docks, but we also had no line of defense. We would need to camp tonight in the forest filled with Theodon knows what. The idea of being alone in the woods without someone who knew the terrain was unsettling. I was suddenly thankful for Reeds thieving abilities.

Laurel stepped out from the house again, her footsteps light against the stone path, and handed me a small rolled up piece of paper. "Here," she said. "When it was apparent your friend wasn't coming, I drew up a map of the Ivy Forest and to the southern docks."

I took the map with a nod, unfurling it in my hands. It was simple, but clear enough. I could see the winding path that led into the woods, the landmarks circled in ink. It would get us to the forest, but after that, we'd be on our own knowing that once we were deep within the trees, navigating may get a bit confusing, map or no map and Reed and I were strangers to this place.

I couldn't help but look at Reed, who was already securing the rest of the bags to the horse. My thoughts lingered on the kiss we'd shared amongst the other things. The way it had felt so right, so natural between us. The warmth of his embrace still lingered, and the taste of his lips was still on my mouth. I was glad we would be on this road together. I just hope he felt the same.

I approached him slowly, my heart pounding in my chest. "Reed," I started, my voice quieter than usual, as I reached for his hand. "About, earlier. The kiss, and the um," I couldn't say it out loud. "Do you regret it?"

His expression softened, and without a word, he took my hand in his, his fingers warm and reassuring against my skin. He smiled, a soft but genuine smile. "No. Not at all. I have never regretted a single moment with you."

I couldn't stop the smile that spread across my face. "I don't regret it either," I whispered.

Before I could say anything more, Reed leaned down, cupping my face gently in his hands. His thumb brushed my cheek, and I felt the warmth of his touch flood through me. Our lips met again, softer this time, more intimate. The kiss was sweet, almost reverent, as though we were savoring the moment before everything changed.

The moment was broken by the sound of Laurel clearing her throat behind us. We pulled apart quickly, both of us flushing with embarrassment, but there was no time to dwell on it.

"It's time. The cloak of darkness is still on your side, and you can't waste it." Laurel spoke with such assertiveness.

I nodded and with one last look at Laurel, we mounted the horse. I sat in front of Reed, positioning myself in his lap in front of him. Laurel waved us off with a sad smile, her face illuminated in the faint glow of the lantern. We would probably never cross paths with her again, but I made a silent promise to myself that I wouldn't forget the kindness she had shown us.

As we left the city and entered the shadowy path of the forest, my heart beat faster. The cool wind blew against my skin, and Reed's body was a solid warmth behind me, his presence comforting despite the uncertainty of the road ahead. The moonlight filtered through the trees, but I could tell it would soon be replaced by the warm glow of the sun.

The mare beneath us swayed gently as we entered the dirt path leading into the forest. The path we followed was clearly one that had been traveled before, a cleared route through the trees that almost resembled a road. It was likely the safest and quickest route, but that also meant it was the most obvious one, perfect for the Ivy Guards, who I was certain had finally begun to stir from the draft. The king would send them after us soon, assuming he suspected we were heading for the southern docks. But where else would he think we'd go? He couldn't possibly think we were planning to hide on the Ivy Isle and live out the rest of our days there. No, he would assume we were making a complete getaway from the Isle. He was smart, but hopefully not smart enough to make the southern docks his first choice for a search.

Freedom was so close I could practically taste it. The full moon would rise tomorrow night, and that's when Hayden said he would arrive. Hopefully, whatever vessel he used to sail here would be small and discreet. Even if the king was able to torture the information from Lars, I doubted that he would have had time to warn anyone near the Isle's edge to look out for incoming ships or boats. By the time the message reached them, Reed and I would be safely aboard an Ember vessel, on our way home.

Well, my home. A home I hoped Reed would want to make his own. I wouldn't stop him if he preferred to return to the Isle of Gust, but the thought of him leaving would crush me.

I glanced over at Reed, his face set in the familiar calm expression I knew so well, though there was a softness in his eyes that made my heart flutter. We'd been riding for hours, the sun now a mere sliver on the horizon. It had been so long since I'd seen a sunrise that I kept poking my head back and forth through the thick trees, trying to steal a glance.

"Are you okay?" Reed asked with a small laugh, no doubt amused at my restless movements.

"Yes," I said, a little embarrassed, "The trees are just in the way."

Reed calmly rested his head atop mine. "You want to watch the sunrise, don't you?" he asked, completely understanding my longing.

"Yes," I replied, a hint of sadness in my voice. "But I don't think we have time."

"We don't," Reed said, only echoing my disappointment. "According to the map, this is where we need to leave the main road, and that will only bring us into the thicker parts of the forest," he added, as if trying not to break my heart.

I knew it was risky, but I didn't know how many more sunrises I'd get to see. Still, he was right, we needed to carry on. We'd already wasted those hours waiting for Lars, and now we just needed to get to the docks as quickly as possible. But there was an aching sadness that lingered in my chest.

Reed nudged the mare gently, continuing to guide the path deeper into the Ivy Forest. Towering, ancient trees stretched their limbs toward the sky, their leaves a thousand shades of green that whispered in the wind. As we trudged on, the forest wasn't getting thicker. In fact, it looked like we were approaching a clearing. It was just a small patch of thin trees before they would inevitably grow thick again, but it felt like the small bit of hope I needed right now. A smile rose on my lips as my head tilted up, catching a perfect view of the sunrise.

"Well, Sparks," Reed chuckled behind me, the vibration filling me with more comfort. "Looks like you will get to see that sunrise after all."

I felt as Reed deliberately brought the mare into a slower trot, though we continued forward. The sun was just peeking over the horizon, bathing the world in soft golden hues. I could feel its warmth, even from a distance, as if the light itself was a promise of something good, something worth holding on to.

I settled back into Reed's chest. The rhythmic beat of his heart lulled me into a peace I hadn't known in ages.

"This is nice," I murmured, watching the sun rise higher, the world shifting with it.

"It is," Reed agreed, his voice soft against my hair. "Too bad we can't stay here in this clearing longer. I would stay in this moment with you forever, if Theodon let me."

I smiled to myself, shifting slightly so I could look up at him. "I think I'd stay here forever if I could, too," I said. "Back home, the sun... it's like another god to us. We worship it almost as much as we worship Theodon. The way it rises and sets, the way it gives life to everything. Without the sun, we would not have the flames, the very thing my Isle thrives on. Do you have anything like that on the Isle of Gust?" I asked, curiously. Fae from Gust were always so secretive. There was so much I didn't know about them, even in written accounts.

Reed's fingers gently brushed through my hair, and I felt his thoughtful silence before he answered. "Where I'm from, aside from Theodon, we worship the air and wind. It's life, it's breath— the very force that sustains all living things. Fire needs it too, even the fiercest flames would die without air. Maybe that's how we are, Sparks. I'm the wind, and you're the flame. Together, we burn."

His words sent a rush of warmth through me, my chest tightening with something soft and tender. I could feel his breath on my neck as he spoke, and for a moment, everything in the world was just him and me, here in this small pocket of time.

"I like that," I whispered, shifting on the horse to see his face more clearly as I reached up to touch his cheek. "Perhaps that's why we were brought together. We truly need each other to survive. To exist."

His lips quirked into that small, private smile I loved so much. "You'll always be my flame, Eli. And that's more than enough."

I was about to say something else, but instead, I just closed my eyes and leaned into him, soaking in the moment. Time seemed to stretch, the rising sunbathing us in its light. It was one of those rare moments where nothing else mattered.

I knew the moment was fleeting. Soon, the trees would become thick canopies against the sky again as we rode toward the dock. But still, the thought raced through my mind, would Reed stay with me on Ember?

"Do you miss home?" I asked, my voice barely above a whisper, waiting for his answer.

"I don't think I do," he said slowly, surprising even myself with the honesty of his words. "Not anymore. Not while I'm with you." Reed's hand brushed my cheek gently, and I met his gaze. His eyes were steady, almost unreadable, but there was something in them, something soft that made my heart race.

Then, without warning, his lips were on mine, warm, sweet, perfect. The kiss was everything, the culmination of everything we had been through, and everything we still had ahead. I sank into it, allowing myself to get lost in him. The guards could be miles behind, but in that moment, nothing else mattered.

When we finally pulled apart, breathless and smiling, I glanced up at the sky and realized the clearing was fading as we rode closer to the dense forest ahead. I would miss the rest of the sunrise, but the smile stayed on my face. Something inside me felt different, lighter, as if a weight had been lifted. He didn't want to go home. He wanted to stay with me. And if we survived this, I would keep him. I would hide him on Ember Isle if I had to. If the king came for him, I would protect him. Always.

The forest grew thicker as we continued on, the trees pressing in around us, their tangled branches heavy with dark green leaves that filtered the sunlight into soft beams. The air smelled of earth and moss, a grounding scent that should've been calming, but instead, it made me feel heavier. Every step the mare took seemed to echo in the quiet, and I found myself fighting the pull of sleep, my eyelids growing heavier with each mile we covered.

I could feel Reed's warmth behind me, his steady presence a constant as I tried to focus on the map Laurel had drawn. The parchment crinkled in my hands as I traced the route with my finger. Laurel's instructions were clear enough, but the thick, twisting paths of the Ivy Forest weren't the easiest to navigate.

"Okay, we need to veer right up ahead," I muttered, yawning so wide it felt like my jaw might unhinge. "No, wait, that's not right... or is it?"

Reed chuckled softly behind me, his voice soft, but with a touch of amusement. "You sound like you're about to pass out, Sparks."

"I'm fine," I said, but my voice cracked at the end, betraying me. I fought to keep my eyes open, squinting at the map, but it was hard to focus. "I just need a moment. The map's tricky with all of the directions that lead through the trees instead of the path."

I shifted slightly on the mare, feeling the comfortable rhythm of her steps, the swaying motion making my body heavy. My limbs had grown sluggish, and before I even realized it, I was tilting to one side. The next thing I knew, I was sliding off the horse, only to be yanked back upright by Reed's strong hand at my waist.

"Easy there, Sparks," he said, his voice soft but concerned. "You almost fell off."

I blinked a few times, fighting the sudden wave of dizziness. "I didn't fall," I said, but I knew it was a lie. I could barely keep myself sitting up straight.

Reed's grip on my waist tightened, pulling me a little closer against his chest. His breath was warm against the back of my neck, and there was something comforting about his touch, like he was a steady anchor in this sea of exhaustion. "It's okay if you want to sleep," he said quietly, his voice gentle, like he was afraid to push me too far. "I can take the map and navigate us."

I tried to sit up straighter, but my body was reluctant. The map felt like it weighed a thousand pounds in my hands. I opened my mouth to argue, but the words tangled in my throat, half-formed and exhausted. "It wouldn't be fair," I muttered, yawning again, my head drooping just slightly. "You can't do all the work while I nap."

Reed laughed softly, and I could feel the rumble of it in his chest. "Sparks, I swear, you're more stubborn than a mule."

"Excuse me?" I lifted my head just enough to glance back at him, frowning in mock indignation. "I am not a mule."

His smile was warm, his eyes soft with affection. "Fine, not a mule. A stubborn little flame, then. But seriously, let me do this. It'll make me happy knowing you're well rested."

I opened my mouth to protest again, but the words slipped away as a yawn overtook me. I felt the heaviness of my eyelids pulling me down, my whole body craving rest. Reed's arms around me felt like a soft cocoon, and I couldn't help but melt into it.

"Reed I…" I started, but sleep tugged at my mind, soothing and inevitable. My thoughts became a hazy blur, and all I could do was rest my head against his chest, surrendering to the comfort of his embrace. I wasn't sure if I'd agreed, or if I just couldn't fight it anymore, but when I blinked next, my eyes did not reopen.

The motion of someone lifting me caused my heavy eyelids to flutter open. I glanced down, realizing it was Reed who was slowly pulling me off the horse.

"Sorry," he muttered, his apologetic. "I was trying to do that gently so you wouldn't wake."

My feet finally met the soft dirt of the forest floor. Though the earth was forgiving beneath me, my legs felt stiff from hours of riding. I staggered forward slightly, struggling to find my balance.

"I got you," Reed said quickly, steadying me with a firm hand against my shoulder.

I yawned, stretching my limbs to shake off the weariness that clung to me. "How long did I sleep?"

"Judging from the position of the sun," he said, peering up into the sky, "I'd say about three hours or so."

Three hours? I'd only meant to nap for a few minutes. But now, as I stretched and flexed my cramped muscles, I realized I must have needed it more than I thought. Looking around, I saw we were still deep in the Ivy Forest. The air was still filled with the scent of pine and damp earth, and the dense canopy above filtered the sunlight into a soft, golden glow. A body of water caught my eye, just a short distance down a small hill ahead. A small, rushing waterfall cascaded down into the creek, the sound of it soothing and almost hypnotic. My skin prickled with the sudden, intense need for a bath.

"Why did we stop?" I asked, my voice laced with the hope that this might be a good excuse to take a quick dip.

"We needed to give the horse some rest," Reed explained, glancing at the mare. "She's due for water and food."

He shifted beside me, and I could feel the weariness in his movements. His eyes were heavy, and there were deep bags under them. He was clearly exhausted.

"What about you?" I asked, noting how tired he looked. "You should get some rest too."

"I'll be fine," he said, brushing it off as he knelt to feed the mare a few carrots from the pack. His body swayed slightly with the effort, his exhaustion clear despite his attempt to hide it.

Like me, he was too stubborn to admit he needed rest. "Well, I'd like to bathe," I said coyly, "and I'll need some privacy for that." Though I didn't mind if he saw me naked, something I wasn't quite ready to admit, even to myself.

Reed raised an eyebrow, clearly not pleased. "I don't feel right about you going there alone."

I pressed my advantage, trying to sound more innocent than I felt. "Please, Reed. I really would like some privacy. You can rest while I clean up."

Reed was quiet for a long moment, and I could see the conflict in his eyes. He didn't want to leave me alone in the forest, but he also respected my wishes, especially after everything I'd been through. His brow furrowed as he weighed the decision, and I could almost hear the battle raging in his mind. He finally spoke, his words clipped and reluctant.

"Fine," he said, exhaling in frustration. "Make it quick. Ten minutes tops. I'll rest my eyes here with the horse, and when you're done, wake me up, and we'll get moving. We still need to cover more miles today."

"Deal," I said with a small smile, planting a quick kiss on his cheek.

I bounded down the small hill toward the water, eager for its cool embrace. When I reached the water's edge, I was struck by how clear and pristine it was. I could see all the way to the bottom, where small fish darted through the gentle waves, disturbed by the rush of the nearby waterfall. The water seemed almost too perfect, too untouched, and for a moment, I felt a fleeting sense of peace.

I quickly shed my clothes, eager to feel the liquid against my skin. I carefully placed my dress on a nearby rock and clutched onto the bar of soap I found in the bag. Laurel, always prepared, had packed some vanilla-rose-scented soap in our provisions. She truly thought of everything.

I dipped a toe into the water, and the coldness sent a sharp jolt through my body. It was shocking but invigorating. Slowly, I waded deeper, allowing my body to adjust inch by inch to the temperature until I was almost fully submerged.

The sound of the waterfall was soothing, a constant, calming presence. If this Isle hadn't been the setting for so many horrible memories, I might have thought of it as a place to visit again. But after everything that had happened, I knew I could never return here, not even if I wanted to.

I scrubbed my body with the vanilla-rose soap, soon surrounded by thick, milky suds. The once clear water became cloudy, but I didn't mind. It felt good to clean myself, to wash away the remnants of our journey.

I swam toward the falls, letting the strong, steady flow rinse my hair. It was probably the last full bath I'd have before returning home, and now, with the shift in my relationship with Reed, I didn't want to smell like the grime of travel. Sure, he'd seen me in worse conditions, both in smell and sight, but after last night, I became more aware of how I presented myself to him. I wanted to look nice, to smell nice. Not that I thought body odor would turn him away. It certainly wouldn't scare me off. Reed could smell like rotted meat, and I'd still crave his touch, still long to be held in his arms. But something inside me was shifting. After last night, I felt like I was growing up a little, becoming more conscious of myself.

After I had scrubbed every inch of my body, leaving barely any soap left, I let myself float on the surface, my mind drifting as the current rocked me gently. I knew I'd been in the water longer than the promised ten minutes, but Reed needed rest, and I was content to let my lost track of time be the reason he got it.

The sound of the water flowing around me was so peaceful. Had I not just woken from a nap, I could have easily drifted off to sleep right there, lulled by the gentle rocking of the water.

I submerged myself completely, enjoying the quiet beneath the surface. Everything was still. Then I heard it, faint at first, but unmistakable. A voice, familiar and filled with irritation, calling my name from above the water. I groaned inwardly.

I surfaced, keeping my naked body mostly hidden beneath the water. Reed stood at the water's edge, arms crossed over his chest, glaring at me as the horse grazed nearby, drinking from the creek.

A scowl was etched on Reed's face as he watched me and I could tell he wasn't pleased. I'd hoped he would remain deeply asleep, but of course, Reed was resilient.

"What are you doing?" he asked, his voice sharp with irritation.

I could lie and say I'd lost track of time, but considering the dire situation we were in, that would only make me seem careless. So I decided to tell the truth.

"I hoped that if I stayed here a little longer, it would give you more time to sleep," I said honestly.

"I told you I was fine," Reed retorted. "You can't just disappear like that, not when Ivy Guards could be hunting us down as we speak."

He was right. My selfishness could have put us both in danger. Who needs sleep when you're dead? And if King Caraway caught up to us, he would slit Reed's throat without a second thought.

"I'm sorry," I said, my voice sincere. "Turn around so I can get changed, and then we can continue on."

A smirk tugged at the corner of Reed's mouth as he picked up the dress I had draped over the rock. "You want this?" he teased, his voice playful and knowing.

"What are you doing?" I shot back, my words laced with challenge, trying to mask the growing warmth in my chest.

"Oh, I don't know," he replied, his tone light and mischievous. "You broke the rules of our ten- minute deal. Maybe I'll just keep this dress for myself." His eyes twinkled with mischief. "You could always ride with me naked, might even make the horse ride faster without the weight of the dress."

I blinked, taken aback by the audacity in his words. This was a side of Reed I had never seen before. He was usually so composed, always polite and restrained, but now he was teasing me, pushing boundaries that I didn't mind being pushed. Either the nap he'd taken had made him more flirtatious, or his exhaustion was making him a little loopy.

"You wouldn't," I challenged, trying to suppress the smile threatening to break free. The idea of being completely exposed in front of him, the male I'd grown so fond of, was both terrifying and tempting. But I couldn't let him see that. I wouldn't let him win.

"No?" He raised an eyebrow, his voice thick with amusement and confidence.

"I am a lady and a princess," I said, standing up from the water, my bare breast exposed to him for a fleeting moment before I quickly ducked back under the surface. "And you will give me my dress."

Reed's eyes went wide, and even from the distance, I could see the flush creeping up his neck. "You may be a princess," he said slowly, as if savoring the words, "but how can I give it back now that I've seen the beauty you've been hiding?"

He had seen me like this before that day in Myrtle's room but it was quick, and the other time I was sure he was able to see my naked breasts, had been in darker moments, in the midst of blood and chaos.

This, though, felt entirely different.

"Reed," I pressed, my voice soft but insistent.

He let out a low laugh, his eyes still full of mischief. "I have to admit, I've been dreaming of seeing that body again since the first time I walked in on you bathing. We really need to stop making a habit of this." His laughter continued as he kept my dress firmly in his grasp holding it hostage.

A wave of confidence surged through me, and I decided I would call his bluff. Fine. He wanted to punish me for losing track of time? I could bite back. It was clear he liked what he saw, and I would use that to my advantage. I could flaunt my nude body, taunt him, and drive him mad, denying him even the faintest of touches. He was a male, and whether decent or not, I doubt he'd last long. It was the perfect revenge.

"Fine," I said as I fully rose from the water, leaving everything on display. "Keep it, but if this is to be the new arrangement, you can look but you can't touch." I let my voice drip with the sultry, seductive tone I'd heard females at the Black Cinder use on males. He didn't stand a chance.

Reed's face immediately drained of color. Was he not prepared for me to play along with his little games?

"Eli," Reed barked, his voice a mix of command and fear. "Get back under the water and don't move."

Panic crept into my chest. Had I made a fool of myself? Was my body not what he expected?

"Now!" Reed's voice cut through my thoughts as he began moving toward the bag attached to the horse. His eyes remained fixed on me as he rummaged through the pack, pulling out one of the swords.

I did as he ordered, but just as I submerged, I heard a deafening roar that seemed to echo from above. I craned my neck upward and froze.

A wolf-like creature stood on top of the falls, its eyes locked onto Reed. But this wasn't any ordinary wolf. The beast was massive, nearly as large as the Loa, with fur that looked like it was sprouting thorns and vines from its ridged back, an evolved predator from the Ivy Isle.

The creature bared its teeth, preparing to lunge.

"Reed!" I whispered, panic rising in my voice.

"Stay down and under the water," Reed commanded, his tone quiet but urgent.

I obeyed, but then a loud splash erupted in front of me, sending a wave of water into my face and blinding my vision. When it cleared, I saw the beast charging through the water toward Reed, sword in hand.

Reed swung the blade at the creature, but it was too quick, dodging with ease and preparing to pounce. My heart pounded in my chest as Reed rolled out of the way, but not before I saw the creature swipe its claws along his arm, tearing flesh.

The wolf-like creature turned its hungry gaze toward the horse. If we lost the horse, we wouldn't make it to the docks in time. And if I lost Reed? No, I couldn't even think about that.

Reed lunged forward, slicing at the creature's ankles. It howled in pain but quickly refocused on him. Reed moved with deadly precision, cutting the horse's reins loose, giving it a chance to escape.

But just as Reed turned his back, the creature leapt, aiming for him. I was frozen, watching helplessly as the wolf-like beast closed in. I couldn't just sit here. I had to do something.

"Reed!" I shouted, my voice desperate. His eyes snapped toward me, giving him just enough time to dive out of the creature's path.

But my attempt to help him backfired. The creature's focus shifted to me and it lunged at the water, charging straight toward me.

"Eli!" Reed yelled, his voice filled with terror as he followed the beast into the water, sword still gripped in his hand.

I didn't know what to do. I was skilled with a bow, but that was it. I had no experience fighting up close. Even if I somehow grabbed Reed's sword, I wouldn't know how to wield it. My only chance was to outswim the damn thing and pray to Theodon that Reed could stop it before it reached me.

I dove beneath the surface, bracing myself for the chase. But when I opened my eyes, the creature had changed course, its attention fixed once again on Reed, who was now swimming towards the creature.

I didn't know how effective his sword's blow would be under water, so I had to try something. With urgency, I grabbed handfuls of rocks from the riverbed, anything I could use as a weapon. When my hand was full, I surfaced, gasping for air.

"Hey!" I shouted, hoping to draw the creature's attention. When it didn't respond, I hurled the rocks at its head.

The creature snarled, its gaze snapping back to me. Perfect. This was what I needed. It was distracted, and now Reed could deliver the killing blow.

I swam backward, never letting the beast slip out of my sight. As it closed the distance between us, I braced myself for the sharp, searing pain of its teeth sinking into my flesh. But then, to my shock, the creature stopped pursuing me. The water around it turned murky, swirling with blood.

My heart raced as I slowly raised my head above the water. Reed stood over the beast, the tip of his sword protruding from its neck.

Panting heavily, Reed remained still, blood staining his clothes. I prayed most of it belonged to the creature, but I feared it didn't all belong to the wolf-like beast.

"Are you alright?" Reed asked, his voice gentle as he withdrew the sword and pushed the lifeless body of the beast away.

I nodded, my gaze lingering on his blood-soaked body. "Are *you* alright?" I asked, my voice rough with worry, though I tried to keep it steady.

"It's not my blood," Reed said, his tone calm as he splashed water over his skin. The blood washed away, leaving his flesh clean, and the sunlight caught on him, making his skin glisten like polished stone.

"I thought I saw it swipe at you," I said, my eyes scanning him once more, desperately looking for a wound. I couldn't find one. In my panic, I'd imagined the worst. He was unharmed, and that was all that mattered, no injuries, no delays, especially with Reed's cursed iron collar still around his neck and at least another day and a half of travel ahead. That collar would need to be the first thing to go once Hayden arrived.

"It nearly got me, but I was faster," Reed replied, his gaze briefly drifting over his own body, almost as if double-checking.

Relief rushed through me, and before I could stop myself, I threw my arms around him. I could finally breathe again now that I knew he was safe. But then something hard pressed against my belly, and I realized, with a jolt, that I was still completely naked. My heart skipped a beat, but I didn't care, not when he was alright.

I dug my fingers into his hair, unwilling to let go. And that was when I felt him harden against my belly even more and a warmth spread between us. There was something about the fear and adrenaline that turned me on, something that seemed to affect us both. Or maybe it was because this was Reed, and I was completely nude. But this wasn't the time.

Reed must have sensed it too. Gently, he pulled away, stepping back with a sigh. "Let's get you dressed, and get the hell out of here," he said, planting a soft kiss on my forehead.

Reed swam ahead, and I followed, trailing behind him as we made our way toward the shore. When we finally reached land, he didn't try to sneak a peek while I hurriedly pulled on my gown. I wasn't sure whether I felt relieved or disappointed by his restraint, but it didn't matter. I quickly slipped the fabric over my wet skin, feeling it cling to me as I followed Reed back up the hill.

Reed quickly retrieved the horse, giving her a few more carrots to calm her down. Once everything was packed and ready to go, we headed back through the thick of the forest.

I knew Reed needed more rest, but it was pointless trying to argue. If I had just stayed the ten minutes like I had promised, our lives wouldn't have been in danger again. I decided not to blame myself and just let it go. Reed didn't seem to hold any resentment towards me; he was just relieved I was safe. I wouldn't waste time fixating on my mistakes. So, I let it go, and we moved on.

We traveled in silence, the adrenaline still pulsing through my veins. I was certain it was what was keeping Reed alert as well. Breaking the stillness, I finally asked, "Where did you learn to wield a sword?"

"My father," Reed replied dryly.

Oh no. Was he angry with me? Or had I touched on a topic he wasn't comfortable with? It made sense for a thief to be proficient with a weapon, in case they found themselves in a tight spot, but Reed wasn't exactly a thief, not a skilled thief anyway. He had only stolen the fish from the Ivy King to feed those in his village. What had he actually done on the Isle of Gust that had made him so skilled with a sword?

"Well," I said, cautiously testing the waters, "he taught you well."

Reed let out a quiet chuckle, though it seemed tinged with bitterness. "I figured, as an Ember Princess, especially a powerless one, you'd have been better equipped with hand-to-hand combat skills. Some way to protect yourself."

"I took up the bow," I answered, trying to sound less helpless than his words made me feel. "Other than that, my place was to hide."

"Hide?" Reed asked, his voice filled with genuine curiosity.

I had shared bits and pieces of my story with him before, but not the full, tragic truth. Still, I trusted him, and I didn't think the darkness of my past would change how he saw me. With a deep breath, I began to tell him what I hadn't before. "Being a twin made Hayden look weak, like there was a chance he didn't possess the full Ember. If word spread, then we could become vulnerable to attack."

"*Does* he hold the full Ember?" Reed asked, his voice full of interest.

"I don't know," I replied honestly. "I think so. He's as powerful as any of our ancestors were, but there's something in me, just a small trace. Enough for little things, just enough to keep me connected to the elemental magic."

"Will you age like a fae?" Reed's voice grew anxious.

I shrugged, trying to keep my tone light, though the reality had always weighed heavily on me. "We'll have to wait and see. I'm only twenty, so the aging process has just started. In ten or twenty years, I'll know more, either I'll stay the same, or my features will begin to change, just like they would with humans."

The uncertainty scared me more than anything else. I didn't know how humans aged exactly, but from the stories I had heard, it could take years before any real signs appeared. For others, the shift was much quicker. I wasn't sure how it would go for me, with the small amount of magic running through my veins. No one knew, not even Kalynda, who had lived for centuries. My life was a mystery, and we would all have to uncover it together.

"So, you said they hid you?" Reed asked, a note of anger creeping into his voice. "How exactly did they do that?"

"When I was younger, they'd send me to our safe house with a guard. But as I got older, hiding turned into confinement. I was locked away in my room, usually when we had important fae over or large events, which my parents hosted more days out of the year than not."

"That sounds… sad," Reed said quietly, his voice laced with sympathy. "Lonely, too. Is that why you don't like being alone?"

"Yes," I sighed. "But it got better as I grew older. Hayden convinced my parents to let me hide in plain sight, pretend I was a palace servant."

"Is that how you learned to cook?" Reed asked.

"It is," I replied, feeling a pang of fondness for the memories of that time. "And I can't say I regret it. In the kitchen, I never felt inferior. It was a craft that didn't require an ounce of magic to excel at. I could simply be myself, and in doing so, I mastered a skill I could truly be proud of and thankful for."

Reed brushed a soft kiss across my cheek, the warmth of his gesture sending a flutter through me. "I'm thankful for that skill, too," he whispered in my ear.

I had been rambling so much about my own life when this was supposed to be my chance to learn about his. I took a deep breath, trying to redirect the conversation. "So, do you have a large family?"

"No," Reed said simply.

"Just your mother and father, then?" I asked, hoping I wasn't pushing too far. I didn't want to cross any lines he didn't want to cross.

"My mother died when I was very little," Reed replied, his voice detached. "After that, it was just me and my father."

I didn't want this to feel like an interrogation, but I couldn't help myself. I wanted to know everything about Reed. "I'm sorry to hear that. What happened to her?"

Reed fell silent for a long moment before responding, his voice quieter now. "She got sick with something... something awful, something she couldn't heal herself from. And I was too young to even understand how that magic worked."

The thought of losing someone at such a young age struck a chord deep in my chest. I couldn't imagine watching someone I loved wither away, knowing I couldn't do anything to stop it. I couldn't even fathom how painful it must have been to be powerless in such a situation. "Where was your father?" I asked gently, silently promising myself this would be the last question I asked about his family.

"He didn't know my mother was pregnant with me," Reed said, his grip tightening around me. "Nor did he know I had been born. My father loved her deeply, but she didn't feel the same. After she left him, she went to the Igneous Mountains on the Isle of Gust to raise me alone. We had a small cabin there, and life was simple, peaceful. But it turns out my father had been searching for her for years. By the time he found us, it was too late." Reed's body tensed, the memory clearly painful.

"You don't have to keep going if it's too hard," I said, my voice soft and reassuring as I placed my hand gently over his. I traced small, comforting circles on the back of his hand with my thumb.

"It's alright," Reed whispered. "When he found us, he came storming in, so angry, his face full of betrayal. But when he saw me, just a small boy standing next to my mother, I could see the moment it all clicked in his mind. He rushed to her side, trying everything he could to heal her. But it wasn't enough. She died that night, and my father took me away. I was all he had left of her."

I understood, more than he probably realized, why Reed didn't have much love for home. I had wanted to think it was because of me, because of what we shared, but the Isle of Gust held more than that, it held bad memories. He had seen what sickness could do, and now, I understood why he risked so much for his people back home. He was trying to protect them from a pain he knew all too well. He was willing to sacrifice even his own safety to prevent that kind of loss.

Not wanting to push him further, I raised his hand to my lips and pressed a soft kiss against it. I wanted him to know that he wasn't alone anymore, that he would never have to face such pain by himself again.

The silence between us was no longer heavy. It was comfortable, warm even, as we shared a mutual understanding. Our lives had not been easy, but together, we would move forward, starting a new chapter.

The day passed quickly as Reed and I lost ourselves in conversations about our homes. He told me about the breathtaking beauty of the mountain ridges throughout the Isle of Gust much like he did those days in the cell, and I shared my stories of the warmth that the Ember deserts always brought to my heart. He painted such descriptive images with his words that I felt like I could see those mountains, feel the powder soft snow between my toes.

It felt good to hear Reed laugh when I shared tales of the mischief Hayden, Adan, and I used to get into. Whether it was sneaking out for midnight swims in the oasis or playing tricks on the guards, those small moments, when I could just be myself with my brother and Adan, were always my favorite. We were free then. No worries, just pure fun.

Reed told me about the challenges he faced learning to control his wind elemental powers. He recounted how he nearly blew away an entire house while practicing, then had to spend weeks repairing the damage he had unintentionally caused.

We continued through the forest, following Laurel's map, taking small breaks when we could. The further we ventured, however, the more barren the trees became. There was still enough cover to shield us, but even the remaining trees looked less vibrant, less alive.

"It's the sickness," Reed said, his voice calm, as if reading my thoughts. I turned to look at him, my mind swirling as I took in the withered trees around us. "It's affecting all the Isles."

Reed had mentioned how it had taken hold of parts of the Isle of Gust, and I'd seen firsthand the emptiness it left on Ember. But now, it seemed Ivy was affected too. I'd never been to the Isle of Mist, but I couldn't help but wonder if they were feeling the effects as well. Mist, with its vast waters, what did this sickness mean for their people? Was their water becoming tainted like our lands? It couldn't be a coincidence. Something was slowly consuming the Isles, and it seemed to have been happening for years. Only recently had the process felt as though it had accelerated.

We pressed on through the forest, the path growing sparser as the sun began to set. I could feel Reed's weariness behind me, his grip on the reins loosening as sleep began to take its toll on his body. His muscles swayed with the rhythm of the horse, and I could tell he was struggling to stay awake.

"I can take over if you'd like," I offered, as I had many times throughout the day. "I swear, I know how to ride; that part wasn't left out of my princess training." I let out a small laugh, hoping to lighten the mood.

But, as always, Reed refused. Maybe it was male pride, or maybe he just didn't trust me to keep us on track.

"We can stop and make camp," Reed suggested after a yawn. "We've put enough miles behind us, especially with this insane route Laurel had us take."

I couldn't have agreed more. I was more than ready to get off the horse and rest, even if it meant sleeping on the ground. Anything to be still for a while.

Reed pulled out a few wool blankets from the pack Laurel had prepared for us. I watched as he laid them side by side, looking unsure of how to arrange them. "Is this alright?" he asked, his voice hesitant.

After everything that had happened in Laurel's room the night before, it was amusing to see him so uncertain about sleeping close to me. "How else am I supposed to stay warm without you right next to me?" I teased, a playful smirk tugging at my lips earning me a smirk from him in return.

While Reed finished setting up the bedding, I rummaged through the pack to see what food we had left. Unfortunately, there were only a few strips of dried meat and a small container of hard cheese. It was hardly enough for a proper dinner.

I wasn't sure what animals roamed this part of the forest, especially considering this was an area where the sickness seemed to be spreading, but I heard the faint rustle of leaves nearby, probably a squirrel or a rabbit. Either would do.

If only Laurel had packed us a bow, I could have gotten us something more substantial to eat before nightfall. Instead, I'd have to rely on trapping. Digging through the pack, I found some rope and emptied the last of the food into my hand, leaving the container free.

"Sparks," Reed asked, his eyes heavy with exhaustion as he studied me. "What are you doing?"

I turned to face him, his posture slumping with fatigue. "I'm going to catch us dinner," I said proudly. "You get some sleep. When it's ready, I'll wake you."

Reed must have been more tired than I thought because he didn't even argue. He just stumbled over to his bedroll, collapsing into the softness of the wool. Before I knew it, a soft snore escaped his lips, and he was out.

I propped the empty container against a tree with a stick, tying the rope tightly around the end of it. My fingers trembled slightly as I made the knot. I couldn't afford to mess this up. Using the last of our food as bait, I carefully placed it inside the container and tucked myself behind a nearby tree, my back pressed against the rough bark.

I waited, crouched low, barely breathing. My muscles ached from the stillness, but I remained silent, my eyes fixed on the trap. I could feel the tension building, thick and heavy in the quiet of the forest.

It didn't take long. A rustling noise broke the stillness. My heart raced in my chest as I caught sight of the creature. A small rabbit, its fur matted and dirty, scurried toward the bait. Hunger was written all over it, its ribs visible beneath its thin coat of fur. I couldn't help but feel a pang of sympathy for it, but I knew this was survival. The scarcity of food in these parts of the forest was even affecting the animals. The poor thing was probably starving, its instincts overtaken by its desperate need to eat.

I pulled the rope slowly, carefully, and the container dropped with a dull thud. My breath hitched in my throat. I had done it. I couldn't help the grin that spread across my face. If Hayden could see me now. I'd always been the worst at tracking, but trapping, well that seemed to be my talent. I could already imagine bragging about it to him when we got back.

I lifted the container with shaky hands. Inside was the rabbit. It was little more than skin and bones, but it would have to do. I murmured a quiet apology before delivering a swift, clean kill. The last thing I wanted was to leave it suffering.

I made my way back to our camp, the rabbit clutched in my hands. Reed was still asleep when I returned, his chest rising and falling steadily in the calm of the sinking sun. He looked so peaceful like that, the soft glow of the sunset playing on his features. For a moment, I just watched him, feeling a quiet warmth spread through me. He was truly beautiful, in a way that left me breathless. And for reasons I still didn't fully understand, he wanted me just as I was.

I let the peace of that thought settle in my chest for a moment before pushing it aside. There was work to do.

I knelt by the twigs I had assembled and set the rabbit down beside me, preparing to start a fire. My fingers brushed against the rough stones, recalling the countless times I'd started a fire without magic. It was something I'd learned early on from old texts about civilization, back when humans still roamed the earth before becoming fae. It had taken time, patience, and more than a few frustrating failures, but there was something deeply satisfying about making fire the old way.

The spark caught, and the flames flickered to life, casting a golden glow on the forest around me. I felt a surge of pride; no magic, just skill.

Once the fire was large enough to cook on but not so big that it would send a signal to anyone who might be nearby, I began to skin the rabbit. My hands worked quickly, the motions instinctive from years of practice. There were no herbs to add flavor, no spices to make the meat more palatable, so I had to make do. I dug through our provisions, fingers brushing past dried roots and bags of grains until I found a small bundle of sage. Laurel had likely packed it for its medicinal properties, but today it would serve another purpose.

I rubbed the sage over the rabbit's flesh, the scent sharp and earthy. It wasn't much, but it would have to do. The crackling of the fire and the faint sounds of the forest were the only distractions as I set the meat over the flames, the heat slowly turning the rabbit golden and fragrant.

Warm hands slid around my torso, pulling me closer as I felt the soft tickle of a kiss brush against the bare skin of my shoulder. The unexpected touch made me gasp, my heart skipping a beat. I must have been so absorbed in cooking that I hadn't even noticed Reed waking up.

"Smells good," Reed whispered in my ear, his breath warm against my skin. "Even in the middle of the forest, your cooking smells delectable."

I couldn't help but laugh softly, despite the fluttering feeling in my chest. "You're supposed to be sleeping," I scolded, a teasing smile tugging at my lips. "It's only been a few hours. You can't possibly be well-rested."

"My nose must have woken me," Reed replied, a playful tone in his voice as he sniffed the air, clearly drawn to the scent of the rabbit roasting over the fire. "Can't say I regret it."

I chuckled, flipping the rabbit over the fire, watching as the heat browned the meat evenly. It was almost done, each side cooked to perfection. "Can you bring me some plates and utensils from the pack, or whatever you can find as a substitute?"

Reed complied without hesitation, and when he returned, I noticed a single knife he'd grabbed.

"Is that really all we have?" I asked reminding myself I should be grateful for whatever we had.

"Yeah, but I'm not exactly opposed to using a stone as a plate and eating with my hands. Unless you're too proper for that, Princess?" Reed replied, his tone mocking.

"Find me a stone," I said, accepting the challenge.

Reed smirked and came back with a flat rock. It was bulky, but it would do.

I sliced into the tender meat, dividing it equally between us, I felt a swell of pride at the satisfied sound of Reed's low moan.

"This is incredible," he murmured between bites, his eyes closing briefly in pleasure.

His words made my chest warm, but it wasn't just the feeling of accomplishment, it was something else that stirred inside me, something deeper with each moan he let out after every bite. As I watched him enjoy the meal, the heat in my belly shifted, and it wasn't from the warmth of the food.

"You may be a princess," Reed said with a grin, his lips still dusted with remnants of the meal, "but cooking was always meant to be your calling."

I felt my face flush at the compliment. "Thanks," I muttered, trying to hide the heat in my cheeks. Then, curiosity got the better of me, and I asked, "What do you think your calling is?"

He paused, chewing thoughtfully, before giving a sly grin. "Other than being devastatingly handsome?" he teased, his eyes sparkling with mischief. "The only other thing I'm good at is fighting."

My brow furrowed slightly. He'd mentioned his father teaching him before, but there was something in his tone that made it seem like it was a subject he didn't want to delve into. I didn't want to make him uncomfortable, so I changed the course of the conversation quickly.

"I wish I knew how to fight," I said, my voice quiet with a hint of longing. "It was something I always wanted to learn, but I was never given the opportunity."

Reed's expression softened, his gaze becoming a little more intense. "Which still baffles me," he muttered, a note of disappointment in his tone. "That your own family left you so helpless."

I winced slightly at the words, not wanting Reed to think badly of my brother. "Hayden did try when we were younger," I said quickly, trying to explain. "But we were both just too young. Neither of us had the patience to teach, or learn, sword fighting skills. It was more like a game than anything serious."

Reed's mouth tightened into a thin line, but he didn't comment. Instead, he set his empty stone aside and stood up, his movements suddenly sharp and purposeful. He marched toward the horse, his face focused and intense, as though an invisible switch had flipped inside him.

"Where are you going?" I asked, a slight edge of uncertainty creeping into my voice. I couldn't help but worry that I had said something wrong.

Without answering me, Reed dug through the bag he had packed and pulled out the two swords, the metal gleaming in the dim firelight. He smiled as he strode back toward me, his eyes alight with determination as he tossed one of the blades at my feet.

"Pick it up," he said, his voice low and almost daring, a wicked smile tugging at the corners of his lips. "We'll start training now."

I blinked, my heart stuttering. Training?

I glanced at the sword, then back at him. It was too dark, and only the firelight illuminated our surroundings. What if I messed up? What if I accidentally hurt him?

"Reed, it's late," I protested, a wave of uncertainty rising in me. "You're tired. I don't think this is a good idea."

"I've never felt better," Reed replied, his voice unwavering. He stepped closer, his eyes locked onto mine, his expression serious. "Pick up the sword, and we'll go over the basics. We don't need perfect conditions to start."

His resolve was unshakable, and a strange, fluttering sensation stirred in my chest. With a deep breath, I bent down and picked up the sword, its hilt cold in my hand. The weight of it felt unfamiliar and strange against my palm.

Reed's gaze never wavered from mine as he began to move, his stance confident as the firelight cast sharp shadows across his face.

"This is going to be interesting," he said, his voice steady as he began to demonstrate the first few moves.

The sword felt clumsy in my hands, as I held it out, trying to mimic Reed's stance, but it just didn't feel right. The blade seemed too long, too heavy, like it had its own mind and was determined to throw me off balance. I glanced up at Reed, whose posture was flawless, his body controlled.

"Come on, Sparks," Reed said. "You're holding it like you're about to give it a hug. You're not going to win any battles like that." He gave a teasing wink.

I shot him a glare, but I couldn't suppress the smile tugging at my lips. "I'm trying, alright?" I muttered, adjusting my grip. "This isn't exactly second nature to me."

Reed took a step closer, his boots crunching softly in the grass as he circled me. The fire flickered behind him, casting a warm glow across his face and making his eyes gleam with mischief.

"Alright, let's start with the basics," he said, his voice suddenly more serious. He reached for his own sword, holding it with a casual grace that made me envious. "First thing's first, your stance." He motioned for me to stand up straight, feet shoulder width apart. "You need to feel grounded. Like the earth is holding you steady. Don't stand too stiff, though. You need to be flexible, like a reed in the wind."

I tried to mimic him, but I could already feel my legs quivering from the awkwardness. I wasn't sure if it was from the unfamiliar weight of the sword or just nerves. Probably both.

"Good," Reed said, watching me. "Now, when you swing, you don't just rely on your arms. You use your whole body, your legs, your hips and of course your core." He demonstrated with a swift, fluid motion, his sword slicing through the air with a sharp whistle. "The power comes from your center, not your arms. Try it."

I exhaled sharply, trying to imitate his fluid motion. My first swing was clumsy, slicing through the air without any real purpose. Reed raised an eyebrow but said nothing, just offering a small, encouraging smile.

"Close, but not quite," he said, his voice teasing. "You're all over the place, Sparks. What's going on up there?" He tapped his temple lightly, and I couldn't help but roll my eyes.

"I'm concentrating," I replied, trying to sound confident, though my stance was anything but. "Give me a break. I didn't grow up wielding a sword."

Reed chuckled softly. "I'm well aware," he said, stepping closer. His proximity sent a shiver down my spine, and I instinctively tightened my grip on the hilt. He stood directly in front of me now, his eyes glinting with amusement. "Alright, one more try. Focus. You need to feel it in your body, not just in your hands. Trust your instincts."

I nodded, trying to push aside the butterflies fluttering in my stomach as I lifted the sword again. This time, I was more deliberate. My muscles strained as I swung, my whole body moving in tandem, trying to remember Reed's instructions. The blade cut through the air with a satisfying whoosh and clinked against Reed's sword as he expertly blocked it.

"Better," Reed said, his voice soft and teasing. "But you've got to use your legs more. If you don't, you'll be like a ragdoll with a sword. Strong, but totally useless."

I gritted my teeth. "You're such a charming teacher."

Reed's grin widened. "You'll thank me when you're not getting your ass handed to you by Ivy Guards."

I rolled my eyes, but I couldn't help the small laugh that escaped me. The way he teased me, even while offering advice, had a strange effect on me. His confidence, his presence, it was magnetic.

I took a step back and lowered my sword, trying to steady myself. "I think I'm getting the hang of it now," I said, trying to sound more confident than I felt.

Reed's expression softened, though there was still a playful gleam in his eyes. "Alright. Let's see what you've got."

We squared off, our swords raised, the firelight dancing in our eyes as we began to spar more seriously. I took a swing, Reed blocked it easily, and then we circled each other, blades flashing in the dim light. I tried to keep up, but I was still slow compared to him, each of his movements was so precise, so practiced, while mine felt like I was still figuring out which way to move.

"Come on, Sparks," Reed teased as he sidestepped another of my attempts, his blade tapping against mine with a soft clink. "Don't tell me you're already winded. I'm supposed to be the one who's too tired remember?"

"I'm not winded," I lied through gritted teeth, taking a sharp breath before swinging again.

Reed parried the blow and took a step forward, his chest nearly brushing against mine. "Then show me what you've got." His voice dropped, making the air between us feel electric.

Our swords clashed again, this time with more force. My heart pounded in my chest, and for a moment, everything else faded away, the crackling of the fire, the rustling of the trees, even my own breath. There was just me and Reed, our swords crossing, our bodies moving in sync, the rhythm of the fight carrying us forward.

And then, just as I swung a little too hard, my foot slipped on the uneven ground. My balance faltered, and before I knew it, I was falling backward. I let out a surprised yelp, grabbing for something to steady myself. My hand latched onto Reed's shirt, pulling him down with me.

There was a brief, shocked pause as we both tumbled to the ground. My back hit the earth with a soft thud, and Reed landed on top of me, his body pressed against mine. We both froze, staring at each other with wide eyes, both of us breathing heavily. His face was mere inches from mine, his wild silver and black hair falling loose around his face, his lips slightly parted.

For a long moment, all I could hear was the rapid beat of my heart in my ears, my chest rising and falling beneath him. And then, just as quickly, the tension shattered with laughter.

Reed let out a low chuckle, his lips curling into a grin as he propped himself up on his elbows, looking down at me. "Well, that wasn't exactly how I imagined our first real fight would go," he said, his voice light but breathy as neither of us moved.

Our laughter began to fade, but neither of us moved. Reed's body still lay on top of mine, his arms digging into the earth on either side of him to prop up his weight.

I stared up at him, lost in those fascinating silver-gray eyes, the green ring around the rim almost hypnotic. I could stay like this forever, unmoving, just staring.

My grip loosened around the sword's hilt, and it fell to the ground with a soft thud as Reed did the same. With my now free hand, I lifted my fingers to his face, wanting to memorize every inch of it. I traced lightly down the scar that angled across his cheek.

"How did you get this?" I asked, almost in a whisper. I had never asked before; truthfully, he was so beautiful that I had hardly noticed it. But now, I was certain there was a story behind it.

"It was a long time ago," Reed murmured, closing his eyes as he melted into my touch. "It was an accident. Do you find it hideous?"

"No," I breathed. "Nothing about you could ever be hideous, inside or out."

In a sudden, urgent movement, Reed's lips collided with mine. The kiss was bruising, more desperate than the night before. So much was left unspoken, so much still undone, and every part of me craved more. But alongside the hunger, a wave of fear swept over me, fear of how much I wanted this, wanted him.

My hands moved over his body, tracing the hard muscles of his chest, his stomach, his arms, he was stunning, every inch of him almost too much to take in.

Reed's hands followed, his fingers skimming over the fabric covering my breast, sending a shock of heat through me.

When our kiss finally broke, we both gasped for air. His hand remained, still cupping my breast, as though it longed to rid itself of the fabric separating us.

"May I?" Reed's voice was strained, almost vibrating with need.

I nodded. He wanted to touch me, free of any confines, and I wanted that too, wanted it so desperately.

Reed carefully untied the lacing at the front of my dress. A cold draft instantly brushed against my skin, causing my nipples to harden. But the chill was quickly replaced by warmth as Reed lowered his head, his mouth finding my nipple. The first teasing nip of his teeth made me gasp, and my back arched instinctively. His mouth on me sent waves of pleasure through my entire body, overwhelming me. I had never felt anything like this before, no one had ever touched me like this, but with Reed it just felt right.

My hand flew to the back of Reed's head, holding him to my breast as my fingers gripped his wild hair, tugging him closer. His tongue circled my nipple, alternating between sucking and gliding over its peak, sending jolts of pleasure through me.

I needed more. My other hand moved to my chest, eager to touch, to knead, but before I could even make contact, Reed's hand captured my wrist. "Did you think I'd forget about this one?" Reed said wickedly, his mouth hovering over my other breast. "These are mine to worship. So, if you need something to do with your hands, I suggest you pray." With a growl, he playfully bit at my nipple, his other hand massaging the opposite breast.

By the grace of Theodon, I needed something to do with my hands, needed to touch him, needed to feel him. I let my hand trail down Reed's torso, feeling every inch of him harden beneath my touch. Finally, I reached the seam of his pants, where his erection pressed painfully against the fabric, straining for release. Slowly, I slipped my fingers into his waistband, desperate to feel him, all of him. But just as my hand met the velvet heat of his cock, his own hand shot down to stop my wrist.

"I'm sorry," I murmured, suddenly worried that I'd done something wrong, that maybe he didn't want this.

"No need to apologize," Reed's voice was thick with hunger as he chuckled softly, the sound low and dark. "But even that light touch made my whole body turn electric. I want this to last, and I don't think it will if you touch me right now. I'm not ready for this to end so soon."

I wasn't sure if I was more confused or impressed. I had barely touched him, and yet he was admitting that the lightest contact almost made him lose control. I knew males could be sensitive, but the intensity of his reaction still surprised me. There was something intoxicating about drawing out such a visceral response, about knowing my touch alone could push him to the edge.

I brought my hands up from their wandering path and ran them firmly down his muscular arms. Reed's lips found mine once more, the kiss charged with hunger and urgency. I wrapped my arms around his back, yearning to pull him closer, to feel his hard body pressed against mine. The thought of crossing that final line with him consumed my mind. I wanted it, but the nerves fluttered in my stomach. I couldn't admit I was a virgin, not after lying about my previous experiences. Perhaps he wouldn't notice?

I could feel the wetness building between my legs with each insistent grind of his hips against mine, our mouths fused together in a sensual dance of tangled tongues. The cool night air did nothing to quell the burning need coursing through me. As Reed's hand trailed down my stomach, slipping lower under my skirt, a new wave of sensation flooded my body.

"Is this okay?" Reed murmured.

It was like something straight out of that dream I had, only now it was a reality. "Yes," I breathed, knowing he would feel the evidence of just how okay I was with this, how desperately I craved his touch. In one swift motion, his fingers pushed aside my panties, exploring me with a gentle touch.

"Fuck," I moaned as he found that sensitive bundle of nerves, sending shockwaves of pleasure through me as his lips returned to mine.

His fingers made the softest, most precise movements around my clit, driving me wild. I needed to break our kiss to catch my breath. His slow, tantalizing touches were creating a pulsing desire at my center.

"Reed," I moaned, feeling like I was on the verge of unraveling.

"Not yet, Sparks," Reed commanded, his fingers slowing to a crawl. "We're not done here. I still have so much more of you to explore."

With that, I felt a finger nudge my opening before slowly pushing into my core. The foreign sensation caused my whole body to press against him, my hips rocking in rhythm with Reed's movements, desperate for him to go deeper.

"Good girl," Reed whispered, his hot breath sending chills through me. "So wet for me already."

"Faster," I begged, my body picking up pace, needing more friction. I wanted to hold off my climax, to reach it together with Reed, but the sensations were overwhelming. With each thrust of Reed's fingers, I was getting closer to the edge. When he added a second finger, I knew I couldn't hold on any longer.

"Reed, I can't," I cried, throwing my head back, my eyes locked on the stars, knowing my release was imminent.

"You can, Sparks. You can, and you will," he growled, his strong arm pressing down on my chest to keep me still. It felt as if he was trying to take control, trying to stop my body from reaching its climax too soon.

I gasped, torn between trying to hold back as he instructed and wanting to give in to the pleasure. That show of his control only made it worse. I liked this side of Reed and craved to see more. If I climaxed too soon, I might not get another chance.

Taking a deep breath, I did as he said and held back my release as his fingers slowed. When he finally withdrew them, I felt a sense of emptiness, not just from holding back, but because I wasn't ready to be disconnected from him yet.

Gazing up at him through hooded eyes, I saw his glistening fingers in the moonlight, and realized that all that wetness was from me.

Reeds' eyes locked with mine, his face filled with a wicked smirk as he brought those two fingers coated with my excitement to his lips. Slowly, he dipped each finger between his lips, licking every last drop of my essence from his fingers. "Delicious," he said, his lips curving into a cruel smile. "Let's see how you taste straight from the source."

I watched as Reed lowered himself to his stomach, his head resting between my legs. His lips trailed gentle kisses along the sensitive skin of my inner thighs as he discovered a sensitive spot I didn't even know existed. The touch elicited a small, involuntary giggle from my lips.

"I'll have to remember this spot right here," Reed purred, pressing another kiss to my inner thigh. "If just this simple touch brings a smile like that to your face, it seems I'll have to give it attention daily."

I would want nothing more. I couldn't fathom ever growing tired of this feeling, this pleasure. Sleep, food, and drink? Those were all distant memories. Who needed such trivial things when one could bask in unending bliss? I was beginning to understand why Hayden spent so many countless hours tangled with lovers.

Reeds warm breath tickled my folds as his face sank deeper and deeper until his tongue glided through and into my core. His tongue moved in slow, hungry circles, much like when he had captured my nipple.

His hands slid down to my knees, prying my legs further apart to grant him better access. Reed's mouth explored every inch of me, as if he were a starving male. His tongue dipped in and out, dragging up my center before resting on that bundle of nerves he was so fond of. Now I understood why they used the phrase "feasting."

I had held back my climax before, but I wasn't sure if I could do it again now that I was already teetering on the edge. My hands slammed into the earth below, as I dug my fingers into the dirt, needing something to ground me before I was swept away by the overwhelming bliss of Reed's touch.

His mouth mimicked our bruising kiss as he continued his thorough exploration. I couldn't take it anymore. I needed the release.

"Please Reed," I begged, hoping this time he would let me let go. "Please," I whimpered.

"Come for me, Eli," Reed commanded, continuing to work his mouth around my center.

My climax came in crashing waves, my whole body shuddering as my muscles contracted and the world became a blur. I opened my eyes to stare at the stars, wanting to give them the show they were undoubtedly watching. When the last of the aftershocks left my body, I felt myself go limp under Reed's touch.

Reed lifted his head, his face glistening with my release. "Even sweeter from the source itself," he said as he wiped his mouth, cleaning the remnants of my excitement with his now shiny palm. He then licked the last traces from his hand. "I don't think I'll ever get enough."

"I want to taste," I moaned, unsure of what was coming over me.

"There's still some of you on my tongue," Reed smiled, bringing his face back to mine as his tongue darted into my mouth. I could taste myself on him, and he was right, I was sweet. Now I understood why males did this, and if Reed's pleasure tasted half as good as mine, then I think I may have found my new favorite meal.

Reed's mouth left mine as he gave my nipples one final suck before completely caging me to the floor. I could still feel the hardness of his chest, despite my skirt being bunched up around my stomach from where Reed had left it after tasting me.

I felt the head of his cock that was now free of his trousers positioning itself just outside the folds of my entrance. All he would need to do was make one small thrust, and he would be inside me. The final line would be crossed, and my maidenhead would be gone. Fear seeped into my mind again, fear of the pain I'd been told would come with bedding a male for the first time, and fear of what Reed might think. I trusted him and knew he would never hurt me or force me into anything, but maybe he wouldn't want to be my first.

I had heard from conversations around the Ember Palace, as well as from Hayden, that some males have a fascination with virgins, almost as if conquering them was a quest to be had. Others, however, did not prefer an inexperienced partner, feeling that being someone's first time was such a monumental moment that they did not want to be the one to experience that, especially without intense feelings involved.

But that was not the case with Reed and I. I had deep feelings for him, and I was sure he felt the same. Yet, this lingering worry still plagued me. Perhaps this meant more to me than it would to him. No, it would absolutely mean more to me than to him. I had chosen Reed to be the first person I would share this experience with, and my heart was ready. I just needed my body and mind to catch up.

Reed rocked his hips forward until I could feel the tip of his arousal at my entrance. I stared into his eyes, hoping he couldn't see the internal battle I was facing. My brow furrowed, likely giving away my conflicted emotions, as Reed spoke.

"We can stop," Reed said, his hand gently smoothing out the worry lines between my brows. "If you're not ready yet, especially after what happened at the Ivy Castle."

We could stop. I could avoid the embarrassment of him discovering my secret. I could use that horrible night with Orrin as an excuse to take all the time I needed, until I found the courage and told him the truth.

But no. I wanted this. I wanted to feel him inside me, to be so connected to him in this moment. I wanted to experience all of this for the first time, with him. With Reed.

I took a deep breath, quieting my mind to listen to my heart. "Don't stop," I whispered. Without hesitation, I felt the head of his cock slip inside.

My whole body tensed at the intrusion, at the sharp pain as a gasp escaped my lips. It seemed I'd remembered to quiet my mind, but forgotten to tell my body. *Great.*

I could feel my body trying to push him out, while all my heart wanted was for him to burrow in deeper.

"Sparks?" Reed asked gently, not withdrawing, but not pushing deeper either, just there, a small piece connecting us. "Are you okay?"

I nodded, but my whole body began to tremble under him. There was no way I was going to talk my way out of this. My nerves and fear were now physically evident.

"You're not okay," Reed said, his voice full of concern. "You're trembling," he continued as he slowly withdrew from me. "Did I hurt you?"

"No," I lied, my body already missing the feel of him, causing my trembling body to vibrate even more. This was not going how I thought it would. "We can try again, but... I think I should tell you something first."

Reed's eyes shifted back and forth, as though he were trying to read me, to understand what was going on

"I lied to you that day at the oasis," I started, my eyes looking away from his burning gaze. "I haven't been with a ton of males."

"That's okay," Reed said softly. "I don't care if it's been twenty males or one that you've been with. Nothing would ever make me think differently of you."

"Well, it hasn't been twenty," I said slowly, preparing myself to tell him the truth. "It hasn't even been one."

Reed was silent for a moment, like he was trying to process exactly what I had just confessed. "You mean you haven't—"

"No," I quickly interrupted, wanting to just get this conversation out of the way. "I've never been bedded by a male. I'm sorry I didn't tell you."

Reed's expression softened, and he pressed his lips to my forehead, placing a gentle kiss there. "Did you think I would see you as less just because you're a virgin? Or that because of that I wouldn't want you?"

"I wasn't sure what you would think," I replied, my shaking body finally calming down now that the truth was out. "I just know some males prefer it when the female is more experienced, and I—"

Reed's lips were on mine, cutting off the rest of my sentence. His kiss moved slowly and passionately, as if he were discovering me for the first time again. When Reed pulled away, I saw a smile forming on his lips as he tucked himself back into his trousers.

"We can still try," I said, hoping I wasn't wrong, hoping he didn't find me unappealing now that he knew. "We can still make love?"

I wasn't sure why I said make love. I should have just said we could still fuck or just have sex, something casual that wouldn't make me sound like the needy little virgin I was. But as the words settled in my mind, I knew I had said the right thing. Make love. Because with Reed, that's exactly what it would have been.

"Oh, we will," Reed said confidently. "But not here, not on a dirty forest floor while we're running for our lives. No. The first time you experience this, it will be where you want it to be. Warm in a luxurious bed, on the soft sands of the oasis, or in a soothing bathtub. Wherever you want it to be, we'll do it."

"Reed," I started to protest, not wanting him to think I was high maintenance. Because the truth was, I didn't need luxury, only him

"No," Reed interrupted me, propping himself up and straddling my waist. "Your first time should be special, and I'm truly honored that you've chosen me to be the one to experience that with. But no arguments. The first time we make love will be on your terms. But..." A wicked smile curved onto his lips as he rose to his feet.

"The first time we fuck, that will be on my terms. Deal?" He held out a hand to help me up and solidify our new arrangement.

I took his hand, and he lifted me to my feet. "Deal."

Reed helped me smooth out my skirt and laced up the front of my dress. With one final kiss, we let the tension that had been building between us disappear as we headed back to our campsite.

The fire crackled softly, its warmth slowly fading as the last embers dimmed. Reed and I had settled on the ground, our bodies wrapped in the wool blankets. The cool night air was a stark contrast to the heat of the flames, but the blankets provided enough comfort to make me feel warm beside him. His arm was draped around me, pulling me closer, his heartbeat steady against my back. I felt the tension in my muscles melt away with every slow breath he took.

The quiet of the forest surrounded us now, only the occasional rustle of leaves and the faint murmur of the wind stirring the trees. It felt peaceful, almost surreal, like we were the only two people left in the world.

Reed shifted slightly, his chin resting against the top of my head. The faint mint scent of his skin mixed with the earthy smell of the forest, and I closed my eyes, breathing him in like it was the last thing I might ever do.

"What are you thinking?" Reed's voice was soft, but I could feel the weight of his words pressing into me.

I took a deep breath, letting the quiet settle around me. My mind had been running in circles all night, but there was one thing that had stayed with me, one thing I couldn't shake.

"I don't want you to leave. I... I want you to stay with me. On the Ember Isle. I don't want to let you go just yet."

There was a pause before he responded, his fingers tracing small patterns on my arm. "I'd like nothing more than to stay with you. But I can't, Eli. I need to go back home. There are things I've left behind, responsibilities I can't ignore."

His words, though soft, stung. I felt the knot in my stomach tighten, but I didn't pull away. Instead, I closed my eyes and let the ache settle in my chest.

"But, if I could wish for anything," he continued, his voice lower now, filled with something soft, something tender. "I would wish to hide away with you. To never let you be alone again."

I swallowed, my throat thick with emotion. I wanted so badly for it to be that easy. For us to escape to some quiet corner of the world where we could just be.

But reality had a way of grounding us. I squeezed his hand, my fingers curling into his warmth, trying to hold onto him as if it would make the distance between us less painful.

Reed cleared his throat softly, as if he, too, was trying to move past the heaviness of the moment. "What are you most looking forward to when you go home?" he asked, changing the subject gently, but I could feel the concern in his voice. He wanted to know, wanted to help me hold onto something hopeful.

I took a moment to think, the images of my family flashing through my mind. The warmth of their embrace, the sound of my brother's laughter, my parents' reassuring voices. The thought of it made something inside me ache with longing.

"I just want to hold my family. I want to hug them and never let go. I want to make up for all the time I've lost. I want to feel like I'm not missing pieces of myself anymore." My words trailed off, and I could hear the exhaustion in my voice. My body was ready to sleep, but my mind was still spinning, still holding on to everything that had been said and done.

Reed shifted beside me, his thumb lightly brushing my wrist. "What do you want to do first when you return home?" I asked through a yawn.

"I think I want to reevaluate my life," Reed replied with a bit of unsureness in his voice. "I want to figure out what I truly want."

I gave a small nod as sleep came for me. His warmth surrounded me, and I surrendered to it, my eyelids growing heavier with each breath.

Reed's hand moved from my wrist to my shoulder. "Get some sleep, Eli," he whispered, his breath warm against my ear. "Goodnight."

I mumbled something in response, my eyes fluttering closed. "Goodnight," I whispered back, the word barely a murmur. But then, just as my consciousness began to slip away, something else escaped my lips, quiet and almost imperceptible. "I love you, Reed," I murmured, unable to hold the words back.

I froze for a moment, hoping it had been nothing more than a dream, that the words hadn't left my lips. I didn't want him to hear it, not yet, not when everything was still so new, so uncertain. I held my breath, willing the moment to pass, hoping I had just said it in my mind instead of out loud. I was truly too tired to even care in this moment. I had meant it. Even if he heard it or not.

But then, just as sleep began to take me completely, I thought I heard his voice right beside my ear. "I love you too, Eli."

I couldn't tell if I had imagined it, or if it was real. But the warmth that spread through my chest, the way my heart fluttered in response, told me that maybe, just maybe, it was true.

And with that, I finally let myself fall asleep, the sound of his whispered words lulling me into a dreamless rest, where I could hold onto that love for a little while longer, safe in the quiet embrace of his arms.

I woke up to the faint crackle of the fire and the smell of something delicious cooking nearby. My blanket was warm and heavy, still wrapped around me like a cocoon, and for a moment, I just lay there, listening to the soft sounds of the forest and the rhythmic sizzle of meat over the flames

When I opened my eyes, I saw Reed kneeling beside the fire, carefully flipping the last of the rabbit meat. His broad shoulders were silhouetted against the growing light of dawn, and I could see the muscles of his back flex as he worked, a quiet focus in his movements.

He didn't notice me watching him at first, so I took a moment to just admire the way he moved. He was graceful in a way that didn't match his rugged exterior, like every action was deliberate and thoughtful, despite the hard life he'd lived. I felt a soft warmth settle in my chest as I thought about the way he had taken care of me, protecting me, teaching me, and in this moment, cooking for me.

He must have sensed me staring, though, because he turned to catch my eye, a playful smile tugging at the corner of his lips. "Good morning," he said, his voice gentle and warm, the same comforting tone I'd grown used to. "Breakfast is ready."

Before I could respond, Reed reached over, grabbing the makeshift stone plate of meat and bringing it to me. He set it down beside me in my bedroll, his fingers brushing against mine for just a moment. The touch sent a pleasant shiver through me, and I couldn't help but smile.

"Thanks," I murmured, my voice still thick with sleep.

He leaned in then, brushing a kiss across my cheek, his lips warm against my skin. The sweetness of the gesture made my heart flutter, and I felt my cheeks flush. When he pulled back, his smile was soft but teasing.

"Did you sleep well?" he asked, his gaze lingering on my face with a hint of curiosity.

I nodded, still feeling the haze of sleep clouding my thoughts. "Yes, I did."

Reed raised an eyebrow, clearly not buying it. "You know," he said, his voice playful, "you mumble in your sleep."

I froze, the warmth of the blanket suddenly feeling too heavy, too suffocating. I'd been half asleep when the words I never meant to slay slipped from my lips. My pulse quickened as I suddenly remembered what I had said. *I love you, Reed.* The words echoed in my mind, and I felt my face grow hot with embarrassment.

"I-I can explain," I stammered, fumbling for words. "It must have been the exhaustion, and my mind was playing tricks on me after we were intimate. I wasn't thinking clearly, I wasn't—"

But Reed cut me off with a quiet laugh. "Is that so?" He leaned in slightly, his voice steady, though his eyes held a glimmer of something more serious now. "Answer me honestly Eli, is it true? Do you really love me?"

My heart pounded in my chest and I realized with certainty that he had heard what I confessed last night. The possibility made me even more flustered. I couldn't meet his gaze, but I managed to whisper, "Yes, it's true. I do love you. At least I think I do, I don't know, I've never felt this way before."

The words felt right when I said them, like a burden lifted off my chest. I'd known it for a while now, but hearing myself admit it out loud made it feel real in a way it hadn't before.

Reed didn't look away. His expression softened, a mix of surprise and something else I couldn't quite place.

"Did I really hear you say it too last night?" I asked quietly. "Or was that just a dream?"

"I did say it," Reed said softly, his eyes locking onto mine. "And I meant it."

I felt a mixture of relief and disbelief wash over me. "But we've only known each other a short time," I whispered, still trying to wrap my mind around the magnitude of what we had both confessed. "And everything that's happened, it's too complicated. It doesn't make sense."

Reed shrugged, his expression almost sheepish, but the sincerity in his voice never wavered. "I know. But I can't deny it, Eli. I've never felt this way about anyone before either. You've completely turned my world upside down, and it's a feeling I'm still learning to process. But it's real. And I'm not going to run from it."

My chest tightened, and I reached out to take his hand, squeezing it gently. "We can learn together," I said, the words slipping out before I even realized what I was saying. But I meant it. In that moment, I wanted to face everything with him. Whatever came next, we'd face it together.

Reed smiled, a little shy but full of warmth. "Together," he echoed softly, his hand still holding mine.

I turned my attention back to the food beside me, my stomach growling in protest. My gaze fell on the small slab of rabbit meat, but as I picked it up to take a bite, I realized something. "Wait," I said, glancing up at Reed with a frown. "There's only enough left for one serving."

Reed's grin turned wicked, and he leaned back with a playful sparkle in his eyes. "Oh, I have other ideas for what I'm hungry for," he teased, his voice low and full of mischief.

I raised an eyebrow, my heart beating faster in anticipation of what he might say next. "And what's that?" I asked, unable to suppress the smile tugging at my lips.

Reed leaned in, his breath warm against my ear. "You," he murmured, his voice rough and full of promise.

Reed pounced on me like a predator and I was his prey. His lips crashed into mine and he lifted me to my feet as he backed me against a tree, eliciting a small gasp when I made contact with trunk a bit harder than expected.

"Sorry," Reed said breathlessly, "I'll make it up to you."

"Yeah?" I replied coyly, pulling him in for another heated kiss.

Reed slid down my body until he was on his knees before me. "Is this where you want me, Princess?" he teased, his voice thick with lust.

I nodded, gazing down at the perfect male at my feet. In one swift motion, Reed hooked my leg over his shoulder and disappeared under my skirts. I braced myself against the tree as his strong hands slid up my thighs.

His face nuzzled between my legs, causing my breath to hitch and my heart to race as he found that sensitive spot. "Fuck," I moaned, feeling his warm laughter against my skin.

His lips trailed higher until he moved my panties aside. My body hummed with excitement as his mouth closed around my clit.

My hips jerked forward as he sucked on my sensitive bundle of nerves, causing a rising wave of pleasure to wash over me. I felt his hand sliding up my leg, settling near his mouth.

"Reed, what are you—" I started, but before I could finish, he sank a finger deep inside me. My whole body twitched forward as I cried out, "For the love of Theodon!" My fingernails dug into the bark of the tree behind me.

His fingers moved in time with his tongue, which was still massaging my clit. When I felt his fingers leave, they were quickly replaced by his darting tongue, lapping at my core and collecting every drop. I couldn't help the moan that escaped my lips as his finger joined his tongue, working together to bring me to the brink of ecstasy.

I could feel myself tipping over the edge as my climax was building with every touch. I remembered that Reed had requested I ask for permission before I could find release, though through my gasps I wasn't sure if I could find the words, let alone if I could form them in a question.

"Reed, can I—," I started before another moan escaped my lips as his tongue hit the perfect spot.

I was so close as I felt the shudder in my body start to take over, all the while my palms dug into the tree behind me as I grasped it so hard, I could feel my skin starting to slice open. With heavy breaths, I was still unable to request the permission I knew he wanted from me, instead I dug my palms even deeper into the trunk of the tree as my whole body tensed before pleasure swept through me, igniting every muscle.

My body went limp, my hands releasing from the tree as Reed's strong hands held me up. Reed lowered my leg as he withdrew from under my skirts, then lifted his mouth to mine, allowing me to taste myself once more. This time, the flavor was different, and I wondered what he had done to evoke this new sensation.

When our kiss broke, Reed's face took on a wicked gleam. "I don't believe I gave you permission to finish, did I, Sparks."

"I'm sorry," I said in a soft giggle below my ragged breathing.

"Next time you disobey me or forget to use your words, I may just have to punish that little mouth of yours." Reed flashed me a wicked smile.

"Deal," I said, holding my hand out to shake his, actually excited for my next moment of disobedience.

Reed took my offer and shook my hand, and only then did I feel the pain. My body must have been consumed by the intense climax, and only after the pleasure had subsided did the stinging in my hands become apparent.

I yanked my hand away as my face contorted from the pain I was now trying to hide.

"What's wrong?" Reed said, his eyes following my gaze down to my palms.

The skin was broken and reddened, but there was no blood. "I guess I got carried away," I said, feeling a bit embarrassed.

Reed brought my palms to his lips, placing feather light kisses on each one. "Pleasure and pain can often intertwine, but I don't want this for you. If I'm ever hurting you, or you're doing something that will hurt yourself, please tell me. No pleasure is worth your pain," he finished, pressing another soft kiss to my hands.

I nodded, and Reed tore a strip from his shirt to bandage my palms. "It's not too bad, but keep them covered while we ride, so they don't split open further."

"Okay," I replied, and Reed planted a final kiss on my lips before we needed to get back on the road.

After breakfast, we packed up quickly, our movements synchronized, working fast to get on the move. The forest was quieter this morning, as though it sensed the change in our journey. I could hear the rustle of the trees above us, but there was an unnatural stillness to everything else. We had to move quickly, though, time was ticking, and we needed to stay ahead of anyone who might be looking for us.

Reed doused the fire, stamping out the last embers with careful precision. We couldn't afford to leave a trace, just in case some of the guards decided to take the same treacherous path through the forest as we did. As the smoke disappeared, I bent down to fold the blankets, my mind still swirling with everything we'd discussed and everything we had done in the last twenty-four hours. There seemed to be a new understanding between us, a knowing want and need we craved from one another.

Reed was moving with purpose, packing the last of our things into the bags, but I caught the occasional glance in my direction, a brief flash of something in his eyes before he focused again. Something soft at first but then it would form into something strange. He assured me he was not ashamed of my nerves from last night, but then why was he looking at me like that? Every smile he threw my way after though, only made my heart settle back into that comfortable place we had built between us. I knew I wasn't imagining the intensity between us, but for now, we couldn't let ourselves linger in that space too long.

"Ready?" Reed asked, standing and brushing the dirt from his hands.

"As I'll ever be," I replied, slinging my bag over my shoulder and glancing at him with a mischievous grin. "Though I insist on taking the reins today."

Reed raised an eyebrow, clearly amused. "You? Riding?" He chuckled, his voice rich with humor. "I thought you were joking when you said you learned. They gave you riding lessons but not self-defense?"

I flashed him a sly smile. "Guess they figured I could just gallop away from any threats," I said with a wink and a laugh, stepping toward the horse. Reed was watching me closely, his expression shifting from doubt to quiet amusement.

I felt a little nervous, now that I had hyped myself up on knowing how to ride a horse, I just hoped I could deliver. Taking a deep breath, I swung my leg over the saddle smoothly and effortlessly as I had done many times with Fintana, the smooth leather creaking beneath me as I settled into place. I adjusted my grip on the reins, feeling the familiar sense of control surge through me.

When I glanced back at Reed, his eyes were wide, his jaw slightly dropped. "Impressive," he muttered under his breath, his gaze lingering on me as I gave him a small, playful shrug.

"Don't look so surprised," I teased. "I told you I did my fair share of horseback riding. Just haven't had the chance to show off."

Reed shook his head, a small laugh escaping his lips. "I'll admit, I was wrong about you," he said. "Maybe I've underestimated you, Sparks."

"You're not the only one," I teased back, nudging the horse forward. "Now climb up here."

For a moment, we traveled in comfortable silence, the soft clop of the horses' hooves on the dirt trail the only sound around us. The trees around us grew sparser as we moved deeper into the forest, the canopy thinning out and giving way to a wider, more open space.

The day continued on and we made short stops to water the horse and stretch our legs. I may have gotten a little cocky in my abilities as my hands cramped after the first few hours of clenching the reins. I wasn't ready to give up so easily though, so Reed and I alternated between who was in control of the horse below us.

The air was starting to warm as we got closer to the beach, and I could feel the subtle shift in the atmosphere. The smell of saltwater and brine lingered in the air, making everything feel a little fresher, a little more alive. I could see the edge of the forest ahead of us, where the trees finally gave way to a wide, open stretch of sand. In the distance, I could just make out the soft, distant glimmer of the water, the rolling waves crashing against the shore.

"We're almost there," I said, breaking the silence as I nudged the horse forward, the anticipation in my chest growing stronger.

Reed nodded, his expression thoughtful. "Yeah, looks like Laurel's shortcut on the map paid off, we're early."

He was right. The dock was empty for now, the wooden planks stretching out into the water, but there were no ships in sight. I guess Hayden really meant by the full moon. That was if he was still coming at all. No. I had to shake that thought. Hayden was coming. Maybe it was a twin thing, but I could sense it; I could feel it.

"We should wait here on the edge," Reed suggested, glancing around at the stretch of beach. "Under the cover of the trees. Keep out of sight until it's time to meet him."

I nodded, relieved by the idea of staying hidden for a little while longer. The beach looked too open with only a few large rocks scattered about where we could be vulnerable if the guards caught up with us or if an Ivy vessel made port.

Reed tethered the horse to a nearby tree, and I immediately set to work, gathering kindling and arranging it into a small pile to make a temporary camp until nightfall. Reed glanced at me with a smile before turning his attention to the water.

"I'll go get us some fish for dinner, hopefully this part of the beach hasn't seen the Isle's sickness just yet." he said, voice warm. "Stay here, keep the fire going. I'll be back soon."

I grinned, watching him walk away. His steps were steady, confident. "Don't take too long," I called after him. "Wouldn't want a beast to attack me again, or worse, attack you."

Reed glanced over his shoulder and shot me a teasing grin. "You'll be fine, with this part of the forest so bare, I doubt any predators would choose it as their home. Just try not to burn the camp down, alright?"

I waved him off, rolling my eyes as I got to work on the fire. The kindling crackled and popped as the first flames flickered to life, the warmth slowly spreading across my skin. The wind was gentle here, the air soft with the scent of the ocean and the earth. It gave me an odd sort of peace.

My mind drifted back to Reed, his smile, the way he touched me this morning, the way he worshipped my body last night. I had finally been honest with him and he was so patient. He was everything I wanted, and I would have had him right then and there last night. It would have made for a great story, a great adventure. The silver lining of this whole experience here on Ivy. He was my silver lining. My prize.

I focused back on the fire and as the flames grew stronger, I settled into the warmth, the sound of the waves in the distance lulling me into a comfortable quiet. I let my thoughts drift, the peace of the moment spreading through me. A peace I realized I couldn't embrace just yet. Not while we were still being hunted by the king, not when I wasn't sure Hayden would make it in time. Not until we were off this Isle.

I glanced over at the horizon, taking a few steps towards the beach to watch the sun set. It was starting to dip lower in the sky, painting the world in shades of gold and orange. I could see the dark silhouette of Reed by the water now, his form moving gracefully as he waded into the shallows. The wind ruffled his hair, and I could hear his deep laugh carried across the breeze.

Despite freedom being so close and danger even closer, there was a part of me that wanted to stay in this moment forever, just the two of us, here in this tiny clearing by the beach. A life I had always dreamed of. I shook my head, pushing away the thought as I remembered everything that led to this moment. No, this was not my dream life. This was a nightmare. One that would only grow worse until we got the hell off this Isle.

I tended back to the fire, my thoughts still going over everything with Reed, everything I would have to tell my parents about what the Ivy King was up to, and of course the things I wouldn't want to say but would surely be asked about, what was done to me while imprisoned.

My thoughts were interrupted by the sound of Reed's voice. "You're doing well with the fire," he said, coming back into view, a string of fish hanging from his hand.

I smiled up at him shaking those thoughts. "I've had plenty of practice."

Reed set the fish down beside the fire, his eyes meeting mine. He knelt beside me, his eyes soft as he looked at the fire, then back at me. "We make a good team, don't we?"

I tilted my head, meeting his gaze. "Yeah, we do." I laughed, glancing down at the fish. "Let's get this cooked before it burns out. I'm starving."

Reed raised an eyebrow. "Starving for dinner? Or something else?"

I shot him a teasing look, my heart fluttering slightly at the flirtation. "Maybe both." I said, earning me a mischievous laugh from Reed.

As the sky began to darken, I glanced over at Reed again, watching him as he set the fish to cook over the fire. The way the light flickered over his face made him look so focused, so sure.

The evening stretched on as we cooked, both of us glancing anxiously toward the sea, hoping to spot Hayden's ship. But so far, it was just the stillness beyond the crashing waves reflecting back at us.

When the fish was good and ready, Reed and I ate in silence enjoying the quiet. After the last bite, Reed cleared our makeshift plates and the air around us grew cooler as the last remnants of daylight began to fade into twilight. The fire crackled softly, its warm glow casting flickering shadows on the trees as I stretched my limbs, content and full. My gaze turned to Reed, who was standing up and brushing the sand off his pants with an almost casual air.

"I think its best that we extinguish the fire now, just to be safe."

"Alright, but first," Reed said, his tone shifting to something more focused, the teasing edge gone. He walked over to where he had left the sword beside the fire and tossed it towards me. It landed at my feet with a soft thud. "Time for another lesson."

I picked up the blade easily, feeling the familiar weight of the blade in my hands. Despite the growing tension in the air of worrying someone would see the flames of the fire, a part of me felt excited. There was something about sword fighting that calmed me, even if it was more about the thrill of learning than actual skill.

Reed gave me a small nod, walking a few paces away, his posture straight and sharp. "Alright, first things first," he said, and I shifted into a more balanced stance, mimicking his movements. He studied me for a moment, then nodded. "Good, you're getting the hang of this. Now, let's work on your strikes."

He drew his sword from his side and held it at the ready. "In sword fighting, you don't just attack with strength; you use your whole body. Let's start with the basics, an overhead strike, also called a 'descending cut.' From here," he demonstrated, "you bring the blade up to your shoulder and strike down diagonally. Think of it like you're trying to split something with your sword."

I mirrored his movements, lifting the sword up to my shoulder, feeling the weight shift. I swung it down with as much force as I could muster. Reed caught my strike easily with his sword, his eyes never leaving mine.

"Not bad for your second lesson," he said, adjusting his grip and holding the blade up. "But remember, it's not just the strength you need, its precision and timing. Try again, and this time, make sure you twist your wrist at the last second. That'll give you the added power."

I took a deep breath, focusing on the technique he'd outlined. I swung the sword again, this time with more control, twisting my wrist slightly as I did. Reed blocked my strike again, but this time, I felt a shift in the balance. My hit had more impact.

"That's better," he said with a smile, stepping back to give me room. "Now, let's try something different, an 'interception' technique. When an opponent strikes, instead of just blocking, you meet their attack head on and redirect their blade. It's about finesse."

He quickly lunged forward, mimicking an overhead strike. I held my sword steady, then, as his blade came toward me, I turned my own at the last moment to meet his and deflect it off course. I didn't expect to land it perfectly, but Reed's sword collided with mine with a soft clash.

"That's the idea," Reed said, a glint of approval in his eyes. "But you'll need to use your opponent's force against them. Watch the way they move, and when you see their strike coming, don't just block. Use your whole body to redirect their blade."

We sparred for a few more minutes, Reed pushing me to pay closer attention to the movements of the sword, to watch how it could shift mid motion. My arms were growing tired, and sweat was beginning to trickle down the back of my neck, but I couldn't help but feel a sense of accomplishment with each new movement.

Then, as I was about to swing at Reed once more, something caught my eye. I stopped mid-swing, my eyes darting over the waves past the beach. A small ship was cutting through the sea, its silhouette framed by the bright light of the glowing moon.

I felt my heart skip a beat, and without thinking, I dropped the sword at my feet, my breath catching in my throat.

Hayden.

33

"It's Hayden," I whispered under my breath, my voice trembling with a mixture of excitement and relief. I took a few steps forward, moving closer to the edge of the forest where the trees met the sands of the beach.

Reed had noticed my sudden shift in focus, and he quickly closed the distance between us, his expression hardening as he placed a hand on my arm to stop me from taking another step.

"Eli, wait," he said firmly, pulling me back gently but with purpose. His voice was calm, but there was an edge to it. "We don't know who might be hiding around here. The Ivy Guard could be waiting for us to show up in the open."

I looked up at him, seeing the intensity in his eyes, and I nodded, the sense of urgency quickly returning. He was right. We had to be careful. Hayden might be close, but we couldn't risk exposing ourselves to anyone who might be watching. Not until Hayden was closer.

Reed motioned toward the trees, and I followed him without question. The fire was still crackling softly behind us, and Reed moved quickly to stomp out the flames. The forest felt denser now, the shadows deeper as the moonlight peaked through the trees.

We stayed crouched for what felt like an eternity, my eyes never leaving the sight of the ship that grew larger and larger as it drew closer.

"It's really him," I whispered, squeezing Reed's hand, "Its Hayden. He really came."

"Did you doubt he would?"

"No, I guess I always knew he would come. I just never thought I'd be the one returning with him. Never expected it to be the both of us." I smiled at Reed, and he squeezed my hand lightly in return, causing my pulse to quicken as our eyes locked for a brief moment. I tore my gaze away from him, just long enough to see the ship approaching.

A crescendo of sounds echoed from the trees behind us. At first, it was a soft rustling of leaves, but soon it built into a louder rhythm, one that vibrated through my chest. Hooves. A collection of pounding hooves, growing nearer with every passing second. It was the Ivy Guard. It had to be. They'd found us.

"Reed?" I whispered, fear creeping into my voice.

"I hear it too," he replied dryly, his hand squeezing mine again, this time so tight it almost hurt. "Eli, listen to me," Reed began, his eyes darting to the trees, searching for any sign of the guards. "Get to the beach and hide. I'll stay here—"

"No! I'm not leaving you here."

"Eli, I'm skilled with a sword. You know this," he said calmly, cupping my face. "I can fight them off or at least distract them long enough for the ship to dock."

"Then Hayden can come help—"

"No, then you'll get on that ship, and if I don't make it there in time, you'll leave without me."

"What?" I asked, confusion flooding me. How could he think I would just leave him?

"There's no need for more bloodshed, and if your brother steps foot on that beach, that's what will happen."

"I'm not leaving you!" I argued, my voice trembling.

"If I don't make it there in time, then yes, you will. Now take this sword with you." He pressed the hilt into my palm. "Use it like I showed you, in case you're found."

"Reed," I pleaded. Before I could say more, he captured my lips in a kiss, one that felt more like a goodbye than a promise for the future.

"Go," Reed ordered, his voice breaking through the moment. "Now!"

My flicker of sadness flared into something fierce. "You better make it to the ship."

"I'll try," Reed said, pushing me toward the beach.

I sprinted toward the beach, sword in hand, my feet sinking slightly into the soft sand with each stride, the rush of adrenaline fueling every step. The jagged rocks loomed ahead, their towering presence a natural shield against the vast, open beach. I dove behind the largest boulder, pressing my back against its cool surface, my breath coming in quick, shallow gasps. I sank lower, curling my knees to my chest, doing my best to remain unseen.

I barely dared to move, my heart pounding so loudly I was certain anyone who might be hiding nearby could hear it, a relentless drum in my ears. My hands were slick with sweat, the sword in my grip suddenly feeling far heavier than it had moments ago. I held my breath, straining to listen. The sounds of hooves grew fainter. Maybe Reed had managed to hide? I didn't hear the echo of metal clashing. Perhaps the guards had turned back, although, if they were indeed Ivy Guards, they surely would have spotted Hayden's ship, its Ember Isle sails unmistakable.

I peered cautiously around the rock, my eyes straining to catch any movement. There was nothing. No signs of life in the dense shadows of the trees. But where was Reed? Something wasn't right. I glanced back at the ship. It was so close now; soon it would be close enough dock. My heart hammered in my chest, a constant reminder of my growing anxiety. I felt small and powerless, hidden away like I always did. I couldn't stay like this. I didn't want to. I wanted to prove that I could do more than hide, I wanted to show that I was capable.

I took a deep breath, and before I knew it, my legs were carrying me through the thick sand, back toward the forest's edge. I had to find Reed. He'd probably scold me for this, but I'd rather face his reprimands than never hear his voice again.

The silence in the forest swallowed me whole, more suffocating than the tense stillness that had hung in the air moments before. Every rustle of leaves, every snap of a twig felt amplified, as though the world itself had slowed down to a crawl. My pulse quickened, my stomach knotted with fear. Each step felt like it echoed in the vast emptiness, and I had to swallow down the rising panic. Where was Reed?

The ship was so close now that I could almost taste the salt in the air, could almost feel the creak of the wooden deck beneath my feet. But Reed was nowhere to be found, swallowed by the cloak of darkness. I scanned the shadows, my eyes darting in search of any sign, any trace, that would tell me where he was, that would assure me he was all right.

What if he's in trouble? What if they've already captured him, and now they're turning back? I needed to find him. I had to know that he was safe.

I pushed deeper into the forest, my voice rising in a whisper that felt small, insignificant. "Reed!" I called, urgency seeping into my tone. "Where are you?"

There was no answer, only the unsettling rustle of leaves in the breeze. But then, in a flicker of moonlight, I saw it. My heart sank. There, in the shadows, was Reed, his form barely visible, and looming over him was a figure, hand pressed firmly on his shoulder, pinning him in place. His sword lay discarded on the ground beside him. It was the Ivy King.

I froze. Fear coiled in my gut. They had him. My stomach churned, bile rising in my throat. I couldn't just stand there, I wanted to scream, to rush forward, to do something, anything, but if I did, what good would that do to have us both caught?

I had no choice. I needed to get help. My best chance was to return to the beach and wait for Hayden. Surely, he'd brought a few guards with him, and maybe they could fight off the Ivy King or at least do something, anything, to stop him from hurting Reed.

I ran for the docks, my legs moving faster than they ever had before. The ship was close, I just needed to reach it. I glanced back toward the forest for a split second, but before I could refocus on the docks, my body slammed into something hard. My mind whirled as I tried to make sense of what had blocked my path.

The familiar scent of leather tickled my nose, and as I looked up, my gaze followed the green and black fabric. My heart stopped. It was an Ivy Guard and I was trapped.

His strong arms wrapped around me, pulling me tight against his chest as he twisted me around, pressing my back to his front.

"Where do you think you're going, little princess?" he sneered in my ear, sending a shiver down my spine. "The Ivy King would like to have a few words with you."

I twisted and squirmed in his grip, desperately trying to break free, but it was useless. He was too large, too powerful, holding me against his solid frame. My feet left the ground as he began marching us back into the forest.

"Let me go!" I screamed, continuing to writhe in his grasp, my legs kicking out in front of me. "Hayden!" I called, praying the ship was close enough to dock, hoping he might hear my pleas.

"Don't make this difficult!" the guard snapped, as he clamped his hand over my mouth.

Panic surged through me like a tidal wave, drowning out everything else. There was no use in fighting back. He was too strong.

I had to do something. I still had the sword in my grasp, but at this angle, I couldn't get a decent strike, not until I was free.

I closed my eyes, focusing on the only move I could make. I dipped my head forward and then threw it back with all my strength. When the back of my head collided with the guard's nose, I heard a sickening crunch while blinding pain filled my senses. Warm liquid began to drip down my neck as his grip loosened.

I collapsed to the ground, my head spinning from the force of the impact, but I didn't have time to recover. I had the sword, and the guard was down. This was my chance. I could make my killing strike.

Dizziness fogged my mind, and I hadn't noticed the quiet shift in the air until three more guards emerged, weapons raised, eyes locked on me. Vines began to slither from their fingers, writhing like living things. I knew that if they didn't strike me down with their blades, those vines would wrap around me, binding me completely and leaving me trapped for good.

I gripped my sword tighter, stepping forward. I'd learned from Reed that survival wasn't just about defense, it was about seizing control.

As the guards approached, the one I head-butted rose, looking as though breaking his nose was merely an inconvenience. He unsheathed his sword, swinging it at me.

Despite my throbbing head, I had enough awareness to step back just in time, narrowly avoiding his strike. I thrust my sword forward, aiming straight for his midsection. He blocked it, but I twisted my body, using the momentum to drive my knee into his ribs. He grunted, stumbling back, but I didn't give him a chance to recover.

I pressed forward, my blade flashing in the dim light. Each strike felt fluid, like the sword was an extension of my body. I ducked beneath his next attack, a vicious downward arc, and pivoted on my heel, slashing at his exposed side. His shout echoed in the air as he staggered back, blood seeping from the wound.

Then, the other guards were upon me. I felt the brush of vines wrapping around my leg.

Without hesitation, I swung my sword down, severing the vines. The moment I broke free, their blades came crashing down. Panic began to rise in my chest, my breath quickening, but I fought to stay focused. I blocked one strike just in time, but then another vine coiled around my wrist, yanking my sword back.

The sudden movement gave one of the guards an opening. His sword slashed across my arm as I twisted away, pain searing through my flesh.

A second vine wound around my other arm, and several more bound my ankles. My body was trapped, pulled taut like a marionette. My arms were forced overhead, and my legs were spread wide, each vine a cruel reminder of my helplessness in this star-shaped form.

"Well, if this isn't a compromising position," I heard one of the guards sneer. His voice was cruel, mocking. I shut my eyes, gritting my teeth, trying to breathe through the pain.

"Fuck you!"

"Looks like you're all wrapped up, ready to be delivered to the king," another guard chuckled, the sound low and menacing.

"Hayden!" I screamed, hoping he had seen what was happening and would come for me.

"Let her go!" A voice rang out from the distance. But it wasn't Hayden, it was Reed.

Relief surged through me. Reed was alive. I couldn't see him yet, but I knew he was on his way.

The guards turned their heads in the direction of his voice, and in that moment, their focus shattered. The vines they'd used to bind me snapped, and the pressure on my limbs eased. I could feel the tension release, and my muscles screamed with joy.

I watched in disbelief as all four guards froze, their eyes fixed on the forest where Reed was now charging toward us, sword in hand.

The astonishment on their faces was clear. They hadn't expected Reed to break free from the king's grip.

A gust of wind exploded toward the guards, knocking them off their feet. Their bodies slammed to the ground around me, the impact shaking the ground.

What the hell just happened?

"Eli!" Reed's voice cut through the chaos. "Get to the ship!"

No. I wouldn't run. I wouldn't hide. Not anymore.

I grabbed my sword, my grip steady now. I took the stance Reed had taught me, my body aligned and ready for the fight.

"Now!" Reed shouted again, closing the gap between him and the recovering guards, their swords raised, ready for battle.

The guards' attention snapped from me to Reed, who was swinging his sword, metal clashing with metal.

"What the hell?" one of them shouted.

"Stop!" another barked, blocking a strike from Reed.

Outnumbered, Reed still fought fiercely, but the odds were against us. I couldn't stand by. I swung my sword.

With all the guards focused on Reed, they never saw my strike coming. My blade cut through the leather of one guard's back, blood spilling as he screamed and collapsed. One down, three to go.

I steadied myself, ready for more. One of the remaining guards turned back to face me. Our swords met with a force that sent a shock through my body. I dug my heels in, using my core to absorb the impact, but his strength sent me stumbling. Still, I held onto my blade.

"You think you can best me?" he sneered. "Cute."

A surge of fury propelled me forward. I slammed into him, forcing him back. His surprise gave me the opening I needed. I lunged, but he sidestepped, and I stumbled past him.

Before I could react, his arms wrapped around my waist, pulling me back. No. I wouldn't be caught again. I twisted the sword in my grip, the blade angled backward. When it slid into his flesh, I knew I had him. His hold on me loosened, and he dropped to the floor, clutching his stomach. *Good*, I thought, let him bleed out.

My attention snapped back to Reed. It looked like he had taken down one of the guards too, leaving just one left.

My body surged forward, running purely on adrenaline as I raced to fight by Reed's side.

The guard's attention was entirely focused on Reed, who was locked in a fierce battle with him. I continued running toward them, my eyes briefly meeting Reed's. The brief distraction made Reed freeze for a moment, and that split second hesitation gave the guard the opening he needed. With a swift movement, the guard's sword slashed across Reed's body, and his scream of pain echoed in the air.

"Reed!" I screamed, my voice raw as I surged forward, desperate to reach him. The guard's gaze snapped from Reed, who had fallen to his knees, blood streaming down his front, to me.

Good. Leave Reed alone and come after me.

The guard charged toward me, and I mirrored his movements. I raised my sword just in time to block the downward strike of his blade. The force of the blow vibrated through my bones, but I managed to keep my ground.

I blocked every strike, but my adrenaline was beginning to fade. My limbs felt heavy, and each movement became more sluggish. With every swing of my sword, exhaustion pressed harder against me. Then, with a cruel swipe, the guard's blade cut across my other arm, leaving a matching gash.

"Run, Reed," I whimpered, my voice barely a breath as exhaustion overwhelmed me. My body was shutting down as all of my energy had burned through.

I couldn't afford to look back at Reed. I could only hope he was still alive, still able to fight. I prayed that his wound wasn't deep enough to keep him down.

The last of my strength was fading as the guard and I stood; swords locked in a tense standoff. Then, I felt his boot crash into my stomach, the pain burning through my core as it knocked the wind from me instantly. I was thrown backward into the soft sand. I couldn't fight anymore. I was drained and utterly exhausted.

My blurry vision met the guard's as he raised his sword above his head, ready to strike.

"Don't worry, Princess," he sneered, spit dripping from his mouth. "King Caraway still needs you alive, but he didn't say anything about how many pieces of your body need to stay intact."

I wanted to retaliate. I wanted to scream, to push him away, but my body refused to move. I was paralyzed by exhaustion, unable to lift a finger.

"Don't you fucking touch her!" Reed's voice broke through the haze, fierce and commanding. A sudden gust of wind swirled around the guard, lifting him off his feet and holding him suspended in midair.

I turned towards Reed, my heart pounding in my chest. His hand was outstretched, palm open, as if he were summoning the wind. No, he *was* summoning the wind. His magic was alive, swirling around him. But how? The silver of his iron collar around his neck gleamed in the moonlight, still securely in place. How could he access his magic with that collar still on?

"Aim your sword up!" Reed shouted urgently.

With the little strength I had left, I lifted my blade toward the sky. In one fluid motion, Reed released the guard, sending him hurtling down toward me. The guard's body collided with my sword with a sickening thud, impaled straight through.

His heavy, lifeless form crashed onto me, pinning me to the sand, my blade still lodged in his chest.

"I've got you, Eli," Reed groaned, as he pushed the heavy guard off of me, freeing my body.

When I thought I had lost all my strength, somehow, I found enough to push myself up and wrap my arms around Reed in a tight embrace. "Reed," I cried, a stray tear slipping down my cheek.

"Let me see you," Reed urged, pulling away from me to frantically search my body.

"I'm alright," I winced as he gently touched the matching gashes on my arms. "Just a scratch." But my eyes couldn't help but drift to him, fixating on the blood staining his shirt, his blood, now smeared across my dress after our embrace.

I placed my palms against his chest, searching for the wound, but there was nothing. Just smooth cool skin beneath the remnants of his torn and bloodied shirt. "I don't understand," I murmured aloud, still confused. "How did you heal? And how did you harness magic?" My mind spun in a whirl of unanswered questions.

"I guess the collar stopped working. Maybe the iron fibers broke down over time."

"What?" I blinked, unsure if that was even possible.

"Eli," Reed said urgently. "The ship is docked. Go now, and I'll meet you there."

"Where are you going?"

"The Ivy King won't stop coming for us. I need to stop him." His eyes burned with determination. "Please, don't argue. Just go. I'll be right behind you."

I nodded silently, understanding now. The Ivy King would always be a threat as long as he was alive. I wouldn't deny Reed his chance at vengeance, not after the king left threw Reed's crew overboard to their watery death, but I didn't want to damn his queens back home. I would allow him vengeance, but not at the cost of an innocent life.

"The life debt." I said, hoping Reed would understand.

"Then I'll simply cut off his limbs to stop him."

"Okay," I said, not wanting to argue and ran to the docks. Once I made it to the ship, I would make sure Hayden and any guards he had with him, helped Reed put a stop to the Ivy King in an non-fatal way. The only way to do that was to reach the ship first.

Through the cascading moonlight, my eyes drifted toward the incoming ship. Freedom was so close. I couldn't quite make out whether the figure standing at the front of the ship was Hayden or not, so I doubt he would recognize me waiting for him on the beach.

It was just as well. With blood still streaming down my arms and the front of my dress soaked in Reed's blood, I was sure I must have been quite the sight.

My legs faltered, stopping in place as I glanced down at the dress, thankful it was already a deep green that would hide the blood, though the stains were still visible. The moonlight cast better illumination here on the beach, and I could finally see the extent of the blood covering me. Flecks of gold shimmered within it, a small relief amidst the chaos. Despite the king's experiments, some of my magic still lingered. As I looked closer, another color caught my eye. The blood on my dress glinted with a strange silver shine under the moonlight.

I pulled the fabric closer to my face, narrowing my eyes to get a better look. The silver shimmer became more and more apparent the closer I inspected it. Had the Ivy King somehow infused his blood with mine? Was that what he was trying to accomplish? No, that didn't make sense. This wasn't even my blood. It was Reed's, from when we had embraced.

Wait… Why would Reed's blood have a silver shimmer?

Reed had healed, but he still wore his collar. He used magic, but that collar had never come off. His blood, this shimmering, royal-like blood, was all wrong.

What in the hell was going on?

Before I could make any sense of it, the sound of hooves pounding against sand pulled me back to reality.

"No!" I heard a familiar voice scream in terror from the distance.

I looked up, and there he was, the Ivy King, charging straight toward me on horseback. My body froze as I struggled to grasp everything happening around me. Caraway grew nearer, and before I could move, he swept an arm down, yanking me by the waist and throwing me over the horse's back.

"Let me go!" I screamed, my voice hoarse with panic, but his grip on me tightened.

"Shut up, you lying fucking bitch!" he spat.

The horse began to gallop toward the trees, but suddenly, there was a force, a pull, that caused the horse to rear back violently. We were both sent flying onto the sand with a harsh thud.

The Ivy King scrambled to his feet as I desperately tried to crawl away from him.

"Where do you think you're going?" he sneered, grabbing my ankle and yanking me back toward him.

I kicked out, thrashing against his grip, but it was no use.

"Let go of me!" I screamed, my body fighting with every ounce of strength to escape.

With one final, frantic kick, he released my ankle. But it wasn't my resistance that did it. Something else had intervened. Vines, thick, twisting vines, had wrapped around his body, pulling him away from me. I followed their path, eyes widening as they led straight down the beach to where Reed stood, his hands outstretched, vines flying from his fingertips.

Reed was wielding earth magic, but how was that possible? He was from the Isle of Gust, wasn't he? I blinked rapidly, trying to process what I was seeing, struggling to make sense of it all, trying to understand what the hell was happening.

Caraway twisted violently beneath the force of the vines, his body contorting in fury before he shot out his own, slashing towards Reed. I watched in breathless horror as their vines collided, a clash of raw power that sent tremors through the ground beneath us. The two forces interlocked, struggling for dominance.

"What are you doing?" the king roared, his voice trembling with effort, each word crackling with the sheer force of his magic. It was as though he was using every last ounce of his strength to hold Reed at bay.

"Leave her alone!" Reed shouted back, his voice strained, his chest heaving. "She's not the one you want!"

I should have been running, should have been making my way to the dock, straight for the ship, but I couldn't tear my eyes away. Something was happening to Reed as his vines remained tangled with the Caraway's. *He was flickering*. It was as if he was blurring in and out of focus, his form distorting like a bad painting, much like when he'd healed me. Was he dying? Was the King's power too strong, draining him of life? My heart pounded, but my gaze stayed locked on Reed, unwilling to look away.

And then I saw it. He wasn't flickering. He was changing.

One moment, Reed stood before me, his shaggy silver and black hair framing his face, his eyes burning with determination. The next, his features shifted, his body growing, aging, until he was someone else I knew. He had ashy blonde hair, larger, broader, a different shape altogether. Lars.

I blinked rapidly, disbelief gripping me. No. No, this wasn't real. But the shift continued. Reed's form flickered between Lars and

Reed, between the two identities, until...*Oh Theodon*, I gasped, stumbling back in shock.

His features sharpened, his face became more angular, his eyes colder. He was taller, stronger, more regal. His dark, coal-black hair fell perfectly over his forehead.

It was Hawthorne. My mind reeled, chaos spiraling within me. Reed... Reed lied. He was never just Reed. He was Lars, he was Hawthorne, and...by Theodon, who else had he been? Every moment we'd spent together, every word, every touch, it had all been a lie. He could have been anyone. He could have been everyone.

Reed wasn't some poor thief from the Isle of Gust. He wasn't who he'd said he was.

He was the Ivy Prince.

A shapeshifter.

How was that even possible?

I stood frozen, my heart pounding in my chest, my world crashing down around me. As I watched, Reed—no, Hawthorne—and the king continued their violent dance, a deadly exchange of power. Each blast of magic tore through the air, shaking the earth beneath my feet.

"Father!" Hawthorne shouted, his voice fierce, desperate. "Let it go! She doesn't have the Ember!"

The words struck me like a dagger to the chest. Oh no.

It hit me with the force of a thunderclap: I had told Reed everything. Everything about me, about Hayden, about the secrets that had weighed me down. I'd trusted him. I'd confided in him. I'd let him do things to me, with me. It was all a lie. Every word. Every moment. Every touch. It had been a trap. A manipulation.

No. No, no, no.

My heart splintered, even as I realized the truth.

The king laughed, a bitter, cold sound that echoed in the night. "She is the firstborn heir of the Ember Isle!" he bellowed, his eyes gleaming with a twisted sort of triumph.

"It's her brother," Hawthorne shouted in return, his voice full of urgency. "The prince, he has the Ember. They lied about it to protect it. The princess isn't part of this anymore."

The truth hit me like a sledgehammer. My world twisted, shattered in an instant. Reed—no, Hawthorne—had known everything. And he had used me all along.

But in that moment, something inside me snapped. The anguish, the betrayal, it all surged within me like a tide.

With one final, immense surge of power, Hawthorne drew on every ounce of his strength, and with a mighty roar, he subdued the king. The Ivy King staggered back, his magic flickering and faltering under the relentless force of his son's power. The vines around him tightened, pulling him down. It was over for now.

But my heart? My heart was still in pieces as I continued to stand motionless in the sand.

I watched as the king slowly rose to his feet, the dark energy in the air intensifying with every movement. His gaze locked onto me, a cold, cruel smile curling on his lips. "Don't tell me you developed feelings for her," he sneered, his voice dripping with mockery. "She set the whole thing up. She and her family tried to deceive us, agreeing to sacrifice the firstborn. I bet they know more about this than they've let on."

I flinched at his words, feeling the accusation press down on me like a suffocating cloak. He wasn't wrong, but I couldn't watch Hayden die. I just wanted to pay for the crime I committed, or at least thought I committed considering the Ivy Prince was alive and well and only a few yards in front of me. But before I could say anything, Hawthorne stepped forward, his jaw clenched tight, defending me as though his life depended on it.

"She just wanted to save her brother," Hawthorne said, his voice steady but filled with undeniable desperation. "She's innocent in all of this. We can still let her go. She hasn't done anything wrong."

The king scoffed, his eyes narrowing with suspicion. "And how do we know for sure she doesn't have the Ember?" His tone was low, dangerous, and filled with rage. "The Ember King and Queen said she was the firstborn. How do you know the secrets she told you are true? It seems her entire family is built on lies."

I could feel my heart hammering in my chest. I wanted to speak up, to say something, but my throat was dry, and the weight of their accusations was too heavy.

"She's a twin," Hawthorne said, his voice cracking slightly, as if revealing this secret physically hurt him. "Eli…Princess Eliane and the Ember Prince were born twins."

The words hung in the air like a dirty secret, and the king froze, his expression morphing from suspicion to disbelief. "Twins!?" he spat, his voice rising with fury. "Another lie! You and I both know that twins cannot exist! Only one child can survive birth!"

Hawthorne stood tall, though his voice was tight, the burden of what he was revealing clearly taking a toll on him. "Somehow, she did. She has a small dose of magic in her; you saw it yourself when you used the star."

I stared at him, my mind racing. He knew all along. He knew what the king had planned for me, knew about the king carving that blade into my chest, the star, the ritual. The hero he'd pretended to be was nothing but a mask, a way to gain my trust.

I could feel the tension in the air thickening, like a storm on the horizon, and I couldn't breathe.

"Her brother is almost here," Hawthorne said, his voice urgent. "He'll trade his life for hers, I'm sure of it. For now, just let her go."

"No." the king spat the word like it was a curse. "If what you say is true, then we still need her. Do you honestly think her brother will just hand over the Ember willingly? She's our leverage now, son. We need her alive. If she is a surviving twin, there may still be a fragment of the Ember inside her, and that's something we'll need. We can't let her go."

His words ended on a sharp, vicious note, and I felt the hair on the back of my neck stand on end. The king's attention snapped back to me, and I barely had time to react before a flurry of sharp, thorn-like vines flew in my direction, aiming to bind me and promising me nothing but pain.

"Stop!" Hawthorne's voice was full of fear, raw and desperate.

I gasped, waiting for the thorns to trap me and tear into my flesh, but the pain never came. The vines never came. And then I felt the air around me crackle, a rush of wind so powerful it lifted me off the ground. I blinked, trying to understand what was happening, when I saw Hawthorne's hands moving, his fingers dancing through the air like he was weaving a spell.

The gust of wind picked up Caraway in a violent swirl, lifting him off the ground and sending him flying backward, crashing into the trees. Hawthorne wasn't just defending me, he was attacking his father, using his power to fight against him. The king was gone and before I knew it, the air was lightly carrying my body down as it placed me gently back onto the sand.

But why? My mind screamed in confusion. Why was he doing this? Was this another act? Another part of the plan?

Hawthorne turned to face me, his eyes filled with something I couldn't read. Was it regret? Fear? But the rawness in his expression only added to the chaos in my mind. I couldn't trust him. I couldn't trust anyone. I needed to get out.

I tore my eyes away from him, my feet already moving as instinct took over. My only chance was to run. I needed to get to the ship, to escape, to put as much distance between me and this place as possible.

And so, I ran.

I pushed through the thick sand, the world around me a blur of movement and panic. Hawthorne's voice echoed in my mind, but I couldn't stop. I couldn't look back.

I didn't know who to trust anymore. But I knew one thing for sure. I couldn't stay. Not with him.

"Eli, wait!" His voice shattered the night air, sharp and desperate. "Please, just listen to me. Let me explain."

I continued to sprint, my legs shaking beneath me. I couldn't let him catch me. I had to reach the ship. I had to get to Hayden. But the sand beneath my feet felt like it was pulling me back. Every step felt heavier than the last, and then, I felt it.

A rush of air slammed into my back, knocking me off balance. I stumbled, trying to catch myself, but it was like the air itself was holding me back. Something wrapped around my legs, thick, snake-like vines, tight and unyielding. Instantly, the memory of Hawthorne's damned vines coiling around my ankles that night in the Ember Palace came flashing back.

My breath caught in my throat as I tried to struggle free, but it was no use. Hawthorne's magic was far too strong.

"Stop," he called, his voice lower now, a mix of anguish and pleading. "Please, just stop running. Let me explain. I didn't—"

But I wouldn't listen. I couldn't risk believing him.

The sand beneath me shifted, and I was falling, tumbling toward the ground. My body hit the sand, but it wasn't the cold impact I expected. Soft leaves, delicate and warm, wrapped around me like a cushion. They didn't hurt me, they cradled me. But I didn't want their comfort. I didn't want his.

I pushed myself up, frantically trying to free my legs, but the vines only tightened.

"No!" I cried, my voice desperate. "No! Don't you dare touch me! I—"

"Eli, please." His voice was so much closer now, and I could hear the tremor in it. "Please, just listen. I'm not going to hurt you."

My body shook with a mix of rage and fear as I looked up at him, my chest heaving. "Tell me you're not him. You're not Hawthorne. I killed him. I killed you. You can't be him!"

It was all too much. The truth, the lies, the betrayal. My heart felt like it was shattering in my chest. I wanted to scream, to lash out at him, but my voice was raw. I tried to stand, but the vines around my legs held me in place, immobilized.

"I'm—" He stopped, his words breaking. "It's true, I'm Prince Hawthorne. I never wanted to hurt you. Please understand, Eli. I have so much I need to explain if you just give me a chance."

I felt my breath catch in my throat as I screamed at him, "No! You lied to me. You tricked me. You made me think I mattered, that I was loved. But I was nothing to you. Nothing!" I wanted to claw at the sand. I wanted to rip him apart, to demand answers. But instead, I felt like I was drowning in my own confusion. "Every promise, every touch... it was all a lie!"

"It wasn't a lie," he said, and for once, he sounded like he was the one breaking. "Let me explain. Just listen to me. Please."

"No!" I shook my head, my voice growing frantic. "It was all a trap! You used me!"

I couldn't breathe. I couldn't think. I was suffocating under the pressure of everything he'd said, everything I thought I'd known.

His eyes softened, and he knelt beside me, reaching out like he wanted to touch me. "Eli, I never meant for you to get caught up in this. I never meant to hurt you."

I recoiled from him, my chest tightening in panic. I couldn't let him touch me. Not anymore.

The vines around my legs loosened, their grip softening. It was as if he was trying to show me that he meant no harm. But I was beyond reason. I scrambled to my feet, my body still trembling.

And then, there was a sudden whoosh of air sliced through the night. An arrow flew straight by me as it pierced Hawthorne's shoulder and he let out a cry of pain, staggering backward.

Relief flooded my veins like fire as I spun around. My brother. He was here. "Hayden!" I screamed.

I saw him then, emerging from the shadows, his face set in grim determination, a bow still raised in his hand. He was here and this nightmare could end.

"Eli!" Hayden shouted as he ran toward me. "We need to go. Now!"

But Hawthorne, was already recovering, his hand on his shoulder, his eyes still locked on me. "Please, Eli, please, let me help. I can't—"

But Hayden wasn't listening. His fire magic surged to life, the flames erupting from his hands with a brilliant, violent crackle. He aimed them straight at the vines Hawthorne had sent toward us. They disintegrated in a burst of fire before they could even touch us.

"Go, Eli!" Hayden shouted again, urgency in his voice.

I didn't need to be told twice. I turned and ran straight for Hayden, my heart still racing, still fighting to understand everything that had just happened. But Hawthorne wasn't giving up. He moved fast, faster than I thought possible, his hand reaching out for us.

"I'm sorry, Eli!" Hawthorne's voice echoed across the beach. "Please, I will tell you everything if you just—"

But before he could finish, a shadow shifted behind him, one I knew all too well. With Hawthorne distracted, trying to reason with me, he didn't even notice Adan sneaking up behind him.

Without hesitation, Adan swung his sword, knocking Hawthorne out cold with the hilt. He crumpled to the ground, his body going limp. Something in me winced in pain to see Hawthorne in such a manner. I shook my head trying to harden those feelings. He didn't deserve my sympathy. He was the sole reason for all my suffering, every horrible thing I experienced, he was behind it all pulling the strings along with the king.

Hayden turned to face me, his brow furrowed with concern etched across his features. "Eli, what happened? How is he still alive? I saw him dead in the oasis that day, he didn't have a pulse."

I swallowed hard, trying to steady my racing heart. The truth was still tangled up in my mind, but I had to say something. "It was all a trick, Hayden. A setup." My voice cracked as I spoke, but I pushed forward, forcing myself to look him in the eye. "The Ivy King, he used Reed. Hawthorne, whoever he is now, he was a part of the plan. The king wanted me to believe it was all real. That Hawthorne was someone else, someone I could trust to get information from me but it was all lies." My hands clenched at my sides, frustration bubbling up inside me. "The Ivy King wants your Ember. He wants to use it for something. I don't know what, but it can't be good."

Hayden's face darkened, his jaw tightening as he absorbed my words. "Does the Ivy King know that I am the one who possesses it?"

I nodded in guilt, "Yes, I confided in Hawthorne about everything, the whole truth, this is all my fault," my voice cracked as I swallowed the lump of coal that settled in my throat.

"No. That asshole manipulated you. This is not your fault alright?"

I nodded again. I needed to be done with all of this self-blame. Hayden was right. Hawthorne was the villain, not me.

Adan's face was hard with a hint of confusion lingering in his features. "We should take the Ivy King prisoner," he suggested.

Hayden shook his head, his voice heavy with the burden of a decision he didn't want to make. "We could. But if we do that, the Ivy Isle will see it as an act of war. They'll retaliate. And they'll go after my parents. They won't hesitate." His eyes locked onto mine, and I saw the weight of everything he was carrying, the responsibility of his family, the threat to his kingdom, and the fear of losing it all. In just these few short weeks, he had really grown into his upcoming role. "I can't risk that. Not for me. Not for my family."

Adan's expression hardened, his arms crossed over his chest as he thought for a moment. "Then what about the Ivy Prince?" he asked, his voice edged with resolve as he looked down at the still unconscious Hawthorne. "If everyone thought he was dead anyway, no one would question it. You could lock him up, keep him out of the way and use him for information without triggering a war."

Hayden's gaze flickered to Hawthorne still lying motionless on the sand where Adan had left him. After a long pause, Hayden exhaled slowly, his shoulders sagging. "You're right," he said, his voice filled with quiet frustration. "No one would question it. And if we take him out of the equation, it might buy us some time. The Ivy King won't have his heir anymore." He looked at Adan. "Take him. Lock him up in the ship's prison. And make sure you put an iron collar on him. A real one this time."

Adan nodded, his expression unreadable. Without another word, he moved forward, bending down to scoop Hawthorne's limp body into his arms. Hawthorne's head lolled to one side as Adan carried him away towards the ship, his weight barely a burden on Adan's strong shoulders.

I watched them go, my stomach in knots. It felt wrong, but at the same time, it felt necessary. This wasn't just about his betrayal anymore. This was about something bigger. Something none of us fully understood.

Hayden turned to me then, his hand resting lightly on my shoulder. "Eli..." His voice softened, his eyes searching mine for something, any sign that I was okay. But I wasn't. I wasn't okay. Not in any way.

I crumbled. The dam broke, and the tears I'd been holding back finally spilled over. I couldn't stop them. I didn't want to. I sank to my knees in the sand, everything crashing over me like a tidal wave.

Hayden knelt beside me instantly, his strong arms wrapping around me, pulling me close. "Eli," he whispered, his voice thick with worry. "Are you okay? Did he...did he hurt you?"

I couldn't speak at first. My throat was tight with grief, with betrayal. I felt his arms around me, his warmth, his steady heartbeat, everything I needed, but it wasn't enough to chase away the hollow ache inside me.

"No," I whispered between sobs. "I'm not okay," I whimpered as I thought on every unnecessary act of cruelness I experienced while in that castle.

"So, he did hurt you?" Hayden said through clenched teeth.

"He didn't hurt me physically. But my heart Hayden, it hurts."

Hayden's grip tightened, but there was a softness in his touch, a tenderness that grounded me in the storm of my emotions. "I know," he murmured. "And we'll get to the bottom of this, Eli. We will, I promise you."

I buried my face against his shoulder, my breath hitching in between sobs. "I don't know what to believe anymore," I admitted, my voice trembling. "I thought I knew who he was. But I was wrong. And I don't know what to do with all this... this pain."

"We'll figure it out, alright?"

I nodded, but even as I did, I felt like I was breaking into a thousand pieces, and I wasn't sure if I could put myself back together again.

After a moment, Hayden gently pulled away, wiping the tears from my face with the pad of his thumb. He helped me to my feet, his hand warm against my back.

"Let's go," he said quietly, guiding me toward the ship. "We'll be safe soon. Just hold on, okay? We're leaving this behind and it will soon just seem like a bad dream."

The wind picked up again, tugging at my hair as we climbed aboard the ship, the wooden boards creaking beneath our feet. But I didn't look back. Not at the shore. Not at the Ivy Isle, still looming in the distance.

I went to the stern of the ship, where the wind was strongest, where the salty air filled my lungs, and I stared out at the vastness of the ocean. My chest ached, but I held my head high. I had to. For me. For Hayden. For everything that still lay ahead.

And as the ship pulled away from the shore, the towering cliffs of the Ivy Isle slowly faded from view, the island shrinking into the horizon. And as it disappeared completely, swallowed by the vastness of the sea, I felt a strange sense of peace wash over me.

The past was behind me now and it was over. Though something tugged at my heart, a thought. I wasn't sure if I wanted it to be over.

ABOUT THE AUTHOR

Lauren Sanatra is a California native who grew up with a passion for theatre and writing for the stage. In 2020, she transitioned from playwright to novelist, channeling her creative energy into crafting stories across all subgenres of romance. A  hopeless romantic, she strives to create love stories that resonate deeply with readers. When she's not writing, Lauren enjoys exploring new places, often traveling to a different destination each month.

@laurensanatra.author *(Instagram)*